RAISING THE TITANIC

A POWERFUL NOVEL OF RESILIENCE,
INSPIRED BY THE TRUE STORY OF ONE OF
AMERICA'S MOST FEARLESS WOMEN

LIGHT & LIFE SERIES

MARTA MOLNAR

ISBN: 978-1-940627-69-4

This book is dedicated to amazing author friend Kaylea Cross for her invaluable help with forensic anthropology. All mistakes are my own.

My heartfelt gratitude goes to Diane, Sarah, Sue, Linda, and Toni for their crucial feedback on the manuscript, and all their much-appreciated encouragement and support.

CHAPTER 1

"My destination is no longer a place, rather a new way of seeing." Marcel Proust

Madison
 August 3, 2024 (Saturday)
 Boston

The sender's email is a string of random letters and numbers, TTP@P1914…, the subject a single word: CONFIDENTIAL.

"Scammers are scum. Scam…scum. Almost the same. Not a coincidence. I can't stand people who waste my time. Is that a sign of getting old?"

"If you're old, then what am I?"

My father and I are on a grocery run at Trader Joe's, in line at the checkout. People waddle forward, like penguins for the fish bucket at feeding time at the zoo.

I move with the flow. "Distinguished."

"You should be a politician." Dad's lips jerk sideways, then back, like a mini seizure—he's typing on his own phone, too distracted to actually smile. "Kidding."

Of course he is. If I were anything else but a scientist, he'd deny paternity.

I should delete the email, but I have the deep-seated curiosity innate to all academicians, so I open it. The text is brief. I hold it up to my father. "I always thought that if I'm ever abducted, it'll involve free art supplies in the back of an unmarked van, but no. This might be it."

He glances at the message, the overhead light glinting off the silver strands at his temples. Even on a Saturday, he's in a button-down shirt and dress pants. I can't imagine him wearing a T-shirt and jeans for anything short of the apocalypse.

"Maybe you're being recruited." His mouth silently forms a letter, then another and another.

"The odds heavily favor garbage." I refuse to feel guilty for wearing yoga pants and a hoodie on the weekend. "What would the FBI even want with me?"

The scant details *are* titillating.

Request for Project Participation—TTP
Location: Halifax, Nova Scotia
Project duration: 6 months
Project status: fully funded

Those last two words grab hold of me, and so

does the fee the next line promises, a BIG fish dangled in front of a very hungry penguin.

Except… "A mysterious organization offers me the perfect bait, with very few specifics, and they want me to leave the country. This is how people get their organs harvested."

We move to the head of the line, Dad saving more thoughts on his phone for his new book on X-ray astronomy, lost in whatever cosmic equation is unfurling in his mind. When he's in the middle of a project, he doesn't stop working. He'll scribble notes in the shower or in the middle of a meal.

He pauses only for another second. "What's TTP?"

"*Thrombotic thrombocytopenic purpura.*" Google is my friend, and my fingers are quick. "A blood disorder that involves blood clots in small blood vessels. That can't be right. Not my field." I scroll, but that's pretty much it.

"Are you going to reply? Some project invites do come with bare-bones information. It's not that unusual." His words carry a heavy undertone of *You've been out of work for too long*.

The undertone is not wrong. With my university position eliminated, my anatomy classes taken from me, I fall firmly in the beggars-can't-be-choosers category. Unemployed is what I am—although my preferred term is *between engagements.*

"Do the police still call you to draw forensics portraits?"

"Not lately." I secretly suspect they've replaced

me with AI. I need to get back in the game, somewhere, somehow. I won't be able to afford my mortgage in a few more weeks.

I need to ask Dad if I can move back in with him so I can rent out my place. Because I'm moving backward now. *Yay.*

I want to find myself again. I want to find my way back to my life as I used to know it, where I'm a confident, productive member of society. I want to go back into the classroom, having spirited discussions with the students, and then at lunch-break grumbling sessions with the faculty. I even miss the odd argument with the administration over their never-ending list of new rules. Every time a text pings on my phone, I still hope it's the dean contacting me to offer me back my position.

As the cashier rings up my purchases, I show Dad the attachment that came with the mysterious email, a twelve-page confidentiality agreement that dares me from the screen. "If I sign, they'll send me a plane ticket. An in-person introductory meeting is scheduled for September second."

"So, what are you thinking?"

"I'm thinking a hard no. Two kidneys are not too many."

"Did I tell you Lori brought up moving in?" His mental gears have shifted, his restless mind already on the next topic.

"Did you pretend not to hear her?" It's his usual MO when a relationship reaches this stage. I'm used to his succession of girlfriends. My mother died shortly after I was born, and no one else has stuck since.

"I can't live with a woman. I don't have time for female drama, honey. You know me. I need my silence and my peace."

The checkout guy finishes ringing up my purchases. The total hurts. I smile to cover the pain, but that hurts too, like I have frostbite on my face.

I read the TTP agreement on the way out of the store, then I sign on my phone with my fingertip. I'm not going to pretend that I have choices.

Hello kidneys, goodbye kidneys.

September 2, 2024 (Monday)
Nova Scotia, Canada

A chauffeur awaits me at Halifax Airport, as promised by the mysterious TTP in their last email. His neatly trimmed beard gives his chin the kind of definition that makes a portrait painter's life easy. Straight nose too, and a face so symmetrical, I want to sketch him.

He holds a sign with my name: *Madison McLain*. He stands at attention, a corporate driver, which makes sense. After all the secrecy, of course, they wouldn't send an Uber for me.

"Dr. McClain." He tosses his sign onto the front passenger seat of the charcoal-gray Lincoln Continental. "I'll be driving you to headquarters. My name is Davey." He commandeers my luggage, then opens the back door for me.

A man around my age sits in the back already.

"Oliver. Hi." He looks like a handyman, in blue jeans and a soft, red-checkered flannel shirt over a faded black T-shirt.

"I'm Madison." I'm in wool slacks and a cashmere sweater, because I'm a professional. I might not dress up for the grocery store, but I do dress up for work. I take my seat. "Are you with the…" I stop short of saying *secret society*.

"I was invited to a meeting." He has a Canadian accent. Might have flown in from Vancouver. I'm not familiar enough with Canadian accents to tell for sure.

His hands are empty. He has no zip ties, and nothing to gag me with either, so probably not a kidnapper.

Oh.

Oh!

An even more horrible explanation for his presence rears its ugly head. *Is he competition?* The emails said nothing about another forensic artist. *Are we both here to interview?* "No."

He tilts his head. "What's that?"

"Nothing." *Wince.* "Bumped my knee."

Davey is stashing my suitcase in the trunk, out of hearing range, so I risk a quick "If after all this, we're just knocked out while some hack doctor…" I make the universally known snip-snip gesture with my fingers. "I'm going to be very disappointed."

Oliver doesn't laugh. My sense of humor goes right over his head. He doesn't correct me with any salient information either.

"What do you know about TTP?" His tone holds zero urgency, and zero anxiety, as if he isn't nearly as desperate for the job as I am. He's comfortably sunk into the leather seat.

"The same as you, I imagine." I'm not letting on that I know nothing. I make a point to appear as relaxed as he is. No reason to sit Victorian-debutant straight. "Mostly, I'm just here to see the aurora borealis." I joke, although, no joke, the aurora is on my bucket list.

"Care to speculate about the project? Or no theories at all?"

How dare he? I'm a scientist. I have a theory about *everything*. "I can hazard a few educated guesses." But I will not bring up the FBI and sound demented. Why would the FBI want to meet in Halifax instead of their headquarters in Washington? "I'm hoping the project involves a dinosaur park," I say to throw him off, although it's not that wild an idea. Four years ago, I was hired to paint a life-size image of a Kritosaurus for a museum, from recently found fossils in California.

"Crossed my mind. We're not far from Fossil Cliffs and Fossil Beach."

He would know. He is Canadian. He has home-court advantage.

As Davey slips behind the wheel, I pop another theory. "Nun cho ga."

I watch the chauffeur in the rearview mirror for a reaction, but he doesn't so much as blink.

"The woolly mammoth?" Oliver tastes my suggestion. "Why not? The Russians are working on bringing them back in Siberia."

The prospect of a woolly mammoth should bring a few sparks into his eyes, but I see none. He's dry and distracted, looks out of the window more than he looks at me. My first impression of him is that he's kind of boring. Maybe that'll work in my favor. Maybe TTP wants a forensic artist with personality.

"Except," I think out loud, "why would we be called to Nova Scotia for Nun cho ga? Canada's thirty-thousand-year-old baby mammoth was found by gold miners two years ago in Yukon Territory."

Quit with the info dump. I'm not interviewing yet. I'm trying too hard.

"They could have shipped her down here. She's a prize. She's the most complete mammoth found in North America."

Oliver's tone is monotone, but I can't hide the wistfulness in mine. "Her fur, skin, and tusks are intact."

"Can you imagine?" The teensiest bit of excitement *almost* sparks.

"Can I? Down to her baby mammoth skull."

If Nun cho ga is the project, my art might end up hanging in the Canadian Museum of Nature. I assess Oliver. One of us is about to win the lottery. I want it to be me.

8

When I'm silent for too long, he asks, "First time in Halifax?"

"Inaugural visit." I looked the place up on the plane. "The most populous city in Nova Scotia, half the size of Boston. Not that it's a competition," I add, not wanting to be *that* person. "Halifax is a great city with a long history."

"Short version: it was stolen from the Mi'kmaq."

He's not wrong.

While stores and apartment buildings zoom by, I sneak in a question of my own. "Where did you study?"

"University of Toronto."

"Boston University." On education, we are evenly matched. I need more information on him before we go head-to-head. "TTP caught you between projects?"

"Have more downtime this year than I'd like. It's the price of being a free agent."

Meaning he doesn't have a university position by choice. He is braver than I am. *What's an unobtrusive way to ask about his relevant experience?*

Maybe if I keep asking questions, he'll keep talking and eventually blurt out something useful.

I nod toward a brick tower. "What is that?"

"The Old Town Clock." Then Oliver comments on the next point of interest and the next, while Davey, our intrepid chauffeur, whisks us through the city, into a modern, not entirely completed, business district.

We pull up in front of an elongated building that

looks like a cubist representation of a whale, dominating the office park, its skin of windows glistening like a wet humpback on a beach. The complex has the kind of lines that blur the boundary between art and architecture and make my fingers itch to sketch a quick outline. But sketching of any kind will have to wait.

I'm so not ready for an interview. How am I going to compete? I only brought my small traveling laptop. I can't even remember if it has my résumé.

The inside of the building is an acre of gleaming marble tile. The open space is pristine, the white walls not yet decorated. We are swallowed whole by the eerie emptiness, alone until a twenty-something security guard shuffles from the back.

"Hey." Gray uniform with an HSS patch, a walkie-talkie at his hip, he has no weapon. Welcome to Canada. "You can leave your bags"—he gestures at the deserted reception desk—"back there."

He waits for us, then escorts us down a hallway, looking bored with us already. He lumbers like a bear that just woke from hibernation. If he does end up showing interest in my kidneys, at least I'll be able to outrun him.

Without another word, he opens a door marked *Conference Room C*.

Four people sit around a long table inside, no scrubs, no surgical equipment. *Relax.* All signs point to a legit assignment.

The fifty-something guy at the head of the table rises with a smile. "Here you are. The rest of the dream team." He's definitely corporate, with a strong Ivy League vibe, someone high up who wants to look like *one of the people* in his matching polo shirt and khakis. Dark hair, dark eyes, he's actually not bad-looking. "Come on in."

A stack of manila folders and a tiny black remote sit on the table in front of him.

"I'm Ramsey Michaels, the executive manager of this enterprise. Dr. Madison McClain, forensic artist," he introduces me to the others. "You might know her YouTube channel, *Looking in the Face of Crime*. And this is Dr. Oliver Green, forensic anthropologist."

Plot twist.

Oliver and I won't be competing.

While my ragged nerves back off from the front lines where they've been preparing for battle, Ramsey gestures at the woman on his right. "Dr. Julia Szabo, archeologist."

She's about forty, with short hair, compact, built like an athlete. I'd be more comfortable with *her* working security than I am with the HSS kid.

"The mayor is lending us two assistant archaeologists," Ramsey goes on, "who are associated with City Hall and local excavations, but for the most part, they'll only be with us on location."

The man on his other side is in his midthirties, showing off a fashionable blue suit that's a little too shiny and a little too tight, charisma rolling off him in waves. If we were on a reality show, this guy would be the host. I know he's a bullshitter, a.k.a. lawyer, before Ramsey introduces him.

"Chad Altman, legal adviser and head of the ethics committee."

The last person at the table is a woman around seventy, classy in a cream-colored knit dress, with the elegance of an aging movie star, her short, wavy hair left silver. I like her on sight. This is a woman who knows who she is and needs nobody's approval.

"Professor Eleanor Dabrowski, geneticist. Eleanor came out of retirement for this project, which we very much appreciate."

Oliver and I exchange a glance. TTP must be something *big*. Our chances for Nun cho ga grow better by the minute.

"The six of us will be the core team." Ramsey indicates the empty chairs. "Please, sit."

"The core team of what?" He's overdoing the secrecy. I assume the others have also signed NDAs to be here. Time to spill the beans.

Ramsey drops into his chair, picks up the remote, then swivels toward the display screen behind him. "I prepared a few slides that will answer most of your questions."

Finally.

The first image is a stark row of granite head-stones against a gray sky. I release my dreams of dinosaurs and mammoths. We are looking at a human cemetery.

"As you might know"—Ramsey stays on the slide —"two thousand two hundred sailed on the most famous ship that ever sank. Of this, one thousand five hundred perished."

Oh.

Oh!

"Three hundred and thirty-seven bodies were recovered, most of them by the Halifax ship *CS Mackay-Bennett*."

This is why we are in Halifax.

"The law required proper preparation of bodies, embalming and so forth, as a condition of admittance into the harbor. The rescue ships didn't have enough embalming fluid, so priority was given to first-class travelers whose identification was more crucial. They had heirs and large estates to settle. Over a hundred victims were buried at sea, most of them crew and third-class passengers."

Drowned in the frigid waves, lost, then found, then dumped back again, trapped forever in an icy grave, far from family and friends.

I shudder as if someone tossed a bucket of ice water on my back. For the families to know that their loved ones were found, yet not being able to see their faces again, being denied the bodies for a funeral—I don't have the words for that kind of terrible.

"Nothing is fair in life, including death," Oliver says under his breath.

Before I can figure out whether that's deep or nonsensical, Ramsey moves on with "Two hundred nine bodies were brought to Halifax, out of which fifty-nine were claimed and taken home at the time. The hundred and fifty unclaimed victims were buried in three local cemeteries. Fairview Lawn, Mount Olivet, and Baron de Hirsch." His tone takes on the solemnity of a bishop. "Most of them were identified either then or later, but forty-four remain unidentified to this day."

"Why now?" Julia Szabo, our resident archaeologist, asks.

Since she doesn't know, she must be an outsider like Oliver and me.

"We have DNA technology that we didn't have before," Eleanor Dabrowski, geneticist, replies, exchanging a glance with Ramsey.

Insider.

I rock my chair closer to the table. "We've had good DNA technology for years."

"Who's behind the project?" Julia clicks her pen twice, *click, click.* "I'd like to know who'll be signing our paychecks." Very to the point.

"TrinovarDNA and Cyntinra." Ramsey's jaw muscles flex, as if sharing even the bare minimum hurts him. "This"—he rolls his head in a circle—"is TrinovarDNA's new facility."

TrinovarDNA has been in the news, gobbling up its rivals one by one, determined to be the largest player in the medical and ancestry DNA analysis game. Cyntinra is in a different industry altogether. They are Netflix's latest competitor in the content streaming arena, a massive entertainment conglomerate out of China.

"It's a philanthropic project." Chad Altman, the lawyer, takes over. An obvious insider. "We will identify the unnamed victims for the blank gravestones. Then the project will find and contact living family who might not be aware of their ancestors' history."

"Media attention will be enormous." I'm not a fan of these types of projects, where I'll inevitably end up spending more time on interviews than working at my easel, but this *is* a once-in-a-lifetime opportunity. "I suppose that's the whole point. Millions of dollars' worth of free PR for TrinovarDNA and Cyntinra."

"Tens of millions," Julia corrects me.

I don't mind it because she's right, and accuracy is important.

"Does this mean a new movie is in the works?" Oliver voices my next thought. "Is that why Cyntinra is involved?"

"What's wrong with the old movie?" *Right. Of course.* "They're making a series." I answer my own question. "A series that runs a few seasons would generate more income than a movie that's a single shot at the box office."

Ramsey brings up the next slide, a photo of the iconic steamship with its four proud white funnels. "The real story had an enormous cast of characters. The movie didn't do it justice. Not to knock it, of course. There'll be people watching our show to see if we find Jack. That's how real that movie was to a certain audience."

Julia clicks her pen again. "If TrinovarDNA and Cyntinra are doing this for PR, why the secrecy?"

"We are only keeping the initial phase confiden-tial." Ramsey's new slide shows an organizational chart with our names and roles. "We didn't want to announce the project until we could announce the core team. Also, I wanted to make sure we had all the permits in hand first."

"Improper interference with human remains is an indictable offense under section 182 of the Canadian Criminal Code." Chad Altman has an odd-toned, dry voice, overly official for his age, as if he were auditioning for a Supreme Court post. He's going to be a laugh and a half. Note to self: don't do anything that requires legal advice.

"These are your contracts." Ramsey hands the three of us outsiders a manila folder each, and then he clicks on to a new slide. "This is our timeline. Exhumations are to start immediately. We will wrap next April."

"How long do we have to think about it?" Oliver asks.

"I need your answers before you leave this room." Ramsey tips his chin down, a teacher looking at the classroom. "Either you want in, or you don't. And before you decide, one more thing... We'll be recording the work you do on the project, so a small camera crew will be present. We'll use the footage for advertising materials, a brief documentary, and other assorted PR."

The idea of being filmed while I work doesn't thrill me, but at least the contract is straightforward. Most of it is a longer, even more comprehensive NDA.

"All communication to the outside world is through our attorney," Ramsey says as we read.

"Nobody other than Chad and I is allowed to talk to the press or divulge any details anywhere or to anyone without prior approval. Including and especially online posts." He looks right at me.

Maybe the others don't have online platforms.

I sign on the dotted line. "I'm a professional."

Our project manager clicks through a few more black-and-white photos of the ship, then finally runs out of slides. Chad collects the three signed contracts.

"Let's toast to a smooth sailing." Ramsey grabs a bottle from the sideboard. "Heidsieck & Co Monopole, the champagne they served on the ship."

Chad Altman brings us glasses, while Julia and I exchange a glance across the table. *Can you believe this?*

"Welcome aboard, ladies and gentlemen. You are about to make history." Ramsey pops the cork. "We are raising the *Titanic*."

CHAPTER 2

Helen

January 1879, Connecticut

"I prefer my horse to any man I have met so far."

"Helen!" My friend Ada grips her seat, as if shock might knock her clear out of our carriage. "Helen Churchill Hungerford, you mustn't say such a thing. You only feel this way because you have not yet met the right suitor. One day, you will, the same as I did." A dreamy smile replaces the distress on her face, her expression pure light and bliss. She could sit model for a fresco for the new church being built down the street, she is that angelic. "Oh, I cannot wait for the wedding." Her sigh is a wish on wings, flying from her lips. "I shall be a princess on my wedding day."

She is so gloriously happy. Perhaps now is not the right time to tell her my secret.

"You are a princess already." We are both daughters of prominent Connecticut families. Mine sailed over to the New World on the *Mayflower* and built a fortune as merchants, while hers assembled an empire of coal mines. "I am happy for you and Philip."

Our carriage stutters to a stop to avoid a coal man who is pushing his cart across the street. Pedestrians and dogs and gentlemen on horseback congest Norwalk, Connecticut. Why, yesterday, we nearly hit a pig.

"The way the streets have been of late…" Ada clicks her tongue as she returns to earth. "I don't see how we shall be on time ever again." She shoots a desperate look through the window, probably imagining the horror of being late to church on her wedding day.

I do empathize. "Papa says the town has doubled in the fourteen years since the Civil War." Up here, people refer to it as the Rebellion, but Papa, who lived through it in Texas, still calls it the War of Northern Aggression. "At least the weather is dry, a boon for January." I curl my toes in my stiff new boots. "We could be mired in mud and snow."

Our carriage rolls on, but only to the corner, a dozen feet away, where I am distracted by a disheveled child on a burlap sack, with a chipped bowl on his lap. The little beggar cannot be more than six years old, straw hair sticking up in every direction, without a hat, gloves, or a decent coat. He keeps glancing behind him, where, in a doorway, his drunk father holds his mother by the arm while he beats her with a stick. The woman's eyes meet mine for a second, but they do not beg for help. Nor does she cry out to anyone else.

She looks away as if ashamed, pressing herself into the corner as if she wants to disappear.

Ada turns her head. "*Really.*"

The coachman does his best to keep to the more civilized parts of town, but he cannot avoid every bad street.

"How unsavory." She yanks the curtain closed to shut out the melee. "I do not understand why these people must be outside all the time. You would think the cold would keep them at home. Anyway, I wish you could meet someone like Philip. Then you wouldn't talk about horses."

Ada's fiancé resembles a horse—an opinion I keep to myself. Our extensive private education and our mothers' unending lectures have left us well-versed in good manners and etiquette.

Too much money and effort have been expended on molding me into a proper young lady, effort I appreciate. I just want to do more with who I've become than merely catching a husband. I plan to use every advantage afforded to me by society to become something scandalous: an independent woman.

The article I cut out of Papa's newspaper a week ago—before one of the maids could discard it—hides like a weapon in my pocket. I shall fight Mama's objections to my plans with *that*.

"I wish to be married on my birthday, in June.

Would that not be perfectly splendid? Love will find you too, Helen. You'll see."

I don't want to argue, but neither can I pretend any longer. It is exhausting to have to keep up with the charade. "I don't wish to marry. I should prefer an independent life of adventure." There. The secret is off my chest at last. Now I only have to inform my parents. Today is the day. I must speak up, before I lose my courage. "I am going to tell Mama and Papa that I wish to attend college."

"Truly! What would people say?"

What indeed. "You should have come with me to visit Mrs. Egerton." I saw our old schoolmistress this past weekend. "Maria Mitchell was there. She is traveling through Connecticut for speaking engagements. She generously stopped to give the girls a brief introduction to science."

"Who on earth is Miss Mitchell?"

"A professor at Vassar College in Poughkeepsie, New York, and an *astronomer*. A woman who believes with all her heart that our sex is capable of anything, including science and math. An independent woman."

"Too much book learning makes a woman sick and melancholic. My brother says excessive reading causes infertility."

Her brother, William, is studying to be a doctor. I don't know enough to argue with him. "All I want is to determine my own fate. I want to pick my own path and then be judged based on my own capabilities and merit. If I fail, I want to fail having tried, not because I never began because others tell me I can't."

"I am speechless." Her mouth, however, very much goes on. "You will settle down once you are married. I am only engaged, and look how happy I am." She beams, and to her credit, none of it is forced. She is that overjoyed by the prospect. "You cannot seriously wish to become a spinster."

"Your dreams are not my dreams, Ada." She will come to understand.

"I suppose it could be worse. At least you are not eloping with an inappropriate gentleman. God forbid," she adds.

We fall silent. Marjori Fielding, the most beautiful girl at school, a year older than us, eloped the winter before we graduated with a minister, of all people, who, according to the headmistress, should have known better.

"Marjori did not die in childbirth." Heat touches my cheeks. "Mama told me in confidence this morning."

"I envy you. My mother would never discuss anything remotely scandalous with me. What happened?"

I shouldn't have brought up the subject.

"Oh, do tell me," my friend pleads. "Or I shall imagine something sordid like being kidnapped by highwaymen."

"We read too many novels." I shake my head as a dull ache builds up in my chest. "The child inside her died at seven months, and her body failed to expel the little body."

"Poor Marjori. Was it one of those… That terrible procedure? Did she die from being cut open?"

"They did not remove it." I shudder, then shudder again.

I do not know what I find more terrifying, being carved up like the Christmas goose or living on with a dead child inside me. I have had a fear of dead bodies for as long as I can remember—I had been subjected at an age far too young to Papa's frightening stories of the war. The thought of corpses leaves me breathless and clammy.

Now, I am the one who has to hold on to the seat. I am light-headed. "Her husband held back the doctor and instructed the family and household to pray for a miracle. Mama said Marjori died of blood poisoning at the end."

I do not know what blood poisoning is, but it sounds as horrifying as the rest.

We do not speak for the remainder of the trip. What is there to say after a revelation as gruesome as that? We merely alternate between horrified and encouraging looks, each wanting to brace the other, but unsure how to accomplish such a feat, until at last our carriage rolls to a stop in front of my parents' house.

The three-story neo-Gothic mansion is the beauty of the neighborhood with its finials and hood moulds, Papa's pride and joy. He can wax poetic for hours about the lancet windows.

The coachman jumps down, giving our conveyance a jolt. He opens the door with "There you go, miss," then rolls down the step.

I work to find my voice. "Thank you, Jenkins."

"See you in the morning." Ada remains in the carriage. We live only six houses apart and have been sharing a ride to church every afternoon to work on the Easter Charity Bazaar with a dozen other ladies of our circle.

Her expression is still haunted. I reach back to touch her lifeless hands that are clasped in her lap. "Don't think about Marjori. Think about something else. Think about Philip. And do try to catch some sleep."

Mention of her fiancé is enough to tease a smile onto her face. "I am too excited. Oh, I might never sleep again."

She has been this way since Philip's Christmas proposal last week.

I wave her goodbye, then stiffen my spine. Today, I shall take my fate into my own hands. No engagement for me.

I climb the steps in a hurry, while appearing not to be in a hurry. *Ladies do not run, for heaven's sake,* Mama always says. If I had a dollar for every time she has scolded me, I would have the largest dowry in the country.

"Welcome home, miss." The new Irish maid collects my hat and coat, her red hair peeking from under her white cap.

She hovers too much, too nervous still that at her

first mistake, she will be dismissed. She is sixteen, the oldest of nine siblings, an important breadwinner in her family. She is missing a finger from an old factory accident and would not be employable in a house such as ours under normal circumstances, but her mother works in the kitchen of one of my mother's friends. Mama found it in her heart to help, as long as Annie keeps her bad hand out of view when we have guests.

"Hope you had a good meeting, miss."

"We are making progress. Thank you, Annie."

Nobody else rushes to welcome me. When one is the second oldest of five, one tends to get lost in the shuffle. Mama is kept busy with the younger children and managing the staff a mansion requires to run smoothly.

"They must have the wool." Her stern voice carries from the back hallway. A foghorn has nothing on her when she is determined. "I do not care if they find it itchy. We are in January."

She must be talking to the nanny about the children's stockings again. Abigail is nine. Fannie is eight.

When we lived in New York, Mama was an acclaimed hostess. Seats at Mary Churchill Hungerford's dinner table were fought over. People asked her opinion on every new marvel and often asked her for introductions. She was a bright light in a bright city, a force unto herself. And now… Well, she is doing her best to build up high-society Norwalk. She has not given up on her dinners.

I do not interrupt her tête-à-tête with the nanny. When Mama is in a mood, it is best to wait until her spirits settle.

An hour passes before she tracks me down in my room. "I want you to pay special attention to your appearance when you dress for dinner tonight, Helen."

My mother is the epitome of a fashionable society woman. Her navy-blue dress is princess line, after the Princess of Wales, who made the style popular. No horizontal seam at the waist, the dress is fitted to be slim, with long vertical tucks, and tight on the hips. No bustle either, but fabric spilling in the back into an exquisite train. She could pose for a painting.

"Do I not always try my best?" I turn the book on my lap cover down. She would be scandalized if she caught me reading *Anna Karenina,* a novel about a woman doing as she pleased, having an affair.

"Your father has invited over a friend."

"Who is it?"

"Edward Candee." Mama pats down her lace collar until it lays so. "His father owns the largest building supply business in the country."

"How exhilarating." I love Papa, but his friends tend to be ancient and boring.

"Mr. Candee's family is from New York."

"Oh." I tuck the book next to me in the armchair. I was born in New York City. We moved to Connecticut when I was three. "Do you think we shall ever move back?"

"You cannot possibly have any memories of those times, Helen. Please, do sit straight."

I shift until I am practically sitting on the book. "I remember the glamour." The sprawling city is a kingdom unto itself, infinitely more interesting than Norwalk. "I remember all the ornate buildings bathed in gaslight."

"You remember that from more recent visits. You are projecting your longing for big-city life onto what scant old memories you truly have. Do be sensible."

"Do you not miss the parties?"

She does. I know it from the abrupt way she steps back, as if the past is a carriage aimed to run her over, and she must jump out of the way. "Your father needs us here." In another step, she is in the hallway. "Wear one of your new dresses."

That light in her eyes…

Ada met her fiancé, Philip, at a dinner arranged by her parents. I am not falling into that trap. I brace myself and reach into my pocket.

She stops on the brink of leaving. "What is that?"

"I have been thinking." I stand, keeping myself between her and the chair and the book. For some time now, I have been taller than she is. Maybe it will serve as a reminder that at the age of twenty, I am no longer a child. "You know how much I loved school, how happy I was there."

"Yes, yes. You excelled."

"I could learn so much more. I want to attend college." The words rush out, along with the air from

27

my lungs, and then my chest tightens, and I can't draw a new breath.

"Oh, Helen."

I present the article I have been saving for this moment. And I have to breathe if I am to tell her the rest. "The University of Oxford is about to admit its first female student in the fall."

Having been born in England, Mama is enamored with all things English. As far as she is concerned, the cream of British society is infallible. She never disagrees with them.

Except this time.

"You are not going to England."

I want, so badly, for our conversation to go well. I need an ally if I am to convince Papa, who shall have the final word.

"I thought of Oberlin College in Ohio," I rush to present an option Mama might find more palatable. "They were the first to admit women on this side of the Atlantic. They have graduated a number of female students already."

"A coeducational institute?" Mama gasps, as if someone has brought up a brothel at a church dinner.

"I wish to receive the same education as men do."

"Do not mention this to your father. We cannot afford for him to have apoplexy. You know the business is at a crucial point."

"But…" *Speak fast. Speak well. Everything depends on this.* "How about Vassar, then? I should love to study geography. I want to learn more about the world I live in. And then someday, I could teach

28

other young women." And not only women of our class. Surely everyone deserves to know that the world is bigger than their kitchen. "You value education. You were the one who insisted that I receive one in the first place. Oh, Mama, if I—"

"A woman ought to be intelligent enough to hold a lively conversation. But as with everything else, enough is enough, and there is such a thing as too much." She waves away the very thought of my ambition. "What brought this about? I know Ada is engaged, and you must feel left behind. Ever since you became friends, you have done everything together." Sympathy sneaks into her eyes. "My child, you mustn't despair."

She hands me back my piece of paper—my dream in black-and-white print—and pats my hand.

At least she is not angry with me. As she moves along, a little smile plays at the corner of her lips.

I save the newspaper cutout in my top drawer, next to an article about Clara Barton. Known for her work during the war, she is giving lectures around the country to draw attention to her disaster relief and humanitarian efforts. I shall most certainly attend when she comes to Norwalk.

Rosie, my lady's maid, bustles in. "Which dress will it be, miss?"

I think about Mama's little smile as she left. "Let me think." I bet Papa has invited one of his *widowed* friends. "I want my short corset, if we still have it."

Rosie is dubious. "The new steam-molded ones make for a slimmer figure."

She is more than a decade older than I am, in the middle of her thirties, too old to be a maid, but since she never married, Mama kept her on. We brought her from New York. She has been working for us since she was seventeen, straight off the boat from England.

"I still feel distended from lunch. The short corset, not too tight. And my pink dress."

Pale pink, the color of childish innocence, high, square neckline, a short train that might as well not be there, and an abundance of ruffles—the dress of a girl rather than that of a woman.

"Pin my hair the same as when I was in school, please," I ask Rosie. "I have been thinking about it. The style flatters my face."

It does not. I was a silly chit then, wishing to appear more sophisticated than my age, missing the mark by a mile, appearing only more childish.

Rosie knows all this, yet she does as I ask.

"Another curl?"

She does balk at that. I already resemble a ruffled curtain. "Are you sure, miss?"

"Oh yes." I might be twenty years old, but by the time we finish, I barely look sixteen. "Perfect."

Maybe too much so. I ponder my visage in the mirror. Mama will never let me get away with this.

The key is not to be seen too soon. And so I hide in my room for as long as I can, until Mama sends for me, at last.

I remain unrushed as I descend the steps.

Mama is sitting on the red velvet settee in the

drawing room. When she sees me, her fan stops in midair. "Oh, Helen."

Frown lines are her nemesis, so she never frowns, as a rule, but her eyebrows twitch. And I know she is going to have words with Rosie, so I silently apologize to the maid. I will make it up to her somehow, I will.

"I suppose it is too late to send you back upstairs to change." Mama presses her fan against her chest. "What were you thinking?"

Papa looks up from the paper, mystified by our exchange. "Is anything amiss?"

An unladylike sound escapes Mama's lips. She has given up on educating Papa on the finer points of fashion, so instead, she scolds me. "I do not know what has gotten into you lately. I swear you wish to give me gray hair." She turns from me as if she cannot bear to look at me. "Oh, very well."

She is not one to easily capitulate, so I enjoy the victory, but not for overly long. I merely won a battle. The war is still ahead. I prepare for my next line of defense. All through dinner, I shall act as a simpleton. I shall alternate between simpering and offering vacant stares. Nothing annoys an old man faster than a silly child. Mama employs a staff of three to keep my younger sisters from Papa.

"Mr. Edward Willis Candee." Mary, the parlor maid, shows our visitor in.

Oh.

Well.

That is… Mr. Candee is not ancient.

31

After a gracefully executed bow, he kisses Mama's hand first. "Mrs. Hungerford. Your house is just as magnificent as my mother always raves about."

Mama's eyes soften. She smiles as if wrinkles no longer matter. She is smitten.

Then Papa's friend claims my gloved hand and touches his lips to my knuckles before straightening. His brown eyes are so sharp and inquisitive, they startle me. "Miss Hungerford."

"Mr. Candee."

"Here you are." Papa jovially claps him on the back before they shake hands.

Mr. Candee joins us for aperitifs, and by the time he escorts me to dinner, I learn that his father is the one who runs the building supply empire. The son manages their Connecticut interests. He is also a member of the Seventh Regiment of the New York Militia. He does carry himself like a military man. He is every inch a gentleman.

While I look like a foolish child. He must wonder where I have left my nanny.

Why, oh, why?

I pull myself straight in my chair in a vain attempt to at least appear taller. I regret my dress, but not half as much as I regret the tragedy of my hair.

"I am certain the depression is over," Mr. Candee tells Papa when asked about business.

"The optimism of young men." Papa toasts him. "I hope you are right, but if I've learned anything, it's that life is full of surprises. I first made myself a name in Texas and had a bright future planned there.

Then I lost my fortune during the Civil War. I had to return North with empty pockets."

"Yet you managed to build a lumber empire"— Mr. Candee's tone carries admiration—"with footholds in Albany and Brooklyn, as my father tells it."

"I had an opportunity to secure water rights in Clinton, Deep River, and Chester." Papa looks at his drink, then back at our guest, obviously torn between modesty and his favorite story. "In truth, at the time, I berated myself for gambling so." He casts an apologetic glance at Mama. "The move could have turned out to be an expensive disaster. Many failed in those difficult years that followed the war."

"Yet clever men prospered, and the economy did turn around," Mr. Candee says with the confidence of our new generation who only know about the war from the papers.

"Only because of all the foreign money that poured into lands in the West, and into railroads," Papa says. "I had hopes for a lasting recovery, a Second Industrial Revolution. Alas, overzealous land and railroad speculation brought us back into depression."

"We are faring better than the English."

I like that at every turn, Mr. Candee is optimistic.

"That much is true." Papa agrees for once. "They are losing their lead against the Continent."

I think I might be the only one who hears Mama's stifled, horrified gasp.

At any other house, the hostess would already

have reminded the gentlemen that such heavy topics impede digestion. Any remotely serious discussion at the dinner table goes against etiquette. Our dinners often veer to complicated subjects, however. Back in New York, Mama hosted parties for millionaire businessmen, politicians, and high-level diplomats.

"Could women not help our country?" I speak up. I must not sit there like a dolt, merely listening to the men.

Papa offers me a fond smile, one of the ones he used when I was young and brought him pretty rocks from the garden. "The ladies are doing their part by being as delightful and lovely as you are. You work very hard at your Easter Bazaar. Your grace and beauty keep us men going and give us something worth fighting for."

I want more. "President Hayes promised to sign a bill next month to allow female attorneys to argue cases before the Supreme Court."

"I cannot imagine what good might come out of that." Papa taps his finger on his glass. "A waste of everyone's time. I fully believe in the education of women, but there ought to be limits set. Unchecked progress never turns out well. Drive a carriage too fast, and the wheels come off, eh?"

"Are you interested in the law, Miss Hungerford?" Mr. Candee is not as quick with dismissal as my father.

"I am interested in a variety of subjects." I'm pleased with myself for managing to sound like an adult, even if I do not look the part.

Papa offers a rueful smile. "I am afraid my Helen is the type of girl who has an opinion on everything. Reads rather more than is healthy."

"Too many books. Is there such a thing?" Our guest responds to Papa, but he keeps watching me. "Any favorite titles?"

His brown eyes have an amber tint, and I am unexpectedly flustered under his keen attention. I cannot remember a book, other than the one I am currently reading—*Anna Karenina*—a title I will not share. I'd be locked in the attic.

"*Little Women*," I rush to say when my brain restarts. "By Louisa May Alcott."

"What do you admire about it?"

Ambitious Jo, for one. And the even more ambitious and spirited Miss Alcott, who writes to support her family. A self-supporting woman who does not rely on others for money and thus does not have to suffer anyone's rules. Thoughts I'd do best not to share with our visitor. "Sisterhood." Before he could ask me another question, I move on. "Mama told me you are from New York, Mr. Candee."

"My father has a building supply store at the foot of East Twenty-Sixth Street and West Fifty-Second Street."

My family is in lumber. He was most definitely invited to dinner for a reason. He must be aware of our parents' machinations as well, yet he is far from uncomfortable. He appears to be happy to be in the middle of this play.

"Do you like New York, Miss Hungerford?"

"I do. I born on Eighth Avenue. The building supply business must be thriving if you are expanding."

"Are you interested in commerce?"

"Should everyone not be so? Commerce is our country's engine. Business enterprise propels growth. Norwalk's population has doubled since the Civil War." I parrot tidbits I have learned from Papa, then fall silent, catching myself, resenting that I should feel a need to impress. Why do I even care what Mr. Candee thinks of me? I am not looking for a gentleman to marry.

"You must agree, then, that better times are waiting ahead."

Mama frowns on my opinions, Papa tolerates them, while Mr. Candee asks for them. My friends have little patience for my philosophizing, as they call it. But Mr. Candee… Oh, this is interesting.

If I am to make a difference in this world, I am going to need educated friends. And as education is still denied to most women, some of those friends must, by necessity, be men.

Mr. Candee has recently moved to Norwalk. We will almost certainly see each other again. His father and mine are good friends. This will not be the last time he comes to dinner. He shall stop by again.

I will *not* be dressed like a child then.

CHAPTER 3

Madison
  September 2, 2024
  Nova Scotia

"We are raising the Titanic," Ramsey repeats.

"Technically, we're raising the dead," Oliver says to me. "You, more so than the rest of us."

Some people find my work creepy, but other than teaching, this is what I do for a living. I resurrect people, paint them back to life from their remains. I find it satisfying, especially when I'm doing police work on an unidentified victim. Sometimes, they let me be in the room when they bring in the family. The news is always a heartbreak. Inevitably, they were still hoping their missing loved one would be found alive, and to find out otherwise is a slap of sharp grief. But at least they have closure, which will eventually bring healing. Even if I'm not there to see that stage, the thought that I helped makes me happy.

In the conference room, we lift our glasses and drink to TTP. The initials stand for…drum roll…*The Titanic Project*. The words are emblazoned in gold on a black background, on Ramsey's last slide. After he sets his glass down, he hands us each a T-shirt with the logo from a box under the desk.

"My grandmother told me once that her aunt was on the *Titanic*—" I swallow the rest. I don't want to have to explain my grandmother.

Of course, Oliver hears me. "Oh?"

"Don't get too excited about it. She also told me she had an affair with Mickey Rooney."

"I smell a bestselling biography."

Ramsey shoots us a quelling glance. "We start tomorrow morning. Normally, there'd be a press release; however, I'm pausing that until next Monday. We have all our permits, but I'd like to have a few bone samples in hand before word gets out about the project. I expect protesters, people who have nothing better to do with their time. We'll overcome objections, of course. I just don't want to be stalled right out of the gate."

"Why would anyone object?" Eleanor asks.

"People will protest anything," I say. "I once painted a Kritosaurus, working closely with the head paleontologist, from an incomplete skeleton, on a project heavily attacked by antievolutionists. They sent me daily death threats because they didn't believe dinosaurs existed."

"May I ask about accommodations?" Julia focuses us on a more immediate concern.

"On the premises." Ramsey indicates the building with a sweeping gesture. "We thought it best to keep everyone together for security."

"Meals?" I love breakfast in bed, my favorite part of staying in hotels on location. It's not the same at home, stumbling downstairs to make coffee and toast and eggs, then dragging it all back upstairs.

"Feel free to order delivery. Save your receipts."

"The email said it's a six-month project," Julia speaks up again. "Any breaks?"

"A few weeks off at Christmas." Ramsey sets down his champagne glass and heads for the door. "Who would like to see the labs?"

Words to cause a nerd stampede.

We're right on his heels.

"Promising." Oliver nods at the plain gray industrial carpet in the hallway as we go. "When the building looks too nice, I worry that they didn't leave enough money for the equipment and the scientists."

I can't say I've ever paid much attention to the carpets. I'll give him this: he's observant.

My phone pings with a text. Gabi from my old lab at the university wants to know if I've landed anything yet. It kills me that I can't tell her about TTP until after the press conference. I so badly want her to share the news with our department head.

Ramsey goes around the corner and stops at the first door. "All yours, Madison."

Since I'm here as a forensic artist, I'm not assigned

a lab. I get a storage room as my "studio," with wall-to-wall gray metal shelves.

The space is about fourteen feet by sixteen, no natural light, only a couple of standing lights, so I wouldn't have to use the overhead fluorescent. The setup will work, and I don't mind the shelves either. I check out the boxes on them.

"You should have everything you need here," Ramsey assures me. "If anything's missing, just ask."

I run my finger over the stack of eight-by-ten canvases. "You want paintings as well as digital reconstructions."

The police don't require that.

"Correct," Ramsey says. "This is a full production. We want portraits of each of the victims, as well as a figure drawing of each person. When the dead were fished out of the water, their clothing was recorded to aid identification. I'll send you the file."

"That'd be helpful. Thank you."

Ramsey moves on, while Julia asks, "How long does it take you to paint a portrait?

"Under ideal circumstances, two days. After the facial reconstruction with tissue-depth markers and the digital mockup."

"How do you know you're done?"

"The portrait is finished when a person looks back at me from the canvas."

We follow Ramsey across the hall into Oliver's lab. His space is twice as large as mine, fully equipped. I've seen plenty of forensics labs in my time, and I'm impressed.

A glass wall divides off extra space in the back that's empty save for a half dozen cardboard boxes stacked in a pile and a small table in the corner. The glass double doors between the two spaces stand open.

"The liquid nitrogen freezers for cryogenic storage will eventually go in there," Ramsey says.

I pick up an osteometric board from a mess of lab paraphernalia. It's for measuring bones. I wonder if one of the boxes in my studio has one too. If not, no big deal. I brought one in my kit. When I travel for assignment, I travel with at least the basics.

Oliver steps up to the NOMAD, a handheld portable X-ray, and pats it. He doesn't say anything, but I can tell he's pleased.

"You'll share the equipment with Julia." Ramsey points to the next table. "Microscopy station." Then the next. "Photography station."

Oliver nods. "It'd be a waste of money to have two of everything."

Eleanor's lab is next, right next to Oliver's, with all the equipment she'll need for gene sequencing. To prevent contamination, we look through the window it has to the hallway instead of going in. Powerful machines hum in their white, plastic casings like doctors in their lab coats, doing rounds. Everything is brand-new, first-rate. Both labs are well supplied, tilting into oversupplied, the kind of labs only private financing can create.

Julia receives a simple office, the smallest of the four workspaces, farther down the hallway. She only pokes her head in. "It's plenty. I'll do most of my work graveside, at the cemetery."

Ramsey turns back. "Your rooms are this way."

He sounds like a camp counselor. His tone says, *I don't know how you miscreants got in, but I'm going to squeeze some good work out of you before your time here ends*. It brings back memories. For most of my childhood, I spent the summers at various science camps.

We march across the lobby, grabbing our suitcases on the way, then file into what Ramsey calls the East Wing. The facility is sprawling.

Our rooms are square, about ten feet by ten feet. Someday, they'll be somebody's office, but right now, each holds a twin bed, a dresser, a nightstand, and a desk with an info packet. Not so much a hotel room as a room at a student hostel. I park my luggage, then rejoin the tour.

"Toilets." Ramsey points out a couple of standard office bathrooms, one for men and one for women. "Showers are on the lab side, standard requirement for any lab that uses hazardous chemicals. I forgot to mention that earlier."

"I'll show them later," Eleanor offers.

We stop at the end of the hallway, in front of the last door, which Ramsey pushes open. "I'll leave you with the break room." He glances at his phone. "I have an executive-level Zoom. We'll discuss the full plan of attack at our first morning meeting, tomorrow."

Once he's gone, we check out the crowded space that holds one table, six chairs, and the minimum of cabinetry, in addition to a fridge and two vending machines.

Oliver sets the time on the microwave. "So, what do we think about TTP?"

I almost play it cool, but then… "I'm excited."

"I am Eastern European," Julia says. "I haven't been excited a day of my life, and I'm not about to start." She opens the fridge, then steps aside to show us that it's empty. "Where did Eleanor go?"

I stick my head out into the hallway. She's walking away with Ramsey. "I think she's going back to her room. You think she's with TrinovarDNA?"

"It'd make sense. She's a geneticist." Oliver steps to the two vending machines that stand pressed together, as if they are too scared to stand alone. "At least these are filled. How do we feel about junk food?"

Julia shoots them the evil eye. "They should call those things what they are, an amusement park slide for carbs. How about we order delivery?"

My heart goes pitter-patter. "Sushi?"

Oliver taps his phone. "Tuna Tangerine?" Apparently, he's already downloaded an app for local restaurants. "Four and a half stars."

"Tuna Tangerine it is," Julia and I say at the same time.

I think we're going to make a great team.

While we wait for the delivery, we squeeze in around the table, and I send a quick message to Dad.

Everything checks out. All is well.

"Feels like my condo kitchen back in Toronto."

Julia runs her palm over the plastic tabletop. "Hugs a little too tightly, but it's not too bad."

"It doesn't encourage lingering." It's like a faculty lounge, minus all the gossip.

"The corporate overlords wouldn't want long breaks." She looks at each of us in turn. "So…why are you here? Really."

"In between engagements," I say.

And Oliver says, "Same."

Julia taps a finger on the table. "I'm hiding from my ex."

"Is he…" *None of my business.* "Sorry."

"Don't worry about it. I'm not afraid *of* him," she tells us without blinking. "I'm afraid *for* him. It's best if he can't find me for a minute."

September 3, 2024 (Tuesday)

The sign at Fairview Lawn cemetery doesn't say CLOSED FOR RAISING THE TITANIC. It says CLOSED FOR UPKEEP.

The sky is a softly brushed pale blue on an endless canvas, the temperature in the low sixties. I don't even have a coat on, just a hoodie. Yet the sunshine brings no cheer. The air is imbued with a sense of loss and tragedy; Oliver and I breathe in heaviness with every breath.

The solemn mood of cemeteries settles on our shoulders, but the usual peace is missing here.

Yellow KEEP OUT, DANGER ribbons flit in the breeze, circling the *Titanic* graves. A noisy yellow compact excavator rules the scene. The machine works on the right side of the grave, while a white staging tent stands on the left.

Exhumations always resemble industrial work sites, and this one is no different.

Technically, only Julia, our archaeologist, and her locally sourced assistants have to be present, but Oliver and I have come over because neither of us has anything to do yet. Eleanor stayed in her lab to double-check her equipment.

In addition to the security guard at the gate, four more are spread out, same gray uniforms, same HSS insignia, as the guards at the lab. They're about the same age too. Looks like HSS prefers hiring college students.

"It's a great day for a...grave digging," Oliver sings to the tune of Billy Idol's "White Wedding," and his unexpected humor surprises a quick laugh out of me.

Is it possible that Oliver has layers?

"Can't believe how fast the project is progressing." I turn my face to the sun, not ready for summer to be over yet. For the dig too, I hope the weather will stay warm and dry for as long as possible. "We only signed the contract yesterday, and today, we're here."

"The remains have to be out before the ground freezes." Oliver watches the excavator. "Ramsey must have had the dig scheduled for a while."

"Had to be awful sure we'd all say yes." Then again, who says no to a once-in-a-lifetime project?

"Or he had a B team lined up, just in case."

"I don't like the thought of that."

We stop to stand outside the yellow-ribbon corral. Julia is having a chat with her assistants, two young women I'd bet are graduate students.

The documentary crew is recording, two cameramen and Maya Carter, the director. Maya is my age, my height, but with the body of a warrior, her braids hanging to her waist, as precise as if they were made by a mechanical engineer. My first impression of her this morning was that here is a woman who gets shit done. Having her in charge makes me feel considerably better about the documentary component of the project.

I watch her from the corner of my eye. I don't look directly at any of them.

Never let your eyes meet the camera, she told us at the morning meeting where we were introduced. *Pretend that we're not here. Viewers prefer a fly-on-the-wall experience.*

"You'd think Ramsey would have invited the media for day one. This whole project was created to build publicity." I speak low enough that the microphones won't pick me up over the machine noise. "He's right about getting some work done before people start throwing up roadblocks, though."

"I ran into him this morning. He was coming from Eleanor's room. He says we're starting up low-key, but the reinterment in the spring will be a huge public ceremony."

"Mm." The heel of my shoe sinks into the soil, and I shift on my feet. The ground is soft. It must have rained in the past few days. I nod toward the granite headstone resting on its side a few feet from the grave. "Looks like a dead seal waiting for the hunters to skin him." Shouldn't have said that. I wave away the words. "Sorry. Cemeteries make me morbid. Ever wonder how the deceased feel about being dug up? What if they don't want to be disturbed?"

"I think they'd want their names on their headstones. They'd want to be reconnected with their relatives."

"That's what I always tell myself when I'm working with the police."

The local contractor who handles the exhumations is working with a skeleton crew of three. Ramsey's idea, probably, to keep the number of people on the job to a minimum. The fewer people involved, the lower the chance that something will leak early. Also, the fewer people, the fewer paychecks. Exhumations don't come cheap.

In the US, they cost about five thousand dollars per body. Disposal of the old casket is extra, but there won't be any casket remnants at this stage. Wood decomposes in a few years, unless we're talking about a desert environment, or wood under water. The fungi that compost wood need moisture and air.

In the desert, they don't have moisture. Underwater, they don't have air. It's really pretty simple.

"How did you end up a forensic artist?" Oliver asks me.

"In a roundabout way. My father worships science. He wanted me to go into medicine. My anatomy professor was the best teacher I've ever had. I got into anatomy because of her. She liked my drawings, introduced me to a forensic artist friend of hers, and I ended up going for forensics with an art minor. I pieced together what skills I'd need."

"Was it difficult to find a job?"

"I worried that it would be." The world needs a limited number of people with my specific expertise. "But I lucked out. Boston PD gave me my first project before I even officially graduated. Most forensic artists are officers without any training in anatomy or art. Your captain points at you at a meeting and says, *We need someone, you're going to a quick class*. Convictions depend on this, so it's more important to know police procedure than drawing. You don't want to muck up a court case by doing something wrong, so few outsiders are accepted. I only managed because of my professor's friend."

"Anatomy nerds unite," says Oliver, a hopeless nerd in every possible way. Even his haircut is nerdy. Too straight. I wouldn't be surprised if he cut it himself.

"What's it like being a YouTube star?" He tilts his head.

"Easy on the *star* part. I don't think fifty thousand

followers make me a celebrity." I only post a couple of times a month, about forensic art, past cases, new methods. "It's a way of keeping me in the game. Brings a few assignments. I'm pretty sure it brought me this. Ramsey must have seen me. Not that many forensic artists have online platforms—"

A young woman pops up from behind a tall gravestone a hundred feet behind the digger. The intruder edges up to the yellow tape, cell phone in hand. Not that everyone doesn't have their phone in hand every minute.

"I don't think she's supposed to be here." I pull my hoodie up to partially cover my face. "Ramsey won't be happy if the media learn of this too early. How did she sneak through security?"

"Five guards can't cover the whole cemetery." Oliver raises his hand to catch the attention of the nearest guy, and the man spots the problem at once, then takes off running.

In seconds, the woman is escorted away.

Maya calls "Break! Five minutes."

The sky darkens as if an invisible hand is brushing on layers of gray to hide the sun. I hope it won't rain.

Julia waves us closer. "We're inches from where we need to be. Come meet Lily Mei Chen and Zuri Williams."

They have muddy gloves on, so we don't shake hands.

"Oliver."

"Madison. How long will it set you back if rain fills the hole?"

"What am I, an amateur?" Julia scoffs. "I have tarps and water pumps. I've done this in the Amazon." She jerks her head toward her tent. "Coffee?"

At the same time, our phones ping.

Oliver's is in his back pocket, mine is in my bag, so he reads the message first. "Ramsey. News of the exhumations leaked. He wants us back at head-quarters."

I glance at my text. "Same."

Julia has to tug off her gloves to read her orders. "I am to stay and finish. Essential personnel only in the cemetery."

Oliver and I are in the parking lot when we're ambushed. A news van pulls up right in front of us. And before we can react, a reporter jumps out of the van—young, beautiful, blonde.

"Excuse me." A microphone materializes in her hand. "Could you tell me who you are and what's going on here?"

Her cameraman—equipment on his shoulder—rushes from the back of the van to back her up.

I hold up my hand to ward them off. "No comment."

We're not authorized to give a statement, so Oliver and I turn our backs on them and walk in the opposite direction, hoping to spot our chauffeur, but the car isn't where he dropped us off. In Davey's defense, we were supposed to stay awhile. He must have gone off for lunch.

"Don't you think the public has the right to know what's happening here? We had reports of unusual activity in the cemetery. Are you involved in any of this?"

"No comment." We hurry away with measured steps, purposeful but not fleeing. Optics are everything. News footage of us running away like thieves would upset Ramsey.

When I can no longer hear the reporter behind us, I glance back. She and her guy are heading toward the dig. "Wish TTP would hold the damned news conference already." Rain begins to drizzle. I reach for my phone. "I'm calling Davey to hurry."

"Too late."

Another news van is turning into the parking lot. *Aw, dammit.*

"This way." Oliver pulls me in the opposite direction before I can send off a message.

We hurry alongside a fence, out to the road, ending up next to a bus stop, at the same time that a blue-and-yellow bus rolls in.

Oliver nudges me forward. "Hop on."

Why not. "At least we'll be out of the rain." I drop into the empty front seat and scoot to the window to make room for him. "We can ride into the city center and call Davey to pick us up there. Lessens the chances of someone following us back to headquarters."

"I have a better idea." Oliver doesn't sit down. "We'll jump off at the next stop."

I try to think of a tourist attraction he might want to show me, but my knowledge of the city is scant, and I come up empty.

We're at the next bus stop in two minutes. I follow him off.

"Come on." He crosses the street.

Apparently, we're going for a walk in the rain.

To the right are railroad tracks, one set next to another and another, running off into the distance. On the far side of the tracks spreads the bay, as gray as the sky it reflects. The sprinkling of white boats are mere specks in the water compared to the container ship that is being loaded in the harbor.

I would think we are in an industrial zone, except, to the left of us, lies a perfectly normal residential neighborhood. "Where are we?"

"Fairview Cove."

"Why are we here?" A flock of seagulls flies over us, and I duck.

Oliver, unperturbed, points at a cottage straight ahead. "I live here."

What is he talking about? "We both came from the airport."

"The driver picked me up at home, then we went to give you a ride."

"You had suitcases."

"I made a bid to work from home, but TTP wouldn't go for it. Ramsey is big on control. You might have noticed." Oliver grabs a key from under the nearest flowerpot that houses a giant of a geranium in exuberant pink. "Come on in."

I look at him.

He looks at me. A few seconds pass before he drops his hand from the doorknob. "Sorry. I didn't even think about that. Do you want to go to the neighborhood coffee shop?"

He understands my dilemma without me having to explain, a point in his favor. I'm a woman, invited into the house of a man I've only met yesterday. Nobody knows where I am.

"Let me text Julia, in case anyone gets worried when they can't find us."

Couldn't wait for Davey. Took the bus to Oliver's house at Fairview Cove. Will grab a cab back to the lab.

"Are you sure this is okay?" Oliver unlocks the door but doesn't open it. "I don't mind going to the coffee shop. "Or… Hey, we have a food truck a few blocks up that sells the best donair in the city."

"Is that Canadian for donut?"

He shakes his head at me as if I'm a lost cause, an uncivilized barbarian, a.k.a. American. "Beef kebab with sweet garlic sauce."

"Ah, for the more sophisticated palate." I find myself curious to see how he lives. "I appreciate the offer, but I'm fine with hanging with you here."

From the outside, the house is a typical rancher, a home you see in any suburban neighborhood in North America, white vinyl siding with gray shingles on the roof, a red front door, and a wide strip of enthusiastic foundation plants. Then I follow him inside, and the living room is a different world altogether. The space is a riot of colors and shapes, a bona fide jungle. An explosion of plants thrives on every available surface.

"I didn't know you were a gardener. Wow."

"Working with dead people for the police and thinking about all the various ways they were killed didn't use to bother me." He shrugs, the movement so slight, I might have just imagined it. "Then Covid came. I watched the news, all the dead being carried out of their houses, and the refrigerator trucks at the hospitals." A pause. "A good friend of mine died." He looks at his plants, then back at me. "I needed to be more involved with life."

The weird thing is, I don't think that's weird. "After the lockdowns were over, I found it difficult to handle skulls. I didn't want to work with bones all day. I needed a mental break. I actually started *painting* painting."

"I was picking up half-dead plants from the grocery store for fifty cents, where they stash them in the corner next to the birthday balloon counter. I didn't want anything else to die, if it was within my power to help." He shakes his head as if it's all silly.

"No, I get it."

A moment of understanding passes between us, a tenuous new link. "Feel free to walk around," he says. "Coffee?"

Neither of us got to drink the cup Julia offered at the cemetery.

"Thank you." I step up to the bay window. "Great

view." And a northern light, preferred by artists. I don't want anything super bright hitting the canvas and messing with my perception of color when I paint. "Great everything."

"I inherited the house from my aunt."

"She must have loved you a lot." I turn back to him. "I told you how I ended up in forensics. What got you into it?"

"I like bringing people back." His smile is half embarrassed, half apologetic. "That sounds creepy. I don't mean it in a necromancer way." He pauses, flinches. "I shouldn't have referenced necromancy. Now you'll think I'm a nerd."

Sooo far ahead of him… Yet the more awkward he looks, the more I want to set him at ease. "Hey, for most of elementary school, I wanted to be a time-traveling doctor. I spent hours daydreaming about going back and fixing my mother." Since I brought her up, now I have to explain. "She died of cancer when I was little."

"I'm sorry." Oliver pauses in the middle of pouring water into the coffee machine. "My parents also passed when I was a baby."

"Do you remember them?" I'd give anything for just one faded memory of my mother.

He shakes his head. "But I can watch them whenever I want to. I have a hundred hours of recordings. They were actors."

I search his face to see if I recognize any of his features from the silver screen. "Would I know their names?"

"Daytime TV here in Canada, nothing huge. They met on set. *The Wind in the West.* I don't think it ever ran in the US."

"What happened to them?"

He spoons the ground coffee in the machine with meticulous care, and its earthy, nutty aroma wafts across the kitchen. "Two idiot small-time criminals figured out actors must have a lot of money and broke in, in the middle of the night. When there was no safe, no stacks of cash, in their frustration, they stabbed my parents." He says the words matter-of-factly, with that blank expression I've always interpreted as bored but now I recognize as controlled emotion. "Then they set the house on fire."

The black smoke of horror fills my lungs. "How did you survive?"

"The firemen whisked me out. I found out later from my aunt who raised me that I was in the middle of my parents' bed, covered with a blanket. I think when my dad heard noise downstairs, he went to investigate. Then, when my mom heard him talking to someone, she must have gone after him to help. She must have covered me up first. When the burglars came up to look for money, they must have thought I was a pillow. Either I was asleep and didn't cry, so I went unnoticed, or I cried, and they knew I was there…"

He leaves the rest unsaid, that the robbers set the house on fire anyway, not caring that they were burning a child alive in his parents' bed.

"I'm sorry. I can't even imagine." But I do, and

the images, the crying baby with flames surrounding him, scratch my eyes until they want to water.

"Anyway." He offers a geeky smile, likely meant so I won't feel like a complete idiot for forcing him to talk about the tragedy. "I am the boy who lived. Milk?"

"No, thank you." I run my fingers over the nearest branch of the nearest plant, a Norfolk pine. I need a minute. It feels stupid to be more emotional than Oliver. "Do you have any siblings?"

"I don't but would have loved to have a couple. I have a cousin almost twenty years older than I am. Javier was out of my aunt's house by the time I came along. He's a successful sculptor. We were too far apart in age to hang out as I grew up, but we've become pretty good friends lately. You?"

"A half brother."

"Are you close?"

"Not really. My father was with the mother for only a year. I think the boy is around twelve. They don't keep in touch."

"What do you paint?" Oliver asks next. "Other than forensic portraits."

"A few aquarelles here and there, strictly as a hobbyist. I've always doodled. For about half of high school, before I found science, I wanted to be an artist."

Actually, it wasn't so much that I found science but that I found that when I talked about science, my father paid slightly more attention to me.

"I'd love to see your art." Oliver glances at the phone in my hand.

"I'm not that good." But protesting feels immature. He opened his home to me and is allowing me free range, sharing with me his most private space and his past. My reluctance is nothing but ego. If I'm terrible, I don't want to hear it. Then again, so what? Even if he laughs at my sad attempts, his opinion isn't going to kill me.

I bring up a picture on my phone screen, three blue teacups against an orange background. I like how the complementary colors give the piece vibrancy.

He says nothing as he inspects the image.

I scroll on to a bagel and a teacup. This one I'm proud of. The teaspoon is the first time I caught the way the light glints off metal.

When Oliver is still silent, I show him a third piece, teacups stacked on a windowsill. I got the glass right, after a dozen tries, there and not there at the same time. Transparent objects and the visual distortions they cause are a trial.

He says, "I see."

He's not going to fake enthusiasm. That's fine. I prefer honesty.

I smile because he shouldn't be made to feel awkward for not lying. "I'm stuck. I need to paint more, but in addition to the forensic portraits, until recently, I was also teaching at Boston University. Once my position was eliminated, I had more time, but I had to spend it on a job search and looking for extra income in the meantime."

I fade back into the jungle in his living room. The myriad shades of green soothe me. The banana trees in the corner are obviously thriving, as are the orchids and the philodendrons, the rubber trees, and many more plants I can't name. All that verdant life feels like a hug. Just standing there in that miniature Garden of Eden is a meditation. The graceful branches and lianas surround me with peace.

When my coffee is done, Oliver brings the cup to me. "What do you think of my green experiment?"

"Thank you. It's like a different world in here."

"That's the idea. When I said I wanted to be surrounded by life, I meant it."

"Will you be stopping by to water? You have to, right? Whether Ramsey likes it or not."

"I have a system set up." He taps a thin rubber hose that runs between the plants.

Once I spot the first, I see a dozen others. "Clever."

"The whole system is on a timer." Oliver points to a gadget plugged into the outlet below the light switch. "Sometimes, I have to travel for work. Sugar? Milk?"

"Black is fine. Do you ever work outside the country?"

"Not really. I signed up once as a volunteer to work on mass graves from the war in Croatia, but nothing came of it. Let me grab a cup for myself. Make yourself at home."

I sip my caffeine and stroll to a doorway. The next room, which would be the dining room in the average house, is a library with wall-to-wall shelving. An explosion of plants rules here too, blessed by an oversized window.

A person's home tells a lot about them. Oliver's house says that I misjudged him. He's not boring. He's a man who surrounds himself with knowledge and life and beauty. I feel comfortable in his space.

I browse his books, a temptation I can never resist. Every time I'm at someone's house, I check out their bookcase. His titles are about plants, travel, and history. "Are you glad you responded to TTP's cryptic email?"

"I am, so far. Forensic anthropology is a synonym for *irregular paychecks*. Another source of income is always welcome. If it turned out to be something I didn't want to be part of, I could always walk away. But if I didn't respond, maybe I'd miss out on an adventure and regret it. People regret more things that they didn't do than things that they did."

"I bet plenty of people regretted sailing on the *Titanic*."

"Touché." My dark humor surprises a smile out of him.

We end up sitting in the kitchen. The entire house is inviting, but the gravity of kitchen tables is irresistible. It's one of the laws of physics.

"I really like your house. Good vibes." Maybe it's the view, maybe it's the plants, maybe it's the man whose low-key, balanced energy keeps me on an even keel.

I want to ask him about the waxy white flowers in the corner, but my phone pings with a text. "Probably Ramsey. He'll want to know when we're returning to the lab."

I tap the message. It's from my department head at Boston University. *Dean willing to admit he made a mistake letting you go. He's ready to hire you back. Return to the mother ship.*

Oliver pauses in savoring his coffee. "Did something bad happen?"

I must look startled. I rearrange my face. "Nothing bad." I can't look away from the words I've spent months holding my breath for, waited so desperately to hear. TTP is a unique opportunity, but it's a temporary project. I need a steady paycheck. Would Ramsey let me out of the contract?

I don't explain my job in academia to Oliver. We're not close enough, don't know enough of each other's previous lives, and I'm afraid he might accidentally let something slip in front of Ramsey. I tuck my phone into my back pocket. I need to think about this.

We finish our coffees, then Oliver calls an Uber, and I'm almost sorry, because his home is the polar opposite of our sterile office building. Yet that is where I live. *Temporarily*.

The streets we pass through are busy, the sidewalks filled with people, skyscrapers reaching to the sky. The economic slowdown spreading around the world hasn't yet reached Halifax.

Oliver leaves me to gawk in peace and doesn't offer commentary.

He only says, "Here we are," when we turn into our office park.

The car reaches our building and rolls up to the entrance where a pack of media hounds lies in wait. As soon as we walk toward them, the pack attacks us.

"Do you work for TrinovarDNA?"

"Why are you opening up the *Titanic* graves?"

"What is your purpose with the remains?"

They block our way to the door.

"How do you respond to people who say you're exploiting the victims?"

CHAPTER 4

Helen

December 31, 1879

The actor is about to dance right off the stage in his thigh-high boots. The set is colorful, the songs gay, the story written to elicit laughter, but it could all turn into tragedy in a blink.

I fan myself. "Thank goodness we have balcony seats."

Mr. Candee received permission from my parents to escort me to the Fifth Avenue Theatre. We are back in New York for the holidays, the guests of the Candees.

The actor dances with so much gusto that several times he teeters on the last board. He keeps me on the edge, and I hold my breath with the rest of the audience. I lose myself in the New Year's Eve premiere of *The Pirates of Penzance*, a comic opera in two acts.

Then the song ends, and the curtain sweeps down for the intermission. Mishap averted.

The lights flicker on, illuminating us all, dispelling the intimacy of the dark. I straighten my spine. Ladies do not slouch. A lady's spine should never touch the back of a chair in public. I want my escort to see me as a lady, want him to forget our initial meeting when I acted like a child on a stupid whim. I want him to see us as friends, which necessitates that he see us as equals in intellect and maturity.

"Are you enjoying the performance Miss Hungerford?"

"Tremendously. Thank you, Mr. Candee."

Despite the lights, we're still in our own bubble. The elegant audience buzzes around us, but we are in our own sphere, like the skating couple in my mother's favorite glass globe ornament on our Christmas tree.

"Please, call me Edward."

We have met half a dozen times by now. He has dined at our house multiple times and escorted me on carriage rides. He is educated, well-read, well traveled, at home in the business world as well as in New York society.

"Only if you call me Helen."

His slight, fashionable mustache twitches upward. "Helen."

I search for something either entertaining or intelligent, but end up with the banal. "Gilbert and Sullivan never disappoint, do they?"

"Never." He stands up and offers me his arm. "Would you allow me the pleasure of treating you to a glass of champagne, Helen?"

"Thank you, Edward."

I rise, and his gaze glides along the folds of my silver sateen dress, down to the hem, then up again, where the sateen leaves my shoulders bare. I accept the arm that's offered. I *will* erase all memory of the childish frock I wore at our first meeting. I am twenty-one. I am very much an adult. I am a grown woman.

The gaslights wave and flicker.

"I was reading about Mr. Edison in the paper. Do you think his electric lightbulb might have a chance?" I ask Edward, in part because I want him to know that I keep abreast of current affairs, and also because he is a well-informed man whose opinions I value.

"Electricity is too unstable. It wouldn't be safe inside a house. Curious children would be shocked to death."

A gruesome thought, but he is likely right. I tend to become excited over every new invention, while he is more sensible.

We have our drinks in the upstairs gallery, champagne for me and brandy for him. People smile at us in an *Isn't that a nice young couple* way. I do not mind. People see what they expect to see.

"Edward." An older gentleman greets him in passing, a gold watch chain glinting beneath his tailcoat. "Do convey my regards to your father. I shall call on him next week."

"Yes, sir."

A man of our own age strolls over in a sharply cut suit. He even walks like a dandy, with a spring in his knees. "And where have you stolen this beauty from?" His eyes spark. "Miss."

Before Edward can even properly introduce us, more acquaintances gather. He knows nearly everyone. He is charming, a witty conversationalist, and his friends are equally amusing and well educated.

I enjoy being part of his set. Instead of weddings and fashion—the most common topic of conversation among the ladies—the men talk about horses, architecture, and travel. I am relieved that I can keep up. I am grateful to Mama for the private education I did receive at her behest, and for her allowing frank and wide-ranging discussion at our dinner table.

The intermission passes too quickly, but it lasts long enough to give me a taste of the life I want: New York, theatre, galleries, museums, travel, intellectual conversations. I want my mind to keep expanding and sharpening. I want my life to be more than worrying about what's the latest trend in curtains. And yet, independence remains out of my grasp.

To move to New York and set up house here would require funds, an income of my own, which would require an occupation. Very few occupations, however, are available or considered appropriate for a woman of my class. It is a conundrum.

The second act of the play is even funnier than the first one. Every time Edward breaks out in a masculine laugh, I feel the warm sound in my chest. He is my window to a life I aspire to create for myself. I am grateful that we are friends.

"I am glad Gilbert and Sullivan decided to hold the premiere in New York this time," I tell him on our way to his beautifully appointed carriage after the performance.

"For the first time, but not the last, I predict." He gallantly hands me up to my seat.

I nestle into the cocoon of velvet and mahogany as he climbs in and sits opposite me. In my dove-gray wool coat, white ermine edging the sleeves and collar, I am protected from the chill of the night. I tug my matching leather gloves higher up my wrists.

"I suppose our theatres are larger and more modern. Although, I do adore the Strand." I have traveled with my parents to Europe multiple times. "But our country has the kind of energy that comes from being new, do you not think? A fast-growing city has its own inspiration. One is caught up in the momentum of innovation."

Our carriage rolls down the wide street that is busy with people even at this hour of the night. The energy of New York buzzes around us, giving credence to my words.

"I believe the reason for the New York premiere is rather practical." Edward watches me instead of the lit-up city. "Every time Gilbert and Sullivan release a new show in England, it is quickly copied and put on stage in American theatres, without any payment to the original creators. By having the premiere in New York, Gilbert and Sullivan cut out the pirates."

I love that he knows everything about everything.

He flashes a rakish smile, and in the dim light of the carriage, he looks like a handsome pirate of the seas, exactly like the ones we have watched on stage earlier. Truly, he is entertaining.

Especially when he breaks into the song of the pirate king from the show, "Oh, better far to live and die under the brave black flag I fly."

I reply with the chorus. "Hurrah, for the Pirate King!"

We dissolve into laughter, finding each other's company more entertaining than the theatre. The way I feel around him is so unexpected, so thrilling, such a gift. I am grateful that Papa has not forced me to marry. A lucky few of my friends have married for love, but most have married *appropriately*, with the expectation that they will be *content*.

I will be more than content with Edward's friendship.

I bring up Edison again, and we talk about his many other inventions, my favorite being the phonograph—surely magic—until our carriage stops in front of Edward's family's mansion at 661 Eighth Avenue.

"The Italianate columns impress Papa no end," I

confess. "Mama called the curtains a poetry of lace." She is dazzled by the Candees' elegance.

The house is lit up for New Year's Eve, with dozens of guests in attendance. I am usually in bed by this time, but tonight, I am not the least sleepy. I do not want to retire upstairs. I would rather not even go inside. I wish Edward and I could stay in our bubble a little longer.

The coachman opens the carriage door.

"Would you give us another moment, Joseph?" Edward says.

"Yes, sir." Joseph closes the door with a soft click.

Edward reaches across the space between us and claims my gloved hands. "I had a tremendous time tonight, Helen."

My heart is beating as hard as if I were kidnapped by pirates. "I had a lovely evening as well."

"I wish for more of your company." He pauses, the flickering flame of the street light next to our carriage reflecting on his open face. "May I escort you to the philharmonics at Madison Square Garden next week? Would you join me?"

"I would be delighted." *Do I sound too eager?*

"Next week, then." But he does not tap to signal the coachman, nor does he open the door himself. He leans toward me instead. "I so wish… May I kiss you, Helen?"

Oh…

My first instinct is to say no.

I am *not* in love with him. My campaign to convince Mama and Papa to allow me to attend college continues. But just because I wish for a different life than what is expected of me does not mean that I must die without being kissed.

I simply want to know what a kiss feels like. Am I not allowed curiosity? We could call it a scientific experiment. "You may."

His lips on mine are gentle and considerate. He is the very best man I have ever met. He kisses me, and I feel adult for the first time, very much a woman. After a bit, I even begin to understand why Philip's courtship had made my friend Ada so restless.

Then Edward withdraws and leaves me a moment—in which I cannot meet his eyes—to gather myself, before escorting me inside. We are immediately surrounded and peppered with questions about the new show at the theatre.

When the quartet Edward's parents engaged for the occasion starts up, he holds out his hand. "May I have the pleasure?"

Swirling in his arms, I am light-headed by the second dance. "We might have packed too many festivities into one evening."

He gracefully guides me back to the sidelines. "We can always hide in the library. My father has a couple of new books I have been meaning to show you."

Mama strolls over, beaming approval. "What fun it is to be young."

"May I fetch you ladies a drink?"

"Thank you, Mr. Candee. Something sweet,

please." Mama looks after him as he leaves. "I don't suppose he has softened your heart?"

I consider my response for so long that she gives up and goes on.

"A pressured marriage when a woman does not wish matrimony is unfortunate. But it is equally sad to remain alone when a woman does find her perfect match."

She *is* clever.

"If I marry, I shall have to give up the future I planned. I wish to travel. I wish to learn. I wish to teach. I would rather keep Edward as a friend."

"Edward, is it? No longer Mr. Candee." She tilts her head. "I see. But do keep in mind, if you do not marry him, eventually, you *will* have to give him up. Sooner or later, he will take a wife. It will not be possible for him to stay your friend forever."

The dreary thought drenches my good mood. But, of course, Mama is right. "I merely want freedom."

"You and I are freer than most of the rest of the country."

"Are we?" How do I explain? "It's as if we live in a world that's a giant palace of endless wonders, but most of the doors are locked against me. How I may wear my hair, what clothes I may wear, what I may study and for how long, what I may do in way of an occupation, what I may do with my free time, the type of man I may marry, and in fact that I *should* marry, have all been decided for me by society."

"A few locked doors aside, would a palace be

such a terrible place to live? Edward would keep you safe."

"Do you know what they call a large building that is well secured with all the doors locked?" How I want her to understand me. If even she cannot, nobody else might. "A prison."

"Must you be so melodramatic, my dear?" She waves my earnest passion away with her fan. "You are very much free to choose whether or not you want Mr. Candee. As much as your Papa wants him for a son-in-law, he loves you too much to force your hand. But you *shall* have to pick. Either your wild dreams, or the man."

"Henry doesn't have to choose." My brother is studying to be a civil engineer. "He is considered fully capable of having a family *and* a career."

I do not pursue the topic further, because Edward returns with our punch in hand.

Later, we dance again, but nothing is as magical and perfect as it was before. Mama's words had taken up residence in my head. They cluck there for the rest of the ball, then all morning the next day. I still can't shake them that afternoon, when I assist Edward in picking the design for a stained-glass window he is gifting to his mother. While we vacillate between flowers and geometric forms, I approach the subject I have been pondering since last night.

"When you marry…"

He stops sifting through the drawings on his desk

and gives me his full attention. His lively brown eyes search mine. "Yes?"

"Would you allow your wife to have a career? A certain degree of independence?"

The moment stretches. I am so breathless, I feel more of a schoolgirl than when I *was* a schoolgirl. *Heavens.*

"I would be dreadfully bored if I didn't marry an intelligent woman," he says. "And if I marry an intelligent woman, I cannot expect her to be satisfied with a life that consists of little more than rearranging rosebushes in the garden." A slow smile makes his dear face even dearer as he hands me a drawing of a rose from the table. "Was that the right answer?"

It wasn't the wrong one. "Yes."

He steps closer, a stubborn hope lighting up his expression. "Does that mean that you will marry me, Helen?"

The question takes me by surprise. I have barely begun to consider the possibility… In a faint, distant future… Yet I have never felt as close to any man, other than Papa. "I wish to attend college."

"You have a keen mind. Of course, you would wish to learn." He seems to want to say more but falls silent instead.

I wait.

"College is not the only way to gain an education," he suggests. "New York has the most splendid new library, the Lenox Library, right on Fifth Avenue."

"New York is far away from Norwalk."

"My father needs me back here. I am moving back, Helen."

New York.

Currently, I am under my father's dominion, and he is a conservative man. Mama is reasonably modern, but she remains his ally in everything regardless. I am but one against two. With Edward, we could be two against the world. I would have someone on my side, forever. When I resolved not to marry, I had but my father's example of a husband. And now…

A door to the future I want opens, not how I imagined it would, but no life has a straight path.

"I haven't thought… I will need time to consider."

He smiles. "Take all the time you need."

He grants me freedom there, which makes it easier to believe that he shall grant me freedom always, as he promises.

Two weeks later, when he visits us in Norwalk, I give him my answer. "Yes."

That night, I write only three lines in my diary, for my feelings are indescribable.

Love is tender.

Love is a rose.

Love is hope.

I am falling in love with Edward.

November 17, 1880

. . .

"Where is that veil?" Mama claps her hands, and the maids scatter like pigeons when a horsewhip cracks. "You are the bride. You cannot be late for church, Helen."

The grand event—except for the church part—is held at my parents' house in Norwalk, Connecticut, on the seventeenth of November, a week after Edward's twenty-fourth birthday. I'm a month past my twenty-second. It is the happiest day of my life.

My union with Edward is so much more than I thought a marriage could ever be. I am gaining a husband who supports my ambitions, a friend, a confidant, a true equal partner. This is what I wish for all women. How did I get so lucky?

"Right here, ma'am." Rosie runs in with the gossamer fabric and sets everything back in motion all over again.

The veil settles over my head. I wanted bobbin lace, same as Ada had, but Mama advised me that tulle is now all the rage. As always, she is right. The tulle is as light as a cloud, and yet still… I am not used to having my face covered. For a moment, I feel claustrophobic, trapped in a net.

I gasp, which sucks the veil against my lips, as if to seal them but, of course, I can breathe. So I breathe, and as Mama prattles on, I grow used to the fabric touching my face. I am grateful that I had not chosen the heavier lace after all.

Mama's hands rest on my shoulders. "Look in the mirror."

"Heavens." I barely recognize myself.

Orange blossoms dot my hair, like Queen Victoria's at her nuptials. The delicate flowers were also Mama's suggestion. My dress is the purest white satin and brocade, with a bustle that still allows my natural form to come through. The fine beading on the bodice sparkles in the light, the long train curved on the ground around me. I am, indeed, a princess at my wedding.

"Perfect." Mama's eyes soften with love. "In but a few hours, you will be a married woman. Now, let us go and dazzle your young man."

The maids stand back. For now, they have done their part. They relax.

I wish I could breathe easier as well, but a new cloud of anxiety creeps under my wedding veil. What if I trip walking down the aisle? What if I faint at the altar? What if I mess up my vows?

What if…

I clench the bouquet in my white-gloved hands, crushing the stems.

I shall not be alone.

The thought allows me to catch my breath. I shall *never* be alone again. With me on life's winding path, there will be Edward.

The church service is a blur, as is dinner, which must end early, since we must be early to bed. Our ship leaves in the morning for Marseille. We shall honeymoon in France.

"Passport. The one thing we must not forget."

Edward holds a small booklet as he walks into the bedroom. We are spending our wedding night at my parents' house in Norwalk, but upon our return, our new home will be in New York.

"And mine?" I assumed he handled the paperwork for both of us. Was I wrong? I have applied for nothing on my own. He told me he was going to arrange everything.

I sit bolt upright in bed, forgetting the cover that I had pulled up to my neck, forgetting my apprehensions about our wedding night.

"I have no passport." Will we have to stay home? Have I ruined our honeymoon? I so do not want to begin our marriage with disappointing Edward.

"It is ours." He shows me the first page. The document is issued to Mr. Edward Willis Candee *and wife*. He sets the important document on the nightstand. "You are a married woman. You will always travel with your husband."

It must have been the same with Mama and Papa, and I have simply not paid attention. As a child, of course, I was included in my parents' paperwork, along with my siblings, when we traveled. I expected it to be different now that I am an adult woman.

Edward shrugs out of his robe. "Ready, my darling?"

Oh. The wedding night. I so want to please him. I so do not wish to embarrass myself.

He lays the navy-blue robe across the chair, then joins me under the covers.

I freeze. My fingertips and toes tingle. One piece

of advice I read said to be shy and demure, as no husband wishes for a brazen wife, but wants innocence. Yet another book on marriage insisted on wives being welcoming in the marriage bed. I almost say *welcome* out loud before I catch myself.

"Are you certain we should keep sharing a bed once we return home?" Nerves push the words from me when I have not meant to say anything at all. "I know we must, tonight, and on our honeymoon…"

"You wish to banish me?" His smile teases.

"Mama disapproves." My parents have toured our house, at 227 West 51st Street, a ten-minute walk from Edward's parents, once it was completed. I had to listen to Mama's advice on more than one aspect. "She is an ardent admirer of Queen Victoria, and the queen's doctors believe that sharing a bed allows the weaker partner to drain the vitality of the stronger partner while they sleep in close proximity."

Edward draws me into his arms and brushes the hair back from my temple. "Do I appear worried, my darling?"

"No." He looks rather…ardent, his expression heated.

"Do you believe all that nonsense, my Helen?"

"No?"

"Then we shall share a bed. I should like to keep my wife convenient, at hand." He laughs.

And then everything is all right. We are in this together. I shall never be alone again.

Edward kisses me, as he's been kissing me every

stolen chance he's had during our year-long courtship, but this time he does not stop there.

I lie flat on my back. I am wearing a lacy night-gown shipped over from Paris, but have left off my matching silk drawers, as Mama instructed.

At the wedding, Ada, glowing with pregnancy, whispered to me that it shall go much easier if I relax. She hinted at discomfort. And that is what friends are for, to tell you the truth. Yet, maddeningly, she would not tell me more.

Relax. I unclench my teeth. *Relax.*

CHAPTER 5

Madison

September 4, 2024 (Wednesday)

Ramsey blows into Wednesday's meeting like a storm off the Atlantic. Then he catches himself, and has his all-is-well, I'm-in-control persona back in place by the time he sits. "We're pausing the exhumations." His voice is even. "Mayor's orders."

He's trying to sell the no-big-deal vibe too hard. We're shut down, and we're only three days in.

"The *Titanic* was never going to be a smooth ride." Julia is unperturbed.

"Is there a problem with our exhumation license?" I ask Ramsey.

"Our disinter and reinter permits are in order.

This shouldn't be happening, but yesterday's media fiasco brought on a shitstorm." He rolls his shoulders. "The hold is temporary. The mayor is being handled. Not to worry."

Chad Altman is not present, presumably laying siege to city hall, waving his legal briefs. But while Chad is missing in action, our numbers are not diminished. The documentary crew is with us again.

I do my best to avoid looking at them, as instructed. "Any idea about how long a delay this means?"

Last night, I told the dean at Boston University that I just signed on to a project that will finish in the spring. He agreed to consider my absence a sabbatical and promised that my position would be waiting when I return home. He will not wait forever, however, which puts a time pressure on me.

"Minor setback," Ramsey says, without committing to a new timeline. "The most important thing is that we've successfully transported the first set of remains to the lab. You can start with that." He clears his throat. "Now, a few words about filmmaking." He carries his gaze around the table. "I've reviewed the footage we have so far."

"How is it?" Eleanor smiles in that serene way some older women do. I used to think it was enlightenment, that you reach an age when you love everybody and everything, but I'm starting to suspect they just no long give a flying fig. Today, she's wearing periwinkle blue jacquard pants in a fleur-de-lis pattern, with a matching silk top, as elegant as ever. And I'm beginning to understand that it's not for us. It's for herself.

"Not bad," Ramsey allows. "We all need to keep in mind that our number one goal is to create something compelling. It's our job to engage the audience. The documentary will run on multiple platforms, most of which have commercials. This means every scene must have a cliff-hanger ending. We do not want viewers changing the channel."

"What does that mean for us specifically?" Julia asks.

"The best cliff-hanger is a hint of something. A hint of a fight, or the brink of a discovery. Nobody will change the channel on the brink of action. They'll want to see what's next, how the fight goes down, or what's discovered."

"You want us to fight?" TTP is definitely not paying enough for that.

Ramsey looks at us like a long-suffering teacher at a class of below-average students. "There'll be disagreements, naturally. All I'm asking is for you to dramatize them. Polite exchanges don't play well on the screen. Don't be afraid to challenge each other."

I don't tell him that, so far, he's the only person on the team I can imagine making me lose my temper.

"There are certain expressions that could help us." He looks at the director. "Maya?"

"If you find anything that might be of interest, say something like…" She pushes a stray braid back over her shoulder. *"What's that? Oh wow. Now that is really something. Would you look at that? Oh my God.* And then a pause. That would make a great place for us to cut."

"So, like, *holy shit,*" Julia enunciates theatrically. "Or… *What the hell*?"

"Kind of, but no." Maya's tone is patient, a teacher fighting to hold on until the end of the school day. "We want the documentary to be widely distributable, and not all platforms allow bad language. There should be no swearing at all when you're being recorded."

"So just… *What's that? Oh wow. Now that is really something. Would you look at that? Oh my God,*" Julia clarifies.

"Not all at once." Maya holds on to her strained smile. She's definitely going out for a drink with her cameramen tonight. "We want our cliff-hangers to be varied. So, use one at a time."

"We got it," I tell her to give her a break. None of us are movie professionals. I'm sure we're not making her life easy.

"All right." Ramsey raps his fingertips on the table. "The mayor's orders are a definite drawback, but I also have good news." He pauses for suspense, overacting so badly that even Maya flinches.

I suspect this will be the cliff-hanger at the end of the scene. The previous few minutes, Ramsey and the director coaching us how to act, will be cut.

"It is my great pleasure," Ramsey goes on, "to share *never-before-seen* materials about the *Titanic*'s sinking. I was able to obtain the notes that Mrs.

Helen Churchill Candee, a survivor, wrote for a memoir that she never finished." He hands us each a stack of papers held together with a black butterfly clip, with more gravitas than golden statues are handed out at the Oscar ceremony. "The *Titanic* part is marked with red sticky tabs, starting on page one-eighty."

Eleanor receives hers first and holds on to it as if to a precious gift.

I note the word CONFIDENTIAL stamped on the cover, then look inside. *Good. It's typed.* I was afraid it'd be photocopies of the handwritten original. I'm not sure I'm up to hundred-year-old cursive.

"This is why we're doing this." Ramsey places a reverent hand over his own copy of the notes. "The people. No matter what obstacles the media and politics will throw into our path, we will not be defeated by bureaucracy."

His voice is rich with emotion. He is in hero mode, playing for the cameras.

I get it. No battle is a great victory if it's easily won. To make viewers hold their breath while watching the documentary, we must struggle against setbacks. The most unlikely win is the greatest win.

Opposition will give suspense to our story. *Will good triumph? Will they make it? Will they succeed? Stay tuned to find out. Wink. Wink.*

Makes me wonder whether the mayor really halted the dig. And if he did, had Ramsey done something on purpose—missing paperwork, downplaying the extent of the project to give city hall reason for a pause? Was the conflict set up for more drama on screen?

"That's it." He beams at us with benevolence. "Now, off to the lab. Let the adventure begin."

The cameras follow us.

We have six more months to go, so I can't be tired of them yet. I'm going to have to learn to pretend they're not there.

The next second, I do forget, because I'm genuinely enthusiastic to begin. Lab coat, masks, gloves, and then we all pile into Oliver's lab.

"Here we go," he says. "This is where the rubber meets the road, or in our case, the bones meet the spectroscopy."

His sense of humor is... He should stick to science. His talent is not in stand-up comedy.

The recovered yellowed fragments are laid out on the stainless-steel table in a sad, gap-toothed puzzle.

Ramsey is at my elbow. "I have the original record, but I want to see what you think without anything that might bias your opinion. You're supposed to be an expert in anatomy."

I've never claimed that, but I'm too excited to care. I look to Oliver for permission. It's his lab. He is the forensic anthropologist.

He nods.

I step up to the remains. "Let me put the bones in order."

It's a matter of science, but also a matter of respect. The victim before me deserves more than the current, jumbled mess.

"Starting with the skull." I work with skulls for the most part, for my forensic facial reconstructions, so they're my strength.

Ramsey watches me. "What can you tell us?"

I wonder if he's testing me and not Oliver, because Oliver is a man and as such doesn't need to prove his competence. I'm not going to get worked up about it. Ramsey can't get to me if I don't care.

"The victim is most likely a woman." I point at the forehead. "Her frontal bone is fairly vertical. Men usually have a lower, sloping forehead. Men have larger skulls and more prominent brow ridges, in general, larger mastoid processes and muscle attachment sites, and their eye sockets tend to be more square. This mandible is more gracile, the chin pointed, and the angle is obtuse, all female traits. There's no gonial flaring. Of course, it's not an exact science. There are plenty of men with smaller heads and feminine features, while there are women who are larger and have masculine features. But considering other traits like tooth size and nasal aperture, I am reasonably sure the remains are female." I'll compare the pelvis in a minute to verify.

I set the cranium at the top of the table, then place the mandible below it.

"And what is that?" The question is Ramsey's way of reminding me to do as we were asked, always think out loud for the cameras. Audiences don't want silence.

"Lower jaw." I gently move the rest of the bones aside to make room for the few pieces of the spine that were recovered. "The cervical vertebrae would go here, then the thoracic vertebrae, and then the lumbar vertebrae on the bottom." We don't have any of those. "Out of the clavicle, scapula, ribs, and the bones of the hands, all we have are a couple of ribs. From the humerus, ulna, and radius of the arms, all we have is a single humerus." The yellowed, brittle bone of the victim's right upper arm.

"As for the pelvis, we have fragments of the ilium, pubis, and ischium. When whole, they make up the pelvic girdle. The pelvic girdle of a woman has evolved for childbirth, so it's another good indication of gender." Unfortunately, to see the pelvic inlet and outlet, I'd need an intact pelvic bone, which we don't have, so I look for the greater sciatic notch. Then the pubic bone, inspecting the angle formed by the pubic arch.

"So, your opinion is that she's a woman?"

"Yes."

I move the last bone in place, a thigh bone. "We have one femur. No patella, tibia, or fibula, nor any of the smaller bones of the feet."

"Any idea of age?"

I lean closer to the victim to see if all the joint epiphyses have fused. The sternal end of the clavicle is one of the latest fusing epiphyses, along with the iliac crest. "Full fusion of the sternal end of the clavicle indicates the individual was likely around thirty." The iliac crest usually fuses completely by about age twenty-five. "The pubic symphysis," I point to the joint in the pelvis, "grows craggier and more pitted as the years go by. There's only a partial ventral rampart on this one. I'd estimate her age at death late twenties to midthirties."

"Care to guess height?" Ramsey's voice takes on the tone of a circus act. I have passed his test. He's now showing me off for the cameras.

I borrow the osteometric board and measure the femur, then pull up the calculator on my phone. Thankfully, I remember the regression formula. The result looks about right. "A hundred and sixty-five centimeters, or around five feet and five inches."

"Oliver?" Ramsey asks.

"Exactly as she said. I think I can go home now." He holds up his hands in a gesture of surrender.

The acknowledgment feels nice, especially since a different man might have served me with resentment.

Ramsey inclines his head to me with grudging respect, then reads from his phone. "Unidentified victim number three in the official record at the time of interment. Female. Height five feet and five inches, weight one hundred and thirty pounds, age about thirty. Brown hair. No identifying marks. Her clothes were a chemise marked J.H. in red thread, gray cloth jacket, red jersey jacket, blue alpaca blouse, blue serge skirt, black stockings, black boots, and gray cholera belt."

The camera crew ever so slightly eases back.

"What's a cholera belt?" Julia asks, her voice softer than usual, as if she's holding her breath.

I know the answer from the excavation of an eighteenth-century cemetery on the outskirts of Phil-adelphia, where the city was relocating remains to make room for widening a highway. The local histor-ical society commissioned me to work with the three best-preserved skulls, reconstruct their faces digitally, and then paint their portraits.

"People used to think that cholera was caused by a person's abdomen getting cold," I share what I learned. "They knitted belts, usually red, six inches or so wide and six feet long, to be wrapped around the abdomen for warmth. The British army had them made from flannel. The belts were in use for a couple of centuries. People still believed in them as late as the First World War."

Eleanor, our geneticist, tilts her head. Another person might sneer at superstition or call previous generations ignorant, but her tone is gentle. "In the face of death, you grab on to whatever hope you can."

"Neither the belt nor any of the other clothes the woman was buried with were in evidence." Julia, our resident archaeologist, speaks up. "Save for a few fibers stuck to various bones that I have collected for further analysis." She points to three petri dishes lined up on a stainless-steel tray on a side table. "And this." Another tray holds a sealed plastic bag that encases what looks like a five-inch piece of gnarled dark leather.

"Must be one of the boots mentioned in the record." I step over for a quick check.

"Hope you can reconstruct it," Ramsey tells me.

"We want the full-size drawings of these people to be as accurate as possible. In fact, let me send you the list of victim descriptions before I forget." He clicks around, then hops back to our current subject. "J.H. was either a second-class or third-class passenger. Only four first-class female passengers died, and we know their names. None of their initials was J.H."

"Maybe a crew member?" Eleanor suggests. "I think the ship had female stewards, and women working in the kitchen."

Ramsey holds up his phone. "I have the crew roster. The initials don't match anyone there either." Then he finally puts his phone away and looks at each of us in turn, pausing for effect. "Now that the cat is out of the bag—"

"The *Titanic* had a cat," Julia cuts in. "Her name was Jenny. She gave birth to a batch of kittens a few days before departure, which everyone thought was a good omen. Ships used to have ship cats to catch rodents. I read about it online last night."

Must be a cat person.

"As I was saying," Ramsey barrels on. "Now that the cat is out of the bag, I'd appreciate it if you started dropping teasers on your social media. Later, as the pilot episode nears, we'll ramp up activity, but for now, a post per platform per day is enough. Positive comments only. The goal is to drum up interest." He looks genuinely pleased with himself. He addresses all of us when he asks, "What do you think about becoming social media stars?"

I nod. This is why he brought me onboard. I can't very well protest.

Eleanor's smile is strained.

Oliver presses his lips together, as if he wants to say something but is choosing to stick with courtesy.

While Julia says, "If I wanted to be a clown, I would have joined the circus."

I love this woman.

I am in bed that night when I pick up Mrs. Candee's notes. I mean to skip straight to the part where she boards the *Titanic*, but her opening sentence catches my eye.

I prefer my horse to any man I have met so far.

Another honest woman, right there.

Instead of turning to Ramsey's red tab, I read the first page, then the second, then the third, then more. The life of a person I never knew comes alive in my mind, what life must have been like for a young woman in the 1870s.

She has an earnestness, a curiosity about life, and a desire to learn. That the bones in the lab are not hers is a relief. I'm glad she survived the sinking and lived to write about her experiences.

Her story swirls in my brain. I watch the twists and turns as if on a TV screen.

Long after I set the printouts on my nightstand, sleep still eludes me. I tug on my jeans and a sweater and walk over to Oliver's lab, to the bones that glint yellow under the lights.

J.H. were the initials on her clothes at the time of her funeral, according to the historical record.

Jane?

I have distant relatives who are Hills. *Jane Hill.* She could be my grandmother's aunt. *If* that story is true.

I pull on gloves but leave the bones alone. Instead, I examine the remnants of Jane's single surviving boot, pulling it from the container of water meant to prevent the material from drying and cracking.

The plain black leather is water damaged and partially decomposed, twisted, and misshapen. I can see no decoration, not even with a magnifying glass —only a simple, functional piece of footwear.

What remains of the sole is worn. A small crack in the heel catches my eye, something I might have missed without the magnifying glass. I grab a stainless-steel pick, the nearest tool, and probe the crack in the old leather. The heel turns under the pressure, not much, barely a millimeter.

I nudge it again. Then I stare.

"A secret compartment."

Ramsey will kill me for not waiting for the cameras, but I don't care. We can reenact the scene tomorrow. The urge to know what's inside is irresistible. With a gloved hand, I turn the loosening heel.

A simple gold band rolls out first. Large. Did it belong to a man? Three silver coins follow, black with tarnish. I lift them to the light and employ the magnifying glass again. Queen Victoria poses on one side, while St. George kills his dragon on the other. All three are dated 1887.

I check the heel for more, but the tiny treasure cave holds no more secrets.

My entire body buzzes as I rush out of the lab.

In our "dormitory" wing, Julia and Eleanor seem asleep. Only two rooms have strips of light under the doors, mine and Oliver's. I hesitate. Oliver could be sleeping with the light on. I should go to bed.

I step forward instead and quietly knock. If there's no response, I won't push it. I swear.

"Come in."

"Hey."

He raises his head from his pillow, lowering his own printout of Helen Candee's notes to the blanket. His hair is mussed. He blinks at me as if his eyes are dry, someone who's been up reading way too late. "Everything okay?"

"I found something."

He sits up all the way, then rolls to standing. He's wearing a T-shirt and cotton pajama pants. "What is it?"

The perfect scene ending for Ramsey.

"I couldn't sleep, so I walked over to your lab. J.H. was carrying a man's ring. I found a gold band and three silver coins in her bootheel." The words rush out of me and conjure up images that turn into a story. "Must have been a widow, converting all her belongings into those three coins in England, hiding her treasure so it couldn't be stolen on the ship, taking what little she had to start a new life in the New World."

"A heelful of hope."

A lovely way to put it. "You should have been a poet."

"I'm afraid I have about as much skill for that as for interpretive dance."

"Pays the same too."

He laughs as he steps into his slippers. "Let's go."

Is this a good idea? Probably not. But it's too late now to stop. I want to go back to make sure I didn't dream the coins and the ring.

We sneak down the hallway like a couple of bandits, hushing each other.

When Oliver sees the bootheel treasure, he lets loose a low whistle. "I looked at the leather earlier, then didn't give it another thought." He picks up a silver coin—with a gloved hand; he's a professional. "Good catch."

"Wonder how much they're worth."

Oliver types the necessary information into his phone with his free hand, using only his thumb. "Around eighteen hundred dollars. But with the link to the *Titanic*, the sky is the limit. Did you tell Ramsey?"

"He can wait until morning."

"These things should be in a safe."

"I left my phone in my room. Do you want to text him?"

I lay out the treasure in a straight line. Oliver snaps a picture, and then he hits Send. Then we wait.

"He might have his phone turned off for the night," Oliver suggests, but barely two seconds pass before Ramsey calls back.

Our team leader's sleep-heavy voice booms through the speaker. "What the hell is that?"

I explain to him about the bootheel.

"Don't touch anything else. I'll be right there."

CHAPTER 6

Helen
  1881

Women do not feel passion as men do. A number of married friends assure me of this, in confidence, after Edward and I return from France and settle into life in New York.

Edward was nothing if not solicitous throughout our month-long honeymoon, and I did my best to accommodate him, despite my *discomfort*. Mama assures me that the duties of marriage grow easier with time. I gain much courage from her prediction. The chafing surely must cease at some point.

I have been misled by the Greeks.

The Greek statues I have seen while traveling the Continent with my parents have been my only refer-ence premarriage. David's odd appendage, carved from white marble, seemed comfortingly manageable in size. No larger than a fingerling potato, something one might eat in two bites—three, if one eats ladylike.

Edward feels rather more enormous, alarmingly so, although, naturally, I have not seen him naked, so I can only guess at that aspect of his body. He turns off the light before he conducts his business. I wonder if his anatomy is normal or if he has a deformity. It doesn't matter, of course. I will love him whatever way he is.

Weeks pass as I busy myself with setting up the household. At night…the conjugal activity does become less onerous when my husband switches from every day to every other day. I should be happy. I *am* happy.

Yet…

Mama was right about New York. My childhood memories of the city were exaggerated. In Norwalk, I had friends. We were somebody. In New York, one is a nobody if one is not an Astor, a Carnegie, a Rockefeller, or a Vanderbilt. I am lonely.

"Your father sends you his love," Edward tells me at the breakfast table. "I had a letter arrive from him while you were dressing."

They often discuss business. I have come to wonder just how big a hand my father had in our marriage. My brother has no interest in lumber. He is a civil engineer who lives and works far away. How my father must have wished for another son. And what would be a better substitute than a son-in-law in the same industry? An empire created by combining their businesses would be a dream come true for him.

"I shall write Mama later." I must not reduce my marriage to a transaction, to strategy. It is not between Papa and Edward. It is between Edward and me. Edward married me because he loves me.

"We must begin entertaining in our own right." He butters another slice of toast. "I must rise in the social hierarchy if I am to grow the company. It is the wives of upper-class men who are the gatekeepers. You must manage to insert yourself into their circle, my darling Helen."

"I shall do my best." We must entertain, but I have been delaying the invitations for a reason. "Our dining room"—along with the rest of house—"is still awfully threadbare. If we invite distinguished guests, we must make the right impression."

"Could you not ask my mother for help? Or yours, for that matter."

Both are enamored by the English style, large furniture, heavy and dark, which they consider elegant. However, the weight of those furnishings presses down on me like rain-heavy clouds, even when I am in the most spacious rooms. "What would you think of the lighter furniture of the Continent? I prefer the light romanticism of the French. The pieces would bring our honeymoon back to us a little."

Edward is lost in his morning paper.

I do not miss our more frequent nightly activities, but I do miss his courting, that I had his full attention, how we spent every day together. Now that he has returned to work, we talk only at breakfast and dinner.

"Choose as you wish." He looks up at last. "The city is exploding with growth, so business is brisk. Greatest country in the world. We are building real wealth here." He turns the page. The back that I see talks about the oil boom, although the article next to it assures that coal is still king. "I will have Henry Piper send over a catalog." Edward keeps reading. "Make your list, and I will arrange for shipping."

"Thank you, dear." I smile, even though he cannot see it. How is it possible to share a house with someone and still miss him? "Do you think I might accompany you to the office one day this week?"

This makes him glance up again. "Whatever for?"

"I would love to meet the employees. I so wish to know more about our business."

He does not say *whatever for* again, but his eyes clearly speak the words. "Are you bored?"

My mind is, if not my hands. I wish to learn about the trade that keeps the roof over our heads. I wish to know how the New York building industry works. There must be some way I can help Edward. We are married. I want us to build a life together. But perhaps I was rash to bring all this up at breakfast. "I have plenty here to keep me busy, of course."

I am still learning how to be a wife, and he is still learning how to be a husband. We shall settle into our marriage. I agreed to this role when I accepted his proposal. And since I have agreed, I shall fulfill my side of the bargain. If I am a wife, I shall be a good wife to Edward. Instead of college, I shall learn from books, and from him and his friends.

After Jenkins drives him to work, I ring for Annie. "I need to dress to go out. And when Jenkins returns, please make sure someone tells him not to unhitch the horses."

"Yes, ma'am."

"We are going to the new import store," I inform her on my way up the stairs. Henry Piper's store is filled with dreary old pieces, wardrobes and divans that would please the most conservative widowed duchess. I want something fresh.

We live in a new, modern age. It is not as if a lady cannot leave her house without her husband or her maid, as in the old days. But since Edward is eager to join the ranks of the leading families of the city, I shall strive to be extraordinarily proper.

The store is worth the effort. I have very much made the right choice by coming in person. Being able to see the color and grain of the wood, to run my fingers over the smooth finishes, I can much more easily visualize each piece in its place.

I begin with two subtly decorated servers.

"Which one would you recommend?" I consult the owner of the establishment, an older gentleman. "You are more of an expert at this than I am."

He preens, then points at the simpler of the two pieces, a light maple. "Eastlake is the new trend."

"Charles Eastlake?" The British architect is Mama's favorite, so I am familiar with his name. There was an article about him in the paper shortly before my wedding, and she insisted on reading it out loud to me. Apparently, Mr. Eastlake honed his skills through three years of exploratory travel through Italy, France, and Germany, learning Europe's architectural and design history.

"Ah, you know of him, madam." The owner's expression warms. "Splendid. May I show you anything else?"

"How about a few French pieces?"

I end up with a secretaire and a large, French enameled and glazed porcelain jardinière for our foyer. A guest bed, twin China cabinets, and several wardrobes go on special order.

We are on our way home from the store when a house fire redirects the carriage to a different street, where a horse accident has us turning aside once more. And then I am in a neighborhood I have never seen before. Only because I read the papers do I recognize where I am.

The tenements.

"I will turn around as soon as I can, ma'am," Jenkins calls back from his seat. He keeps mumbling, likely thinking that I cannot hear him over the noise of the street. "Lazy bastards. Damn micks and dirty dagoes coming here to take over."

I am stunned by his vehemence. He is usually an even-tempered man.

Threadbare laundry hangs on a tangle of lines over our heads. I do not wish to know what the brown sludge is in the gutter. The sidewalk is covered in dirty, skinny children.

"My goodness, they are all very young."

Only a handful are over the age of five, and most of those are girls, in charge of the little ones. The few older boys I spot are all missing fingers or even limbs. One has lost both eyes, and his face is covered in burn scars.

"The older ones are at work." Annie looks at her lap. "Some factories don't hire on younger than ten, but plenty will put them on the line at seven or younger."

"Surely, that cannot be safe. Would they not make too many mistakes?"

"What damage they cause is deducted from their wages. And if they suffer an injury, they are fired." She hides her hand, the one with the missing finger, under her skirt.

I consider my carefree childhood in Connecticut, chasing butterflies with my nanny in the garden. "How much work can a child possibly do?"

"Twelve hours a day."

"For how much?"

"A dollar a day, ma'am. Adds up, it does, six days a week."

I do not dare to think how much I spent today in but a few minutes. "Are there many more neighborhoods in the city like this?"

"Most of the city's like this, ma'am."

As if he could hear us, Jenkins calls back, "I'm sorry, ma'am. These tenements keep popping up like rat nests."

We pass a gaunt woman selling aprons on the

corner, then another one pushing a laundry cart. An old crone stirs something in a steaming barrel that stinks to high heaven. Even when we leave her behind, the air does not improve. I hold my handkerchief over my mouth against the foul smells that permeate the air.

Annie is not as sensitive as I am. Her nose remains uncovered. "No indoor plumbing," she tells me, "and a dozen family members to a room sometimes."

Unimaginable.

I can see that the people around us are doing their best. At one door, a young woman with a baby tied to her back is sweeping out dust. At another building, an old woman is washing down the front steps, on her knees, moving stiffly but not pausing to rest. I do not know how she will rise. She will have to be helped.

"A dozen to a room sounds terribly crowded." How can we have all those riches—the coal, the oil, the gold, and silver—and not have enough to feed these poor children?

"When typhus sweeps through, or cholera, or tuberculosis, for a while, they are less tightly packed," Annie says to ease my distress.

"How do you know all this?" She has only ever lived with us in Norwalk. She has never before been to New York.

She glances at her shoes, embarrassed. "I have cousins a street down, fresh over from Ireland. On my day off, sometimes, I visit them."

I had no idea. I suppose, I have not given a great deal of thought to what the maids do on their day off. "What made them come here?"

She thinks for a spell. "Death came to their cottage and kicked down the front door, so they had to run out the back."

Jenkins cracks his whip at a couple of gaunt little boys. "Damn Paddies. Out of my way!"

Then he finds an unclogged side street and whisks us away.

I should feel relieved to be back in air I can breathe, but instead, my body and mind are heavy through and through, as if I have absorbed all that wretchedness. "I do not understand how people can live like that."

"It's better than where they're coming from, ma'am."

How is that possible?

Soon, we are in a neighborhood I recognize, and I call out to the coachman. "Stop, please. I wish to walk a little."

The small bookstore I spy turns out to be my deliverance. Books always settle me, even just their touch and their smell. I can sink into a story as if it's a comfortable armchair.

I browse for a while, then ask, "Anything new and popular?"

"These two shelves, madam." The fair, wide-faced proprietor has a Swedish accent.

I page through a travel diary, then a sentimental romance, and then the next book I pick up puts my jumbled thoughts into words.

Progress and Poverty, a book about the increase of want with increase of wealth.

Precisely what I have been pondering in the carriage. How is it possible that the more the economy booms and the more wealth our country has, the more poverty spreads?

The author is Henry George. I carry the volume to the counter. "I should like this one, please."

"Ah." The proprietor nods with approval as I pay. "A gift for your husband."

His wife wraps up my purchase. She pulls a sheet of paper from under the counter, slips it under the book, and hands them to me together.

I think it an advertisement and inspect it only once I am seated in the carriage. HAVE YOU EVER THOUGHT ABOUT HOW DIFFERENT THE WORLD WOULD BE IF WOMEN HAD A SAY?

I am so surprised that I hold it out to Annie. "An invitation to a suffragette meeting." Oh, but the title sounds tantalizing. "I wish I could attend without causing a scandal in our circles and harming Edward's business.

Six months pass in a blur.

I occupy myself with the house and attending social events. Edward gains new clients; I make new friends. Lenox Library becomes my favorite place in the city. I am becoming a confident hostess, but the evening before we are to hold the first gathering with music, I worry about the musicians.

"Do you think the quartet will have enough room?" Our dining room is spacious, but we have a large guest list.

Edward swallows his mutton cutlet and rosemary potatoes. Our cook, Mrs. Reid—recommended by Edward's mother—is a marvel. Her blackberry tart is waiting its turn on our Eastlake server that turned out to be precisely what the room needed. "They will be all right. Stop fretting, Helen."

I cast about for another subject. We cannot talk about the children, as we do not have any yet. Edward is not interested in household matters or my new friends. No husbands are; it is only natural. They have more important matters to occupy their minds.

At long last, I land on "Mary Eloise says Walter is concerned about the stock market."

Edward frowns, indicating I hit on the wrong subject. "My sister should not gossip about her husband. The topic of fashion would be more appropriate for conversation when you two are together. You mustn't concern yourself with money matters and other things women do not understand."

I must think about *something* beyond dresses. Even with all the time I spend on running our home at a standard that will raise Edward's status, and all the dinner parties I give to court prominent men with whom he wishes to associate, I have hours left to fill each day. I do spend some by reading, but most of the books I want to read I can neither purchase nor borrow from the library without raising eyebrows. I try to read Edward's papers, after he's done with them and before the maids have a chance to discard them.

"I thought about joining the National Woman Suffrage Association. Not something I'd ever bring up to our friends or guests, of course. I'd merely attend a meeting here and there. They seem to have the most interesting speakers, true women of accomplishment." I have been seeing more and more of their pamphlets. I must admit, their arguments make sense.

Edward looks at me over his wineglass. "Does the life I provide for you not satisfy you?"

Now I have further displeased him, which was the last thing I wished. I was merely attempting to make conversation so we would not sit at the table in silence. "Or I could become more involved with charities. Clara Barton is holding a fundraising event for the American Red Cross." She founded the organization earlier this year. "She saved a great number of lives in the Civil War. She worked directly on the front lines, with bullets still flying sometimes. They called her *The Angel of the Battlefield.* I heard her speak before, back in Norwalk."

He sets his glass down too quickly, clinking the bottom against his plate. "When you are a matron, you may find yourself a worthy cause. For now, you must focus on your highest calling. You need not have any occupation beyond providing me with a son. To that end, it would be best if you did not exert yourself."

"Yet while we wait for that blessing... Edward, I wish to find my place in the world, as you have."

"Your place in the world is by my side." His expression is one of mild bewilderment. "You are my wife. My success is your success," he explains with exaggerated patience, the way my mother used to explain to my little sisters why they couldn't wear their favorite boots to bed.

"Of course. I am so proud of you for all you do at the company. We are so very lucky, but, you see, there are thousands in great need in this city. I am compelled to contribute to *something*."

"Lucky?" Aggravation snaps in his tone. "I am building the company into an empire with my own two hands. The poor are poor because they are lazy. The wretched masses need to stop drinking and start working harder. You should see some of our so-called employees. They are not worth half of what I pay them. *They* are lucky I have not fired them yet. Workers ought to be happy they have work. If they do not like it, they are free to quit."

"And starve their families? Children are starving already. Right here, in New York, in the tenements. From what I have seen"—from the safety of my carriage—"the poor work so very hard already. I wonder if raising their pay might not help matters. They seem to spend their wages on food and lodgings, putting it all back into the economy. While some of our friends tend to gamble on speculative investments on the other side of the world, half of which fail, and then all that money disappears."

He stares at me, as astonished as if the umbrella stand had offered an opinion on hydraulics. "What do you know about the economy?"

Precious little, although I certainly wish someone would teach me more. "Would it not be stronger if we could all contribute? I mean, I know women of the lower classes work terribly hard, but is it not possible that middle-class and higher-class women might also have something to add?"

My husband draws his eyebrows together. "Babbling feminine nonsense."

"At least, in Norwalk, Ada and I used to volunteer—"

"You are a married woman now." Edward changes tone. He leans back in his seat and smiles at me with indulgence, as if I am being very silly indeed. "A woman's priorities change once she has been properly wedded and bedded, darling Helen. No thought should interest you more than fulfilling your duty of giving me an heir. Ada is not volunteering either."

She had her son, little Philip, two weeks ago. She sent a letter describing the child down to his last soft lock of hair. Her obvious joy and contentment fills me with happiness. "I cannot wait to be back in Norwalk to see them."

We are to travel by train next week and stay five full days. Edward does indulge me.

After dessert, we rise from the table, and my husband offers me his arm. "Shall we retire to the sitting room?"

He has his usual glass of port, while I ask for my usual cup of tea, regretting my contentious dinner table topics. I shall allow him to direct the topic of conversation for the rest of the evening. While I wait for him to say something, I sip my tea in silence.

"Sir. Ma'am." Our butler enters with a silver tray that holds the evening paper for Edward and a letter for me, silver letter opener included.

"From Mama." My fretful mood disappears. Truly, I am like a child at the prospect of a puppy every time an envelope arrives. Mama writes the best letters. She catches me up on family events, and she is not above sharing a bit of gossip either. She often makes me laugh. Yet this time, by the time I read the third sentence, I am blinking away tears.

"What is it?" Edward lowers the paper. "Is it your father?"

"Ada." I have to wipe my tears so I can read on. "She developed a blood clot. She is gone."

I shouldn't have had to say that sentence for at least another fifty years. My ears buzz so loudly, I barely hear the words come out of my mouth as I speak them.

My best friend is dead, her life extinguished forever, and part of my world ended with her. We have gone from children to young ladies, then to married women together. We were closer to each other than we were to our own sisters. We pledged to raise our children together, to grow old together.

A week passes before I find out more, and then only because Annie receives a letter from her own mother, who is also in service, still in Norwalk.

"I can see that something happened." I watch her in the mirror while she combs my hair in the evening. Edward has not joined me yet. "Why do you look sad?"

"It's about Mrs. Alexander."

"Ada?" Annie always loved her. All the staff did. She had sunshine for a temperament and never a bad word for anyone in service. "I miss her. I am going to miss her letters. I cannot imagine not seeing her when I go up to visit my parents." I draw a slow, steadying breath so I will not start crying again. "A chance blood clot. It is almost inconceivable."

"One of them ladies' ailments." Annie hangs her head.

I nod a few times before I catch the meaning of her words. "What do you mean?" She is more knowledgeable of these matters than I am. Her mother works in a kitchen, but when the need arises, she assumes the role of the midwife, a skill she brought with her from her old country, Ireland. "Do working women not suffer from the affliction?"

"Not so much. Not ever, really. My mother says it has to do with the lying-in. Peasant women are back in the field the next day. Women who work the cotton mills too. But the doctor had Mrs. Alexander on strict orders to stay in bed for a month."

"Does lying in bed cause blood clots? I always thought of rest as restoring."

"I don't know, ma'am. 'Tis what my mother says. Mum says it's best to be up and about after."

"All midwives know this?"

Annie nods.

"Why do the doctors not?" I propel myself from my chair. I would throw my silver brush across the room if it was not clutched in Annie's hand.

It's best to be up and about after. This one piece of knowledge would have saved my friend, if only she had been allowed a woman to tend to her during birth instead of a man.

Edward is my husband, and his expectations for an heir are not unreasonable. I do my best. I am always accommodating in bed. Never do I make myself unavailable, not even in mourning over Ada, or when my sweet sister Fannie dies six months later, at ten years old, her little body ravaged by scarlet fever.

I cry alone while Edward is at the office, then, before he arrives to dinner, I refresh myself. No man wants to come home to a desolate mess.

At first, he is encouraging in our attempts to conceive.

"This will be it," he tells me each time he rolls off me.

To make up for my ineptitude at conception, I organize even more frequent dinner parties for prospective suppliers and business partners.

Edward's business booms, nearly doubles. He takes the accolades as his due, and I let him and never bring up my contribution. At least he is happy at work, even if my continued failure at home frustrates him no end.

The first year of our marriage passes without the arrival of an heir.

Our lack of success dims the joy of celebrating our first anniversary. Edward is in a dark mood throughout dinner. And later, in the bedroom, once Annie leaves, instead of the usual, smiling *Shall we retire to bed?* he asks with a dour expression, "What have you done, Helen?"

"Whatever do you mean, dear?" I tie a green silk ribbon in my hair, his favorite color. The neck of the new nightgown I am wearing to please him is edged with green embroidery, Rosie's fine work.

"Where is it?" Edward whirls around in the middle of the room, then charges toward my wardrobe. "You must be doing something to prevent my seed from taking hold."

The implication chills me. "Please, be reasonable, dear. I would never. I wouldn't—"

I want children, desperately so. And even for women who do not, nearly a decade has gone by since Congress passed the Comstock Act that criminalized birth control.

"Dr. Mensinga's device." Edward's eyes bulge as he throws my dresses onto the floor. "Is that what you have? The cap?"

I move to go to him, but the strength leaves my legs, and I drop onto the bed. I know he is under a lot of pressure, both about the business and an heir, from his father, but… "I do not even know what you are talking about, Edward."

"Do not pretend!" My favorite pink robe flies past my head.

"Perhaps the fault is with our method?" I ask to distract him. "I have heard about a book…" From the suffragist Elizabeth Stanton, which I absolutely cannot reveal at that moment.

He pauses in his destruction. "What book?"

"*The Science of a New Life*, written by John Cowan. Dr. Cowan"—a supporter of women's rights, which I will also not mention—"believes that husbands and wives must practice abstinence. Only one attempt at conception must be made, at two-year intervals, on a cloudless day, in either August or September, to harness the sun's electricity. All that energy is then focused on creating a new life." I clear my throat. "The doctor also has strong opinions on the evils of tobacco."

"What nonsense. I shall not give up my cigars. He sounds like a charlatan." My husband throws my clothes about the room like a madman.

Only when the wardrobe and my set of drawers are empty does he cease his violence. He does not come to bed. He throws himself into his armchair and slams back a glass of brandy instead. We have a silver tray in our bedroom with a crystal decanter. We have a tray like that in nearly every room of the house now, in fact.

I wait under the covers, dreading what is sure to come next, but after another glass, he storms out of the room, and seconds later, I hear him calling, "Tell Jenkins to have the carriage ready."

A quick sob escapes me, and I do not know if it is a sob of relief or despair. Either way, the tears keep coming. I hold back any further sound. I do not want Edward to hear me.

Long minutes pass before the front door closes behind him.

And here I was, thinking we were happy.

I slip out of bed and pack my dresses away with shaking hands. I do not want the maids to see the mess in the morning. I do not want them to gossip about our fight.

I am as shocked as I am embarrassed.

An hour passes before I am back under the covers. I bury my face into my pillow and replay our earlier interactions, then our last few conversations. He has been spending less time at home, and when he is at home, he has been talking to me less. Stories of men who grew tired of their wives fill my head, overheard from my mother's friends through the years, stories of the mistresses who replaced them.

That cannot happen to us. It will not. Temporary frustrations aside, we love each other.

I tell myself that over and over, then I doze, waking to the rattle of our coach rolling up to the house. It's dawn. A soft light fills the room.

The front door is opened, then Edward's shoes tap upstairs. I close my eyes and listen to him undress.

The mattress dips under his weight.

The covers reach my chin. He tugs them lower. "I am sorry, Helen." His voice is rough. "I do not know what came over me." His breath smells of whiskey. "With the business growing, I have that much more strain on me at the company."

I open my eyes. His are bloodshot. He looks truly contrite and wretched.

Tears overwhelm me. "Oh, Edward."

He kisses my cheek and squeezes my hand. "You know how much I love you. I swear to you, I will not lose my temper like that ever again."

He kisses my lips, and while he kisses me, he tugs up my nightgown. "Helen."

I am exhausted, still shaken from our quarrel the night before, but I do not push him away. I should not. I cannot. He is my husband.

Thanksgiving, 1882

We are at Thanksgiving dinner at Edward's parents' house the following year when I overhear two maids on the stairs while I am in the water closet.

"Are you certain?" one of them whispers. Her voice is so low, I cannot identify her. They sound alike, in any case. My mother-in-law's housekeeper is Scottish, so most of the maids she hires are also from Scotland.

"Aye," the other one responds.

"What will you do?"

"Hide it for as long as I can."

"But are you truly certain?"

"My mother says the first sign is aching breasts."

"She should know, with the six she had."

The maids move on, but I catch another word. "Seven."

I stare at myself in the gilded mirror as the realization that I am with child unfurls in my mind.

My breasts have been aching so much of late, I can no longer sleep on my stomach. And my courses are late by weeks, although that happens often. Yet as I return to the dinner table and think about it, I cannot deny that lately I am always tired. And I have been craving relished pickles, a condiment I normally cannot stand, while I can barely look at meat. I have also been weepier, although Edward could not be more kind and gallant. Our fight is truly in the past.

When I return to the table, he jumps to his feet and pulls my chair out for me. "Here you go, my darling."

He has reformed since that terrible night of wild accusations and has not raised his voice at me since. There have been no further outbursts of violence. He is my sweet husband again.

I smile up at him as I take my seat. I cannot wait until we are home alone and I can share my good news with him.

"I passed Andrew Carnegie on the street this morning." Julius, my father-in-law, is always dressed like a banker, his expensive waistcoat stretching across his abdomen, the thick gold chain of his pocket watch fashionably draped on top. "I lifted my hat to him, and he nodded back at me." Emotion thickens his voice, as if the brief acknowledgment from one of his betters is the greatest achievement of his life.

His wife, Evelina, and my sister-in-law, Mary Eloise, both ooh and aah, but it's not enough.

His attention settles on me. "Are you unwell, Helen?"

I forgot to smile and clap. "Mr. Carnegie! I can scarcely imagine."

"But?" He will not let it go. I have hesitated too long.

"I only wish that when our country has so much wealth, the Carnegies, the Vanderbilts, the Rocke-fellers…" I cannot forget my ride through the tene-ments last year, those poor women and children. "Should the most fortunate not care for the least fortunate?"

"You have not joined one of these silly women's groups who delude themselves into thinking they shall save the world, have you?" He laughs, a rolling belly laugh. "What innocent nonsense. Do not concern yourself over how the country is run, Helen. Leave that in the hands of better-informed men."

"We are in need of another footman and two more maids." My sister-in-law injects before anyone can derail the conversation into an unpleasant direction again. She enjoys living beyond the means of her husband's purse, so her father tends to finance her fancies.

"Soon, my dear," her embarrassed husband, Walter, shushes her. "When my railroad investments pay out."

Nobody has learned from the depression, which mercifully ended three years ago. Half the people we know still speculate in railroads, although safer investments, like government bonds, are widely available. Sir Francis Bacon has famously said, *Knowledge is power*. I am not certain. Knowledge is frustration when one does not have the agency to act on one's knowledge. Maybe I should stop reading the papers.

"Is not speculation too risky?" I ask as I pick up my crystal goblet.

"Investment is not something for ladies to worry about," my father-in-law chides me mildly from across the table. He is most tolerant and humors my attempts at entering manly subjects.

My sister-in-law's husband glares at me, however. "I expect to make a fortune on the Nickel Plate Road. Vanderbilt bought it for seven million last month, a mere nine days after they ran the full length from Buffalo to Chicago for the first time. He knows a deal when he sees it, and I do too. Mark my word, Ward McAllister will have to edit his list to make room for me."

McAllister published his list of New York's four hundred most important citizens-its bona fide high society—in *The New York Times* in February. The Candees did not make the list, a sore point I know not to bring up under any circumstances.

My mother-in-law tut-tuts. "No business talk at the dinner table, or we shall all have terrible indigestion. How about the theatre? What do you think of Edwin Booth? Quite the star of every stage he graces with his presence."

The conversation swivels to Broadway, then to the arts, to the Impressionists in Paris: Degas, Monet, Renoir.

My father-in-law harrumphs. "To call the dreck they throw at a canvas *art* should be illegal. Where is the sharpness of the lines? They simply figured out how to sell unfinished art for good money. Every time I look at one of their pieces, I feel as if I ought to put on my reading glasses."

"I rather like the dreamlike quality and the softness of the colors." I also love the gaiety of Toulouse-Lautrec's Moulin Rouge scenes, scandalous as they are. "My favorites are Mary Cassatt and Suzanne Valadon. The way they paint women as if they are real people, as if I could meet them on the street…"

The men shoot me patronizing looks. I will not argue. Their ready dismissal of any opinion I share does not matter. I shall leave the conversation to them. I can barely think past my important news, in any case. I am in a blessed condition. For the rest of the evening, my thoughts revolve around that, and I barely hear half of what is said around the table.

An eternity passes by the time Edward and I are finally alone in our carriage, on the way home.

"Darling?" My heart flutters as I attempt to look into his eyes. Unfortunately, the interior is dark; I can only make out the shape of his head. This will not do at all. I wish to see the joy on my husband's dear face.

For now, all I say is "Wonderful dinner."

"Don't you ever," he responds with vehemence through gritted teeth, "talk like that in front of my family. It was the most ignorant, most unladylike display I have ever seen. Do you want people to think that I cannot control my own wife? Where do you get all that dreck?"

"I read your papers." That he barely scans. And I have begun to read others too that I send Annie out to fetch. "I am sorry." Oh, tonight of all nights, I do not want to make him mad. "I should not have spoken like that. I am sorry, Edward."

"You are not to go into my study or the library without my permission again."

"Of course." I do not want to ruin this precious moment. As soon as we are at home, I shall share my secret, and that will put him in a better mood. We shall celebrate.

When we stop in front of our house ten minutes later, however, he does not step out of the carriage and offer his arm. "I am off to the Club. Good night, Helen."

The Manhattan Club, founded by President Van Buren's son, is where Edward hobnobs with people like the ex-governor of New York and other politicians, along with prominent financiers and diplomats.

"Could you not stay home tonight?" I nearly reach for his hand, but he is still full of bluster. If he shrugged off my touch, it would merely add to the distance between us. "I wish to tell you something,

121

darling."

"No apologies needed. In the future, just try to think before you speak."

A lady does not argue in the street. I can share my news with him over breakfast. I shall not be jealous of the time he spends at the Club. He must meet with the right people as frequently as he can. Who knows who might stop by for a post-dinner whiskey and cigar.

Jenkins helps me out.

Edward calls after me. "Get some rest so you are in a more amicable mood in the morning."

I smile back at him, although I don't know if he can see me in the dark. "Enjoy your evening, Edward."

The coachman silently escorts me to the door and knocks for the maid.

"Can I fetch you anything before you go up, ma'am?" Rosie must be curious why I am coming home alone, but she does not ask. She turns more solicitous instead. "A cup of hot tea? A bed warmer?"

"No, thank you, Rosie." I head for the stairs. I refuse to cry in front of the staff.

Annie, my lady's maid, helps me undress, removing layer after layer of muslin and silk. I shall soon need a maternity corset and new gowns. And that is only the beginning. We shall also have to have the nursery room furnished, and a wet nurse and a nanny in the way of new staff. The prospect of a child, and how happy Edward will be with me, puts me in better spirits by the time I climb into bed.

I almost tell Rosie to have a note sent to the doctor in the morning to ask him for a visit, but I do not wish to cause speculation in the servants' quarters. I want to tell Edward first.

He is about to be a father.

I am about to be a mother.

1883

The months of my pregnancy are a second honeymoon, despite the physical discomforts. Edward cuts his evenings at the Manhattan Club by half. When we are in Norwalk, he barely stops by his beloved Wee Burn Golf Club. He showers me with furs and jewels. All previous unpleasantness is forgotten.

Even my stern father-in-law pats me on the back. "I knew you would give my boy an heir. You'll make sure it is a boy, won't you, Helen?"

I am as nervous about disappointing him and Edward as I am about childbirth. My heart overflows with joy, gratitude, and excitement, but sometimes I wake up in the middle of the night and think of how, over the years, two of my friends have died in childbed.

Edward must have friends who lost wives, because when I am in the fourth month, after an examination, he pulls Dr. Klauz aside in the hallway, outside the bedroom door. "No reason for concern, is

123

there, Doctor?"

"I wouldn't say so. Mrs. Candee is young and healthy. Medicine has improved greatly over the past few decades. Seven out of eight women survive childbirth these days."

They do not realize that I can still hear them. Then they move along, and I truly cannot catch anything more. What else has the doctor neglected to tell me?

My parents are solicitous. This will be their first grandchild. My older brother, Henry, has not yet married. He is still working as a civil engineer in the Rocky Mountains.

The last of winter flies by. Spring is over before I can blink. Ida, Edward's middle sister, gives birth to a daughter, Annie. Once she is home from the hospital, I pay her a visit.

She has a plethora of well-wishers, her sisters and her female friends. She is surrounded by a roomful of small, rambunctious children. I have so many questions, but I must wait for the right time. When everyone else eventually goes downstairs for tea, I stay behind.

"How are you?"

"Still exhausted." Dark circles frame her eyes. She looks away, her mouth turning down at the corners. "My father-in-law is, of course, disappointed."

"Everybody wants a boy for the firstborn." I commiserate. "Edward is obsessed with an heir."

"Phillip is sure we will succeed the second time around. Mama is encouraging. Papa… Well, I am used to disappointing him. I married a dentist."

We share a smile. I move closer and sit on the chair next to her bed. "How was it? Truly?"

She hesitates.

I wait with my hands on my distended abdomen. Sometimes, the baby moves, the slightest of flutters. I do not want to miss the moment. "It is only that I am so woefully unprepared."

Ida looks away. "She was breech."

A dozen horror stories spring to mind, whisperings I have overheard at home from my mother's friends and from the kitchen staff. "Turned the wrong way?"

Ida refuses to meet my eyes. "I labored for two days."

"Lucky you were in the hospital."

"The doctor tried to turn the baby"—her thin frame shudders—"with the most primitive methods."

Her voice is so filled with anguish, I take her hand. "I am so sorry you were hurt."

"You do not understand, Helen." She squeezes my fingers. "The pain was unbearable. I lost consciousness twice and had to be revived."

I cast about for something encouraging to say. "At least you have a healthy child."

Her voice is strangled as she says, "She had to be delivered with forceps."

I do not know what those are or dare ask how such a procedure is even managed.

Ida's fingers go limp around mine. "A few days later, when I was well enough to use the water closet in the hallway on my own, I looked in on the woman in the next room. The poor soul could not stop wailing. The doctor chose forceps for her as well and crushed her baby's skull." Ida closes her eyes shut. "Her little daughter was dead."

Black horror clogs my throat. I am swallowed by a swamp of darkness. We have a vaccination to prevent smallpox. And brain surgery for epilepsy. With all the innovation around us in our modern age, how is it possible for childbirth to still be medieval? Does nobody care about women? I wrap my arms around my growing middle in a helpless gesture, then drop them. I must not worry and make myself sick. What shall happen to us is quite out of my hands.

"The woman in the room on my other side," Ida goes on, as if she cannot stop talking, "couldn't tell me anything at all. The whole time I was there, she was insensate from childbed fever."

I lean over to hug her, and I hold her. I need to feel her in my arms to reassure myself that she is here. "You are home now. You are safe."

"I am convinced," she whispers in my ear, "that we've barely escaped death." Then she releases me. "Forgive me, Helen. I should not have told you any of this. What a terrible sister-in-law I am. You must not let my blabbering frighten you." Her dark-rimmed eyes beg. "For you, it shall be different. I am fretful only because I have not been sleeping well."

"I am grateful for the truth." Am I? Oh, I suppose I am. "You have done me a favor. I would rather know what to expect."

For the rest of the day, I can think of little else. I am awash in anxiety even as Edward escorts me to the park. I am in no mood for an outing, but it will be my last one before my own confinement, so I do my best to enjoy this last bit of freedom I am allotted.

"Doctor Klauz and I have decided that you will give birth at the hospital, like Ida," Edward tells me as we stroll around the abandoned bandstand arm in arm. "It is the most sensible course."

My maternity corset is so tight that I cannot breathe, but necessary, for it is highly inappropriate, a terrible breach of etiquette, to appear visibly pregnant in public. I focus on filling my lungs with air. Then the meaning of his words hit me.

"Ida was only transported to the hospital because she had difficulties at home," I manage to gasp out, taking a few more steps. "Edward, I have concerns about the maternity ward."

"You have not been volunteering at the hospital again while I have been at work, have you?" His voice is that mix of disappointment and censuring that parents use with their children.

"Of course not." After a handful of times, he forbade further visits out of concern that I might catch something contagious. Merely out of his love for me, he said.

"Stick to the Ladies' Christmas and Easter bazaars, Helen. I donate plenty of funds so that you can be on the committee. Let the wives of those who cannot afford to help with money face the unpleasant tasks." A smile sweeps the strict expression off his dear face, and the next second, he is his charming self once again. "I work hard so you do not have to see any ugliness. I want the best for you. You know that."

"Of course." I cannot fault him for loving me too much.

"In any case, after your confinement ends, you will not have time for charity work. You will be raising our son. I know you wish to be a good mother."

"Of course, Edward."

He pats my lace-gloved hand. "Dr. Klauz says you have nothing to worry about. God created women specifically for this task."

He told you more than that. Seven women out of eight survive childbirth, the doctor said, which means one in eight ends up dead.

"It is only that…" I drop my eyes to the toes of my shoes that flash from under my dress with every step. "Mothers are more likely to die at the hospital."

"Superstitious drivel invented by midwives scared of losing business. Dr. Klauz has warned me about them. Where did you hear their nonsense?"

"From a health pamphlet."

"Distributed by the suffragettes? I forbid you to have any contact with those women. Ida is back home, comfortably resting in bed with her daughter. I thought seeing her would reassure you, my darling." Edward waves our coach over. "Let us go home so you can rest. And do not worry about the hospital.

128

Dr. Klauz and I know what is best for you. I would not risk my heir."

"Edward?" I ask as he hands me up into the coach. "Do you think I am starting my confinement too soon?"

He sits next to me. "You should welcome rest."

"It's only that…" I adjust my hat, which I knocked askew on the door. "I so wish to see the opening of the Brooklyn Bridge on the twenty-fourth."

"I shall go see it myself, and then I'll tell you all about it afterward." His face is flushed with New York pride. "The structure is magnificent, isn't it?"

We have, of course, seen it built and have ridden past numerous times in our carriage.

"A true shame that John Roebling didn't live to see it completed," he adds. "He deserves all the accolades. In any case, his son, Washington Augustus, has done a remarkable job in the end. At least the project stayed in the family. That must give him comfort, if he is watching from heaven."

"I heard his wife, Emily, guided the construction to completion. Was not the son terribly ill?"

"Who fills your head will all this fantasy?"

"I forget." One of the local leaders of the suffragettes was giving a speech about it in the bookstore the last time I visited.

"I swear, you would believe anything. No more suffragette pamphlets." Edward guesses the source. "I mean it, Helen."

"Do you not think women should have the right

to vote?" I ask carefully, only because the more pregnant I have grown, the more indulgent he has become. "Surely, an educated female teacher or librarian knows more about current affairs than an illiterate, drunkard dockworker."

"The few educated women, maybe. But the rest?" He scoffs. "Where do you draw the line? What would be the requirement? Other than marital state, of course. Unmarried women should most certainly not vote at any age."

"Why not?" Some of the smartest women I ever knew were my unmarried teachers at school. I still remember their lessons.

"I thought that should be obvious." Edward screws up his eyes as if I am being very silly indeed. "Spinsters do not have a husband to tell them what to think."

"Some women might have their own opinions."

"The best argument yet against them being granted the vote." He pats my hand. "Now, no more about this nonsense. An agitated mind is harmful to women's delicate health."

I have argued as far as I dare to argue. I let him take me home. "Of course. You're right, Edward."

I make confinement easier by engaging in small acts of rebellion, like reading books on politics and economics in Edward's library when he's not home. I spend hours poring over the latest atlases and studying geography. I leave off my corset. The thrill of all that is brief, however. Soon, the days grow endless. At least my imprisonment is temporary. My pregnancy will end soon—in the middle of June, according to Dr. Klauz. Soon, I shall have a baby.

At the end of May, I am forced to read in the papers about the Brooklyn Bridge's dedication. Edward cannot attend in my place after all; he is too busy with his work. Emily Roebling rides the first carriage over from the Brooklyn side, taking a rooster with her as a sign of victory. Her contribution is openly acknowledged in Abram Hewitt's dedication speech.

Edward does not mention any of it, and I do not bring her up. He so hates being wrong.

I, on the other hand, am thrilled that Mrs. Roebling is given credit. History shall celebrate her. People will admire that bridge and say, *Look what a woman can accomplish.* I would not be surprised if they renamed it after her at some point.

Alas, the next news of the Brooklyn Bridge is anything but happy.

"Twelve people are trampled," Edward informs me, coming home from work a mere six days after the bridge's opening. "Some fool started a rumor that the structure was collapsing, and it caused a stampede. See? I was right." He claims my hands and draws me to him. "You are safer at home. I can scarcely think that you could have been out on that bridge, promenading with your lady friends, and I could have lost my heir."

I smile at him. How concerned he is about us only proves that he loves us. He is a good man.

"I have enough to worry about at the office." He releases me. "Our suppliers are competing to see who can raise their prices higher. They don't appreciate that without me, they would be nothing. And our customers are too damn closefisted and fickle. How they complain about every small defect, for heaven's sake."

"I am truly sorry."

I stay inside for the rest of May and for most of June as well, growing larger and heavier. My time of trial begins on June twentieth. We already have the nurse Edward hired, ready on staff. The pain spears me all at once, far from the promised, gradual progression I hoped would allow me to catch my breath.

"Ah!" I stand from the dinner table, cradling my abdomen, then sink immediately back.

"Is it time, my darling?" Edward is at my side in an instant.

I draw a long, uneven breath. "If you would be so kind as to send for the midwife."

"I will take you to the hospital."

"I wish to go upstairs."

"We must have the coach," Edward calls over his shoulder to the butler. "Now."

Since my husband refuses to help me, I head

toward the stairs myself on shaky legs. I extract myself from the dining room, but then, in the hallway, the next contraction bends me over. I am far from ready, but the baby is most definitely coming.

"This way." Edward does his best to turn me toward the front door, but I cannot move another step. "Helen!"

The pain abates at last. I catch my breath. "You must see that I cannot ride in the coach like this." I grip the baluster and climb the first step. "Please, help me to bed."

"You cannot—" Liquid splashes from under my dress to the oak floor and cuts off the rest. He jumps back. "Ah—"

I would be mortified if pain weren't tearing through me with iron claws. "I have no time." I must make Edward understand. "The child is coming too fast."

"Are you certain?"

"Edward!"

Annie on one side, my husband on the other, they half drag, half push me up the stairs, where Rosie is already preparing my bed. Then, once Edward leaves, the maids help me undress. I am to give birth in a white nightgown gifted to me by my mother-in-law for the occasion, even if it is too tight around the arms and uncomfortable and makes me feel as if I am tied to the mattress.

On my nightstand awaits a stack of issues of *The Ladies' Home Journal*, a brand-new magazine that began publication in February, and the sight nearly makes me laugh. I understood childbirth moves at a slow pace, so I have prepared a few distractions. Now that the time has arrived, however, I find that I am not in the mood for articles on home management.

Breathe, breathe, breathe. Do not think about the pain. Think about how happy Edward shall be to have a son. "Aaah!"

I know women must bear their children in pain to pay for Eve's sin. The minister at church gives that sermon at least once a year, but only now do I comprehend how blindingly unfair that is. I am not Eve. What have I done to deserve this?

"Where is the midwife?" I beg as soon as the pain abates enough for me to speak.

"I am sure she is on her way, ma'am." Annie tries to soothe me.

Then the door finally opens, but no midwife appears. Dr. Klauz strides into the bedroom, a gaunt grandfather whose face is always pinched with disapproval. This occasion is no different. He is cross with me already, I can tell.

"I understand you refused the hospital, Mrs. Candee." He clicks his tongue at me as he sets his black leather bag on the bench at the foot of the bed. "Your husband caught me just in time. I was finishing my last autopsy of the day."

His stained sleeves are rolled up to the elbows, his fingernails crusted with blood and Lord knows what else. His glasses are speckled with a grayish matter.

"Time for the examination. If you would be so kind, please part your knees." He rolls up the covers, and then his hands are on me. "You might feel a slight discomfort, Mrs. Candee."

CHAPTER 7

Madison

September 5, 2024 (Thursday)

My serendipitous discovery of the ring and coins in J.H.'s bootheel is reshot the following day, from beginning to end.

I start with hair and makeup—a quick fix from Maya—then it's back to bed, where I toss and turn for the cameras.

"Slower," she calls from the doorway. "We don't want a blur of movement, just obvious indication that sleep isn't happening. For the narrative."

I roll over, look at the ceiling, and sigh, in new navy-blue pajamas instead of my old beige shorts and T-shirt. The camera loves the color blue—and they're also a good contrast against the white bedding—so Maya had the pajamas brought in.

"Cut!"

Next, they film a few seconds of me padding down the hallway. Then we set up in the now perfectly lit lab.

"Silence on set." She calls out the date for the record. "Lab scene."

The clapper board snaps.

I turn the bootheel with one camera filming from my left, and another over my shoulder. The only way the cameramen could be any closer would be if I were giving them a piggyback ride.

"Ooh! What is that?" To my own ears, I sound fake, but nobody tells me to tone it down. "Is that a glint of gold?"

"Cut!"

I must have delivered my cliff-hanger right. I am allowed to sit while Maya checks the footage, and my mind strays to Helen Churchill Candee and all the women who died in childbirth back before *germ theory* was a thing.

I managed to drink my morning coffee and read a few more pages of her notes before Ramsey showed up with the camera crew. Now, as I wait, I worry about Helen.

I learned about childbed fever at college. In the 1800s, hospital doctors would go to assist at births straight from autopsies, without washing their hands. A Hungarian physician, Ignaz Semmelweis, figured it out in the end. He begged other doctors to disinfect their hands and instruments with both soap and a chlorine solution before they entered the maternity ward. They called him crazy for imagining that little invisible organisms were responsible for the deaths. They had him committed, and the guards at the asylum beat him to death.

The only thing people hate more than change, our professor said with Semmeilweis's mustachioed image projected behind her, *is to have their beliefs challenged.*

"Madison?" Maya calls me back. "The light wasn't right. Could you please do it again?"

The filming eats up the entire day. It *is* a crucial scene. People don't find *Titanic* treasure every day.

That evening, while I'm burning through the next chapter in Helen's story, my phone pings. Julia wants to friend me on Facebook. I accept, then scroll through her recent posts: Prague, Krakow, Bucharest. She's quite a traveler.

I check for Eleanor. She doesn't have a Facebook page, as far as I can tell. I spy on Oliver next. Most of his posts are about plants and gardens. I don't look up Ramsey. I don't care.

I record a three-minute update for my YouTube channel. So far, I've posted cemetery footage, then a review of our equipment. I updated people about the first set of remains we have out of the ground. Any big discovery, however, I am only allowed to hint at, per Ramsey's orders.

As I'm about to put the phone down, a message pops onto the screen from Oliver.

In my lab. Got a minute?

Did he discover something new?

I'll be right over.

"I've completed the biological profile," he tells me when I get there. He tugs off his gloves as he stands next to the remains. "I agree with everything you said in your initial assessment."

The biological profile consists of an official determination of age at death, sex, ancestry, and stature, among other descriptors.

"Trauma and pathology?" I ask.

"No physical trauma. Considering known history, she likely died of drowning. I'm going to give Eleanor a sample for isotope analysis."

Isotope analysis could determine diet, geographic origin, and even her migration history. "That should be interesting."

"She's not why I asked you over." Oliver walks through the glass double doors to the back room, where three blank canvases lean against the wall. "What do you think?"

Each canvas is taller than I am. "About what?"

"Painting something for yourself." He taps the tip of his shoe against an open cardboard box that contains a jumble of paint tubes, along with brushes and turpentine.

"I paint things for myself all the time."

"How do you feel about going big?"

"What's wrong with my aquarelles?"

"You said you felt stuck."

"I hate when people use my own words against me." I rifle through the box. "These are oils."

"So?"

"The medium of the masters, permanent. If I'm using watercolor, I can pretend I'm playing, like in kindergarten. Oils are too much pressure. If I moved up to that level, I'd better paint something worth looking at."

"You use acrylics for your forensic portraits."

"That's different. It's science. I follow the bone structure, and the muscles and the ligaments that outline the face. It's basically paint by number."

"I don't believe that."

"There used to be more art to it. We used to sculpt faces in 3D with clay, but now it's all computer models. Except special projects like this, where the client wants an actual painting, but even then, I just copy the computer-generated image onto an eight-by-ten canvas." It's the only time anymore that I do anything *by hand*.

"Do you want more?"

"What I want doesn't matter. In a few years, forensic artists will be replaced by AI." I want to shrug it off, but I can't quite do it. For the most part, I don't think about these things, but now that he brought it up... "Why does everything have to change all the time? Are we sure it's a good thing?"

"Change is literally the human condition. We were made to adapt."

RAISING THE TITANIC

"Right until Armageddon, when we adapt no more. Extinction. The end."

"That took a dark turn fast. How about, we focus on the here and now, where you're one of the last true artisans in the field of forensics?"

I like the way he makes it sound as if I'm part of a grand tradition. "It's just a job."

He shakes his head. "What would you do if you didn't limit yourself?"

What are you going to do next? My father's question, always. He's never happy with where I am. He always wants me to be one rung higher on the career ladder, have an article published in an even more prestigious journal, gain tenure at the university.

My good mood sinks. I step back. "You don't know anything about me."

"I know more than you think. You showed me your paintings. Javier says the creation mirrors the creator."

"Who the hell is Javier?"

"My cousin."

Right. The sculptor, the cousin who's twenty years older than Oliver, whose mother raised Oliver after his parents' murder.

I say nothing.

Oliver gestures at the canvases and paint supplies. "I had him bring a few things over. Since he's an artist, when someone's grandmother who used to paint dies, or someone's kid starts, then gives up, they gift Javier the leftovers. He has a basement

141

full of stuff. He says to let him know if you need anything else, and he'll bring it by."

"I don't need a guardian, or a benefactor." I don't want to owe a stranger any favors. "Also...the creation mirrors the artist? I paint forensic portraits. Does that mean I have dead people inside me?"

Oliver hesitates for a couple of seconds before he asks, "Have you ever painted your mother's portrait?"

"No. Not that it's any of your business." I have a handful of photos of her set aside for *someday*. I'll get there when I get there.

His lips start to move, then go still, as if he changed his mind about what he was going to tell me next.

I wait him out.

"Let me ask you another thing," he finally says. "Are you a tea drinker?"

"No."

"I thought so. So far, I've only seen you drink coffee. May I ask why you paint teacups?"

I've waltzed right into that trap.

"I'm comfortable with still lifes, for one. And in the unlikely event that I'll ever rent a table at an art fair, I'll do better if my paintings have a sellable subject."

"Do you want to hear what I think?"

"Will it bother you if I resent you for it?"

"No."

"Then, go ahead."

"For work, you paint what your clients ask for,

understandable. But outside of that, by focusing on what will sell at some future imaginary art show, you are keeping yourself boxed in."

"What makes you an expert on art, exactly?"

His eyes smile. "I've put in my ten thousand hours listening to Javier."

"I don't think you can be an artist by proxy."

"All I'm saying is, screw what other people might want from you, what will make people you've never even met yet happy. Try for the limitless. Wallow in whatever makes your heart sing."

He drops that on me—*Wallow in whatever makes your heart sing*—and walks back to the bones. Who the hell does he think he is?

September 6, 2024 (Friday)

"I can't believe we've been here for almost a week." Eleanor sticks her head into my studio. In navy silk pants and a fitted white top, she looks like Audrey Hepburn at one of her UNICEF Goodwill Ambassador appearances. "Am I bothering you, Madison?"

"No." The camera crew has come and gone already. Maya deemed us too boring and took her cameramen to the cemetery to interview some of the locals who invariably show up every day. Now they'll be given a chance to say, on film, what they think about the dig. "How are you?"

"Okay. I have a little time. My machines are running."

She extracted multiple samples yesterday in front of the cameras—some from a molar, some from the one available femur—for DNA segmenting.

"I just gave the skull back to Oliver." I play with the sketch on my laptop. Compared to Eleanor and Oliver, what I'm doing is little more than a party trick. "I have all the photos and measurements in the modeling software. Progress is being made."

"Every scientist's favorite phrase. Mind if I sit?"

"Please."

She slides onto a barstool and smooths out her lab coat. "Are you reading Helen's *Titanic* notes?"

"Reading her notes, but haven't reached the *Titanic* part yet. I started at the beginning."

"What do you think of her?"

"Smart, observant, and compassionate. I don't know how she didn't tear her hair out from frustration, living at the time when she did."

"Those women fought hard so we could have something better. We have rights now because of them." Eleanor peers at the computer model of the skull on my laptop screen. "And this one. Who was she? I wonder what her life was like. We might find out, once we find her family."

I almost bring up my Jane Hill theory, but the chances of us being related are one in a million. I called my grandmother about it and ended up leaving a voicemail, which she probably won't check.

She hates cell phones. She'll call me when she'll call me. *If* she'll call me back.

Eleanor watches me add virtual muscle to the virtual bone. "I am so glad that I can be part of one last great adventure," she says. "Something worthwhile. Something people will remember."

"You'll have many more adventures." Although, I don't know what could outdo the *Titanic*. I have a feeling that despite Ramsey, the project will turn out to be spectacular. We might end up chasing this high for the rest of our lives. "People have climbed Mount Everest at your age."

"Not me. For me, this is it. My last big gig."

"You don't know that."

"I do." Her smile is serene. "I'm not going back to chemo again. I've decided."

My hand slips off the mouse. "Oh, no. I'm really sorry, Eleanor. I didn't know."

"Pancreatic cancer." She doesn't flinch, doesn't look away. "I thought I beat it." She lifts a hand, palm out, a dam to hold back the torrent of stupid platitudes and false hope I'm about to offer on reflex. "I've accepted my fate. To work on a project like this… I like the idea of going out with a bang."

"What can I do to help?"

"Don't tell the others. Especially Ramsey. I'm enjoying being here with young people in the beginning of your careers. I don't want to turn what time I have left into a pity party. I'm hoping for a celebration. The best thing you could do for me would be never mentioning my diagnosis. Pretend you don't know. Please."

"All right. Celebration it is. How about a party on Sunday to toast that we successfully survived our first week?"

She snaps her fingers, her eyes sparkling. "Any excuse for champagne."

I don't know how she musters this kind of strength, but if she can smile, so can I, or at least I can refuse to cry. My tears are the last thing she needs. "What was it like to study genetics when you first started?"

She laughs, and her eyes brighten, as if remembering makes her feel younger. "I was the only woman in class. Some of the men didn't think I belonged there, and a few let it be known, loudly. At least by the time I was working on my PhD, some of my colleagues were gentlemen. That's how I met my husband. Apparently, even men mature. He defended me against the jackasses." Love shines on her face like bioluminescence. "We had forty happy years together. It's more than most couples receive."

I try to picture having all male classmates and all male professors. "Both of my mentors at university were women. They dragged me through the parts where I wanted to quit. They still give me references when I need recommendations for a project. How did you make it without all that?"

"I clung on out of sheer stubbornness. In my first class, the professor told me he didn't believe in educating women because they'd have children and never work a day in a lab. He told me I'd never be another Walter Fiers. That professor didn't know, but he gave me a gift telling me that. I knew I'd make it, just to prove him wrong."

"Who is Walter Fiers?"

"First person to sequence a gene, bacteriophage MS2 coat protein, in 1972, the year I started college."

I wasn't even born yet. "I didn't realize genetics was so advanced back then." *Cringe.* I didn't mean to sound like I think she's really old. "Sorry."

Eleanor waves away my apology. "Every time a big-money startup comes out with something new, they act as if they'd invented the field of genetics. But my generation did achieve a few things, and we women contributed."

"I didn't mean—"

"Nettie Stevens discovered sex chromosomes in 1905. Charlotte Auerbach discovered mutagenesis. Barbara McClintock received the Nobel Prize for her discovery of mobile genetic elements." Satisfaction rings in Eleanor's voice. Her eyes shine with pride. "So there."

I'm glad the camera crew is not with us, and we don't have to cut and replay every few minutes. It's nice to be with Eleanor like this. I enjoy our nerd one-on-one.

Later that evening, in my room, I keep thinking about her instead of sleeping. I would never have guessed that she's sick. She is a remarkable woman. I have never seen anyone face death with half as much courage as she is.

Her illness is so incredibly unfair. Of course, cancer is unfair to everyone. It makes me want to scream. It makes me think of my mom.

I end up walking over to the other wing again. The night guard is on his phone in the lobby, a different college kid. He looks up, blurry eyed.

I wave at him. "Just me."

He barely nods back before his eyes are glued to the screen again and his thumb snaps back to scrolling.

In the low light, all the white marble looks gray. The empty, unfinished building is eerier at night than during the day. A metaphor for my life: half done, intending to accomplish something big and important, outcome unknown.

I shake off the thought. The more tired my brain is, the more it tends to think its every thought brilliant.

The light is on in Oliver's lab. Mongolian throat singing music filters out into the hallway. I can't decide if he's weird or eccentric. What's the difference between the two, anyway? He procured art supplies for me. He means well. I can't be mad at him.

"Hey." I stick my head in the door. "Sounds like you're either strangling a hippo or having a party."

He is standing over Jane's bones. "Can't sleep?"

"In a weird mood."

"How weird?"

"I was thinking this building might be a metaphor for my life."

"When you're in a weird mood, everything is a metaphor for life."

I can't tell him that I'm worried for Eleanor, so I say, "I've been antsy all day," which is also true. "Maybe I'm growing old and starting to feel when the weather changes."

"What are you, twenty?"

"Huh. Didn't peg you for a schmoozer. Anyway, I'm just walking around to burn off some energy. I might work a little too."

"Want to paint here?"

No. Then again, I don't really want to withdraw to the solitude of my storage nook of a studio either, only marginally better than spending the night staring at the ceiling in my room. "Maybe?"

The unwieldy canvases are leaning against the wall in the back room where I left them. The closer I walk, the larger they look. "An ocean of opportunity. To screw up, that is."

"Why not jump in?"

"Like I said, oil is not my medium."

"What do you have to lose?"

"Dignity? Self-respect? The illusion that I'm not a complete hack?"

He returns to his work, accepting that although he brought me the supplies, he can't make me paint. It's that whole horse-and-water thing.

"I'll think about it." I think about it. I usually sketch from the middle out. The middle is at my waist. "Can I use the small table in the corner?"

"Go ahead. Do you need help?"

"I might be just a woman, but I can still deadlift two pounds." I flex my biceps.

I drag over the table, and then a blank canvas and I are eye to eye at last. The new setup should help, but it doesn't.

"I've never done anything like this before."

"When you start saying that regularly," he says without looking at me, "you know you're an artist. That's what my cousin Javier always tells his students."

Freaking Javier.

The white nothingness is intimidating, an endless desert full of quicksand, waiting for me to step in so it can swallow me. "I don't know what I want to paint."

Especially with Oliver there, watching. I can't ask him to close his eyes, so I close mine. Then, eyes closed, brush in hand, I stand there like an idiot. *Oh, yeah. This is great.*

"I heard music," Julia says from the door. "Is it all right if I join?"

I've barely seen her today. "Sure. What's up?" She's been at the cemetery all day. We can't dig up new remains, so she's been going over previously processed territory for anything she might have missed. "Are you limping?"

"Pulled my back climbing out of the grave."

"Sounds like something a zombie would say. How bad is it?"

"Couldn't bend over if Jason Momoa was standing behind me."

I want to be her friend forever. I want to talk her into moving to Boston. We could go for long walks and get ice cream.

She looks around. "I've been trying to figure out if I could cook anything on a Bunsen burner. The samosas I ordered for dinner weren't that great. I'm hungry and I'm tired of takeout. What would you think about making something?"

"Unconditional yes." Best idea I've heard all day. "S'mores? We might be able to scrounge the ingredients together from the vending machine."

"I was thinking more along the lines of mutton stew."

Oh. Well. "I like ambition, but I'm not sure how realistic a stew is tonight. We could borrow the chauffeur tomorrow and go grocery shopping."

"Sounds like a plan." Julia walks over. "This doesn't look like it's going to be a forensic portrait. What are you painting?"

"No idea." But no matter what, I can start by covering the white. I pick up ultramarine blue and squeeze some onto a stained, old palette, and then a blob of burnt sienna, side by side.

"Ooh." Eleanor is at the door, in a champagne-colored designer sweat set that drapes softly over her figure, which must be her informal wear for relaxing in her room. "Is this one of those wine-and-painting parties?"

"It could be. I was planning a party for Sunday to celebrate that we survived our first week," I tell the other two, "but we don't have to wait."

Other than Julia, we've barely left the building since we've arrived. The media circus isn't worth it. Every time we try, we're surrounded by reporters. Ramsey no longer minds the publicity—he now encourages interviews, and we've each given a few—but it gets frustrating. The reporters are relentless for details we simply don't have yet.

"I had my cousin Javier drop off a few things for me yesterday," Oliver says. "He included a few bottles of wine."

Good man.

"The vending machine has chocolate puffs," Julia adds. "Chocolate-covered marshmallows. Madison wanted s'mores," she explains to Eleanor.

Eleanor brightens. "I'll bring the graham crackers I have in my room."

I wonder if she got into the habit of carrying crackers for treatment-caused nausea. I feel bad for her. And on top of that, I feel bad because I'm not contributing to the festivities. "I'm sorry. I have nothing."

"You can be in charge of the music," Julia delegates.

"Classic rock it is." We exchange a glance that says Mongolian throat singing is more of a mood thing.

The makeshift s'mores are amazing, gone too quickly. We keep to the back room. Julia brings over her knitting, and Eleanor opens her crossword puzzle on her phone. Oliver assists. I paint. We talk about previous jobs and projects, when we're not talking about the *Titanic*.

By midnight, when the party starts to break up, my canvas is covered in swirls of blue gray. It's nothing, literally a field of nothingness, but I find the rhythm of the brushstrokes soothing.

"Progress," Oliver says behind me.

"How can it be progress if I have no idea *what* it is?"

"The universe is full of mysteries."

"And you're full of…wine," I tell him.

September 9, 2024 (Monday)

I'm the last one to arrive to the meeting room Monday morning, walking into silence instead of the usual chatter.

Has another big discovery been made? Has Julia found something at the cemetery over the weekend? I've braved the press and spent Saturday and Sunday riding buses and discovering the city, seeing little of the rest of the team. I had a bout of cabin fever and wanted to escape the building.

Ramsey barely nods at me when I drop into my chair. "Good morning."

Is he mad at me? I'm not even late.

Maybe he found out about our little team get-together Friday evening. But why would he care? Because we didn't invite the cameras? We deserve a private moment. What business is it of his if we have some fun? We're not hostages.

He looks at each of us in turn. "The artifacts are gone."

The words are spoken with theatrical gravity, as if written by Shakespeare.

"What artifacts?" Oliver's question draws the cameras.

Ramsey flattens his palms against the table. "The ones Madison recovered."

"The coins and the ring? Where were you keeping them?" I hold up a hand in a conciliatory gesture. "And I'm not implying blame."

"I locked them in a drawer in my office." The fingers on his right hand curl into a fist. He presses the fist against the table, but stops short of banging. "They should have been safe."

"Did we have a break-in?" Julia asks for clarification.

Ramsey's jaw moves as if he's chewing his tongue. "Not that we can tell for sure. Not all of our security cameras are operational. The parts of the building that aren't finished don't have electricity. The cameras that are working, we did check. They didn't catch the thief."

We stare in silence, the one thing we were told not to do while the crew is filming. We can't help it.

"Security doesn't think the building was breached." Ramsey's words snap over our heads like a whip.

I don't like what he's implying. He'd better not be

saying what I think he's saying. "Do you think one of us stole Jane's things?" He looks confused, so I add, "J.H."

"All I know is…" He looks me in the eyes and holds and holds without blinking. "That the items are missing."

"Would it be wrong to murder Ramsey?" I ask Julia that evening.

We're all back in the future freezer space in Oliver's lab, but Friday night's party mood is definitely missing.

"Murder is always wrong." Julia is roasting sausage on a fork over a solitary blue flame. "But sometimes it's necessary. We have a DNA expert on our side." She glances at Eleanor. "I bet we could figure out how not to leave a trace."

Eleanor is playing Scrabble with Oliver, who brought the board game from home. He stopped by to check on his plants over the weekend.

The room is semifurnished. We have scavenged another table and four chairs from the unused rooms of the ground floor.

Oliver drops five of his seven letters into place with a satisfied air. "Philodendron." He writes down his score. "We could always quit."

"You got tomorrow's lottery numbers up your sleeve?" I keep my eyes on my blue-gray canvas, brush in one hand, wine in the other. "We're responsible for punitive damages if our actions result in a delay to the project, per our contract."

In my peripheral vision, I see Julia turning the sausage over the flame.

"Somewhere," I say in my best PBS narrator voice, "an OSHA inspector sits bolt upright in bed, unsure what woke him."

"We don't have OSHA. We have CCOHS in Canada, but what they don't know won't hurt them." Julia rotates the sausage again. Fat sizzles; the savory aroma of frying meat fills the air. "Makes you think of a county fair."

"I don't know. I'm starting to get prison-yard vibes. We're in a guarded building, accused of crimes we didn't commit."

"He hasn't called in the police." Oliver, permanently unruffled, waits for Eleanor to make her move on the board.

Julia places the roasted sausage on a paper plate and replaces it with a raw one over the flame. She's making one for each of us, with crusty peasant bread and fresh sauerkraut delivered from an Eastern European specialty shop. "Maybe he doesn't want bad publicity."

"I thought all publicity was good publicity." I look at Eleanor, curious to hear what she thinks.

Eleanor says nothing.

September 10, 2024 (Tuesday)

• • •

At our morning meeting on Tuesday, a woman I haven't seen before is sitting next to Ramsey.

Oliver is missing. He wasn't in the break room for breakfast either. Last night, he said something about quitting. He'd better not have. Or…has he been pulled from the project? Does Ramsey think Oliver is the thief?

No way.

The stranger is around midthirties, smartly dressed in a crisp dove-gray shirt and maroon wool skirt. A detective? She doesn't look tough enough. Julia could take her. I have faith in my team.

Ramsey says, "The mayor agreed to remove the temporary ban on exhumations, as long as he has a staff member present to keep an eye on what we're doing. Please welcome our friendly observer from the mayor's office, Jennifer Martin."

Ramsey introduces each of us in turn.

"Thank you for the warm welcome." Jennifer offers a politician's practiced smile.

She has to be putting us on.

Julia looks as if she'd as soon trip the woman into an empty grave as welcome her. I've never been good at hiding my emotions either, so I'm sure my expression is the same. And Eleanor won't even look at Jennifer; she keeps looking at Ramsey.

We already have the damn cameras. None of us wants an *observer*, someone looking over our shoulders and questioning our decisions, someone reporting on every move we make. We have PhDs.

We don't need a supervisor. We're not freaking interns.

As I'm about to voice my thoughts, Oliver stumbles in. "Apologies. I overslept. Phone battery died in the night, so my alarm didn't go off." He blinks the sleep from his eyes. Draws back. "Jenny?"

Jennifer Martin's next smile is *not* political. It's soft and sweet and, *well, well, well…*

"Hello, Oliver," she says.

He pats down his hair. "What are you doing here?"

CHAPTER 8

Helen

 June 21, 1883

My daughter arrives into this world on June twenty-first, hours before the first light of dawn, with eyes wide and a fierce cry. She is ready to gulp down her share of life.

In the end, Dr. Klauz does not assist much. Edward keeps insisting on consulting in the hallway and refilling their glasses with whiskey. By the time my daughter is born, both men are drunk. I'm grateful to be able to give birth in private.

After Rosie cleans me up, the nanny washes the baby, and when we are tidy enough to receive the new father, he visits us. His eyes are unfocused, his gait uneven, but I shall forgive him for imbibing. He must have been so worried.

"Our first child. Look, darling." I present the baby. "A difficult labor, but neither of us perished."

"A girl. Dr. Klauz told me," Edward says with a grimace as if something bitter is coating his tongue.

"Is she not beautiful?" I cannot tear my eyes from our daughter's perfect little face for long. She is so pink and fresh into this world. I am so proud of how hard I fought, how tough I was, how I brought forth this new life. She is a miracle. She is my every thought, even pushing the fear of childbed fever from my mind. "See how sweet she is?"

Edward's eyes are bloodshot, his stare accusing.

I shift so he can see our little daughter better, and for a moment, I grit my teeth. The pain does not vanish after birth, another detail among many that nobody remembered to mention beforehand. I feel as if my body has been torn into pieces. Only the joy that fills my heart keeps me from weeping outright. My emotions are in such disarray. I must not annoy my husband. "Edward?"

He turns on his heels, calling back over his shoulder, "As you will not be able to come downstairs, I am heading over to the club for breakfast."

Rosie hurries in, and I catch the pity in her eyes before she drops her gaze. She is carrying the silver tray Edward and I bought in Paris on our honeymoon, steam rising from a blue-and-white china bowl that was a wedding gift. "The cook sent a bit of broth, if you think you might be able to eat. All the staff send their congratulations, ma'am."

No sooner does she set the tray on the bedside table than the nanny—a buxom Scandinavian woman whom Edward hired through a domestic staffing agency—appears for the baby. I release my special bundle with reluctance. How is it possible to feel so happy and miserable all at once, feel as if I accomplished something momentous, and at the same time, I utterly failed?

I so wish I could have made Edward happy.

I sip my broth, too weak to do it justice. Then I sink back into the pillows and let sleep claim me.

Mama's voice outside the door pulls me awake, as she arrives in the late afternoon with my father in tow.

"Oh, my poor lamb." She rushes to my side. "I hope you did not suffer much."

I had a telegram sent when my labor began, and they caught the first train out of Connecticut.

My little girl is brought in, and both Mama and Papa kiss her head before Nanny gives her to me.

Papa beams, although he is not entirely at ease in a room full of women. He keeps glancing at the door. "And where is the proud father?"

"Celebrating at his club."

"As he should." He pats his pocket watch but does not check the time. "Very well. I believe I shall join him for a brandy and a cigar."

The nanny leaves the baby with me, and Mama abandons her chair to sit on the edge of my bed, as close to her first grandchild as she can get. Her smile is full of wonder and joy.

I imagine our expressions mirror each other. "I thought Abigail would join you."

Mama's smile falters. "Your sister is in bed with pneumonia. We had to leave her behind this time."

Abigail caught scarlet fever at the same time as Fannie, but Abigail was fortunate—she survived. Her constitution suffered, however, and she is more prone to fall prey to any new malady.

Mama pats my hand, her gaze shifting between the baby and me. "I am glad to find you well. Bringing forth the next generation is a dreadful business."

"You could have warned me."

"It is rather better not to know ahead of time, don't you think?"

Maybe. "I cannot imagine how you survived the five of us."

"I have done my best to forget." She coos to the baby, who watches her with curious, slate-gray eyes, as peaceful and bald as a little monk. "What will you name her?"

For a moment, I consider Mary, but it would be strange to speak to the little baby using my mother's name. And, also, Mary is rather old-fashioned.

"I considered Evelina. Naming our child after Edward's mother might soften the disappointment that he did not receive the son he wanted. But then, Edward's parents live a few blocks away, and they have yet to call. You and Papa came at once from Connecticut."

Mama gives a satisfied nod, proud to have won

the grandparent race. "I have had our bags packed for the past two weeks."

My in-laws' delay is no mystery. When Edward sent word of the birth, he must also have informed them of the gender of our baby. Well, I am not disappointed with her sex. She is most precious to me, and most welcome. "I shall call her Edith."

If my mother hoped for Mary, she gives no indication, but she does ask, "Why?"

"I like the meaning. *Strong in strife.*" I consulted William Arthur's *Dictionary of Christian Names* as soon as I discovered that I was in a blessed condition.

"Surely, she will not see strife. Edward's business thrives. His father cannot brag enough about him to yours, every time he comes up to Norwalk." Mama's gaze drifts to the bedside table, then returns to me. "Where is his birthing gift?" She touches her fingers to her emerald necklace. "Your father always gave me jewelry."

"He has not had the time yet." I look away. "The day has been hectic."

"Of course." Mama's smile is unconvinced and unconvincing. "He has trouble settling into fatherhood. No doubt he wanted a male child first, a proper heir." She pats my hand again. "Don't you fret. You shall have a boy next."

I could cry at the prospect of having to go through the ordeal of childbirth again. Yet this is my lot as a woman. Edward's mother had to keep going after three daughters—Ida, Ella, and Annie—to finally have Edward.

"I cannot." I look at my mother, stricken by the thought. *How will I survive?* "Mama, I cannot."

After Edith's birth, Edward avoids me through the summer, but in the fall, he returns to our bed. Knowing the outcome he desires, I am no longer able to relax. To make matters worse, he is no longer gentle.

When several months pass by without results, the accusations begin all over again.

"Is that an herbal?" He grabs my teacup from me one morning to sniff at the amber liquid. "What are you drinking?"

"Ceylon tea."

"Liar." He throws the cup against the wall, where it shatters, leaving a stain on the wallpaper. The brownish droplets run down the pink roses and their ivory background, as if someone has murdered a rose garden.

I will not be able to hide that stain from the staff. And now our tea service—part of the blue-and-white wedding set—is no longer complete. Yet more than a teacup is broken on this morning. So is my trust. This is no longer just the odd mood on Edward's part, a cold shoulder, a raised voice here and there—he has progressed to violence.

That night, he apologizes and promises it will not happen again.

I no longer believe him, and I am right to be skeptical. The next time he loses his temper, he shoves me against the wall.

I am a mother, so I hold strong for my daughter.

I don't allow myself to shatter.

I am no china cup.

May 7, 1886

Three years after little Edith joined our family, I go into labor again, on the seventh of May, 1886.

I hide my pain for as long as I can, staying in the bedroom, claiming fatigue.

Annie checks on me. "Is there anything I could fetch you, ma'am?"

"No, thank you. But would you be so kind as to open the window? I should like some fresh air."

"Yes, ma'am."

The clatter of traffic and the chirping of the birds might mask a few small moans when I can no longer contain them.

"And Annie, would you, please, see what fruit the greengrocer might have? I have a particular craving for cherries."

I want her away. I have already sent Rosie to the seamstress. That way, they will not be entering my room every other minute.

"Cherries it is, ma'am. Maybe Mr. Tiller still has some of those he had shipped in from New Jersey last week."

My plot succeeds. Edward is at work. By the time Rosie and Annie return, I am in full labor. Rosie runs for the doctor, Annie for her friend who was a sought-after midwife in Ireland before the family boarded a ship for America. She reaches me first. I spare myself the hospital again. Dr. Klauz arrives so late, he misses the birth altogether.

"Forgive me," he apologizes to Edward, who burst through the door only ten minutes before him. "I was at Schurz's office to relieve the pain of his gout. The interruptions were never-ending. Cables are flying in to the *Evening Post* about the massacre, as you might imagine."

Exhaustion presses me into the mattress like a lead blanket. Blood flows between my legs into the rolled-up towel Annie's mother placed there, my lifeblood leaving me. Yet I am triumphant. I have given Edward an heir.

"If workers are granted the eight-hour workday they demand," Edward's tone is laced with anger, despite the happy family event, "what will they ask for next? We will never see the end of it. Working men should be grateful for the work they have. If they do not appreciate the bread on their table, they can quit and starve to death."

A reasoning I have heard too often. He is wrong, but I cannot muster the strength to care. He congratulated me on delivering a healthy boy but did not linger by us, as though producing an heir was merely an item to be completed. He did promise a necklace, rubies, an heirloom from his grandparents, and now he seems impatient to move on to his next task.

Dr. Klauz harrumphs. "They are already talking about a minimum age for children in the mines and the factories. Anarchy. If the poor cannot send their children to work, they will have no motivation to have any. And when the factories have to close for lack of labor? Do these people want our economy to collapse? How they can be so selfish is not only beyond comprehension but downright un-American."

Edward pours him a glass of brandy while making sounds of agreement. "What do the cables from Chicago say, then? Do they know yet who threw the bomb at the police at Haymarket?"

"Some agitator." The doctor knocks back half the glass. "Seven officers dead. Protesters were killed too, although not enough, if you ask me. Dozens are injured on both sides, from what I've heard."

"An example must be made."

"Oh, there will be, my good man. The police are hunting the anarchists as we speak. Any that are caught will be hanged."

My eyes flutter closed. *Blood, blood, blood.* Behind my closed eyelids, all I see is red.

Edward names his much-awaited heir Harold. The name means *leader of an army*, popular among British royalty.

I do not want my son, my Harry, to ever fight in

MARTA MOLNAR

war. I want him to grow up gentle and kind, and I tell him so when we are alone.

As soon as I heal enough to walk, I escape the bed, against the doctor's orders. The moment Edward leaves for work, Rosie helps me dress. I do not have the wet nurse over during Edward's office hours either. I feed little Harry myself whenever I can.

Once my three months of confinement end and I can leave the house again, I visit Kerstin, the wife of the owner of the bookstore I secretly frequent. I heard rumors about the kind of help she offers to women on the side. Now that I have done my duty and gifted my husband with an heir, I very much find myself in need of such help.

"This is it?" The linen bag of dried leaves and twigs she hands me in her kitchen, in the tidy apartment above the store, is less than impressive.

The potent scent of dried herbs fills the air: rosemary, thyme, oregano, mint, and dozens of others. They hang in bunches from the ceiling above our heads.

"I will also make you a tinful of suppositories, but you will have to return for those. You insert those…*after*." She gives me a meaningful look. "It would be better *before*, but if he notices, there'll be hell to pay. *After* works too, but make sure to also partake of the tea."

She is a big-boned blonde Swede like her husband, with an open gaze and an open heart. Yet I

168

cannot look her in the eyes. I have never had such an intimate talk with anyone in my life.

"Thank you," is all I manage.

"Be sure you hide everything."

"I shall." If Edward found out my secret, it would be the death of me.

"Be careful." She means it not just for myself, but for her as well. She is risking her life to help me. If anyone found out, she would end up in prison.

"I promise."

Downstairs, I buy a book, a French travelogue. The last thing I want is for Jenkins, our coachman, to become suspicious.

But, of course, he babbles to Edward.

"I hear you have been to that store again that caters to suffragette nonsense."

I lift my book from my nightstand and show him, the most innocent topic imaginable.

"I want you to understand this," he tells me in a tone I have never heard from him before but I am used to from my father. "A woman is under her husband's authority at home, and under the government's outside the home. If you flout the government's authority, people will think you must flout my authority as well. I am *somebody* in this city, a prominent businessman. Do you want to damage the store's reputation, Helen?"

(Seven Years Later)
    1893, New York

. . .

Who am I to whimper when queens are falling from their thrones?

"She will be reinstated, won't she?" I ask Mama, who is visiting. "They say President Cleveland is going to launch an investigation, as soon as he is inaugurated."

"He probably will, but I expect to happen what always happens when rich men stand to gain money and a woman stands in their way." Mama glances at me over her knitting.

She has arrived at the beginning of the week with my sister, Abigail, who sits quietly by the window. We are surrounded by the most exquisite furniture money can buy, our chairs upholstered in periwinkle brocade threaded through with gold. Since Harry's birth seven years ago, Edward has been most generous. The new curtains are a matching shade of lighter blue. Unfortunately, they fail to stop the cold draft that seeps through the frames of our tall windows.

Outside, a light snow sifts over New York City, and I feel, at the same time, close to and a million miles away from the Pacific, where a group of American businessmen recently deposed the queen of Hawaii.

"In any case"—Mama returns her gaze to the wool yarn and adds another line of brown to the shawl she is to gift to the Ladies' Bazaar—"President Cleveland will have enough problems with our own country."

The economy is in a free fall once again. Some of the railroads are failing, and there have been runs on banks in a number of states. Papa, who stayed at home in Norwalk, is in a panic.

Yet, despite all that is going wrong right outside my front door, my thoughts are stuck in Hawaii. Maybe because the country had a queen until very recently. And, of course, England has Queen Victoria. I cannot understand how elsewhere women can sit on thrones while I cannot even vote in my own country.

"Every woman is a princess on her wedding day, then a queen of her household. But Lili'uokalani is a *real* queen. How unbearable it must be for her to lose her kingdom."

While I muse about the fate of a collection of islands I shall never see, Abbie is reading a letter by the window from her beau, lost in her own world. I envy her and fear for her at the same time. I pray that disappointment will not crush her, but that she finds a happy life. As always, she is far too thin and pale, looking years younger than her age. I hope she isn't lovesick.

Mama glances at her, then lowers her voice as she asks, "How long has he been gone this time, Helen?"

"Two months."

"And not a word?"

"None." Embarrassment prickles my cheeks. I fear that people will judge me, believe that I have done something wrong. God knows I do not wish for Edward's volatile company, but at the same time, I question what is wrong with me that makes my husband not want to be with me.

"You could start over." Mama looks straight into my eyes. "A new life."

Her words surprise me into silence. Several seconds tick by before I can form a response. "I am a thirty-four-year-old woman with two half-grown children. What life could I possibly have? The best I can hope for is that he returns before the gossip grows any worse."

Mama considers me at length. "Maybe if you sent him a note? Where is he?"

Now my cheeks burn. "He could be back in Denver. He has gone there a few times to establish a new store. With the economy as it is, there is some urgency. I do not think he is in New York. We would run into each other. I would see him."

Mama adjusts her needles. "You do not have to settle for this."

Seconds tick by before I catch her meaning. *Divorce.* Or, at least, I think that is what she means. My children laugh upstairs, their sweet voices echoing down the staircase. Despite all, they are happy.

I draw my shawl tighter around me. "And what about the casualties?"

"There are always casualties in war."

How true that is. "Queen Lili'uokalani conceded to save her people's lives. She could have deployed her army, but she did not." I read that in Edward's papers, which are still delivered.

"Oh, for heaven's sake, forget that queen, Helen. You could leave Edward. You should come home to Norwalk with the children. *You* could choose to fight instead of surrendering."

Mama is sixty-two years old, lucky to be unfamiliar with violent outbursts and drunken, flying fists. Her fights are imaginary.

"The law makes it nearly impossible for a woman to divorce her husband. I would have to prove adultery or cruelty, and provide eyewitnesses in court." I consulted an attorney in secret.

"If he stays away much longer, you can claim desertion."

"How on earth do you know the rules of divorce?"

"I am friends with everyone who is anyone in Connecticut and New York. It is rare, but it does happen. Don't you read the papers?"

I *am* familiar with a few high-profile cases, but… "I am not certain I am quite that modern. I do not know if I could bear the shame of failing."

"Victoria Woodhull did it. Twice," Abbie joins in from the window seat.

I did not realize my sister was listening.

"She also ran for president. She is hardly the average woman. Edward will come home, and then we shall talk. We are two intelligent people. Surely, we can solve our problems."

An awkward silence follows. Abbie moves to the walnut-inlay writing desk to respond to her letter, and she is immediately lost in her own world again.

Mama does not push any further either, although I sense that it is merely a strategic retreat and not a full surrender.

She examines her knitting. "How would you feel about us staying another week? We could go to the theatre again."

I miss the theatre. A married woman attending alone always generates overmuch speculation, so I have been avoiding Broadway. "Oh, please, do stay. Edith and Harry would be delighted. And so would I."

"It is settled, then. Your father is in a state. I would rather stay out of his way. He is convinced that the *Narconic* sank."

I shudder. When I was three years old, I almost drowned in the bathtub. The gaslight went out, and my nanny ran off for a candle. When Mama came up to see how we were getting on, my head was under the water.

"I am not familiar with the *Narconic*. Did Papa invest?"

"A cargo steamship of the White Star Line. Goods from Liverpool to New York, then American cattle on the return trip to England. It has gone missing in rough seas. Henry keeps muttering that she shouldn't have sunk, a new ship, less than a year old."

"*Four steel boilers!*" Abbie imitates Papa's voice from the writing desk.

When we cannot suppress a laugh, Mama shakes

her head. "Your sister and I know more about steamers than we care to. This is what happens when a man is obsessed with them and his only son moves to the Rocky Mountains."

At least Papa spends time with his children. He often accompanies Mama to see us. My heart squeezes for Edith and Harry, who are forced to do without such fatherly niceties.

When they fly downstairs to take tea and cake with their grandmother and aunt, I am more determined than ever to save my marriage to Edward. Edith is nine. In a decade or so, she will want her father to walk her down the aisle. And Harry is almost seven, a boy in need of a man in the house as well.

To convince Edward to come home, however, first I must find him.

How difficult could it be to hire a private detective?

1895, New York

"Can you prove the infidelity, Mrs. Candee?" The honorable judge peers at me over his bulbous nose like a vulture from atop a chimney. I have never seen a king, but I imagine he would look very much like this man: imperial, inspecting me as if he were holding my life in his hands.

He does, in fact.

The detective I hired did find Edward; however, the report Mr. Mason handed me was such that… Mama was right. I deserve better. I can no longer accept Edward as my husband.

"Mrs. Candee," the judge repeats. "Can you *prove* infidelity?"

The courtroom smells like wood polish and the scent of tobacco that wafts off all the men present. My head buzzes. I might faint. *I am not here alone*. I grab on to the thought, and I nod toward the man who has come with me to court. "Mr. Mason."

"The private detective you hired?" The judge laughs. "He can hardly be impartial now, can he? Seeing how you pay him."

"One cannot hire a detective without payment"— for heaven's sake—"as one cannot engage a coachman or maid for free."

The judge's face freezes, its angular panes hard as hammered iron. "Control your outbursts, Mrs. Candee."

I am not to argue, no matter how unfairly I am being treated—the first rule I learned today. "I apologize, Your Honor."

I am not in my best form, overwrought not only by the proceedings but also by news of my sister, Abigail. Mama's letter is heavy in my pocket. Our family doctor in Norwalk has diagnosed my sister's prolonged illness as female hysteria and has sent her to a sanatorium by the sea.

I do not agree. Abbie does not imagine her chronic cough, nor her fevers, nor her weak spells when she can barely rise from bed. At each visit, I am convinced that her body is fighting a disease in a battle that sometimes she is winning, but mostly she is losing. If all she needed were rest, she would have long ago recovered.

"You cannot prove adultery," the judge pronounces. "Do you have proof, then, of cruelty and inhumane treatment?"

"He drinks."

"So do most gentlemen. And we might smoke a cigar too, now and then." The tone is patronizing, impatient. "If a glass of port or whiskey is a crime, we would all be in prison. Are you one of those *dries*, those meddlesome women who want to prohibit alcohol in their neighborhoods?"

"No, Your Honor. But, you see, my husband drinks overly much. And when he drinks…" Embarrassment might kill me before the hearing is over, an outcome the judge would probably prefer. "He is violent."

"Do you have proof? Injuries? Bruises?" He looks at me as if he wishes to inspect them.

Blood rushes to my face. "I did have bruises, on multiple occasions. But not at present. He has been gone for some time, as I have said."

"And you still bring up his mistakes." The man glares. "A wife who holds grudges forever. You might see why your husband does not wish to return home. I suggest you mend your ways and resolve to be more pleasant."

"I have been nothing but accommodating. I hired the private detective to locate Edward so I might convince him to give our marriage another try, but Mr. Mason's report made painfully clear that all hope was gone."

"Mr. Edward Candee is a prominent businessman in this city. As such, he is a levelheaded fellow. You must have done something to provoke his displeasure. Are you a shrew? Do you give voice to your thoughts when you disagree with him, Mrs. Candee?"

"It is difficult to argue when he is not present."

"How old are your children, again?"

"Edith is twelve, Harold nine."

"And you would tear them from their father at such a crucial time?"

"*He* has abandoned us. We have not seen him these past two years."

"And so you wish to desert him. You should do well to remember that Christ counsels us to forgiveness and patience. In any case, you cannot sue for divorce on the grounds of abandonment until you have been abandoned for three years or more. Your impatience to leave your lawfully wedded husband is unseemly indeed."

"My husband is keeping company with *another woman*." *Lord, help me to remain calm.* "He gambles. He engages in other sordid activities. If you would only look at the private detective's report, Your Honor."

Magnanimously, the judge waves Mr. Mason over, but he barely pages through the thick stash of papers I obtained at great cost before he hands them back.

He breathes in scorn and breathes out disapproval as he raises his gavel. "I will not break up a family over such trifles. A woman's purpose is to support her husband. So has God ordained, and so this court confirms."

The gavel comes down with an aggressive *bam*.

For several moments, I stand frozen.

How can the proceedings be over so quickly? The judge is deciding about my life, the lives of my children. Should he not have more questions? But no, this has been my chance. And now it is gone. I am trapped. The law has spoken.

The whole time I have been standing before His Honor, my spine was as if made of wool yarn, soft and ready to fold. My legs trembled and still tremble under my dress. Yet now that the merciless verdict is pronounced, I do not faint as I feared, nor do I fall into hysterics.

To leave me was Edward's choice.

The judge now decided to sentence me to further suffering.

When shall I have a voice in any of this?

"Accept your fate," the man still lectures, "and go forth with more humbleness hereto, Mrs. Candee. You must understand that God put the weaker sex under the dominion of the stronger one for a reason."

A colony of ants is crawling through my veins.

Butterflies flap their wings in my ears. Another woman might reach for her smelling salts, but I refuse to as much as sway. I square my shoulders and look him straight in the eyes. "No."

"What is that?" A thunderstorm builds in his voice.

"Mr. Candee has abandoned us completely." Heat creeps across my face. "Physically as well as financially."

I had to let Jenkins go, the coachman. And the cook too. The butler disappeared at the same time as Edward, likely gone along with my husband. All I have left are Annie and Rosie, who take turns cooking our meals and keeping the house in order, which is no joking matter. My circumstances are dire. In New York society, one is either on the way up or sliding back. One does not lay off staff. I have already been passed over for invitations to multiple events.

The judge scoffs. "How do you and the children sustain yourselves?"

I wish he hadn't asked that. "I write."

"Write what?"

"Articles for *The Ladies' Home Journal* and *Harper's Bazaar*. Also, for the *Woman's Home Companion* and *Good Housekeeping*. And for Scribner's." A few months ago, out of desperation, I submitted a few short pieces, expecting rejection, but they were accepted.

Open disbelief sits on the man's face. "And you are an expert on what subject?"

"I write about childcare, affairs of the home, and household management."

He cannot find fault with that, but he is far from being won over. "Are you telling me you are supporting your family off your scribbles?"

"I support my family from my *work*. Yes."

"Nonsense. I am sure your husband contributes. I happen to know him from the Manhattan Club. He is a fine fellow. No doubt he is a good father and a good husband. Case dismissed."

Then, down comes the gavel for the second time, in case I missed the first.

This man has such power over me. I burn with the unfairness of it all, but I politely withdraw, lest he end up punishing me for insolence. I cannot afford a fine at the moment.

All the way out of the building, the same question circles in my head.

In a world built for and ruled by men, where does one go for justice as a woman?

I recall the poor woman I saw once in a doorway, back in Norwalk, her husband beating her with a stick, while their small child was begging for food a few feet away. I witnessed the scene with my friend Ada, from the safety of our carriage.

At the time, I thought that woman and I inhabited different worlds. I was wrong. We are one and the same. None of us—no woman—holds true agency over her life. And we shall not either, until we gain political power. Women must gain the vote. The suffragettes are right.

When I arrive home, the children are upstairs. I close the door behind me, but I can take no more than half a dozen steps. I lie down in the foyer, on the middle of the carpet. Annie and Rosie are not around, thank heavens. They must be in the kitchen. I spread out my arms and legs, the least ladylike pose for certain. I do not care if I am behaving in a way that is unseemly. I feel dead.

I close my eyes, and for a moment, I imagine I am already locked up in my coffin. I give myself over to defeat. Then the children's laughter reaches me through the ceiling, and I awaken.

Somewhere else, there must exist a life that is *more*. A life filled with joy, a life where I could have some modicum of power over my fate. I close my eyes again, and this time, I imagine that I have that life, envision what such freedom might look like.

In France, women may have their own bank account. They may open one without their husband's approval, Mama told me in her last letter. I could move to Paris.

Except…

I do not wish to leave my friends, my sister and brother, and Mama and Papa. I am not ceding the country of my birth to Edward. As much as this land is his, it is also mine.

I shall not run away from the oppression of my sex. I will fight so that my daughter's life shall be better, so that when she grows up, she shall have the same rights as her brother.

My eyes open.

"Ma'am?" Annie steps into my field of vision and peers down at me, worry wrinkling her forehead. "Are you all right? Shall I send for Dr. Klauz? Is anything amiss?"

"All is well, Annie." I sit up. "I was lost for a minute, but no longer. I know where I am going."

CHAPTER 9

Madison

September 10, 2024 (Tuesday)

After Jennifer finishes thanking us for adding her to the team, Ramsey starts a slideshow. The man is enamored with PowerPoint. If anyone gave him a lectern and a laser pointer, he'd faint from the thrill.

"While we want to identify all the unidentified remains," he says, "I am hoping to find one person in particular. The discovery would be a major news event. His story has everything: wealth, romance, subterfuge. If we were to find him, he might merit a movie of his own. It would significantly increase the value of our project."

John Astor was the richest man on the *Titanic*, on his way home from his honeymoon with his bride, but Ramsey already told us that Astor's body was found, so this has to be someone else.

"Victor Peñasco y Castellana."

The photo on the screen is that of a young man who holds himself with a quiet confidence, accessorized with a walking stick and leather gloves, his kind eyes looking straight at the camera.

I wonder how Oliver knows Jennifer.

"Victor was twenty-four years old, traveling across Europe with his wife, Maria Josefa, on a honeymoon that is estimated to have cost half a million to a million in today's dollars." Ramsey pauses to give us time to fully appreciate those numbers.

"That is a lot," Eleanor says.

Ramsey moves on. "Victor's mother asked them to stick to the Continent and not embark on an ocean trip, but they could not resist the inaugural voyage of the *Titanic*. They booked passage, leaving Victor's butler behind in Paris to send prewritten postcards to Victor's mother so she wouldn't suspect anything."

"I can see where this is going," I whisper to Julia, at the same time as she whispers, "Mama's boy," to me.

"When the *Titanic* sank," Ramsey rolls along, "the mother had no idea her son and his bride were on the ship. She kept receiving French postcards in the mail."

"Were they both lost?" I ask Ramsey.

He clicks on to the portrait of the beautiful young bride. "Maria Josefa survived. She and her maid were in lifeboat number eight. Victor's body was never recovered. According to Spanish law, Maria couldn't remarry for twenty years, and neither could she inherit after her husband. All the money, including her own considerable dowry, would be locked away from her."

"Was the law the same for men whose wives disappeared?" Julia words it like a question, but her face clearly shows what she thinks.

The next slide reintroduces us to the looming granite gravestones of the cemetery, their dark gray outlined against the pale sky.

"Maria's family bought off the authorities." Ramsey's tone turns scandalized, for the cameras. "Her maid identified one of the unclaimed bodies as Victor. That way, Maria could be officially declared a widow."

Julia asks, "If they had Victor here in Halifax, wouldn't the maid have recognized him? If she didn't find him here, we're not likely to find him, are we?"

"She might not have been shown all the bodies." Ramsey shrugs. "Or Victor's face could have been damaged when the ship went down, with deck furniture and other debris flying."

I don't want to think about faces all smashed in. "Did Maria remarry?"

"To a baron, six years later. She had three children with him."

I hope she found happiness. I hope she married for love. She must have. With Victor officially declared dead, she would have received her money, so she wouldn't have had to marry for funds.

The cameramen circle around Ramsey.

Right.

That's the point. These little stories are meant to spellbind the audience. They're not for us. Whether we know about Victor and Maria makes no difference for our work. Ramsey is trying to jam as much story, as much intrigue, into the documentary as he possibly can. He's not my favorite person on the team, but he's a clever man.

I wonder what the cliff-hanger will be at the end of the scene once it's edited.

I bet it'll be my question: *Did she remarry?*

Cut to commercial.

After our morning meeting, Jennifer drives Julia and Oliver out to the cemetery. We don't see them again until late in the afternoon when they bring the second set of remains back to Oliver's lab.

I'm close to finished with Jane Hill's portrait, so I head over. One cameraman is in attendance. A third grave has been opened up, so the other cameraman is still at the grave site, along with Ramsey, who is delivering a monologue today about how TTP came into being. Maya, our director, is going back and forth between the two locations.

At the lab, Oliver is dictating into his phone from the original rescuers' records. "Victim number five in the roster, the fifth body pulled from the water.

Female. Height, five feet and nine inches. Weight, around 170 lb. Age estimated at forty. Dark brown hair. No distinguishing features. Personal effects found on the body were a crucifix, snuffbox, medallion, and three rings, two of them silver, one turquoise. None of the items were located upon exhumation." He clicks off the recording. "Let's see what we have here, and then I'll add my own notes."

He begins to lay out the skeleton in anatomical position as I would, skull first. This one is crushed, with several pieces missing.

"I thought," Jennifer says from a respectable distance, her arms wrapped around her, "that if you are embalmed, you don't decompose."

"Nothing stops time," Oliver scans the rest of the scant bones we have for this victim, unbothered by the mayor's spy watching. "Nobody cheats Mother Nature."

I observe the easy rapport between them. They're not in a current relationship. I think she's Oliver's ex.

"Embalming only slows decomposition," I put in, because I resent the supervision, and the stiff way Jennifer holds herself says the topic bothers her. "But even with embalming and the body buried in a coffin, decomposition of soft tissue still occurs. In five to ten years or so, all we have left are the bones."

"And then we have the bones forever?" She sounds hopeful. "I saw a documentary about prehistoric burials from hundreds of thousands of years ago. Some still had skulls."

"That greatly depends on the burial environment.

A lot of conditions would have to line up right. Under ordinary circumstances, even the bones turn into dust after a century or so. In some countries, they recycle cemetery plots after a hundred years." I look at her mouth. "Your teeth hang on the longest."

"I see." She steps forward, caught up in the topic, then immediately steps back. She has goose bumps on her neck. "The *Titanic* sank a hundred and twelve years ago. Is that the urgency for this project? Is it a now-or-never type of situation, where you have to do it while there are still a few bones left?"

"It wouldn't be wise to wait much longer." Oliver brushes the dirt off a clavicle.

We watch him clean the bones, each of us lost in our thoughts. Who was this woman? What dreams drew her across the ocean?

Jennifer is the first one to break the silence. "I'm sure you find my presence here irritating."

Obviously, I don't hate her, but... "We didn't expect to be monitored." It does chafe.

The camera closes in. Behind the cameraman, Maya's eyes glint. She's itching for a catfight. The cameraman too. His lips are pursed, he's wishing so hard.

"It's not that the mayor thinks that your team isn't up to the task." Jennifer attempts to defuse the tension. "But he has to deal with the opposition party. Whatever he does is immediately declared evil and untenable. He has to show that he has everything in hand. Because of the initial secrecy, as people are finding out more about TTP, it's quickly becoming unpopular. Ramsey neglected to bring the local stake-holders onboard. A project like this needs more than a handful of permits to succeed. He should have made a public announcement before he started digging."

She sounds too reasonable. Her tone is too conciliatory. The cameraman, refusing to give up hope, turns his lens on me. I might still fly off the handle. Wouldn't that be great for ratings?

I say nothing.

"If I were you," Jennifer tells us, "I'd absolutely hate the supervision. If it helps, I didn't ask for this either. You're obviously professionals. I don't think my presence here is necessary. How about I stay quiet and stay in my own corner?"

Oh, the camera will love that.

I don't want to like her, but she has a sincerity about her that's disarming. I hate when I'm all set on disliking someone, and they keep being nice, ruining the dynamics.

I shake my head at her. "I would have preferred if you turned out to be unreasonable and tried to take over. I don't want to like a politician. It feels wrong."

Her response is a quick laugh, then she busies herself with her laptop. She might be taking notes; she might be on social media. I don't care, as long as she doesn't interfere with our jobs.

I snap a few dozen pictures of the bones for my own work and jot down the skull and jaw measurements Oliver dictates into his phone, for the record. The skeletal remains are the most deteriorated we've seen so far. Half an hour passes without us exchanging a single word.

Maya taps the cameraman on the shoulder. "Let's check on Eleanor."

Once they're gone, Jennifer flashes us a grin. "Wow, we're so boring, we drove them away."

Oliver smiles back.

Are they in some kind of a relationship? Am I the third wheel? I slip my phone into my pocket. "I'll go and start on my sketches."

"Do you use software, or is it still all done by hand?" Jennifer follows me to my studio.

I did not expect that. I must have misread the vibe.

"Software to a point, but computer imaging carries me only so far. The program can't quite make a person look *real*, real. When an assignment allows for it, I like painting the final image onto canvas. To me, it's still the best way."

"Worth the extra effort?"

"It is to me. It's almost as if a living artist is able to transfer some of their own essence to the painting that helps it be more lifelike."

She doesn't laugh off the sentiment as crazy, which I appreciate. "I get it."

"So…" *Do not ask.* "How do you know Oliver?"

"A million years ago, we used to date."

Interesting.

I pull J.H.'s drying painting off a shelf, flip my laptop open to her digital reconstruction, and show the two side by side. "I can see the difference, but I don't know if other people can. I could be biased."

"You're not." Jennifer leans in. "You brought her *to life*. I don't know how anyone can create a likeness from a skull." She straightens and looks at me. "How much of this is guesswork?"

"More than I'd like. For starters, I have no way of knowing if she had freckles, or scars, or moles. We'll see how good I am once we find her family, if they have old family photos."

"I bet it'll be close."

"Hope so. I'm working off anatomy. There's a method to it. It's not that difficult, really."

"I'll take your word for that."

She's easygoing, curious, upbeat. I can understand what Oliver saw in her. Maybe this project will bring them back together. They're both nice people. I'd be happy for them.

"How does it work?" Jennifer asks. "What's the process?"

She's got me there. Who doesn't like to talk about their work? I'm rarely asked for details. Most people have an aversion to the dead.

"First, I send the pictures of the bones from my phone to the computer. Then I start building up the face. On the screen, computer magic attaches the detached mandible to the skull. Next, I add red muscles line by line using depth markers from a specific forensic database, then yellow fat for padding, then tan skin, then eyes."

"How do you know her eyes were brown?"

"The log mentioned brown hair. I matched the eyes, but I can change them if genetics end up indicating otherwise."

A roughly painted image of the woman whose bones I've held just minutes ago looks at me from the screen. She's a decade older than I am. I've started thinking of her as hopeful, but the program gave her a neutral expression. She's neither happy nor scared to be resurrected on a laptop screen. I feel connected to her, like I do to J.H., which is not a rare occurrence. When I work on a case, I always wonder about the people the bones once were, my mind filling in the gaps.

"I think she was married. The snuffbox the record mentioned must have been her husband's. He gave it to her for safekeeping when they still thought all the women would have a place in the lifeboats."

And then the lifeboats were lowered half empty, before second- and third-class passengers could jump in. I haven't reached that part in Helen's memoir yet, but I have seen the movie.

"You made her real in a few minutes." Jennifer's hushed, awed tone is gratifying.

"That's the plan." I click over to J.H.'s file to show the progression of images, and I page through, forgetting that I have pictures of Jane's bootheel treasure in there.

"What's that?"

Too late, I slap the laptop closed. "Uh… Couple of things we unearthed with the first body."

"From the *Titanic*? Does anyone know you found this?"

"You mean, did Ramsey tell the mayor? I have no idea. You'd have to ask Ramsey."

The fact that the police haven't shown up yet says that our project manager slash producer wants to keep the discovery, then subsequent loss of the artifacts, private, maybe reveal it only when the documentary comes out. In entertainment, timing is everything. He'll do whatever offers the best plot twist. He'll do whatever will earn him the highest number of eyeballs, the highest number of clicks. Promo is his top priority.

I don't want Jennifer to ask any more questions about the found objects, so I switch to the first topic that pops into my head. "So, you and Oliver…"

"He's a great guy."

"Yet you're no longer together."

"No big story there. Nothing scandalous happened. I have political ambitions, he doesn't."

No, I can't see him campaigning. He's not a performer. He's too chill. "As simple as that?"

"I can appreciate him and, at the same time, understand that he's not for me."

"That sounds like something he would say. Why is everyone more mature than I am?"

"He's rubbed off on me." Jennifer smiles, then she reaches toward the stack of printouts on my desk. "What's this?"

The red CONFIDENTIAL stamp does draw the eye. In my defense, my desk doesn't have any drawers. "Notes for a memoir by Helen Churchill Candee, one of the survivors of the *Titanic*."

"May I?"

"I signed an NDA that says we can only share information with people on the team."

"I'm on the team. Ramsey said so."

"All right." What am I going to do, tackle her? It's not like we're talking about military secrets. "The *Titanic* story starts at the red tab."

Last night, before I turned out the light, I got to the part where Helen wants to divorce her abusive husband but can't. Out of curiosity, I looked up when no-fault divorce became legal in the US.

Ronald Reagan (then governor) was the first to sign it into law in California in 1969. Other states were slower to follow. In New York, no-fault divorce didn't become legal until 2010.

Footsteps in the hallway interrupt my musing.

Oliver appears in the door, wide-eyed instead of his usual Zen. "Our woman is a man!"

September 12, 2024 (Thursday)

The next two days are a blur. The local news is on-site to prepare interviews with us. Ramsey is in full PR mode.

After Oliver pieces together enough bones to make a final and firm determination that the victim he's working on is a man, not a woman, as the original record stated, all we do is reshoot the scene in various ways. Ramsey and Maya are so happy, I wouldn't be surprised if they burst into song. Their fondest dream has come true. They have a major *Titanic* plot twist.

"It explains the snuffbox," Eleanor tells me Thursday evening.

We're walking from the dorm wing to the lab. I keep the pace to an easy stroll, although she doesn't look tired or breathless. She stopped by my room unexpectedly, as I was about to put on pajamas and settle in to read, and asked how I was coming along with my portraits. I offered to show her.

"Who do you think our mystery man is?" she asks as we cross the lobby. "And why was he wearing a dress?"

"He must have seen that only the women were allowed in the boats, run down below, and put on his wife's clothes. In the dark, with a bonnet covering his head, he figured he wouldn't be discovered."

"He didn't make it into a boat, though. Something must have happened."

"Either he was discovered, or by the time he ran back up to the deck, all the boats had been lowered. I can't even imagine the sheer desperation of those who were left behind. To know that you're dying that night." I open the door of my studio.

"Surprise!" Oliver and Julia are already inside.

"Happy Birthday!"

Warmth floods through me. "How did you know?"

Old friends from the university have been sending greetings on social all day, but I didn't expect an in-person celebration this year.

"Facebook." Julia hands me a ship-shaped balloon. "We decided you should have a cake." She steps away from the desk behind her, revealing a blue-frosted round ocean with the *Titanic* outlined on top in black and white, portholes neatly lined up. I inhale. The air smells like birthday cake.

I laugh to dispel the tears that want to gather in my eyes. I'm not going to embarrass myself by crying. "Don't mean to sound ungrateful… But isn't the whole sinking-ship symbolism too early for thirty?"

Eleanor laughs. "If you're a sinking ship, what am I?"

I wince. "Sorry."

"Oh, Madison. I'm just kidding."

The four of us about fill the small space. And, of course, there are more. The portraits on the wall watch us. The faces I claimed back from the past celebrate with me. This party that I didn't expect touches me in a multitude of ways.

"The ship brought us together." Julia's tone is uncharacteristically sentimental. "And I am glad."

Oliver picks up the green bottle of champagne that sits next to the cake. "Let's drink to your birthday. And to us, in this place and time, together. Although, sadly this is not 1907 Heidsieck & Co Monopole Gout Americain."

"I'm afraid you have cheap friends," Julia adds.

I have *good* friends, and I appreciate them. "Thank you. For all this." Friends were the last thing I expected to find when I flew to Halifax. "I can't tell you how grateful I am that we met."

"Don't get carried away." Julia hands me a package wrapped in newspaper. "You might hate the presents."

I open the gift. "A hand-knit, authentic cholera belt in red." She must have worked on it after retiring to her room in the evenings, to keep it a surprise. There's a sting behind my eyes again. "You shouldn't have."

"Something to remember me by. You can use it for a scarf."

Oliver gifts me with a set of brand-new brushes. "The right tools make all the difference. Javier says quality materials are never wasted on any artist, no matter what level. Have faith in yourself."

His faith in me is a gift in itself. "Thank you."

Eleanor's present is a book about Violet Jessop, a survivor of the *Titanic*. "I bought it when I decided to join the project. Violet was a stewardess on the ship. Many other ships as well. She's seen everything. Her life story makes for a fascinating read. I think you'll enjoy it."

She envelops me in a motherly hug, and I sink into it with gratitude. "Thank you, Eleanor."

Oliver opens the champagne with a soft pop, and then we have a party. I'm having a genuinely good time with people who two weeks ago were strangers. How did this happen?

We're on to the finger sandwiches when my phone rings.

I check the screen. "It's my grandmother." I step out into the hallway and take the call. "Hi, there."

"You haven't been to see me." Her voice is crackly, as if someone has grated her vocal cords with a cheese grater, a courtesy of a lifetime of cigarettes.

"I'm in Halifax for a project, remember?"

"Betty's granddaughter lives in New York, and she visits every weekend." She hacks, just an opening salvo, just a little.

"New York is a two-hour drive from Philly. I'm a little farther than that."

"Well, when you find the time, bring vodka and smokes. The price goes up every time I blink. You know why? The damn Communists want real Americans to fail."

I no longer talk to her about alcohol and nicotine being bad for her. Nothing I can tell her would make her cut back. Life is finite, and we only have so many phone calls and visits left. I don't want to waste them on fighting. "How is your back?"

"Hurts like hell. Everything hurts. You know I have a bad heart. Could stop any minute. I suppose, then everyone will be happy. You won't have to put yourself out visiting me."

Dad says if Grandma had a *These are my favorite things song*, the items on the list would be: *vodka, smokes, and guilt trips*. They don't see eye to eye. Grandma Miller is my mother's mom. My dad's parents were older. I never met them.

My father liked Grandpa Miller, who was an engineer by training—although he never worked in the field—but Grandpa Miller died of a heart attack a few years after my parents were married. Grandma Miller makes dollhouses and dollhouse furniture for her Etsy shop, an occupation unfathomable to my father's scientist brain.

"Have you had any new tests lately?" I ask because she has a minor arrhythmia. It's not nothing, but it's not terminal either, and quitting smoking and drinking *would* help.

"Why should I? What are they going to do about it, give me another pill? It's all a conspiracy to make the pharmaceutical companies rich."

"How is Betty doing?" Grandma's neighbor is the only person she still socializes with.

"In for eye surgery." She coughs, for a full ten seconds this time. "Has your father thrown out his latest whore yet?"

"He and Lori broke up last month. I think he has a new girlfriend."

An even longer episode of hacking commences. "You think he'll ever learn not to pick his women from middle school?"

She likes making my father sound like a creep. He's been trying to replace my mother, over and over, ever since he lost her. He goes for women who are like my mother was when he met her in college: young and excited by life. At the beginning, it wasn't so weird. Now that I'm thirty and the women are younger than I am… I'm starting to see what my grandmother means.

Julia bursts from my studio, on the phone as well. She walks in the opposite direction as she furiously whispers something to the person on the other end.

"Anyway, happy birthday," my grandmother says. "Get yourself a man."

If she cross-stitched, I'd have a sofa lined with pillows with that slogan.

"Why?"

"I was married by eighteen."

"You were lucky to find the right guy so early."

"My father left my mother with six children. I was the oldest. I became their second parent. I wanted to be an architect, but there weren't that many women architects back then. I had a scholarship." She coughs. "Had to waitress instead, to help with the bills."

I know the story. My grandfather used to come into the restaurant for lunch. He owned the Ford dealership on the corner. "But you were in love with Grandpa."

She cackles. "Was I? He was thirty-seven, and I was eighteen. Anyway, I could stop waitressing, and he didn't mind helping my mother and my little brothers. Then we started having our own kids."

I run the numbers in my head. My grandmother was forty when my youngest uncle went off to college. What was a forty-year-old housewife without an education going to do in the seventies?

Certainly not become an architect. Her window of opportunity had closed, if ever it had been open.

What would she be like if her life had been different? Would she be less abrasive without alcohol? Without cigarettes, would her face be pink instead of gray? I try to picture her in slacks and a crisp shirt, running a business, no cursing, no empty bottles in the trash. I can't.

"How is work?" *Cough. Cough.*

"Coming along."

"Your mother wanted to be an artist. She always scribbled. Once she drew fishes with a marker all over my tablecloth."

I've heard the story before, so I know it well. I also know that there's no use in wishing that life turned out different. "Hey, I've been meaning to ask you. Was your aunt really on the *Titanic*? Do you remember her name?"

"Of course I know my own damn aunt's name. Lilly. She wasn't on the *Titanic*. She was on the *Lusitania*. Sank in 1915."

"Are you sure? You said *Titanic* before."

She thinks about it. "Was I drinkin'?"

"Good point."

"Don't get smart with me. When are you coming to visit?"

"As soon as I can. Definitely Christmas."

"Hmpf."

"Thank you for calling for my birthday."

"Hmpf."

"All right. You take care of yourself."

She hangs up first. I slip my phone into my pocket and turn back toward my studio.

Julia is also walking back. "You come here, I'll smack you so hard, you'll have teeth coming out of your ears." She stabs the screen with her finger to end the call, then she gives me a shrug. "It's the only tone he respects. Ex-husband."

We stroll back into my birthday party together.

A single pink candle is now lit on the cake.

"Happy birthday!"

"Make a wish!"

I already have, and it has come true.

The university offered to give me my job back.

So why am I not ecstatic? In addition to a return to job security, I'm currently working on an interesting project, surrounded by good people.

For a second, I grasp for what more I could possibly want for my birthday. I should know what I want by now. I am thirty. It's a major milestone. I'm officially, indisputably an adult, but there are still so many things in my life that I'm unsure of. I wish…

I wish I could find my true self this year.

The thought comes out of nowhere and has way too much of a woo-woo, spa-retreat, meditation vibe. Yet there is also truth to it. I went into premed to please my father, veered into anatomy because I liked a professor, ended up as a forensic artist by sheer coincidence. I want to put more intention into my life going forward.

What I want is to take the rudder.

I think about that as I blow out the candle.

Dad doesn't call. He doesn't usually remember. It's all right, doesn't make him a bad father. His research absorbs him. He's putting the finishing touches on his groundbreaking new paper.

I can handle his inattention, or at least handle it better than when I was a kid. I always had food and clothes and a roof over my head, but I always suspected that there was more for other children. Some had less too, for sure. I wasn't abused. I don't feel unfortunate, but I've always fantasized that had my mother lived, she would have loved me. Of course, I don't know that. Maybe she wouldn't have. Maybe she would have beaten me with a stick. I know plenty of people who had bad mothers. We always idealize the things we want but can't have.

Eleanor rises from her chair and stretches. "I'd better retire to bed. It's almost eleven."

Julia rises too. "I need my beauty sleep."

They both give me hugs, and then only Oliver and I are left.

"I should pack it in too." I stand, but then stay right there. "So…" *Don't poke your nose into it.* "What's it like having your ex-girlfriend here, supervising?"

"Jenny is great. She isn't going to give us any trouble. She's reasonable."

"I can't imagine being friends with any of my exes."

"Do you have a lot of them?"

"Two. One high school, one college. With the second one, competition got the better of us. All forensic artists in a given area tend to compete for the same few positions."

"That must be difficult."

"What do you do about your competition?"

"Nothing. If you don't pull on the line, there's no tension."

I'm not sure what that means, but it sounds impressively deep. "Is that a fishing metaphor?"

I can see Oliver fishing, sitting contemplatively by the mirror surface of a deep blue lake. He's surrounded by an aura of peace. I can't imagine him having a fight with anyone, or shouting, or pushing someone out of his way. At a time when men are obsessed with hypermasculinity and being the alpha male, the macho man, I'm beginning to find Oliver's low-key, steady vibe attractive.

I turn to my wall of portraits, but I'm picturing the giant canvases in his lab. I haven't made any progress since I began. I'm frustrated with the nothingness of the gray-blue swirls of my first attempt. "I wish I had talent. I wish I were a real artist. I wish I were *something*."

Especially because I'm not the scientist my father wishes I were either. I might have the degree, but in my heart, the passion isn't there.

Oliver looks over from the birthday table. *Is that his third slice of cake?* He sets it down and walks to me. "First of all, you're not a thing. You're a spiritual being on a journey. Like how you can look at a long hike you took and think, the beginning was cold, the middle was muddy, I was scared on the north side of the hill when it got dark… But the hike is none of those things. It's how your soul was built up while you were walking."

Honestly. "I have no idea what to do with someone like you."

"You could always…"

Kiss me, an inner whisper in the deep cave of my mind finishes for him.

We're standing too close to each other, too still.

CHAPTER 10

Helen

   1895, New York

After the judge rejects my petition for divorce in New York, I begin planning my future, but then the unfairness of divorce laws loses its importance when my mother calls, my father having finally installed a telephone.

"Oh, Helen." Her voice is thick with tears as she struggles with composure. "I… We've… That poor little lamb."

I know what she is going to say, even while the dark words remain unspoken.

"Abigail."

My mother sobs. "She is gone, Helen."

My own throat seals shut, the stunned silence so long that I fear our call might be disconnected. "How?" I finally manage the single word.

"Now they say it was an infection all along. Dr. Taylor was wrong about hysteria."

I curse Dr. Taylor and his damned diagnosis. I curse his prescription of a rest cure. I see Abbie, sitting by the sea in the sanatorium, in agony, while the infection ate its way into her bones and stole her away from me.

"She—" Mama dissolves into sobs.

"I am so sorry." Anger flares, the flames licking higher and higher, a bonfire of fury.

I am mad at the doctors, but I am mad at myself as well. I should have done more. I should have asked Dr. Klauz to consult, but he has refused to come to the house since he found out about my attempt to divorce Edward.

My tears fall unchecked. "I am so sorry, Mama."

The merciless axe of death cut our family tree in half. It is an unthinkable devastation. When I think of how Abigail must have suffered, I am nearly driven to murder.

"Abigail told Dr. Taylor, more than once, that she wasn't simply being emotional because she reached the age of a spinster," Mama tells me. "I wish he'd listened."

"So do I." I am familiar with my sister's attempts. She recounted their conversations to me in her letters. She could feel the disease inside her. I believed her. Dr. Taylor did not. I even called him, demanding an alternate treatment plan, to which his response was that I too had succumbed to hysteria, which obviously runs in the family. He offered to place me at the same sanatorium if I traveled up to Norwalk and placed myself under his care.

For the first time in a long time, I wished Edward were still with me. If Edward called the doctor, man-to-man, he might have been able to convince him.

I fear running into Dr. Taylor when I am next in Connecticut. I might not be able to hold myself back from screaming at him. *A woman knows her own body!*

I sink into despair. Even when the sun shines, I cannot see the light. Day and night, darkness surrounds me. Were it not for my children, I would hide myself in bed. For their sake alone, I maintain the appearance of being whole, but I am only a shadow of myself.

Months pass before I am able to shake off my malaise, but once I do, I remember my new dream. Freedom, for myself, and for my little family. I am going to live the kind of life that was not granted to my poor sister, Abbie.

I will not be defeated by His Honor. I will not be beaten down into the ground. I will not be controlled. The judge is not in charge of me, and neither is Edward.

When the bookstore holds a new suffragette meeting, I attend. I sit in the front row and do not care who might see me.

"Our main goal for this year, as last year, and the year before, is to gain the vote," the first speaker tells us, the mother of seven, a hatmaker. "Until we can vote, politicians will never represent us. Only once we have the vote can we champion a woman's choice of how many children she wishes to conceive. Yes, contraception," she says to applause, "as a way to improve our health and economic condition. And once we have the vote, we will challenge divorce laws too. We will make sure that any woman is able to leave her abusive husband."

By the time she finishes, we are all much encouraged.

The next speaker—a young widow of twenty whose husband was killed in a factory accident—informs us that a group has formed to defeat us, the New York State Association Opposed to Woman Suffrage.

Their efforts are bewildering.

"But we are not trying to take anything away from anyone," I tell the matron next to me, a Mrs. Teichman from Oklahoma Territory, who is visiting her sister for the week. "Why should any decent human being be opposed to us gaining rights that could save our very lives? Is it true that divorce is more freely allowed where you live?" I overheard her talking to the woman on her other side at the beginning of tonight's meeting.

"Ninety days, Mrs. Candee. All you need is ninety days of residency before you can appear in front of a judge and be granted a no-contest divorce. In Oklahoma Territory, no proof of infidelity or abuse is needed."

"And the dissolution of marriage is valid anywhere in the country? Even here in New York?"

"Indeed, it is."

For the rest of the week, I see her round, freckled face in front of me, smiling proudly.

When Papa's business was ruined in Texas, he moved to New York, and he built a better dream. *One does not lie down and accept defeat at the first cut of the sword.* And then, when he saw more opportunity in Connecticut, he moved us there.

I ask Kerstin about it at my next visit to the bookstore.

"We came here from Småland," she tells me. "No one owes loyalty to anyone or any place that makes them wretched. At home, we were starving. Here, Anders and I have this." She indicates the store with outstretched arms. "If you need to go, you go."

I take her advice. I am surviving, but I do not wish to merely survive. I wish to thrive.

"To blazes with New York and its arcane laws," I tell my bags as I pack our basic necessities. "There are yet more progressive places in our country."

We are leaving for Oklahoma Territory.

"Move back home to Norwalk," Papa begs over the phone. "I am lonely."

Come to France. The West is too uncivilized, darling. You will all be massacred by outlaws, Mama predicts in her letter from Neuilly-sur-Seine, Île-de-France, where she moved after Abigail's death. She will not tell me why. I suspect an indiscretion on my father's part, but maybe only because I have had to deal with Edward's indiscretions.

In any case, Mama left Papa and has no plans of returning.

I am leaving New York and will not be swayed.
Let freedom ring.

1895, Guthrie, Oklahoma Territory

"Will Guthrie be very different from New York?"
Edith is apprehensive.

We travel by train in a first-class car; Rosie and
Effie, the new maid, traveling in third.

Neither of my children has lived anywhere other
than the house where they were born. Edith is stuck
in that awkward phase between girl and woman,
taller than her age and beautiful with her doe eyes
and russet hair, already drawing curious looks
from men.

Whenever we disembark at a station to stretch
our legs and I notice one approach, I step between
them.

"I should think so. New York is a city nearly three
hundred years old. Fort Amsterdam was built in 1624
on the southern tip of Manhattan Island. I believe
Guthrie is rather new."

Mr. Haggerty, the gentleman traveling in the same
compartment with us, nods. "Guthrie was estab-
lished on the Southern-Kansas Railway as a railroad
station only nine years ago." He is a land investor
from Philadelphia, traveling on business, smartly
dressed in a three-piece suit. "Deer Creek, that's what
they first called it."

The name sounds pastoral, peaceful, but the closer we are to our destination, the more tension stiffens my limbs. A place that would allow me my freedom sounded like heaven when I was trapped in New York, but what if it will merely be a different hell, a rough frontier town that lacks any semblance of civilization and safety? And I have dragged along my children…

"Hawk!" Harry calls out everything he sees in passing. "Black birds! Deer! Rabbit!"

"Don't forget the prairie daisies." Mr. Haggerty points at a large patch of blue and white blooms, then at some purple flowers that have hairy leaves. "Buffalo peas."

"What's that?"

"Blackjack oaks. And those are pecan trees."

As thrilled as Harry is, Edith watches the wild, untouched landscape without a trace of excitement. If her eyes hold emotion, it is worry. "Do you think they hold balls in Guthrie?"

"Your coming-out ball is still a few years away. It is too early to worry about that yet, my darling."

"Do they have theatres?"

"I am not certain. I know they have a post office and a pharmacy. I have corresponded with Mrs. Lillie, the wife of the pharmacist. They will be providing us with lodgings."

The Royal Hotel would not reserve us rooms on the excuse that they are always full. Could be the truth, or could be they saw my request for a woman with two children and assumed I was coming for a divorce. Just because it is allowed in the Territory, it does not mean everyone approves.

The pharmacist's wife sounded kind in her letters, but I know little about her husband. He might yet turn out to be the same kind of man as Edward. I am putting my life into Mr. Lillie's hands, and not just my life either. Beyond Harry and Edith, I also have the maids. Rosie became my lady's maid again when Annie married—seduced clear off her feet by a widowed ice delivery man with eight children.

Annie always had a good head on her shoulders. I have known her since my family moved to Norwalk from New York. She did what needed to be done without having to be told. But the new maid, Effie, whom I brought instead of a nanny to help with the children, is only seventeen. She's the only daughter of a coal miner and a washerwoman, and proud beyond words to be in service, to have moved up so high in the world.

"If Guthrie used to be a railroad station on the Southern-Kansas Railway, then aren't we in Kansas?" Harry is mesmerized by anything that involves trains.

The pinched expression that invaded his handsome little face when Edward left us is gone. Every time Mr. Haggarty rolls the window down for a breath of fresh air, Harry stands on his seat and sticks his head out into the wind. He is as playful as a puppy. He has been happier on this journey than I have ever seen him.

"A few years after the train station sprang up,

they had the Land Run of 1889," Mr. Haggerty tells him.

"What's a land run?"

"Oh, you should have seen it, young man." Our travel companion puffs up. "At noon, cannons were shot, and fifty thousand settlers broke into a run toward the Unassigned Lands. By the time the sun dipped to the horizon, they had settled two million acres of Indian Territory and turned it into Oklahoma Territory. Ten thousand settled right in town, and that is how Guthrie became the capital."

"What happened to the Indians?" Edith has a predilection for focusing on the most tragic part of any story.

While at the same time, Harry asks me, wide-eyed, "Will there be a land run in New York?"

My son is worried about what shall happen to our home while we are away. He might inherit it some-day, depending on Edward. All our property is in Edward's name. I was shocked to find out that—despite my sizable dowry and my father's generous contributions to building and furnishing the house—I own next to nothing.

"Of course not," I reassure my son. "Nothing will happen to our home, my darling."

"New York is a civilized city," Mr. Haggerty chimes in. "Before the land run, this here country was empty."

I nod, unthinking, but then we pass a group of Indians, a family with two skinny horses, who make it obvious what great nonsense Mr. Haggerty is speaking. I must have a conversation about this topic with the children later. I do not wish them to remain ignorant on the subject, but I do not wish to contradict Mr. Haggerty directly. In my experience, men do not take well to correction, especially in public.

"Cotton," he says, identifying an obviously worked field with a shack in the middle. Then comes another farm, with a slightly larger farmhouse. "Corn." Then, "Alfalfa."

We must be coming closer to town.

"What is that?" I marvel at a spiky bush.

"Yucca," he says as the train whistles.

Outside our window, buildings rush into view, first wooden shacks, then larger wood houses, then even taller, proper brick buildings. The children are immediately distracted.

"A river!" Harry jumps up.

Mr. Haggerty leans closer to the window. "Cottonwood River, that is. And the meandering Cimarron is even wider. Shame that one is salty, on account that it flows through the salt plains."

Our compartment shakes; metal wheels screech on the rails.

"Guthrie!" the conductor bellows.

Mr. Haggerty opens the compartment door for us but doesn't follow. Our destination is not his.

Our new home is certainly rougher around the edges than the old, but it is nearly as large as Norwalk. What I expected to be a frontier town is on its way to becoming a city. The afternoon sun paints the buildings golden. Even though we're in town, there's a sense of openness, endlessness. I draw a long, slow breath.

"Welcome to the Queen of the Prairie." A sharp-eyed man in a bowler hat greets us on the busy platform, a head taller than I am. When he makes a quick bow, he nearly smashes his nose into my forehead. "You must be Mrs. Candee, with her children. Allow me to introduce myself. Foress Ball Lillie, the pharmacist. You have been corresponding with my wife, I believe."

His coachman, a burly, red-cheeked Irishman, helps him with our luggage, rougher with my leather valise than necessary.

Edward would shout at him. I let him be. "Thank you so much for everything."

Rosie sits up front with the coachman, while Effie, who is so slight from having grown up without sufficient nourishment that she might as well be an elf, sits with us in the carriage.

"Harrison Avenue. And this here is my little empire." Mr. Lillie points out his pharmacy.

Lillie's Drug Store the sign proclaims on a two-story brick building topped by a bona fide tower in the middle.

I give him his due. "It is the most impressive establishment on the street."

"I fill prescriptions," a proud smile lifts the tips of his mustache, "and sell whatever else my customers might need. Stationery, paint, wallpaper, Bibles. You come in, and I promise you will not miss anything from your big city, Mrs. Candee."

I evaluate his gestures, his tone when he speaks to his coachman, the look in his eyes when his gaze drifts over us. What kind of man is he? Can I interpret his words as kindness, or are they merely masculine bragging? Will we be safe under his roof? When I smile back at him, I am careful to look grateful instead of inviting.

The streets are laid out in a perfect grid. I note a butcher and a general store as we pass. The Blue Bell Saloon… *Oh, a girl up front is lifting her skirt—*

"Look at your shoes." I clap to distract the children. "Oh, look, how dusty we all are from our journey."

Harry and Edith barely glance at themselves. They are too busy gawking. In all fairness, Guthrie offers a lot to see, and most of it is strange. Despite its orderly layout, the town is rather chaotic. If they have traffic rules, they must keep them a secret. Wagon drivers cut each other off and curse at each other without any care whose children might hear. Loose dogs chase after horses, and… "Is that a giant chicken?"

"A turkey. But we are thoroughly modern," Mr. Lillie assures me. "We have electricity, municipal water, and underground parking for horses and carriages. We are perfectly civilized, Mrs. Candee."

I am willing to give him the benefit of the doubt until a crusty fur trader rides past us with a jumble of wolf furs in the saddle in front of him. And I spot two more saloons, plainly visible from where I sit.

Then my chin nearly drops when a *woman* drives a stagecoach past us, wearing buckskin!

The mixture of familiar and wild is disorienting. Yet, have I not crossed a great divide on purpose? Have I not come here to be free? Little by little, as we progress down the street, a sense of wonder fills me. As our carriage rattles over cobblestones, it sounds like the rattle of falling chains.

"Oklahoma is still a new territory," I tell the children. "You are seeing a country being born, and how many people can say that? Is it not splendid?"

I have arrived into a different world, one that might very well make me over into a different woman. In New York, as a fashionable young bride, I was a specimen, like one of my father's perfect butterflies, kept carefully under glass. What shall I be here?

We turn left on Drexel Street, then right on Oklahoma Avenue, where we meet a gang of cowboys herding cows in the opposite direction, toward the train station, stirring up dust. The ground trembles, while the earthy smell of sweat and manure fills the air. Mooing echoes between the brick storefronts.

Edith presses closer to me. Harry whoops and looks ready to join the men on horseback. Effie shrinks deep into her seat.

"It is rather overwhelming," I admit.

"More grand than you expected, is it not?" The pharmacist glows with satisfaction. "Grand enough for statehood, I promise. And someday, we shall have it." Then he looks us over once again, thoughtfully—

a woman traveling with her children, without her husband. "I hope I am not being presumptuous, but once you are all settled in, might I introduce you to a friend of mine, Henry Asp? He is the best lawyer in town. If you'd be needing one, Mrs. Candee."

The cattle pass, and the dust settles. Our carriage rolls on.

"Thank you." I drop my gaze to my lap, but then I raise it again. "Yes. I would love to meet Mr. Asp."

The coachman stops the horses in front of 1409 Oklahoma Avenue. The well-appointed brick house with a white picket fence, one of the nicest on the street, says something about the Lillies' standing in the community. The house itself is not enough to make me relax, however. Edward had plenty of standing in New York, yet it did not hold him back from hitting me, and worse.

A rosy-cheeked woman rushes down the steps, followed by her maid, and distracts me from my thoughts.

"Mrs. Candee. Welcome," the woman greets us with genuine warmth, leaving behind cold ceremony. "How much you all have been expected. I have such a good feeling about you. I have since I received your first letter. Your stay with us will be a happy one, you will see. You are going to love our Guthrie."

Mrs. Lillie is older than I am, yet sprightly and obviously happy, beaming at her husband. This, at last, convinces me that he cannot be a bad man.

"This here is Magda." Mrs. Lillie introduces her maid. "Magda, help with Mrs. Candee's luggage."

The girl, Effie's age, hurries over to my maids, then Mrs. Lillie ushers us in.

The scent of cinnamon draws us farther into the house that is modest in comparison to our New York mansion but gives the impression of a happy home, filled with plants and keepsakes. It feels welcoming and safe. I am blinking back tears, I am so relieved.

"Mr. Lillie came from Dighton, Kansas, did he tell you? For the Run of 1889." Our hostess leads us up the stairs. "His first drug store was a tent." She laughs an honest, earthy laugh.

She is modest, but as I ask a few questions, I soon find out that her husband is the first secretary of the Territorial Board of Pharmacy. He is about as famous as one can hope to be in Guthrie.

Our rooms are sufficient, comfortable even, but were they worse, I would accept them still. I am here for a divorce, not for a holiday.

As we settle in, so many questions remain. Will Mr. Asp, the lawyer, agree to represent me? How long will our lives be interrupted before I can finally appear in front of a judge? Will the judge grant me my freedom, or have I risked my family for nothing?

1896

"I will not have my reputation be tarnished by the stain of divorce." Edward towers over me. Since I have last seen him, a few silver hairs have appeared at his temples. He is also a smidgen thicker in the middle. A number of things about him changed, but his voice is just as sharp as the last time we fought.

Judge Frank Dale summoned him to Guthrie. The very last thing in this world that I wanted, but now, here he is.

My newfound bubble of safety pierced, I stand too, putting Mrs. Lillie's coffee table between us. "Surely, you would rather be free of us to pursue other interests."

"I could have you committed." He is staying at The Royal Hotel, which managed to find a room for him. "No sane woman would act as outrageously as you have."

I hope he cannot see the tremble that runs through me. "You would not leave the children without a mother."

My words make him think. If I were gone, he would have to handle the caretaking. He questioned, straight upon arrival, Edith and Harry about whether they had been treated well in his absence. He must have hoped to use negligence against me in front of the judge, but our children assured him that they were perfectly happy. He sent them upstairs without further inquiries into their health, or budding interests, or schooling.

"I wish for nothing that is yours, Edward. Only what I brought into the marriage, what remains of my dowry."

"I will give you nothing. You do not deserve it, nor could you handle your own finances." He casts me a pitying look. "What do you know about money?"

I do not point out that I have been earning and managing the household on my own for years. Instead, I appeal to his vanity. "Think of your reputation in New York if you were to cast me aside without means. Do you not wish to remain well regarded?"

This gives him pause. He cannot afford to be shunned by New York society. If they turned their backs on him, his business would be ruined. He ponders my words for several seconds as he paces, then he stops and erases the deep frown from his forehead. "Can we not go back to the way things were?"

He has not simply been thinking. He has been *calculating*. He has been adding up how a divorce might affect his joint business interests with my father and with his more conservative friends.

He tilts his head as if cajoling a child. "Is our marriage so bad?"

Oh, that voice. Oh, that look in his eyes. How I once loved this man. There is something irresistible about the familiar, the lure of the once-happy past.

Yet I resist. I hold my ground. "Yes."

"Dammit, Helen." His sweetness melts away. He leaps for me, and as I am hindered by my voluminous dress, he manages to grab my arm. He shakes me so hard, I lose my balance and crash into the coffee table. "Come to your senses, you blasted woman. You owe me obedience. I *am* your husband."

I scramble up, but he catches me again and throws me onto the sofa, at the same time that the dining room door bursts open.

"Here is that cake I promised." Mrs. Lillie sails in with the three maids on her heels.

I rise and step toward the fireplace. I should have been standing there this whole time, with the cast-iron poker within easy reach.

"A larger slice or a slighter one, Mr. Candee?" Mrs. Lillie holds a knife. "Have you had lunch?"

Edward knows a stalemate when he sees one. He is surrounded by five women, two of whom are carrying heavy trays, one who is armed. I doubt he misses my hand inching toward the poker either; he fenced in college.

"Mark my words, you will regret this, Helen." He strides to the door, brushing Mrs. Lillie out of his way. "You will rue this day, I swear it." He slams the door closed behind him.

"Oh, dear." Mrs. Lillie collapses into the nearest chair, then startles at the sight of the knife in her hand, as if she forgot she had it. She lays the knife gingerly on the tea tray. "How I wish Mr. Lillie were home. He would have shown that brute… Oh, my nerves. Today of all days!"

She has been in a state since we all woke up this morning. Half a dozen ladies from the Chautauqua Literary and Scientific Club of Guthrie are coming over for tea to invite her to serve on a committee.

"Would you mind locking the door, Magda?" I ask her maid and step away from the poker. I clasp my hands. "Mrs. Lillie, please accept my apology." I hate to have brought strife into her home. "He is gone now, and he will not be back. The man cannot stand losing. He will pretend that he won the exchange and taught me a lesson here." I force a smile I do not feel. "Let us turn our attention to your wonderful event, shall we?"

"Oh, Helen." She is on the verge of tears. "I only want everything to be perfect. What if I say something silly? What if they look around and decide I have no taste? Oh, please, help me. I want them to feel that they are back East."

A distraction might be perfect for both of us and the maids as well. Effie still looks ready to flee.

"All right." To settle everyone down, I must project confidence. "We shall make them think they are at the Brunswick Hotel on Fifth Avenue." I turn in a slow circle in the middle of the room. "You have a lovely parlor. They need to see more of it. Let us pull these heavy curtains aside as far as we can. Nothing is more elegant than an airy room filled with light."

The maids remove the hastily put-together refreshments, then quickly return to do our bidding. The extra light reveals a few spots of dust here and there that were previously undetectable, but Magda quickly solves that problem. Then we march on to the dining room to search out possibilities for improvement there. I envision the grandest houses I have visited in New York and Norwalk and think about what was different about them.

"Your furniture is Victorian, Mrs. Lillie, isn't it? With a few Gothic and Neoclassical pieces mixed in." I suppose there are not that many furniture stores in Guthrie yet, and they probably don't carry everything. "We could remove the pieces that do not match anything else. That will ease the overcrowding. The dark pieces with those heavy carvings have so much work put into them, and they are truly lovely, but the latest style is simpler. Victorian Eastlake, they call it."

"Oh? Is Eastlake near New York?"

"Charles Eastlake."

"Never heard of him. Won't the room look half empty? I don't want the ladies to think that we cannot afford furniture."

"Restraint is at the core of elegance. You would not want them to think that you are trying too hard. I know their set. If they believe that you are rushing to please them overmuch, they will consider it as proof that you are of a lesser class. You must pretend you do not care."

"Yes." She wrings her hands. "As you say. I can see how that might happen. Do I have time to hire men to do the moving? Oh, how I wish Mr. Lillie were here."

"We could attempt a quick rearrangement of the pieces ourselves." Since I have given birth twice, I stopped believing that women are the weaker sex. "After all, this is Oklahoma Territory." I place my hands on my hips. "Does that not make us pioneer women?" Other than two Gothic pieces, we only have those half-column plant stands and little tables that are jammed in everywhere. "We can surely muster up some strength."

And we do.

After my confrontation with Edward, the physical labor is most welcome. As is the reminder that I do have skills and knowledge others appreciate. The work helps me to burn off my anger and frustration. With Annie and Effie and Mrs. Lillie's maid, all of us putting our backs into the work, a miraculous transformation begins. By the time teatime rolls around and the ladies are about to arrive, the downstairs rooms are fit for a New York mansion. I surprise even myself with the transformation.

Mrs. Lillie is speechless. "Oh," is all she can say, with her hand over her heart. "Oh." And then, "You are a treasure, Helen."

Mrs. Lillie's tea is a grand success. Compliments on the house abound. And when she graciously credits me for my assistance, several ladies inquire if I might help redecorate their homes.

How wonderful it feels to be thought of as capable, to discover that I have other skills beyond writing magazine articles. The prospect of having more than a single source of income makes me feel sturdier. I am steadier standing on two legs. When we moved to Oklahoma Territory, a whole new world opened to me, and this is a new window yet.

. . .

Our court date is January eleventh, in the middle of the grayest winter I can remember.

"On what grounds do you wish to divorce your husband, Mrs. Candee?" Judge Frank Dale demands.

The courtroom in Guthrie is no less intimidating than the one in New York, even if the walls here are knotty pine instead of mahogany.

"Abuse and cruelty," I respond, as coached by my lawyer, Mr. Henry Asp. Infidelity did not sway the New York judge. It is common enough. "My husband is an alcoholic. He is a domineering and violent man. I fear for myself and my children."

"And how do you respond, Mr. Candee?"

Edward's vicious glower makes me grateful for the distance between us, the judge's presence, and my attorney next to me.

"I deny all charges. She speaks utter nonsense. The woman is fit for Bedlam. I should have used a heavier hand in showing her discipline. It is an oversight I plan on remedying, Your Honor."

"I see. I know only too well what is happening here." The gavel crashes down.

Why? But I have not had the chance yet to fully present my case. *No.* Oh no, please. Shock freezes me to the spot. The word *Bedlam* is lodged in my lungs like a blood clot. I thought Edward wasn't here to claim the children. If I lost Edith and Harry, the pain of it would kill me.

It cannot be.

How is this possible?

I came to court with such hope. Mrs. Lillie told

me this morning at breakfast that she had a *feeling* everything would go well. But no, my freedom has never been farther. I shudder when I envision the revenge Edward will exact from me for dragging him to court. If only—

The judge looks right at me as he pronounces his judgment. "Divorce granted. Custody of the two children granted to Mrs. Candee."

One moment, I stand near fainting from fright, the next from relief. I sway on my feet, blood rushing loudly in my ears with the speed of a river. Mr. Asp has to touch my elbow to steady me.

On Edward's face sits the same disbelief. This might be the first time anyone naysaid him. He is a New York gentleman, with plenty of cronies in the city, but out of his element in Guthrie.

I cannot think. Then slowly, slowly, realization dawns on me. Fifteen years after Edward and I said our vows, our marriage is no more. My ordeal is over. Finished.

Mr. Asp escorts me through a side door so I do not have to go near my former husband. I do not turn for a last look. I refuse the hate I know sits in his eyes. I will not give him the satisfaction of being able to shoot me his silent threats one last time.

In fact, I do not see Edward again. I only hear later, through Mrs. Lillie's maid Magda, that he took the first train back to New York, without asking to say goodbye to the children.

I am free. *I am free!* The whole sordid business is finished, but I am not ready to leave yet. I stay. I keep nothing of Edward but his last name and Edith and Harry. I choose to remain Mrs. Candee so I can have the same last name as my children.

The very next charity bazaar I attend, I donate my wedding ring.

When I first arrived in Guthrie, I expected to be lonely and scared, as some had predicted. My father-in-law told me, should I divorce, I would starve without a man, and that I would run back to Norwalk to my parents' house with my tail between my legs.

None of that happens.

I make new friends.

I am far from being the only woman in town who has come to Oklahoma Territory to divorce her husband.

We meet in the shops and invariably end up talking. Many of the women are less fortunate than I am. Papa spared no expense on my private education. I can keep writing articles for the magazines to support myself and my children, but most women cannot do that. No life training is given whatsoever to young women of a certain class. How to make a living is the biggest worry among my new friends.

"I do not know if I can afford the rent for the full ninety days," Annabelle, another abandoned wife, recently arrived from Philadelphia, confesses at one of our luncheons. "Sorry." She covers her face with her hand. "I shouldn't talk about money. I know it's terribly gauche. I apologize."

"Nonsense." I speak up first from our gathering of eleven, all sitting around the table. "We must be able to speak openly about these matters."

Those of us who have been here for a while have relinquished monetary etiquette. Society's insistence that mentioning money in front of women is vulgar is, in fact, not meant to protect women. Such rules are meant to keep us ignorant of money matters and thus dependent on men.

"It is not as if we can take in laundry," Cornelia says on my right, twenty-three, here with her little daughter from Boston. "We are ladies."

Annabelle sets down her glass. "Even if we all were willing to turn into laundresses, nobody would bring us their shirts. They would feel too uncomfortable."

"We are given no opportunity to support ourselves." Amelia, from Albany with four children, glances around, lost. She is twenty-seven. "And yet if we fail, we face the horror that our children might be sued away from us by our husbands."

That is one fear I do not have. Edward continues to care little about Edith and Harry. He has not contacted them since he left, too busy with his latest woman. I do not envy her. If anything, I pity the poor wretch.

"You speak French very well," I remind Amelia. Her mother was French. "Business is booming in

Guthrie. People with money wish to educate their children. You could acquire private students."

I thought about it myself, as I speak both French and Italian, courtesy of my travels and education. But my magazine articles and the rare interior design engagement are sufficient to support us, for now.

Amelia blinks at me. "But I am not a school miss. I would not know how. I have never—"

"You need not be a school miss. You could be a private tutor. Chat with your pupils about any subject you wish, anything that interests them. Fashion with the girls and horses with the boys. Or the other way around. Teach them songs. Read Victor Hugo."

While Amelia brightens at the idea, Annabelle grows more despondent.

"My French is terrible. I hated my French tutor. He had wandering hands and appalling breath."

"You have the best eye for color of anyone I know. I adore your aquarelles." I tap my fan on the table, energized by the subject. "What does anyone in the Territories want more than anything?"

Mabel's face lights up. She is twenty, no children, ran away on her honeymoon when she realized her much-older, impotent husband's greatest joy was torturing her bloody in bed with various implements. "To convince everyone that people here are as sophisticated as people back East."

"Right." I love her quick mind. I love that she has not withdrawn, has not lost her spirit. She covers her scars and goes about building a new life. I know she will succeed. "Look at the houses. Look at the gardens. The fashion. Where can you help?"

"I am not a seamstress. Neither am I an architect."

"But you could be a fashion advisor for the wives of the nouveau riche. You could assist with the ordering of their wardrobes or their furniture, and then advise on their husbands' art collections."

She lifts her dainty chin, a smile settling into her eyes that are somber more often than not. "You know, I think I could."

"And you, Helen, can invent occupations for all of us lost souls," Annabelle teases, then grows serious in the next blink. "You will, won't you? Nobody else will help us. We shall have to help each other. Which reminds me. I wish to invite you all to meet Margaret Rees at our next suffrage meeting."

I have heard of the fiery suffragist leader who founded the Woman Suffrage Association of Oklahoma, but we have not been formally introduced. She's rather revolutionary and brave. Other women call her the Mother of Equal Suffrage. Men call her other things.

"By all accounts, she's an exceptional woman," Mabel gushes. "I would love to meet her. We could sign her petition."

"Do we not have plenty of problems already without involving ourselves in politics?" As I say the words, I hear them in Edward's voice in my head. "What can we do from here?" I stop myself before I can say *Politics is best left to men.*

I am recovering from my former life, but I have

not yet fully recovered. It is more difficult than I thought to truly leave behind my husband. I *will* do it, however. In New York, I have gone to a few lectures, but I have only been a passive listener. More is needed of me if I want to affect reform, and I do want change. "I shall be there, is what I meant to say."

However, it is not the suffragist movement that I think about after our luncheon. It is Annabelle's suggestion that sticks with me.

Could I write a book? I suppose I shall not know until I try. I *have* written dozens and dozens of articles that were well received.

A book is different, however. My only contacts are magazine editors. I do not personally know a single author who is a woman, although, of course, there are a few. I shall find out more about how such a thing is accomplished.

That very night, after the children go to bed, I settle in at my small desk by the light and pull a dozen sheets of paper from the drawer. I dip my pen into the inkwell, then write my title on top in oversized letters.

How Women May Earn a Living
By Helen Churchill Candee

The ink-blue words on the white paper are a declaration. I feel as if I have spoken an oath. My intention is stated plain and clear.

I move to the next page and write the number *1* in the top right corner. The word *Introduction* goes on the top of the page.

Apprehension tingles through me, the fear of being tested and failing. I start writing anyway. When I have a paragraph, I lean back in my chair to read it. The apprehension goes away.

For the first time in years, I am content and happy. I have forgotten this feeling.

I write the first page, then the next. I have the introduction finished by the end of the week. Then I write the first chapter, thought by thought, keeping in mind the women who need my help. I picture them, and then I picture talking to them.

As the filled pages multiply, satisfaction saturates my days, the joy of knowing that I can accomplish something big. Is this what men feel in their offices?

Later, when I look back at this time, I marvel at the short period of perfect idyll. I can scarcely believe how quickly everything then shifted.

Most people do not understand how little it takes to drop from heaven into hell. Life can turn on something as little as discarding a whisper of an instinct or ignoring a warning.

CHAPTER 11

Madison

October 1, 2024 (Tuesday)

"We will not be able to wait until March." The dean from Boston University delivers the bad news over the phone. "Circumstances have changed, and we need you here sooner, Madison. The first of the new year, the latest."

It's eight in the morning, and I'm on my way back to my room from breakfast—a bowl of oatmeal. My brain is only half on the dean because I'm wondering why Oliver wasn't in the break room once again. We usually all have breakfast together.

My momentary insanity of wanting to kiss a fellow team member has passed. I almost leaned in, two weeks ago that night in his lab, but caught myself and held back. If I leaned in and he ducked, I would have died of embarrassment.

"Let me see what I can do," I tell the dean. Our team here has already processed seven sets of remains from the *Titanic* disaster. If we can keep up the pace, if no further roadblocks pop up, *maybe* I can leave TTP earlier than planned.

After we hang up, I go in search of Ramsey. I want to tell him about the opportunity that dropped in my lap, want to ask him how he'd feel about me leaving early.

The half-completed building makes me think of my grandmother who wanted to be an architect but ended up putting on five-course dinners for her husband's most important clients instead. It saved her mother and her little brothers, but she had to have wondered how her life might have turned out if she'd been able to go to college.

After a grand party, once everyone was gone and she finished the cleanup, my grandfather in bed already, I can see her taking a cigarette and an unfinished bottle of wine, sitting on the porch under the stars, building houses and skyscrapers in her head.

My mind is decades in the past as I give a quick rap on Ramsey's office door, then open it. "Hi."

"Madison?" He sweeps what looks like loose change into his top drawer. "Good. I was about to find you all. I hear you have little get-togethers in the evenings. It'd be great to show a more personal side of the team. Maya and the cameras will be there tonight to film."

I'd protest, but I'm distracted by a glint of gold, that unmistakable undertone of shimmering amber and ochre. A piece of his change missed the drawer, dropped to the floor, and rolled out from under his desk.

"What's this?" *No way.* Anger replaces my spinal fluid and expands, makes me grow an inch. "I know this ring." I snatch up the gleaming metal and hold it on my flat palm, a lawyer in a courtroom submitting evidence. "You said it was stolen."

Oh, he's not going to get away with this.

He has that bullshit, magnanimous-boss smile on as he says, "I can explain."

He doesn't even have the decency to look guilty.

"No. Let me." I was stupid not to have seen it sooner. "You invented the theft." Of course, he did. *Of course,* he freaking did.

"It's a plot twist. I couldn't tell you all ahead of time. The camera would have picked up if your reactions weren't authentic. Disappearing treasure makes for good drama, all right? Nobody wants to watch a boring documentary."

"You made us look like thieves for ratings?"

"Don't knock ratings. In the world we live in, ratings are everything. This project is going to make you famous, Madison. The more popular the documentary is, the more you'll benefit. Don't you want people to recognize your name the next time you apply for a job?"

"I'd rather be known for my actual work than my TV credits. And I'm pretty sure I'm speaking for the others as well." I set the ring on his desk with a clang. He's lucky I don't throw it at him. "I don't even know if I want to be involved with TTP at this stage."

"You can't quit. You signed the contract. And you can't tell the others about this. We can make a great documentary together, Madison. Don't ruin it."

I am ruining things? "Tomorrow, at the morning meeting, you need to admit, on camera, that you misplaced the artifacts. You need to clear the rest of us."

"How would that look?" He spreads his hands, his tone and expression asking me to be reasonable. "I'm the producer."

"That doesn't make it all right to destroy our reputations. You realize that would also degrade the entire project, right?" He must know that. The question is, does he care? "Who did you pick for the fall guy? You must have had someone in mind."

He palms the ring. "One of the security guards." He follows that with a *come on now, I'm not a bad guy* pout. He could have been an actual actor. "With his agreement. The boy will be well compensated."

I think of the kid who let us in on the first day, probably desperate to pay off his college loans. "I don't want to be part of a hoax. I'm neither a liar nor a cheat."

He drops the ring into the drawer, and this time, it doesn't roll away. "Like I said." He shoves the drawer shut. "I'd appreciate it if you could keep this to yourself for the time being. For the plot twist to work, everything has to unfold according to script."

"You have a script?" *Of course,* he has a script. "You should have told us. We haven't agreed to any of this."

"Madison… Don't."

"Covering for your lies is not in my contract." I don't quit on the spot, not because I owe Ramsey anything, but because of the nameless graves, the still-faceless victims, people who deserve better than they received from fate.

I don't quit, but I do walk away.

"We are raising the *Titanic*!" he calls after me.

Raising the Titanic is his favorite phrase. For him, it means the perfect headline, publicity, money. To me, the words symbolize doing the impossible, righting a wrong, undoing—in what limited way I can—something that never should have happened in the first place.

I cloister myself in my studio for the rest of the day. Because if I run into Ramsey again, *so help me God.* Also, I need to settle down before I tell the others about the ring and the script. I'd rather tell everyone together, which means I have to wait until Julia returns from the cemetery.

It helps that, for once, nobody pops in during the day to check on me. Eleanor is glued to the equipment in her lab, and the documentary crew keeps Oliver busy. I find out why he wasn't there at breakfast. They're filming a spotlight on him today. Eventually, there'll be a spotlight special with each member of the team. *Eye roll. Hurray.*

It's lunchtime, indicated by my stomach's growling, by the time I realize that I've completely forgotten about Boston University and the dean.

I eat lunch at my desk, putting finishing touches on two more faces on the computer. The moment I put that final dab of white, the glint, into their eyes, never grows old. They look back at me as real people for the first time.

"Hi."

The woman is of Asian descent—her skull profile nearly a straight line—around fifty years old; the bone spurs in her shoulder, the only other bone I have for her, indicate heavy physical labor. She has two healed cracks in her skull and one in her cheekbone. Either she's been in multiple accidents or has been severely beaten. I'd love to know how she ended up in England, how she got on the ship. She was halfway to freedom when... My heart hurts for her. She deserved a better end.

The man is around twenty, front tooth missing, possibly lost in a fight; European, judging by the narrow nasal aperture and protruding ridge of his nasal bones. Did he travel alone? He might have had a family, of course. People married early back then.

I'm so engrossed, I work past five, and I am the last one to arrive in Oliver's lab. Our nightly get-togethers have become a thing none of us would willingly miss. This is where we find out what happened at the cemetery that day and where we can freely say how we feel about the cameras and having to pose and repeat things a hundred times for the documentary. Except, of course, tonight. Maya is there with her cameramen and Ramsey.

"What's wrong?" Julia picks up on my mood as soon as I walk in.

Ramsey cuts her off. "Look what I found." He shows off the maquette of a ship, *not* the *Titanic*. "Ladies and gentlemen, meet the *Mackay-Bennett*, the ship that brought the dead to Halifax."

The cameras zoom in.

"The CS *Mackay-Bennet*, launched in 1884, was a cable ship that laid cable and carried out cable repair in the Atlantic. She was one of the first steel-built ships."

"What did they use before?" I picture a Viking ship. "Wood?"

"Iron," Oliver says. "But those had a problem with rust. Steel was a big step forward."

"Cable ships often assisted other ships in emergencies. In February of 1912, two months before the *Titanic* disaster, the *Mackey-Bennett* rescued the crew of a vessel that also sank in icy waters, the schooner *Caledonia*."

"I detect a pattern here." Julia sips her wine. "I think if I lived back then, I would just have left the ocean to the mermaids."

I fetch myself a glass, while Ramsey says, "After the *Titanic* sank, the White Star Line asked the *Mackay-Bennett* to collect the bodies. They paid the crew double. The *Mackay-Bennett*, with a large hold designed to store literal tons of cable, left the harbor with one hundred coffins."

"Why a hundred?" I ask, aware that Ramsey is playing us. He has information he wants in the documentary, and he's using us to squeeze it in. "Didn't you say that fifteen hundred passengers perished?"

"I suppose they didn't expect to find them all." Ramsey is appropriately solemn, careful not to look at the cameras. "Or maybe Captain Larnder had trouble scaring up more than a hundred coffins in a hurry. He also took with him a priest, Canon Hind, from All Saints Cathedral, embalming supplies, and equipment enough for seventy, and an embalmer called John Snow."

The ship also carried one hundred tons of ice, we're told.

Eleanor is the one to speak up this time. "Why carry ice to a field of icebergs?"

Ramsey doesn't have the answer.

"To store the bodies?" I guess. "They probably didn't want to go close enough to an iceberg to harvest a few chunks. They didn't want to sink themselves."

"The ship fought inclement weather for four days before it reached the victims." Ramsey rolls along. "We know about the recovery efforts from the diary log of twenty-four-year-old Clifford Crease, naval artificer, which is on display in the Public Archives of Nova Scotia."

I want to see that before I leave the city. "What's a naval artificer?"

"A highly skilled member of the Royal Navy who's undergone several years of apprenticeship in handling electronics and mechanics," Julia reads from her phone.

Ramsey raises his voice slightly for the cameras. "The *Mackay-Bennett* arrived at the site of the tragedy in the middle of the night, so they had to wait until dawn before they could look for the bodies. Captain Larnder ordered lifeboats to reclaim the poor victims, many of whom were not poor at all, of course, in the literal sense. Isidor Straus was the owner of Macy's Department Store. John Jacob Astor's son offered one hundred thousand dollars for the return of his father's body."

"Wonder how much that was worth back in the day," Julia ponders, then looks that up too. "The average house cost around two thousand seven hundred dollars."

Even Ramsey pauses at that, but not for long. In another second, he's sailing on. "First-class passengers received embalming and a coffin."

Naturally.

"Second-class passengers were wrapped in linen shrouds and kept cool on the ice. Third-class passengers and crew, a hundred and sixteen bodies, half of whom could not be identified, were weighed down and received a sea burial."

Every time I think about all the dead left behind, a shiver runs down my spine.

"While many crew members and second- and third-class passengers were returned to the water,"

Ramsey says, "band leader Wallace Hartley, who was recovered with his music case still strapped to his chest, was not assigned to a watery grave. His body was saved and returned to England. The rescuers, on their own, also saved three third-class passengers and stowed them in the hold: two adults, and an unidentified two-year-old."

"I've wondered about the rescue crew before," Eleanor says. "What grim work they had, risking their own lives in the field of ice, knowing that no matter how hard they worked, they weren't going to find anyone alive."

I hope the city has a memorial plaque or monument to them somewhere. They should be remembered.

"All in all, after seven days of hard work," Ramsey consults his phone, to make sure his figures are right, "the men reclaimed three hundred and six bodies of the fifteen hundred and seventeen who perished. Another twenty-two were recovered by other ships. The *Mackay-Bennett* arrived home to Halifax with one hundred and ninety victims, who were laid out on the ice rink of the Mayflower Curling Club."

"That might be the most Canadian thing I've heard in a while." I'm trying to picture it. I'm too ashamed to admit that up until curling became an Olympic sport a while ago, I didn't even know it existed.

"The crew split Astor's one-hundred-thousand-dollar reward, setting aside enough to pay for a little white coffin, grave, and headstone for the unidentified and unclaimed child whom they called Our Babe. Clifford Crease pulled the little body from the icy waves, and for the rest of his life, each year, on the anniversary of the sinking, Crease visited the little boy's grave."

Who's crying? I'm not crying.

After Ramsey and the documentary crew leave, we drink the last of the wine Javier, Oliver's cousin, dropped off the week before. We've talked him into weekly deliveries. Turns out, in addition to being a sculptor, he's also a wine aficionado. His choices can be trusted.

I pour myself a glass of pinot noir from Unsworth, a name I wasn't familiar with until now, an oversight.

"Did something happen?" Eleanor asks. "You looked upset when you came in earlier."

She's one strong woman. If she's in pain, she never shows it. She never lets us see her without a smile on her face either. I don't want to stress her out. And yet, she deserves to know what I've discovered.

"The good news is, the missing artifacts turned up." I take a drink, appreciating the hint of cherry. "The bad news is…" Another sip, and then I tell them about Ramsey's script, the setup, the games he's playing. "Is it wrong to murder someone? I can't remember what conclusion we came to last time we talked about it."

Oliver sets his glass down with a hard click, uncharacteristically letting his Zen slip. "I have half a mind to pack up and leave."

"We all could." While Julia doesn't vocally support murder, her serenity is deceptive. Her tone carries a distinct chill that brings to mind an ice blade.

"Except for our contracts." Eleanor's shoulders slope, as if all energy left her, as if her muscles are too tired to support her bones. Instead of angry, she sounds hurt and disappointed. For the first time since I've met her, she looks frail.

I hate to agree with her point, but she's right. "Our contracts and the fact that we all do want to add names to those headstones."

Julia rubs the pad of her thumb on her wineglass. "I wonder how much TrinovarDNA and Cyntinra know about Ramsey's script. Did he tell them ahead of time that he's going to fake a robbery for ratings? Bad publicity could throw a negative light on the project. If Ramsey set this up on his own, without clearing it with anyone…"

"We could go over his head." The thought does cheer me up for a moment. "Except, if they have to replace him, it'll slow us down." And the schedule needs to speed up, if anything.

Boston University is waiting for me. I keep my mouth shut on that subject, however. I'm not ready yet to tell everyone that I might have to leave.

"He's not a bad person." Eleanor's tone is oddly apologetic. "He wants so much for the project to succeed." Her eyes beg for understanding. "He just made a mistake. It's my fault. He'd be different if I'd raised him."

Julia's head snaps up. "What do you mean, if you'd raised him?"

CHAPTER 12

Helen
April 28, 1897

"Are you certain the waters won't rise?" Mrs. Lillie passes the salt to her husband. "The rain has been relentless. The bargemen say the Cottonwood is about ready to burst. I have a bad feeling about that river."

My children and I have been living with the Lillies for nearly two years. I am used to Mrs. Lillie's *feelings*. She is right often enough for me to respect her premonitions.

Her husband, however, is a man of science. "We are perfectly safe." He finishes his ale, which he prefers with dinner over wine when we are not entertaining. "We've had April rains this heavy before."

Fat raindrops tap against the windows, replacing the usual evening song of the whippoorwills. I have still only heard the birds, but have never seen one yet. And I will not tonight. They must all be hiding from the weather.

Mrs. Lillie looks out into the gloom, her expression pinched. "The hog man put all his hogs into train carts to Santa Fe."

"And everyone is calling him a coward." Her husband cuts another bite of his roast, unhurried, attempting to enjoy his dinner. "I am a prominent citizen. I cannot afford to look like a nervous ninny. We have never had a dangerous flood in Guthrie."

I'm about to remind him that the town is only eight years old, and rain like this might only come around once a decade, but he holds up his hand and gives us his final word on the subject.

"The mayor says we have nothing to worry about. He is confident. He is set on statehood. We have all worked hard to build Guthrie up to be the kind of city that could be the capital. The mayor would not ignore an impending disaster that could undo all our efforts and set us back years. If he thought there was going to be a flood, he would be out in the streets right now, organizing precautionary measures."

"Of course, dear."

The soft patter of the rain turns into insistent drumming by the time we finish dinner. Effie takes the children up to bed. The adults linger for conversation, spending another hour discussing local matters, but then the wind starts up, incessantly rattling the shutters, and we follow after the children.

Rosie assists with my dress. I sit still while she combs my hair, her even strokes relaxing. I am happy here.

The children and I have started a new life in Guthrie. My friends here have become close to sisters. The Lillies are becoming family. I even attend the Trinity Episcopal Church with them.

Without the high-society matrons of New York to judge me, I am turning into a new person. I dare more. I do more. I am reinvented. My articles are published in all the top women's magazines and payments arrive regularly in the mail. I am turning into a self-sufficient woman—a woman of means. I have even invested in a small property. I fall asleep every night thinking about the house I wish to build.

I am growing to love Oklahoma, so different from back home, where Caroline Astor is seeking to recreate Europe from the cream of New York, fast establishing an American aristocracy. The group of wealthy men who will forever stand above the rest of us to rule us has already been chosen. I prefer the frontier that still has its gates open to all. I find it more American. Freedom and opportunity are still there for the taking.

"Do you miss New York, Rosie?" At one point, I shall have to discuss my long-term plans with her and Effie.

"No, ma'am. I like Guthrie better. There is adventure in the air here."

I can see why she would feel that way. The lines between the classes are more blurred, more of a gap-toothed fence than the solid wall that class distinction is becoming in New York. A poor fellow from the tenements might come here—and I have seen it happen—gain land, build his own house, be his own man. I know a maid who came from Boston with her mistress and stayed behind when her mistress returned home. She opened a bakery, and now she is a well-heeled woman.

Has Rosie ever thought about leaving my employ? If she ever does, I shall not object. She deserves a new start as much as anyone else.

"Thank you, Rosie." My toilette complete, I release her to retire to her own bed.

The wind dies. Even the rain eases. Its soothing music lulls me to rest. I am content as I consider the future, lying on fresh linens.

I wake toward dawn to a terrible roar and people screaming. It is as if hell's mouth has opened outside.

I bolt upright in bed and call out, "What is it? What is happening?"

Then my wrap is around me, and I leap to the window. The rain is a deluge again, obscuring all but the glow of the electric streetlights, small, scattered ghosts in the dark night. A moment or two, and my eyes adjust.

People are running from the west end of Oklahoma Avenue, some in their nightdresses.

"Lord have mercy."

A wall of water at least eight feet high rushes behind the fleeing people, thick with flotsam I judge to be pieces of houses up the street.

I grip the sill. "The river left its bed!"

I do not remember the time I almost drowned in the tub as a small child; I only know of the incident from Mama, but I feel imaginary water closing over my face, and it paralyzes me for a moment.

I shake off the frozen terror and run for the children in the smaller room next door. "Up!" I drag them from their beds. "Go up to Rosie and Effie." The maids sleep on the third floor. "I have to wake Mr. and Mrs. Lillie."

We meet our hosts in the hallway. Either they heard my shouting or they heard the river. "Careful." "Go." "Hurry." We scramble up the steps, the maids already awake and rushing to help, reaching for Harry and Edith. Everyone is wide-eyed with panic.

"We are all right." I finally tie my wrap around me. "We are safe."

Then the lights go out, and everyone shrieks.

"Shhh. We are up high. We shall not be harmed." I do not tell them that some houses have already collapsed. I have seen the water carry away what was left of them. Papa's words come to me, wisdom he learned in the war and often shared. "Panic does not improve any problem."

We none of us want to be separated, so we end up in Rosie's room. Even Magda crowds in there. Mr. and Mrs. Lillie hold on to each other as they sit on the narrow bed. I stand sentinel at the small dormer window, the children pressed against my side, unwilling to be too far from me.

"What do you see?" Mrs. Lillie's voice shakes.

"Very little. Shadows. The streetlights are out too."

The rush of flood lasts ten minutes that feel like ten years, with me staring blindly into the night while my mind's eye paints the most terrifying images. Then the roar of the water abates, followed by a terrible silence that lasts only the length of a few ragged breaths.

"Heaven help us." Desperate cries reach us from the street. "Help! Help, for heaven's sake!"

Rosie gathers herself enough to light a candle on the dresser, where it illuminates the clock. "It's six in the morning." Her voice is not her own. She is in a daze.

Mr. Lillie rises to his feet. "I must go. There will be a great many injured. I must open the pharmacy for supplies."

Mrs. Lillie sobs as she releases her husband's hand. "Be careful, dear."

The pitiful pleas for help outside rend my heart, especially the sound of children crying. I move toward the door. "You stay here with Mrs. Lillie and the children," I tell Rosie and Effie. "I shall be back as soon as I can."

"Take the candle." Mrs. Lillie calls after her husband. "We will light another."

My boots are in the corner. Rosie must have brought them up for polishing, God bless her. I quickly step into them.

Everything downstairs is wet. Two of the front

windows are broken out. Inches of mud cover the carpet.

"We are locked in." Mr. Lillie yanks on the door handle in vain, over and over. "The door is obstructed."

I pick my way through the ruined furniture and grab the fireplace shovel from the debris. "Here. Would this help?"

"Yes."

I hold the candle while Mr. Lillie shovels the mud aside, and when he is finished, I help him pry the front door open.

Our street is bedlam, utter screaming madness. We step out into the rain. The first gust of wind blows out our candle. I stick it in the foul mud that covers the front step.

Mud-caked carriages lie turned over. A coal cart is crushed on one side of the street, a potato cart on the other. The mud sucks at my boot. A horse whinnies pitifully, washed out of some stable and dropped on our corner. He is down on his knees, one of his front legs broken. He struggles with all his might, but he cannot rise.

"Shh. Shh. You poor thing." It breaks my heart, but there is nothing I can do to help. He will have to wait to be delivered from pain until someone with a pistol comes by.

A portion of the people who were running away from the river earlier are now cautiously making their way back. Men are calling for their wives.

Women are calling for their children. Everyone is soaked to the skin, a straggling army of wraiths.

"Have you seen my Bobbie?" one desperate soul demands of me through chattering teeth.

Another, with eyes that burn with anguish, asks, "Have you seen my Mildred?"

I can but mutely shake my head.

Mr. Lillie turns toward his pharmacy, and I almost immediately lose sight of him in the darkness.

I have had a fear of dead bodies all my life, although I do not remember the Civil War. I suppose I have heard too many stories from Papa. *No matter.* I must forge ahead. The need is too great. I shall not allow myself to be scared.

The first drowned I see is a little girl of around seven, her nightdress twisted around her slight body, her eyes and mouth full of mud. A sobbing woman darts past me and grabs the child into her arms. I give thanks to God for the safety of my own children and march on.

An old woman lies lifeless in a doorway straight ahead. I close her eyes and whisper a quick prayer, then spot another pair of children, in front of a collapsed house, still hanging on to a muddy blanket. The water must have washed them straight out of their bed. I am too late for them too.

All I can do is whisper a last blessing. "May angels carry you to heaven."

Closer to Cottonwood River, more of the dead are men. They must have already been working on the water. The night and the rain close in around me, suffocate me. Horror binds my feet. I want to run back to the house and hide in a silent corner.

Then, somewhere nearby, a child cries, the most pitiful sound that exists in the universe.

"Where are you?" I stumble forward and spot the little boy clinging to the top of a lamppost. He cannot be more than four.

"Mama! Mama!"

I pray that his mother is not one of the drowned. I stand under him and hold out my arms. "Come, I shall catch you."

He hangs on all the tighter.

He reminds me so much of my Harry at that age. His heaving sobs break my heart. "Jump. I can tell you are a brave boy. Do you want to go to your mother?"

He shrieks as he lets go.

We walk up to the corner where a sodden maid, distraught to tears, grabs him from me. "Freddie!"

I keep moving, soaked through and shivering. In Norwalk, I would be frozen by now, but the weather down here is milder, the temperature probably close to fifty. Not a murderous cold, but I am still chilled through. The devastation around me is such, however, that I forget about my own minor misery.

"Here. Let me see." I crouch next to a woman with a bleeding leg. She is sobbing too hard to tell me what happened. I move to rip a strip off the bottom of my nightgown to stop the bleeding, but of course, the hem is soaked in mud. I fish a clean handkerchief from my pocket and wrap the wound tightly with the piece of white cloth. "That should do." I help her to her feet. "Can you walk? Do you know where Mr. Lillie, the pharmacist, lives?"

She nods, her teeth chattering.

"Go there and ask one of the maids to give you a dry blanket. Tell them you were sent by Mrs. Candee."

People keep staggering forward from the lucky houses that were spared, staring at the destruction, slack-jawed. Some run straight toward the river, where they know the need for help will be the greatest. Others turn right back in.

"We need clean water boiled, and bandages and wood for splints." I try to wake those who stand frozen in place. "Someone must run for the doctor."

"Which one?" A young woman wrapped in tartan stumbles forward. She smells like wet wool, while everything around her smells like river muck.

"Any doctor you know."

I reach the other side of the street and look north. A wooden bridge that has not been there before blocks the intersection.

"Out of the way." Muddy rescuers carry even muddier wounded victims past me.

I whisper a prayer after them. I do not know how far they will have to carry their burden before they shall find a dry bed.

I head toward what appears to be a small dog and end up picking up a mud-covered toddler. He is dead. I wipe his little face with my sleeve, then set him on a porch that is still standing by some miracle.

"I am sorry I must leave you," I whisper to the little angel. "But you will be found here."

The destruction by the river knocks me breathless. And to think that warnings have been sounded, but the men who lead our town ignored them, for fear of appearing weak. How many would die tonight for the sake of stupid pride? A dozen? A hundred?

"I am stuck! I am stuck!"

I climb onto ruins to help an old woman. As I reach higher ground, I stop a dozen feet from her yet. I can see the river at last.

The rushing water is carrying a little house away —mother, father, and baby on the roof. I cannot tear my eyes away from the woman who could be my sister, we are so alike in appearance. She has my figure, the shape of my face, and even my hair.

Several men attempt to save the family, throwing ropes to them, but the little house disintegrates before our eyes. The wooden abode dissolves in the river as if it were made of paper.

As the mother goes under, my body violently shudders, as if it is my face the waters are closing over.

I must move.

People need my help.

"I am coming." I scramble over the rubble. "I am here."

CHAPTER 13

Madison
    November 1, 2024 (Friday)

By the end of October, we have thirty-nine of the
forty-four victims out of the ground, and Eleanor has
analyzed the first set of DNA. J.H. has a third cousin
in TrinovarDNA's database, with 1.47% DNA shared,
five segments. She also has a bunch of fourth cousins,
less than 1% of DNA shared with each. She's definitely not my grandmother's aunt.

For now, Trinovar is holding back J.H.'s record, so
her cousins remain unaware, but she *has* living
family. With a little luck, family records combined
with census records will give us her name and might
even tell some of her life story.

"Remember your nondisclosure agreements,"
Ramsey tells us at the morning meeting on Friday, his
hands folded behind him like a ship captain's, as he

stands at the head of the table. It's the first of November, but deep in the building, we're locked away from the blustery winds of the bay. "None of this can leak. We're releasing all the data, all at once, in the spring. I want to make it a major event. All announcements and press releases will be tightly coordinated with the release of the TV series on April 14th, on the anniversary of the *Titanic*'s sinking."

The frequent reminders are unnecessary. We've had NDAs before. We're not stupid.

"The last of the remains are coming out next week," he says, moving on. "We've already had frost a few times. In a couple of weeks, the ground will start freezing. The window of workable ground conditions is closing."

The rush will affect Julia and her two assistants the most, along with the equipment operator and the documentary crew. We'll all help to make sure the remains are safely transferred to the lab, but once that's done, I'll have all winter to paint the victims' portraits, while Oliver will assemble and catalog the bones, and Eleanor will test and analyze them. We have sufficient time until April, so the work shouldn't put her under too much stress.

Ramsey sits and shuffles through his papers.

Now that I know Eleanor is his mother, I can see the similarity. It's in their smiles and the tilt of their heads when they're concentrating.

Eleanor apologized for keeping their relationship a secret back when she'd accidentally let it slip a month ago. She asked us to understand that she meant no deception. She just didn't want the rest of us to think that she was a nepo mom, that she hadn't earned her spot on the team. Understandable. Knowing her other secret, I find I can't be mad at her for anything.

"That's it for this morning," Ramsey says. "But if you could stay a little longer, we need to reshoot a brief snippet from yesterday's meeting." He consults his notes. "Actually, we don't need Madison." He looks up at me. "You're free to leave."

On my way to my studio, I call my father. I haven't seen him since the beginning of September, the last time we went grocery shopping together, when I received TTP's initial email. Since it'll be a while before we can do that again, I make it a point to talk to him over the phone every couple of weeks.

"You have a minute?"

"Hold on." A keyboard clickety-clicks on the other end. "Let me finish this thought."

I wait in silence, and after a few seconds, he comes back on the line. "What's up?"

"Boston U offered me my old job."

"When are you coming back?"

How easy it must be to always know what you want, to be so certain of the right choice. I am not him, however. "I haven't decided whether to accept yet."

Silence stretches on the line, as if my enormous stupidity needs its own space and more than a few seconds to digest. "Why would you even hesitate? This is what you've always wanted. If you play your cards right, you'll get tenure, and then you're set. The whole rest of your life falls into place. You'll have a pension from the university. Do you know how rare a pension is in this day and age?"

"It makes sense. I know. I'm not declining. I'm just thinking about it." I walk into my studio. "How are you? Everything all right?"

"My publisher is lining up media appearances for the book. In addition, they want me to set up lectures at the most relevant universities where I have connections. Did you want anything else? I have a Zoom in five minutes with my editor."

I don't expect him to ask how my work is going. His work is groundbreaking. Mine, well, it's for a TV show. I feel like I'm his graduate student, at most. "Okay, Dad. Take care."

I open my laptop and back up all the computer images I created so far. A few years ago, I lost a month's worth of work to a computer crash. Since then, I make sure my backups have backups. I'm not going to be caught flat-footed again.

Once that's done, I start measurements on my next skull. Male, fifties, Southern European, narrow nasal aperture with a pronounced nasal bridge. I grab paper and pencil to sketch him.

Minutes turn into hours. At lunchtime, Eleanor sticks her head in. "My machines are running. Are you busy?"

"Always, but I need a break. Want to order something to eat?"

"I was going to check how Julia is coming along

at the cemetery. We could grab some food on the way back. We need to get out of this building and see some sunshine. We need vitamin D."

"We should ask Oliver to come with us."

"He's gone. Ramsey released him for the afternoon. He's receiving an award. Apparently, he designed and implemented an accessible garden for a local retirement home where people of all abilities can grow their own vegetables. Did you know he gardened?"

"I did, yes." I picture what an accessible garden might look like—wide rows and raised beds.

I text for the chauffeur, since I don't want to drag Eleanor around on the bus. Davey immediately texts back. I think he secretly likes to hang with us.

"Car will be here in ten minutes. Want to wait outside?"

The initial media frenzy has died down, so they're no longer camped in the driveway. They even left the cemetery. The excavations are the same day after day, and the reporters accepted that they're not going to squeeze another press release out of Ramsey until he's good and ready.

As we walk through the front door, I want to ask Eleanor how she's doing, if the meds she's taking are bothering her with any side effects, but I promised I'd pretend that all is well, so I ask something else. "Do you have any other children?"

"A daughter, Ella. She's married, in Australia. Her husband's family are Ngunnawal. They live in Canberra, so I don't see them often."

"Grandchildren?"

"Not yet." Her voice is whisper soft. "They're trying."

I hope Eleanor will live to see her first grandchild. I watch her as we walk a few steps down the sidewalk. Is she slower? Does she look more tired? I wish I could do something to help.

"What do you think of Oliver?" she asks, as if she can tell what I'm thinking and wants to change the conversation in my head.

Oliver. "He's unnerving. The way he talks, he should be a bald old man in an orange robe, but he's not."

"No. He's not a Buddhist monk." Eleanor laughs. "We live in a benevolent universe."

I don't know how she can say that while dying of cancer.

Eyes closed, she turns her face to the weak November sunshine that's a fading brushstroke of amber dragged across the gray-blue canvas of the sky. "He likes you."

"He likes everyone."

"You know that's not what I mean."

"I'm not here on a husband hunt. We're colleagues."

"I don't think anyone would mind. Ramsey wouldn't care. I doubt he'd notice. When he's on a project, he's all zeroed in."

"Why did you name him Ramsey?" My turn to change the subject. "It's not a common name. Was he named after his father?"

"After jazz. Ramsey Lewis got me hooked. Eighty records, five gold, three Grammies. The man knew what he was doing. I named my daughter Ella, after Ella Fitzgerald. I like the freedom of jazz music, the improvisation." She spreads her arms, bliss lighting up her face, as if she's standing in the bow of the *Titanic*. "It makes you feel limitless." She runs her fingers through the curls at her nape as she says that, then she shakes her head. "Can't get used to this new hair." She offers a small smile. "This is how it grew back. Before chemo, it was dead straight."

Then she tells me about Billie Holiday, giving me a music education I sorely lack. She talks, and I listen, until Davey pulls up next to us at last.

As always, he's neatly dressed, his beard neatly clipped. The man cares about his appearance. "Ladies. Where to?"

"The cemetery, please."

"You should listen to 'Stormy Weather,'" Eleanor says once we're on our way. "Ethel Waters was one of the best." She waves the words away. "Sorry. You just wanted to know how Ramsey got his name." She laughs. "I got carried away. What do you listen to?"

"I tend not to have music on. Growing up, we didn't have music in the house. I don't mean in a super-religious, cult kind of way. My father is a scientist, and he believes that you can't think while listening to something. You'll end up humming or silently singing the words. To be engaged in active problem solving, a person's brain needs complete silence, is his theory."

"Sounds like a man of strong opinions. You might want to tell him about Shakespeare. He wrote his plays in pubs, with drunks carousing around him."

"My dad is convinced that multitasking causes attention deficit disorder. I wasn't allowed to have the TV on in the background if I was reading. No Saturday morning cartoons either. They cause short attention spans, according to several studies. In hindsight, I know he was right, but at the time, I just wanted to be like all the other kids."

"What does he think of millennials who always have their phone in hand these days?"

"He's expecting civilization to crumble. The fall of Rome all over again."

"What do you think, Davey?" Eleanor asks.

"Not impossible." He raises a hand from the steering wheel and waves it around. "My granddaughter… Eh."

"What's your father's field of study?" Eleanor inquires next.

"Astronomy. His lifelong goal has been to be the first to discover alien life and to receive the Nobel Prize."

Davey perks up. "E.T.?"

"He'd settle for a microorganism."

"I was still hoping I'd achieve something in microbial genetics." Eleanor's smile is undiminished, but somehow, the car fills with sadness. "Then one doctor visit, and my entire world changed. We only recognize how short life is when it's too late." Her eyes glint with mischief. "Except for Buddhist monks and Oliver."

I'm saved from having to respond because we're at our destination, and Davey pulls into the parking lot.

The cemetery is open. They opened it right after Ramsey's initial press conference, once the cat was out of the bag. Now, only the *Titanic* section is closed off with yellow KEEP OUT, DANGER tape. Our security guards are still on duty.

"They'll probably be here until the reinterment." Eleanor veers off instead of heading to the tent area where Julia is deep in discussion with her assistants, Mei and Zuri. "I'd like to see something else first. Come with me?"

She navigates by the little map on her phone screen, guided by a red dot.

"Who are we looking for? Someone famous? Is Ramsey Lewis buried here?" I'm proud of myself for remembering his name. I'm going to listen to his music.

Eleanor says nothing, just keeps walking toward the back, where the graves are gap-toothed, the rows not yet filled. She stops by a spot of faded, weary grass between two new granite markers that haven't yet been dulled by the salt-laced winds.

"I just wanted to see it," she says softly.

"Who is buried here?"

A bird chirps in a nearby tree. Another responds. The barely there breeze dies, and the air goes still.

"I bought the plot for myself online yesterday."

Eleanor's smile is serene. "If not now, when? I have to start making plans. I want to be ready."

This is only the second time she's referred to her condition and where it will eventually lead since she revealed to me that she's ill. My throat tightens, my eyes burn—all the stupid clichés. I want to be able to give her more than this, but I have nothing that would truly help or make a difference. I lack any special powers of healing.

"When are you going to tell Ramsey?" When she first shared her condition with me, she said nobody knew about it, not even him. Back then, I didn't know he was her son. Now that I do... Well, it's different, isn't it?

"When I'm ready." She looks out over the cemetery. "We've only recently reunited. I had him at nineteen. I was incredibly naïve. One of my professors seduced me, then he and his family pressured me to give the baby to him and his wife. They threatened to sue for custody if I didn't agree. I was a college student with no income. I was a nobody. His family had connections..."

"I'm sorry."

"At first, they told me it'd be better for the boy if I didn't visit, didn't confuse him. And there was always the threat that the father would arrange for me to be kicked out of the university, if I made him angry. Then, when I was working on my PhD, I fell in love and married the best man in the universe. For the few visits I was allowed with Ramsey, they told him I was a distant aunt."

"That's so sad."

"I accepted whatever conditions I was offered." Her eyes are filled with regret. "Before our daughter Ella was born, my husband and I focused on our careers. And our travels. Malaysia, Morocco, a caravan through the Sahara, the monasteries of Japan, the Galapagos Islands. Anyway, Ramsey was a teenager by the time he found out the truth. He was, of course, told that I abandoned him. He was mad at me for that, and for getting married. He thought I should have waited for his father to have an epiphany and make us a family." Her soft voice turns heavy with heartbreak. "Whoever says teenage girls are emotional has never met a teenage boy."

"I'm glad you got a chance to build a relationship with him as an adult."

"Me too. It's a gift I don't want to ruin by bringing cancer into it. I want to enjoy a few months of could-have-been, before it's over."

"Would it be okay if I hugged you?" I ask, unsure if it's for me or for her. Maybe the brief physical connection will comfort both of us.

"I'll never turn down a hug." She opens her arms. "And thank you for coming with me. I didn't know how seeing the spot would make me feel. I'll be alone here plenty. It's nice not to be alone just yet."

The lab coat she usually wears to work exaggerates her frame. I never realized how slight she was underneath. Or under the light coat she's currently wearing. Once I have my arms around her, it's obvious that her shoulders are too slim, her entire skeleton too delicate. Cancer, that slithering monster, is stealing her away. I'd do anything to be able to steal her back. I imagine Ramsey will feel the same once he finds out. As I think that, I dislike him a little less. My heart starts to hurt for him.

"Why here?" I ask as we release each other.

"TTP is my last adventure, and being able to have a last adventure makes me happy. My family is from Cincinnati, but nobody is left there. My husband's ashes were scattered over his favorite patch of ocean in Florida, where he went for blue marlin every year. I don't like fishing. I get seasick." A rare melancholy shadows her expression, but only for a few seconds, then she's smiling again. "As soon as I walked into this cemetery back in September, I knew this would be it."

"I'm so sorry." About her illness, the shortness of time, about things I can't even articulate.

"For a long time after I was first diagnosed, I was obsessed with reaching the finish line of *cancer-free*. I wanted to reach it with the religious fervor some people have for reaching heaven. The fight consumed my life, not just the minutes at the doctors' during treatment, but the minutes I should have allowed myself to be free. Marcel Proust said, *My destination is no longer a place, rather a new way of seeing*."

I wait for her to explain.

"I can control how I see, even if I can't control this disease." She pats my arm, as if I'm the one who needs to be encouraged. "I choose to see that there are still choices left to me. Spending my last few months working with my son, picking my resting place, what I leave behind. I used to think that the second the doctor said the test was positive, all my choices were snatched away from me. Now I look to identify choices I still have, and I celebrate them."

She's so…*heroic* is the word, that it leaves me speechless.

"Sometimes I wonder," she says, "if it's someone absentminded up there, and he only remembers to glance down occasionally. *What are they doing down there? Are they bored? They're probably bored.* And then he pushes a button."

The birds in the tree sing, a laugh-like trill.

"What if God has gone on vacation," Eleanor suggests, "and left generative AI in charge? And it just keeps tossing us plot twists without any thought and consideration for the plot, its main objective being to keep things *interesting*. Anyway. I'm full of silly thoughts these days. Let's see what Julia is doing."

All the way to the white tent, I turn her words around in my head, how strong she is, how resolutely she's making her plans.

I'm good at plans. I'm good at setting goals, charting a path, cutting the work into manageable chunks, and putting in the effort. I've always thought of the finish line as a productive career with a stellar list of publications, tenure at Boston University, then a retirement where I'm still teaching classes part-time. But this is the real finish line: a small plot with a little grass on top.

I can hear my father's voice in my ear: *Madison, don't be morbid. How and when we die doesn't matter, as long as we leave a legacy.*

At the same time, I know now that my plan for life is not really *my* plan for life. It's *his*.

All this time, I've been climbing a ladder that's leaning against the wrong wall.

As the birds chirp around us, I feel very deep for having thought that thought. Oliver would be proud of me. Then he'd say something like *Stop climbing ladders already. Just fly.*

"Hey!" Julia springs up from a crouch next to the current grave she's excavating. White privacy screens are up all around her now to protect the dignity of the dead from any curious onlookers. "You won't believe what we found."

Before I can ask what it is, the director jumps up out of nowhere and shouts, "Cut!"

CHAPTER 14

Helen
   (Eight Years Later)
   1905
   Washington, DC

"I hear you survived the Guthrie flood." Edith Roosevelt's eyes fill with sympathy. "What a terrifying night that must have been for a mother with her children."

The First Lady of the United States is one of fifty dinner guests at my home in Washington DC, near DuPont Circle. She is three years younger than I am, a progressive, along with her husband. I have hope I might win her to the side of the suffragettes. She is an intelligent woman.

"We were some of the lucky ones. A hundred souls lost." The memories chill me straight through still, every time. "Six bridges gone, and countless houses." That feels the most surreal part. We know human life to be fragile, but one expects bridges and buildings to stay where they are planted.

"Two hundred thousand dollars' worth of property washed away. I read the report the president received. The devastation must have been complete. Was that when you moved to Washington, Mrs. Candee?"

The Italian ambassador dances past us with his wife, the Marchesa Cusati, and I step closer to Mrs. Roosevelt to leave the dancers more room. "First, I moved back to New York."

The Lillies' house was badly water damaged. We helped with the cleanup, but left shortly after. If we remained, our presence would have been a burden. And, too, my bubble of paradise was pierced the night the Cottonwood River left its banks. It was time for us to leave. I had learned what Guthrie was meant to teach me.

The First Lady fans herself. "Were you not worried that you would run into that beastly husband of yours?"

She knows some of my story. Divorce is still rare, especially in our social circles. *The New York Times* wrote *two* articles about the whole scandal, dissecting my marriage to Edward.

"I was born in New York. New York is as much mine as it is his. I was not going to let him have the city."

"Brava!" Mrs. Roosevelt toasts me with her champagne.

"Freedom is a terrible thing to waste."

"Thus, first you conquered the West, then New York, and now us. No." She cuts me off when I would protest. "False modesty does not suit you, Mrs. Candee. Everyone I talk to sings your praises."

The quartet begins a new piece. New couples form on the dance floor. Everyone who is anyone in Washington is at my party tonight. Everything must be perfect. I glance at the sharply dressed servers who are circulating with drinks. Nothing needs my attention. All is well.

"I suppose I have made some headway."

"Yes. Your magnificent tome, among other accomplishments, *How Women May Earn a Living*."

My book was published in 1900, right as we stumbled from the old century into this one that is still bright and new and filled with possibilities. *No more wars,* is what everyone is saying, *just progress and prosperity and peace*. "I felt the advice was needed."

"Very much so, but your *Oklahoma Romance* is my favorite. The very first novel ever written about Oklahoma Territory, and it is written by a woman." She toasts me again. "Quite an accomplishment."

I published that book a year after the first one, the same year I lost Mama. I needed to lose myself in the story, in a different world. The subject is a land claim dispute after the Land Run of 1889, a fiery disagreement between a young doctor and a politician.

"I read a review," the First Lady tells me, "that

called you the most important female writer of Oklahoma Territory."

"I shall find it and frame it. So I can show it to people who told me to stick to articles about etiquette and recipes."

"Thank goodness you did not. What do you think Oklahoma Territory's chances are for statehood?"

"Very good, I hope. Several government officials have asked for my support. And I do support them, with all my heart. Oklahoma gave me my freedom."

"Very well." She carries her gaze around the room. "I must say I am glad that you settled down here, in the capital."

"Once my father died, there wasn't much to keep me up north. As much as I like New York, living there was awkward. Edward and I have too many mutual friends. Some looked at me askance for the divorce, some because I earn my own living." *How vulgar!* "I could succeed in New York, and I did, but… *Everything is allowed to me, but not everything is to my benefit*, as Saint Paul says. I have the right to live where I can be happy."

"You are a wise woman." She shifts her gaze back to me. "New York's loss is Washington's gain. Are you writing anything new?"

"A book on interior design. *Decorative Styles and Periods*. And then I mean to tackle antique tapestry. I am planning on traveling to Europe to research the topic. I hope to spend several months on the Continent. I enjoy a good transatlantic voyage."

"Is there anything you don't do? A trustee of the

Corcoran Gallery of Art and the Archaeological Society." Her smile holds a hint of mischief. "Yes. I have taken the liberty of acquainting myself with your illustrious achievements."

I don't bring up that women's rights, in fact, are the most important reason behind my move to Washington. If I am to change the course of history, I must be where the decisions are made. To win a battle, one must first show up on the battlefield.

I must be familiar with the terrain and the players. So, I have taken a page from my mother's book and transformed myself into a sought-after hostess.

I want to talk with Mrs. Roosevelt about the subject of women's rights later, in a quieter environment, when I am not hosting a large event. I very much respect her and the president, who are working on breaking some of the worst monopolies that are strangling our country. They both believe in protecting the rights of working Americans.

"Is that your Edith?" Mrs. Roosevelt follows my daughter with her eyes as Edith swirls by us on the arm of her husband.

Harry is here too, somewhere. He is almost twenty, formed by the years we lived in the West. He is adventurous and fearless.

I am proud of my children. "In all honesty, all I have achieved means little compared to the fact that my children are happy."

"Certainly." Mrs. Roosevelt has five children of her own, and she also raised her stepdaughter, Alice, from the president's first marriage. "But you are as accomplished outside your home as inside its well-decorated walls. A celebrated hostess and author, and the inventor of a whole new occupation. What did you call it…"

"Interior designer."

"Well, nobody can deny that your taste is impeccable."

"I give credit for the house to Nathan C. Wyeth. He is a brilliant architect. The furnishings are mere embellishments."

"I must talk to the president about you. I find that I am not quite finished with redecorating the White House. Separating the public business area into the East Wing from our family areas in the West Wing is working. I know people question my addition of the tennis court, but it *is* necessary. To be healthy, the president must keep himself in good physical condition. I am finished with major changes for the most part, but there are still areas where your exquisite touch is exactly what I need. Would you be willing to advise me?"

The unexpected honor feels as if I have been gifted an award. "I would be delighted."

And that is how I end up working with the architect remodeling the West Wing, after my book *Decorative Styles and Periods* is published. I enjoy collaborating with Mrs. Roosevelt, and after her with Mrs. Taft, who is an ultraconservative and not a proponent of women's rights, unfortunately. Yet, despite our different opinions, we develop a friendship. Of course, everything requires twice as much time as expected. It is 1912 by the time I am ready to go to Europe to research antique tapestries.

"I have you booked on the *Olympic* on the way over, Mrs. Candee," my agent tells me, a young man new to the company. "And on the way back, if you end up staying until April, I could book you a cabin on the *Titanic* for her maiden voyage. The largest and fastest ocean liner ever, the most luxurious ship the White Star Line has ever built. The Guggenheims and the Astors have already booked passage." He lowers his voice, as if just speaking the names is an honor. "You would be part of a historic voyage."

"Sounds splendid. However, I do not wish to put an end date on the trip. Let us leave the return flexible, shall we?"

"You might regret it, if the cabins sell out. The inaugural voyage of the *Titanic* will be a one-of-a-kind experience. Are you certain you don't want to secure your place, Mrs. Candee?"

April, 1912
    France

Harry has been injured in a plane crash.

Edith sends only that single sentence to my Paris hotel. The terrible news reaches me in the evening, after dinner, the telegram handed over by the concierge.

Europe suits me. So does travel. So does research. Anything that engages my mind thrills me, but that thrill evaporates the second I read those words on the paper.

It's the beginning of April, my preliminary research for the tapestry book finished. I planned on staying another week to visit Mother's grave in Neuilly-sur-Seine, Île-de-France, but now… All thought of further travel is immediately discarded.

Six years ago, on a trip to the Mediterranean, I nearly died from typhoid fever. I was less scared then than I am now. Nothing matches the terror of something bad happening to one's children.

"I will be checking out in the morning," I tell the man behind the front desk. "Please arrange for a carriage to Saint Lazarre train station."

"Of course, Mrs. Candee. And I will send up a porter."

"As early as possible please. Seven?"

Upstairs, I ask my maid, Giselle, to pack. I inform her of my departure and pay her in full, adding a small bonus to the amount. She cannot travel with me, as I have no idea how long I shall stay or when I might return here. I should be able to manage a six-day voyage without her assistance. I shall hire another girl once I reach New York.

I cannot sleep, the cold fingers of worry squeezing my heart. I slip from my bed at seven and stare out into dawn's awakening light. *Dear God, I rarely ask for anything, but I am begging you now. Save my son.*

Another telegram arrives at breakfast. *Harry is expected to fully recover.*

I can breathe again. His condition must not be as dire as my worst imaginings. I am going anyway. I am his mother. My place is next to him.

I say goodbye to Giselle, have the coachman drive me and my luggage to the train station, and then I travel to Cherbourg harbor posthaste.

"One ticket on the first ship to New York, please."

"That would be the *Titanic*," the man behind the glass says, his eyes as bright as if he were taking the trip himself.

The very ship my agent wanted to book for me for my return trip, before I ever embarked on this journey. News of her maiden voyage has been all over the papers. My train carried so many of her passengers, the conductor called it the New York Express.

"One first-class cabin, please."

"Yes, madam. You will travel on the grandest vessel ever built. The harbormaster says the passengers will be talking about this voyage for the rest of their lives. You are very lucky."

I am that. My Harry is not seriously hurt, and now the magnificent *Titanic*.

"The accommodations," the man smacks a kiss at his fingertips. "Madam, you shall want for nothing. Her wonders have no end."

We shall see. Then again, she *is* an international

sensation. Who knows, I might even squeeze a magazine article out of the voyage.

April 10, 1912
  Cherbourg, France

The *Titanic* is late arriving to France from England.

"Cherbourg harbor is the world's largest artificial harbor in the world," the harbormaster brags to the two hundred and eighty impatient passengers to entertain us. "It is a modern wonder, ladies and gentlemen."

Yes, yes, so everybody says. We might be listening, but nobody is looking at the man. All eyes are on the Astors' party.

"Do you know who that is?" the woman gawking next to me whispers, titillated.

"I think most everyone recognizes John Jacob Astor." He might be the most-known man in the world, rich enough to buy the *Titanic* a few times over.

"He is returning from a honeymoon in Egypt with his new wife. And that's his valet. His wife travels with her maid and her nurse." My fellow traveler says nothing about the energetic terrier running circles around them, one of the numerous dogs waiting for the ship, but she does have further information on the couple. "The marriage is a sensation, so they thought that while the fuss dies down, they would go abroad."

"I am not certain I caught the whole of their story." I was at a convent out in the French countryside, studying centuries-old tapestries, when the papers wrote about the Astor marriage.

"Second wife, of course." She falls silent. Opens her mouth, then closes it again. She can't quite bring herself to say the word *divorce*. Instead, she says, "Eighteen years old, for a man who is almost fifty. She is a year younger than his son." Her voice trembles with the scandal.

"And the other man?" He wears glasses and a thick mustache. "He looks familiar."

"James Clinch. One of the former Mrs. Astor's famous Four Hundred."

Mr. Astor looks around bored—I suppose he is not often made to wait—his young bride disinterested and listless. She appears to be in a blessed condition, so she must be tired. She should be able to rest soon. No doubt they shall have the grandest accommodations available on the ship.

"Who is the other woman with them?" She is old enough to be the new Mrs. Astor's mother. I hesitate over her straight nose and curved eyebrows, the way she stands, as sure of herself as a general. She looks familiar too.

"Margaret Brown. I heard she was with the Astors' party in Cairo."

Margaret Brown. Of course. I have heard her speak

before. She is a member of the National American Woman Suffrage Association.

I am about to say something to that effect, but our ship finally glides in through La Passe de l'Ouest. I check my watch. It is six thirty in the evening. In the crush forward, the woman next to me and I are separated.

Fifteen passengers disembark in the aptly named tender *Traffic*. On the return trip, the small boat ferries third-class passengers from the harbor to the ship, along with the mail. I board the *Nomadic*, another White Star Line tender, that carries the first- and second-class passengers, along with provisions from France. Cases and cases of exquisite champagne and cheeses rush to the *Titanic*'s storerooms, among other delicacies that can only be found on the Continent.

"Everything is so obviously, ostentatiously, tediously first-class, do you not agree?" a girl of about seventeen asks her father next to me, in French, affecting a world-weary ennui.

He pats her hand with indulgence. "When I am dead, you may give away all your inheritance, dearest."

Then they both fell silent. The closer we get to our ship, the more obvious it becomes how, well...*titanic*, the *Titanic* is, a veritable mountain rising out of the sea. The black side could be smooth granite, the white chimneys snow-clad peaks.

Our tender is quickly secured. Crew hurry around, shouting to each other in a multitude of languages, as they escort us onboard. It's as big a cavalcade as a world fair.

"The Tower of Babel," the world-weary girl complains. "I do hope the voyage will be more civilized."

"Careful with your metaphors, my dear." Her father offers his arm. "Do remember how that story ended."

The Tower of Babel collapsed.

I expel the thought from my mind as I weave among passengers, stewards, and porters. For a moment, I end up by the railing. A small crowd fills the harbor, men and women waving handkerchiefs and shouting farewells, although I suspect half of them have nobody onboard. Many must have come merely to see the much-advertised *Titanic*.

A ridiculous number of flower bouquets are carried up the ship along with the luggage. It is customary to send ladies flowers to their cabins upon departure. Alas, my cabin shall remain unadorned. I have no beau and, in any case, none of my friends and family know that I am on the *Titanic*.

I move along the E Deck and find my cabin, which could compete with a room at the Waldorf Astoria, offering an ornately carved wooden dressing table, a firm sofa, spacious wardrobe, and a washstand topped with white marble—the amenities of first class.

My single stateroom offers me rest as we journey to Queenstown, Ireland, to pick up mail and the last group of passengers. For the first hour or so, a slight queasiness assails me, as usual when I first board a ship, but then it passes, as always.

At dinner, I end up next to a dashing gentleman. He is impeccably dressed, tapping his heels together as he bows to my hand. "Major Archibald Butt, at your service, madam."

He is at least half a decade younger than I am, although I would not admit to being fifty-three unless I were put under oath. "Helen Churchill Candee."

"I am aware. I saw you at the White House when I was military aide to President Roosevelt. I am currently military aide to President Taft. I am glad to make your acquaintance. How lucky we are to be here. I thought the voyage might be delayed due to the coal strike in England. No coal is to be found in the harbors. I do not know how the White Star Line managed to fill up her belly, but I am glad they did. She *is* rather splendid."

I think he would go on, he is that excited about the coal, but two other gentlemen arrive at our table. The major is quick to introduce us. "Colonel Gracie. Edward Kent. This is Mrs. Candee."

The colonel kisses my hand with old-fashioned ceremony instead of a quick dip, while Mr. Kent can barely tear his eyes from our surroundings. I cannot entirely blame him. I am the lesser attraction for certain. No mortal woman could compete with the *Titanic*.

The first-class dining salon on D deck is all white plaster and mirrors and stained-glass-covered portholes, clever solutions to make the room bright and make us feel as if we were in a European grand hotel's dining room. It wouldn't be out of place in any of the finest castles I have seen in France and England, and neither would be the diners, the gentlemen in white tie and tails, the ladies in our best gowns and jewelry. Everybody is eager to make a good first impression.

"I wager the room could hold five hundred passengers," Mr. Kent says with awe. "It spans the full width of the ship and is over a hundred feet long." I am not certain a man has ever looked at me with as much admiration as he grants the sleek columns. "Absolutely brilliant." Then he finally *sees* me and quickly kisses my hand. "I apologize."

"Edward is an architect," the major tells me, humor glinting in his eyes.

"Analyzing grand structures is an occupational hazard." Edward offers an apologetic smile.

"I know what you mean. I am an interior designer myself." I enjoy seeing a man so enthusiastic about his vocation, so thrilled by it after what must be decades in the field. It is the opposite of my former husband, who enjoyed complaining about suppliers and customers and regulations more than he enjoyed going into the office.

"A designer?" Mr. Kent nearly forgets to release my hand. "Then you understand."

"I could be quite content spending the entirety of the voyage in this room, studying the details."

Interest and admiration glint in his eyes. "I hope

288

we shall have the opportunity to experience the ship together. I would be very much interested in your thoughts."

I incline my head. I appreciate a man who can appreciate me for my brain and not merely for my figure and my face.

The major introduces the next gentleman who strolls up to our table. "Hugh Woolner. Mr. Woolner is an investor from London."

Then a couple walk over, and the major executes a quick bow for the wife before shaking the husband's hand. "Mr. and Mrs. Harris, from New York, theatre directors. And this is Mrs. Candee, writer and friend of both First Lady Roosevelt and First Lady Taft."

The wife is a beauty in the middle of her thirties. "Please, call me René. How do you like the ship? Is she not a marvel? Did you know we have a Turkish bath? I am planning on taking advantage of every amenity every chance I have."

"Henry Harris, at your service." The husband is next. "How very curious that you worked with two administrations so different from each other. Isn't Mrs. Roosevelt a progressive and Mrs. Taft a conservative? How do you manage to keep good relations with both? Surely you can only agree with one or the other."

He is not the first person to wonder.

"I was a child during the Civil War. I do not remember much of it, except for my father waxing poetic about which side was the patriots and what being a patriot meant. As an adult, I gave the question thought. For me, patriotism is the love of one's country."

My fellow travelers nod.

"And what is my country if not other Americans?" I go on. "I am determined to prove my patriotism by loving other Americans, *all* of them. Even the ones whose beliefs differ from mine. It is my quiet rebellion when others want to divide us and tear us apart."

Usually, at this point in the conversation, I can see in the women's eyes that they might agree or that they also have opinions, but they act dazed and confused and fan themselves. The men tend to look at me as if I am a curious specimen, a frog giving opinion on Darwin's theories, for example.

René claps. "Well said."

"A woman with an opinion on politics." The major's tone is thoughtful, on the verge of impressed. "And what does your husband say to that?"

"I am divorced," I say without a hint of shame. "I had a brute for a husband, and so I left him."

Nobody offers a single word of criticism, although I am not sure the men know what to make of me. Still, the trip looks more promising than before. I might have found a few open-minded new friends. One pair of fine male eyes, in particular, holds admiration instead of puzzlement: the eyes of Mr. Kent, the architect.

The conversation veers to other subjects.

The men discuss the Chinese emperor's abdication and the formation of the Republic of China. The consensus is that nothing will come of it. China is too far behind the West, in any case, and too far away to ever be any trouble. The prediction is that they shall go the way of other great empires and crumble. The military men around the table are especially certain.

"I had the queerest encounter after the incident at Southampton," René tells me as our drinks are served, talking around her husband, who is seated between us. He is fully engaged in the discussion on the Orient.

I lean forward to see her better. "What happened?"

"Did you not see our near collision with the SS *New York*?"

"I boarded in Cherbourg."

"The SS *New York* broke away from the RMS *Oceanic* in front of us. Her steam wasn't up, so she couldn't turn."

"Goodness."

"Luckily, one of our tugboats, the *Vulcan*, threw a rope over and over until the crew of the *New York* caught it, and then the *Vulcan* tugged the *New York* to a safe distance from our stern. Still, our departure was delayed by an hour."

"That explains the long wait in Cherbourg."

"The mishap settles the *Hawke-Olympic* incident," her husband, Henry, puts in. "Proves that the water displaced by a ship this size can, in fact, pull a smaller ship into its wake."

"Proves that the *Olympic* is unsinkable, in any case," the major says, joining our discussion. "The

Hawke pushed eight feet into her hull and ripped a forty-foot gash below her waterline. Two compartments flooded, and still the *Olympic* pulled into harbor under her own power. Give thanks to God, ladies and gentlemen, that we are on her sister ship. Like the *Olympic*, our *Titanic* is also impossible to sink."

We all toast to that. "Hear, hear."

Then the men are back again on the topic of international affairs.

"As we pulled out of the harbor," Rene tells me, "a bizarre woman with the most horrible visage came up to me. She looked right into my eyes. *Bad omen,* she said. *If you love life, disembark at Cherbourg, as I certainly will.*"

Henry's tone is indulgent as he puts in, "Every once in a while, I must remind my dearest wife not to be overly superstitious."

"She appears to have heeded your advice." I love seeing a couple who are as obviously in love as these two are. "Otherwise, you would not be here now."

"I am more than ready to go home to New York." René shakes her head. "But that woman… Can you imagine saying such a thing to a stranger?"

April 11, 1912

The sky over Cork Harbour is overcast when we reach Queenstown in Ireland the next day, shortly before noon. Wind whips about the harbor, the chill what one would expect for April. I stand by the railing with my chin tucked into the fur collar of my coat, lured on deck by the splendid cathedral that overlooks the town.

"St. Colman's Cathedral." Edward Kent appears by my side and touches the brim of his hat in greeting. "They started building it forty-four years ago. At three hundred feet, it will be the tallest church in Ireland when it is finished."

Since he is an interesting conversationalist with something to say instead of simply commenting on the weather, I forgive him for the name Edward, the same as my former husband's. He did not choose the name, after all. I shall let it pass.

"You are an architect." I remember from his introduction at dinner. "From New York?"

"Albany."

Despite it being barely spring, his face is sunkissed. He sports the sort of jaunty mustache that some women adore but which has never been my weakness. "Did work take you abroad?"

"Pleasure. Two months shared between France and Egypt. My working days are over. As soon as I reach home, I am officially retiring." His brown eyes sparkle in the sunlight. He has an infectious, joyous energy about him. "I am ready to live."

With a trim body that hints at sport, he cuts a fine figure. He is about the same age as I am, certainly no more than a couple of years older, dressed in a stylish dark suit, every inch a gentleman. Standing next to him, I feel something I have not felt for too long, an awareness that I am a woman and he is a man.

His eyes track the two tenders that are making their way to shore. "I predict they will have to start building larger harbors to accommodate ocean liners like ours."

"It would have been nice to be able to board the ship on a ramp rather than from a boat."

Our tenders—one aptly called *America*, the other *Ireland*—let off their passengers, then lift off several large crates of mail, nearly losing one to the water as the pallet wobbles. They manage to save it in the end, then the tenders load up with new passengers next.

A gust of wind grabs on to my hat. "Oh!"

Mr. Kent catches it for me before it can hit the deck. "May I escort you below, Mrs. Candee?"

"Yes, I am refreshed enough. Thank you. I wanted to read a little anyway, before lunch."

I do not see him again at the midday meal, but at dinner, I am seated next to him, by sheer coincidence. He is already there when I am escorted to my chair. His eyes dance with mischief as he stands.

"You look like a man with a secret."

"Just heard a bit of ship gossip, Mrs. Candee." His smile is lively, conspiratorial. "We had a *deserter*. I overheard two stewards talking in the corridor outside my room. A stoker from below hid under the mail and abandoned the ship."

"My goodness." I blink at him. "Do you suppose that wobbly crate earlier wobbled because the weight was more than expected? And to think that we watched and suspected nothing."

I laugh at the outrageousness of it.

René and her husband step up to the table from behind us. "What's this about a deserter?"

I am reminded of her strange story about the baleful woman who spooked her in Southampton. Maybe the woman shared her premonitions with the stoker too and scared the poor man off. And now there he is, in Queenstown, with no pay and no references. For shame.

Hugh Woolner, the charming London investor, arrives, distracting us.

"Mrs. Candee. I trust your first day on the ship was pleasant." Woolner's unwavering gaze holds mine. "I find that the beginning of a voyage is like the beginning of a theatre play." His voice dips as he sits on my left. "Anything could happen."

Is that an innuendo? I am so surprised, I stutter. "Yes, I…love a journey."

The seats around our table fill up quickly. Drinks are served, but Mr. Kent, on my right, holds a hand over his glass. "Thank you. Not tonight."

I catch myself staring at him. Those are words I have never heard from my former husband, that other Edward, when it came to wine.

While I recover, across the table, Archibald Gracie clears his throat. "As I said, I was a colonel in the 7th New York Militia." And he launches into a summary of his recently published book, *The Truth about Chickamauga*.

My former husband was in the same regiment. I do not bring that up, however.

The gentlemen are spellbound by the talk of war. René leans back in her chair and whispers to me behind Hugh Woolner, gesturing at him, "A widower at forty. Is it not a shame?"

I struggle with a smile as I whisper back, "The shame is how shameless some people are with their matchmaking."

Oh, I am going to enjoy this voyage.

CHAPTER 15

Madison
   November 4, 2024 (Monday)

"What is it?"

The mysterious object one of Julia's assistants found in the grave has been brought into Oliver's lab. Julia has cleaned it, photographed it, and sent a small sample off-site to be examined by XRF, X-ray fluorescence.

We're looking at the enlarged image, gathered around her laptop. The artifact is a faint, unrecognizable ghost of its former self, corroded, the edges crumbling, definition worn down by time and groundwater.

Oliver points to the bottom left corner. "This used to be a round part."

Julia zooms in and then clicks around. "Let me improve the resolution." She taps on the image. "Is this a fleck of red?" A small bit of pigment that adheres to the warped metal in fragile flecks. "Looks like red enamel."

"A flattened lunch box?" Ramsey suggests. "The grave belongs to a young boy, according to the record."

"Why would he take his lunch box into the water?" Although, in the chaos... But... "Did they even have lunch boxes back then?"

Ramsey's phone pings. "XRF results are in." He pauses for effect, and to allow the cameras to focus in on him. "The object is made of *tin*."

He makes it sound like the discovery of a lifetime. As if it's a pound of pure gold, dated to the time of the pharaohs, something that will rewrite history.

Julia squints at the laptop screen. "It's a toy."

I look closer too. "Here's another round bit. Wheels?"

"Tin toys were popular in 1912, including toy cars," Julia says.

She opens a new window on her laptop and shows us half a dozen examples.

"According to the record, nothing was found with the victim but the clothes he was wearing." Ramsey isn't ready to jump onboard with our hypothesis.

"Someone who handled the little body might have been a parent." Eleanor turns to him. "He might have seen his own boy in the victim and slipped that toy into the coffin."

We share a moment of silence, interrupted when Ramsey's phone pings again.

He ceremoniously checks. "Another text from the XRF."

"Cut!" Maya calls from the corner. "Let's end on a moment of suspense."

That little boy haunts my dreams. I keep waking up. (The additional XRF identified resin and red pigment, confirming that the object, which we now all believe to be a red toy car, was painted with enamel.) I think about the brevity of life, about Eleanor, then about my own life too, of course. *She achieved tenure.* Is that what I want on my gravestone?

My work is important. Of course, it is. I teach students, and I help the police. I've made a difference in the lives of dozens of families. Yet I have more inside, long-held dreams bubbling up from the depths of me.

My phone screen shows three a.m. by the time it dawns on me that it's not all or nothing. Few things are black and white. I can keep doing what I've been doing *and* I can also paint.

I want to make art that's more than filling in the blanks, more than merely expanding on measurements and bone structure that already exist. I want to paint what's at the heart of me.

I slip out of bed and stumble down the dark hallway, across the empty lobby. Wind throws rain against the glass, turning the night spooky. Stray leaves cling to the window, staring at me from outside. The guard must be walking his rounds. He's nowhere to be seen.

He's escaped being blamed for the theft of the gold ring and the silver coins. After Eleanor talked to her son, Ramsey admitted on camera that he misplaced the items, calling the incident *much ado about nothing*.

The cavernous place makes me feel as if I'm alone in the middle of the night, on a giant, abandoned ship. A cold shiver runs up my spine. *The last person left on the* Titanic.

I am at the crossroads.

No, that's too dramatic. Aren't we all at the crossroads, in one way or the other, always? Every single day, a new choice could be made, a choice that would affect the rest of our lives. For the better, or…

I could easily turn the wrong way and hit an iceberg.

What if I sink?

I could let go of safety, the university job, and jump, just to miss my aim. I could end up with nothing.

But here is another truth: the greater tragedy might be to never gather enough courage to leap.

In my studio, I squeeze paint onto the palette. And I speak my intention to the universe out loud, putting on notice whatever gods and spirits can hear me. "I am ready."

I stand there. No divine whisper fills my ear. No muse pops in to visit.

Right away, I face the first, not insignificant, problem. The things I want to paint cannot be painted. How does one paint infinity?

I close my eyes, and I wait until I'm on the ship in the middle of the ocean, under the limitless sky. I am on the top deck, all alone. I marvel at the endless water around me—above me, the stars. *There.* Infinity it is.

I paint what I see.

It's nothing, and it's everything.

"I don't see a big market for my art." My giant canvas of dark whirls and smattering dots of light is a disappointment at first glance in the morning. "Who would want this?"

"Do you want it?" Oliver asks without looking at me. He's standing directly in front of the painting, with his hands in his pockets. "What if I pulled out a wad of hundred-dollar bills right now and said *I'll pay you ten thousand dollars.* Would you let me walk out with it?"

"No." I don't have to think about my response. It hits me at a visceral level that this piece of art is mine, a gift from me to myself.

"Good."

"Yeah. A great way to make a living."

"It's a great way to make art."

"Artists sell what they paint."

"Not everything."

"Easy for you to say. You're sticking to a field that actually pays."

"People who look for solutions, find solutions;

people who look for excuses find excuses." He watches me. "You think I am a forensic scientist?"

Of course…

"You're a gardener." The truth hits me. "And a philosopher."

"A gardener who likes to philosophize." He says this so modestly, as if people like him are a dime a dozen. "Go for what you want, always. If you can go for it with all your life, great. But if you can't do that, at least go for it with all your heart. If your passion won't pay the bills, then do something that does, but pursue your passion as the most important part of your day." Intensity flares in his eyes, not monk-like at all. "You're not going to box up the fire inside you and toss it away. Please, promise me that."

I want to kiss him more than I've ever wanted to kiss a man.

CHAPTER 16

Helen

April 12, 1912 (Friday)

Our first morning at sea, I step onto the Sundeck, and who do I run into but Edward Kent. His tailored navy wool suit is pinstriped, the single-breasted jacket matching his waistcoat. I do appreciate a man who is mindful of his appearance.

Could our many meetings in such a short time be a coincidence? Was he waiting for me, perhaps? As I enjoy his company, I do not protest.

"Mrs. Candee." His smile is brighter than the crystal chandeliers of the first-class salon. "Would you be interested in a stroll?"

"Thank you, Mr. Kent."

We walk by the railing. Land has slipped out of

view overnight. The sea is the color of the sky. We are in a bubble of mist, but far from alone. Couples, children, staff, and dogs ebb and flow around us like the tide.

"Penny for your thoughts?"

"In Cherbourg, the ship dwarfed the harbor. Now we are but a speck on a vast ocean. Everything is a matter of point of view…" I clear my throat. My former husband, the other Edward, used to mock me if ever I turned philosophical or brought up anything I read or, at the end, shared any independent thoughts at all.

Edward Kent simply says, "Very much so."

He is such easy company. I relax and look out over the water. "Calm seas today."

"I spoke to Captain Edward Smith earlier. He expects conditions to stay this way. Everyone predicts a smooth journey." He takes in the vastness of our universe. *"My soul is full of longing for the secret of the sea, and the heart of the great ocean sends a thrilling pulse through me."*

"Henry Wadsworth Longfellow," I say without thinking, then wince. Edward Candee hated it when I acted as a know-it-all.

Yet Edward Kent's eyes light up. "Ah, you are a connoisseur of poetry, madam. Well done."

"Poetry is nearer to truth than history."

"Plato." He laughs. "What a treasure you are, Helen. May I call you Helen?"

"You may, Mr. Kent."

"Please, call me Edward."

"Edward." It should be awkward, but it isn't. Edward Kent is nothing like my former husband. Not for a second could I confuse the two men with each other.

We walk all the way to the front, and I am mesmerized by the way the sharp bow cuts the waves. I have crossed the Atlantic both with my parents and as a young wife many times before, sailed on many ships. The *Titanic* outpaces them all. The water rushes by at such a speed… "I did not realize how fast we were going."

"Twenty-two knots. The captain is determined to make up for the small delays that occurred at our departure."

I clasp a hand over my hat, probably ruining a feather or two. I shall have to add an extra hatpin next time, or rethink the wide-brim hats I prefer. On deck, the wind is ever present. With my other hand, I draw my coat closer around me and hide in the safety of my ermine collar. "At least we are high up enough so the salt spray cannot reach us. How cold do you think the water is?"

"Forty degrees at the most. This *is* the North Atlantic. Wouldn't be surprised if overnight the temperature dropped into the twenties."

"Should we be worried about ice?"

"This might be the *Titanic*'s maiden voyage, but it's hardly Captain Smith's. He has forty years of experience at sea. Even without him, but especially with him, you may take my word for it"—Mr. Kent fondly pats the railing—"unsinkable, she is."

"Everybody keeps saying that."

He opens his mouth, then hesitates.

"But?" He cannot possibly harbor any doubts, can he? He just pronounced her unsinkable.

"As an architect, well, the builder of any structure is loath to give guarantees. There are always unforeseen circumstances. One can dig a foundation down to thirty feet, build the strongest building possible, then find out that at thirty-one feet lurks the loose sand of a sinkhole. Four years ago, I saw a three-story building disappear like that." He snaps his fingers.

"Good thing we are on water then, and not on sand."

He turns from the ocean and takes in the length of our enormous ship. "Puts in mind a book I read five or six years ago. It's the darndest thing. Let me think." He raps his fingers on the side of his hat. "*Futility*! That's it."

"Was that the name of the ship?"

"The title of the book. Oddly, the name of the ship was *Titan*. And just like our *Titanic* too. Seventy thousand tons, around eight hundred feet long, carrying three thousand people."

"How many people are on the *Titanic*?"

"Two thousand two hundred and twenty-seven." He smiles. "See? Nearly twins in everything."

"Maybe someone at the White Star Line read the book about the *Titan* and named our ship after her."

"I should hardly think so. In the novel, the *Titan* sinks."

The northern wind finds its way under my scarf and touches my neck with an icy finger.

"Shall we continue walking?" Edward notices that I am shivering, and he offers me his arm. "Movement will warm us up."

"Yes, please. Let us discover our floating palace."

On the Boat Deck, the uppermost deck of the ship, we pause by one of our two cutters, just behind the Bridge. The smaller emergency boats are swung out, one on each side, so they can be lowered faster in case anyone falls overboard.

"We have two of these with a capacity for forty people each, then fourteen clinker-built wooden boats that can each carry sixty-five men." Edward gestures at the three nearest ones, all lined up, sitting on their wooden chocks. "We also have four canvas-and-cork collapsibles that will each take almost fifty souls, according to Captain Smith. The problem with the *Titan* was that she did not have enough lifeboats. A ship such as ours would not make the same mistake. It is the greatest ship ever built."

April 14, 1912

Edward waits for me on Sunday too, at the top of the stairs. "Good morning, Helen."

"Good morning, Edward."

As soon as I reach him, he offers me his arm.

After a short walk, we find our way outside.

A child's squeal draws our attention to the Steerage Deck below, where a young mother is taking the air with her children. She is tall and sturdy, wrapped in brown wool, her blonde hair whipping in the wind. Her chin is up, her eyes look straight into the future, as if she is challenging fate. She is as wild and free as a goddess out of a Norse myth.

"The mother has the bearing of a Viking, does she not?" Edward's mind runs along the same thoughts as mine.

I watch the children swarm around the woman. "The sea air is rousing a ferociousness in the little ones."

"A family ready for a new life in a new land."

Edward's words make me think. I am simply on my way home from a European research trip, but the immigrants in third class travel under different circumstances. They have left behind everyone and everything they knew, all they had. They are facing the unknown with nothing but their trust in God and their own abilities to build a better life for themselves on the other side of the ocean.

"What courage she has." I wish them all the best.

"How do you feel about seeing the rest of the ship? The parts we missed yesterday."

"By all means. We shall have plenty of time to sun ourselves on deck chairs after we are retired."

"Retire, yes. Retiring to a chair, no. I aim to drink life's cup to its empty bottom, my dear Helen." His brown eyes smile with an invitation that says he'd very much prefer not to drink that cup alone.

The wind is cold, so other than us, only a few wool-coated gentlemen brave the elements, escorting their ladies wrapped in sables.

"Shall we try the Hurricane Deck?" Edward offers.

Everyone has the same idea this morning, however, so we find the Hurricane Deck—a partially enclosed promenade on the A Deck—crowded. A number of new acquaintances wave at us. If we stay, we shall be drawn into conversation. I would rather spend a few more minutes just the two of us. "Have you tried the gymnasium yet?"

"I have only seen it in passing."

We climb the stairs to the Boat Deck, then make our way to starboard.

"Welcome, madam. Sir." The young gymnast in charge of the place, dressed in all-white flannel, ushers us in. "Allow me to introduce you to our equipment. As you know, purposeful movement is the key to health. A nice ride for the lady on the stationary bicycle?"

The eager little gymnast leads the way. He is so earnest, so full of goodwill, as if our health is of the utmost importance to him. This might be his first job on an ocean liner. He must feel lucky indeed to be working on the *Titanic*.

"What is that?" I am distracted by a bulky contraption to my left.

He immediately switches course. "Our electrical camel. Another popular choice, ma'am."

"Perhaps I should start with something more

familiar." I step up to the mechanical horse. "This one, please?"

He gallantly helps me up into the stirrups.

"The punching bag, sir?" the boy offers next to Edward.

"Thank you, my good lad, but I shall row."

The rowing machine is the nearest piece of equipment to my horse.

The gymnast is a wonderful assistant and explains how everything works, and then off we go on our unlikely adventure, Edward rowing in the middle of the ocean, while next to him, I am riding a horse. Only on the *Titanic*.

"The White Star Line certainly did not miss a trick, did they?" I laugh, holding on to the reins. "What will they think of next?"

The exercise is an unexpected delight, especially when Edward challenges me to a race. I am breathless by the time we finish, neither of us able to determine who secured the win.

I shall have to return again, but without Edward. This demonstration aside, there are separate hours set for ladies and gentlemen.

Next, we discover the F Deck. The temperature dropped a good ten degrees while we were inside the gymnasium. Most of the crowd has cleared. We pass by the pool, which is reserved for the ladies in the morning. Afternoon hours are for the gentlemen.

When the wind picks up, we ensconce ourselves in the salon in a pair of velvet armchairs by the heartwarming fire, sitting in companionable silence. Anyone observing could easily think we are a married couple. When Edward smiles at me, the light of the fire dances in his eyes.

I could sit here like this forever.

We only separate when his friends find him and demand his presence at a poker table somewhere. Edward Kent, Edward Colley, Mauritz Steffansson, James Smith, Hugh Woolner, and Colonel Gracie formed a coterie shortly after boarding. They joke that I am an honorary member, but I do not go with them.

I chat with René Harris about New York and the theatre, and find out that she is as much of a theatre director as her husband. How wonderful it is to make friends with an intelligent, intellectually curious, successful woman.

Then, when René leaves, I am drawn into the company of two ladies who bustle into the salon to escape the cold: Margaret Brown and Emma Eliza Bucknell. We even end up lunching together at the Café Parisien on the B Deck.

The row of windows on the starboard side fills the space with light, white trellis covering every available wall space, including the ceiling.

"I'm told the designer meant to recreate a Paris café," Mrs. Brown shares, "and by George, he got it right."

We sit in wicker chairs at wicker tables, the café being less formal than the main dining room, although, the waiter tells us, the menu is the same.

I order roast duckling, and then for dessert, the vanilla éclairs.

"Certainly, madam."

Once he is off to carry our orders to the kitchen, Margaret Brown fixes her gaze on me. "I keep seeing you in the company of Mr. Kent. He is a rather pleasant gentleman."

"He is." Alas, my thoughts about him are too jumbled to be publicly shared, so I change the subject. "Will the Astors not miss you at lunch?" She has spent most of her time in their company so far.

"Madeleine is feeling under the weather. They are having lunch delivered to their quarters."

"I hope she soon recovers." In her delicate condition, she deserves some rest.

"Now, as far as the rest of their circle is concerned, I prefer not to spend my time with them," Margaret adds. "They offer their false smiles when I am with Jack and Madeleine, but those same socialites turn a cold shoulder when I walk into a room alone."

"Whatever for?"

"I am as wealthy as they are, but, you see, my late husband didn't inherit his wealth. He made it in gold mines. As for my own pedigree, I am the daughter of Irish immigrants, born in Missouri. And for that colossal mistake, I shall never be forgiven. I used to be a shop girl, working in the carpets and draperies department." She laughs.

"Mrs. Bucknell does not seem bothered."

"Oh, but I am the daughter of a reverend. I was

born in India. I exonerated myself by marrying a Bucknell, but as I am his third wife, it still counts as a scandal."

I have been buried so deep in my book research, have spent so many weeks at remote locations, I have nearly forgotten what high society is like. I suppose since certain ladies have no other occupation, they have plenty of energy for enforcing the social order. What a waste of everyone's time.

"I heard you were in Egypt." I address Margaret again.

"Yes, the land of the pharaohs. Alas, my little grandson is sick, so I am hurrying home."

I tell her about my Harry's accident, then we talk more about the vagaries of high society, then husbands, then our experiences on the ship so far, and I tell them about the gymnasium and the mechanical camel. They immediately want to see all those marvels, so after lunch, I walk there with them.

The little gymnast is as eager as before, wanting nothing more than to see us entertained. His hair is tinged with red, twin dimples in his cheeks. He is impossible not to like. I predict a great career for him with the White Star Line.

Once we separate, I peek into the reading and writing room and find half a dozen ladies inside. The pink silk curtained windows look out to the Promenade Deck. The sun drenches the room in light. I need to catch up on correspondence with family and friends, so I pick myself a free desk.

Only after completing seven full letters do I

return to my quarters for a well-deserved nap. The bugle wakes me at six, our warning that it is time to dress for dinner. *Let me see, which gown. Yes. The flattering black velvet.*

The bugler plays again at seven to signal that the dining room is open. Nothing is left to chance, but I still manage to be late, due to too much woolgathering, thinking about Edward Kent as I dress. Yet I am not the last one at our table.

"I see the Harrises aren't here yet."

Hugh Woolner beats Edward to pulling my chair out for me. "I am afraid there has been an accident with Mrs. Harris."

"René? Oh no." We have only just met, but I already think of her as a friend. Friendships happen faster on shared adventures, in a closed environment.

"It only just transpired," Edward tells me. "As you know, we gentlemen played some poker today. The game stretched into the afternoon." Guilt sits on his face. He obviously feels terrible about having been involved. "In Mr. Cardeza's room on the B Deck…"

Mr. Thomas Cardeza is the grandson of one of the founders of the Fidelity Trust Company. We were introduced yesterday. He is onboard with his mother, who, as unlikely as it is, is rumored to be a big game hunter in Africa.

I wish very much to meet Mrs. Cardeza, but this is not the right time to beg for an introduction. "What happened?"

"Henry was at the game, and he asked René to sit

in. We were trying to keep out a cardsharp, you see, and wanted all the seats taken. When the bugle sounded, we all hurried to our staterooms, and René slipped on the stairs."

The moment everyone finishes dinner, I stand. "If you will excuse me, I would like to visit Mrs. Harris."

Edward insists on escorting me, of course. He offers me his arm and I accept. He is extra careful with me on the steps. On the short walk, he shows me in a dozen different ways that he cares. The stirrings of a new beginning flutter behind my breastbone.

Dare I trust my heart to such fragile hope?

I shall have to consider it later. René comes first.

The Harrises' stateroom is C83. As soon as Henry invites us in, I rush to my friend's side. "What happened?"

She is propped up in bed, her dinner tray next to her, her arm in a thick bandage, held on a pillow on the top of her blanket.

She glances away, embarrassed. "I slipped on a grease spot."

Wrath throws dark sparks in Henry's eyes that suggest he might challenge the whole staff to a duel. "Someone dropped a tea cake, and it was poorly wiped up. I have already talked to the head steward. He apologized and sent in cleaners, but obviously too late."

"Is it broken?"

René winces as she shifts. "I'm afraid so. Could have been worse. I fell only half a dozen steps. If I fell from the top of the stairs, I would have broken my neck."

She seems the type of person who always looks on the bright side of life. I would be more upset.

Her husband shakes his head as if to shake off the image his wife's words conjured. "Do not say that, dearest."

I take René's good hand. "Are you in a great deal of pain? How do you feel?"

"Almost relaxed."

Not what I expected. "How so?"

"This is it, the arm, you understand? The accident. The bad omen that strange woman warned me about in Southampton harbor has been hanging over my head all this time, and now my bad luck has happened. It is over. I can draw an easy breath. Nothing but smooth sailing ahead. I can enjoy the rest of the voyage."

"That is one way to look at it. I am not certain I would suffer as stoically as that."

"Nonsense. You would not fret like a child. I have no doubt you are of sturdier stock. And I shall not fall into weeping either. Tell me about dinner. I want to know what everyone wore and everything that was said."

I do my best to entertain her, but Edward and I only stay for an hour and then leave her to rest.

"Ready to retire?" The way Edward's eyes bore into mine while he awaits my response makes it clear that he very much wishes to hear *no*.

"I find myself rather restless. I am so disappointed for René. She was eager to enjoy all the ship has to offer."

"Then let us enjoy the entertainment on her behalf, so you can at least tell her about all the marvels later. We could listen to the lounge band." His smile is flirtatious, but then he grows hesitant. "Unless you think we should be careful spending so much time together. I would not wish to subject you to any gossip."

He is a true gentleman to worry about my reputation.

I accept the arm he gallantly offers. "Let wagging tongues wag."

Edward's friends, Edward Colley, Mauritz Steffanson, James Smith, Hugh Woolner, and Colonel Gracie, wave us over as soon as we walk into the lounge. They secured extra seats. We give them an update on René, chatting until the musicians start, with Wagner.

After the first piece, the audience is invited to suggest their favorites, and the band obliges each.

"May we have Dvořák?" Edward shouts his request.

Later, I ask for Puccini.

We are tremendously entertained, happy and carefree, even if my mind does frequently turn to my injured friend.

"I hope, since René's injury is limited to her arm and she is able to walk, she will be able to enjoy at least some of the rest of the voyage," I tell Edward while the staff serve coffee.

The band plays on until late, but even then, our coterie is loath to leave. Edward Colley returns to his cabin to sleep, but the rest of us, Mauritz, James, Hugh, Colonel Gracie, and Edward Kent, move to the restaurant one level up.

Only one other table is occupied, by the boisterous party of Major Archibald Butt, President Taft's military aide. He and his friends are having a grand old time, judging by their raised voices and ruddy cheeks. Glasses clink with toast after toast. They certainly aren't feeling the arctic chill that has me drawing my scarf more tightly around me.

"I should have brought the cashmere one instead of the sateen."

"Waiter!" Edward calls as he pulls my chair out for me. "The lady will have a scotch with lemon to warm her up," he tells the server, who appears as quickly as if he were hiding behind a column. "And the same for me."

I mean to stay for one drink, but a few minutes turn into more. We discuss politics, then literature, then art, then a famous New York actor's latest shenanigans. Our laughter fills the restaurant, competing with Major Archibald Butt's entourage. I would dearly love to stay for more, but it *is* late, and it *is* cold, even with the scotch.

"I truly must retire," I tell the men.

"I wish you would stay, my dear Mrs. Candee, but if you must leave us…" Colonel Gracie carries his gaze around the table. "For the rest of us, may I suggest a cigar and another game of cards in the smoking room?"

"Allow me first to escort the lady to her cabin." Edward never for a moment ceases to be a gentleman.

The deck is nearly deserted at this late hour.

"Look." He points up. "The North Star."

I stop and follow the line of his arm with my eyes. He is but an inch from my back, blocking the wind, radiating warmth. "How do you know?"

"It stands above the north celestial pole. Keep looking. While the stars appear to move across the sky, the North Star stands in place, because the celestial pole is in line with the Earth's rotational axis."

"I see." Even with him so close, it is too cold to be standing still. I shiver.

"Colley will be thirty-seven years old tomorrow," he tells me as we resume walking. "Should we do something for his birthday?" he asks, as if I am his partner, as if we are a team.

"Let me talk to my steward. I am sure a cake could be arranged."

"What would you like to see tomorrow?"

We hash over our options, chatting all the way to my cabin, where he claims my hand. "Helen. My dearest Helen, I—"

A reckless thought races through me. *Should I invite him in?* No, there will be time. We have all the time in the world, so we only kiss. And then we kiss again.

He never lets go of my hand. "My feelings for

you… I know it is too soon, but I wish to ask you something."

He is entirely too serious, as if he just made a momentous decision, and I am suddenly filled with apprehension. "I am quite up to my ears in assignments. My son has been in an accident. I want to be honest with you, Edward. I am not entirely certain I have time for *feelings*."

"Saying that one does not have time for love is like saying one does not have time for air."

Love.

Too soon, indeed. Too fast. And yet, Edward Kent has wormed himself into my heart. Neither of us is young. If we found something here, we would be fools to waste any more of our lives without each other. "Ask me after breakfast?"

"As you wish, Helen." He kisses my hand, his lips lingering on my knuckles. When he straightens again, his eyes hold the world. "I will see you in the morning, my dear."

I nearly change my mind again and ask whether he wishes to stay the night with me, oh, scandal of scandals. An urgency drums through me, silly, really; tonight is not our only chance. Long nights stretch before us under the arctic skies, and I am not a blushing maiden, after all. I am a grown woman. A *divorced* woman. Yet I don't invite him in. I want it all: the stolen kisses, the agonizing wait, the whole courtship. "See you in the morning."

I retire to bed thinking about the man, his intelligence, his warmth, his gentleness, and his impeccable manners. Lord knows I was not looking for a shipboard romance, but then the Lord brought me Edward.

My heart drums a poem of a single word, repeated. A word that holds every possibility in the world, and yet it is a word most precarious.

Tomorrow. Tomorrow. Tomorrow.

I feel twenty again. Tomorrow, Edward Kent will ask me something, and I cannot wait.

CHAPTER 17

Madison

    November 8, 2024 (Friday)

By the end of the first week of November, all the remains from the forty-four graves are safely ensconced in Oliver's lab. Carefully marked boxes—each a sealed secret—are stacked on every surface. They hide the stainless-steel tabletops that no longer reflect the bright fluorescent light overhead.

I borrow a new box, scan it, then return it. Computer imaging comes first. Sometimes I miss the Manchester method, the tissue-marker straw and the careful recreation of the eleven major muscles of the face, but I also appreciate efficiency.

"Let the bones speak their truth," I incant my motto out loud into the empty space. It's not so much the art part of being a forensic artist, but that uncovering-the-truth part that has always been my main motivation for all the projects I've undertaken in the past, and it's no different with this assignment.

I've been working late every day, in part because the story of the *Titanic* is drawing me in more and more each day, and in part because I want to stay away from Oliver. Entering into a relationship with a coworker on a project as high-profile as this one is inadvisable. I even drag the large canvases over to my studio at one point.

In the end, work distracts me a little too much. One evening, as I brush my teeth and look into the mirror, my old university sweatshirt catches my eye. The once bold red lettering has faded into a ghostly pink on the washed heather-gray background.

"Dammit."

I've forgotten to respond to the dean's offer. How is that even possible? That job has been the most important thing in my life for the past decade.

It's nine p.m., too late to call, so I send an email. The dean can read it when he saunters into his office in the morning.

Thank you for the offer, but I am not able to return to my previous position at the university. I've decided to explore other opportunities and take my career in a different direction.

I should say life, but he wouldn't understand that. *Life* and *career* are synonymous to him, same as for my father.

Relief dances through me, but anxiety is stomping close on relief's heel. I'm trading safety and stability for a dream I can barely make out as it shifts and floats like fog on the water.

After I close my laptop, I pick up Helen Candee's notes and read the next twenty or so pages. The impending sense of doom is seeping in among the lines, like seawater between the boards of an old ship's hull.

When I can no longer stand the suspense, I look up the *Titanic*'s voyage on my phone. After Ramsey's multiple presentations on the subject, I know a lot of what happened, but I can't remember every detail. I want to check the dates.

The Atlantic swallowed the great ocean liner on the night of April 14th.

I turn out the light—my eyes are too bleary to read more, and too teary too, now that I know Helen will not see Edward Kent for breakfast.

Tomorrow. Tomorrow. Tomorrow. The word echoes through my brain, bounces inside my skull.

None of our tomorrows are guaranteed.

That thought has me turning on the light and leaving my bed. At home, I don't normally meander around the house after midnight, I'm pretty attached to my sleep, but TTP has made me nocturnal.

The strip of light is on under Oliver's door. I knock.

"Everything all right?" He puts down his book. "Do you need help with anything?"

"Thank you for telling me to paint."

"My pleasure."

I step inside, nerves tingling through me. "I'd like to kiss you."

The Dalai Lama has never been more serene. "This is unexpected."

My face flushes. What am I doing? I step back. "I'm so sorry. Could we forget about this?"

He rises and steps after me, moving with a supple grace. "Unlikely."

My choices are to run or stay. I don't know which one is more embarrassing. I don't want to run.

Oliver takes another step, then another. "I was waiting to ask you out until the project was over. I didn't want to make you uncomfortable at work if you weren't interested."

I'm standing on the threshold of his room, on solid ground, but I feel as if I'm falling.

He leans in.

And then he kisses me.

It's the kind of kiss I normally don't allow myself, the kind that doesn't consider project schedule or career plan, doesn't hold back half, so if this doesn't work out, all of me won't be broken.

In seconds, we go from tentative to all-consuming.

"Would you like to stay?" His voice is raspy.

"Not tonight."

He releases me immediately. "Any time." A smile plays on his lips. "Please, do visit."

"Good night." I manage to step back out into the hallway.

"Good night."

I close the door behind me, then I plod over to my studio, electricity sparking across my skin. I could have asked him to come with me, but with Oliver present, I might not see what I need to see in the canvas, and I want to do this.

In front of me, still invisible, awaits a path I want to take. I lean the second large canvas against the wall.

The empty whiteness is intimidating, the mocking challenge of a milky-eyed blind god. *What do you want?*

CHAPTER 18

Helen

 April 14, 1912

I float on the warm sea of a pleasant dream, where I am in Edward's arms. A tender smile blooms on his handsome face. *Oh, Edward—*

A metallic groan yanks me back to reality.

It is the middle of the night. Under me, around me, the ship is trembling, then the noise and the shaking stop, over with so quickly that I question if I merely dreamt both. I stay in bed, trying to sort dream from reality.

Outside, in the hallway, doors open one after the other.

"What is it?" The same question is asked in various male voices.

"All is well, aye." I recognize the Scottish brogue

of one of the stewards. "We shall be moving again in a minute."

Only then do I realize the silence in the background. The engines' rumble is missing. The ever-present background noise of our journey that lulled me to sleep earlier is absent. Tension tightens my chest. *What happened?*

I flip the switch, and light floods the room, a good sign. As long as we have electricity, nothing can be seriously wrong with our systems, can it?

The clock tells me I have been asleep for only an hour. It seemed so much more. I dreamt a whole other life that—

"If you please, gentlemen, I must ask you to return to your cabins." The steward again, outside. "The captain will send word in a minute."

He answers every question thrown at him, reassures every inquiring passenger with utmost patience. *Nothing to worry about*, is his message to all, but I push off my covers and slip my dress over my head. I fumble with the endless row of buttons, while the steward's voice fades as he moves farther down the hallway.

About to step out the door, I glance in the mirror. *Oh Lord,* m*y hair.* I coil the braid at my nape and pin it in place. *Good enough.* I am not heading to a beauty contest.

Outside my door, in the hallway, a handful of male passengers are milling around, some in their pajamas, some still in their evening clothes. None appear worried in particular. A few grumble at the disturbance, yawning behind their hands.

The steward is gone, and I do not know any of the men well enough to quiz them in the middle of the night. I wish I were next door to Edward. Then again, it hasn't been that long since I've seen him. He is probably still in the smoking room, playing poker.

I could use his reassurance.

I step back inside my room. *Boots, coat, hat.* Then I am ready for the cold.

We run into each other on the A Deck.

"I was coming to see you. I worried that you might have been startled out of sleep," he calls out as soon as he spots me. "All is well."

His quiet confidence is contagious. The tension eases in my chest and shoulders. "Do you know why we stopped?"

"A minor problem down below." He takes my hands. "We spoke to one of the quartermasters. He was certain that we have nothing to be alarmed about. One of the engines might have temporarily overheated."

A couple of gentlemen walk by, probably on their way to reassure their wives. They tip their hats as they pass. I should follow them back down and return to my cabin.

Edward offers his arm. "How about a turn on deck to calm your nerves? We could walk close to the wall and keep out of the wind."

Truth is, as much as I need sleep, I'd rather stay with him.

"Without enough rest, I shall be exceedingly miserable in the morning. If I stay out now, you'd best avoid me tomorrow," I tease him.

"Remember, you promised to have breakfast with me. I am afraid I am going to have to hold you to that promise, Helen. I cannot imagine any mood that would prevent me from seeking your company."

We walk through the Hurricane Deck, then end up on the Boat Deck, passing by the exercise room again. The door is closed, the little gymnast no longer on duty. Other than us, only a handful of gentlemen meander the deck. Most of the passengers have gone back to sleep.

The giant funnel rattles next to us, steam shooting from its mouth with a deafening roar that makes me jump. Then a second chimney starts up, mercifully farther from us. Then the third spews a swirling white cloud upward.

I have to shout to be heard. "They haven't blown this violently before!"

"When the engines stop, the men in the furnace room must let off the steam as a precaution, to prevent an explosion. Look." Edward leads me away, pointing toward the bow of the ship. "No smoke at all from the fourth chimney." He smiles. "The fourth one is merely for decoration, added for symmetry's sake."

His calm demeanor steadies me. If he is talking ship minutiae, we must not be in dire straits. He is right. The engineers are merely letting off steam. A perfectly valid explanation exists for everything that is happening. Precautionary measures are being taken. All is well with our magnificent *Titanic*.

And yet… I shift my weight to my left foot, then the right, then back. "Is the ship listing starboard, or am I mistaken?"

The slight list scares me less than Edward's expression, which turns serious by degrees. The ever-present lightness in his brown eyes vanishes. His gentle humor is so much a part of him that without it, I scarcely recognize him.

"Helen." He draws me toward the steps. "We must go." He leads me down the steps to the A Deck below.

In that short a time, the ship is listing noticeably more. We stop a dozen feet from the stairs. Edward's eyes hold a grim resignation. He takes both my hands. For a long moment, he says nothing, then quietly, "I don't mind going."

I almost ask where, then… "You cannot possibly mean…" He does. *God save us.* "My children need me."

I very much mind going. And how are we talking about *that* now, when a minute ago we were at *All is well*? A violent shiver runs through me.

"Best warm up inside." Edward launches into action again and steers me to the smoking room.

"Ladies are not allowed." Has he forgotten?

"Never mind that now. There is a fire in the grate."

I have heard mention of it before. The smoking

room has the only true fireplace on the ship, the others being electric.

He ushers me through the door without hesitation, and his breaking of convention alarms me. It tells me we are no longer operating under ordinary rules. We are in an emergency.

After midnight, the smoking lounge is deserted, although the gentlemen's cigar smoke still hangs in the air.

I follow Edward to the fire. "What is happening? Do you truly think we are in serious trouble?"

He rubs my hands between his, draws a long breath, carefully planning his next words, but before he can speak, a young man bursts in with a snowball in his hands. "We struck ice!"

The boy is so carefree, so thrilled, that my momentary dread vanishes. "Just ice?" He hands me the snowball, and I smile at him—nearly laugh—then I smile at Edward. "Captain Smith said, more than once, that ice cannot sink our great ship."

All is well, indeed. The snowball in my hand is melting already, from the heat of the fireplace.

Buoyed by the good news, we follow the young man outside with lighter hearts. We are safe from a fate too dark to contemplate. More people are out on deck now. I suppose, like me, they have given up on trying to fall back asleep. Like me, they searched for reassurance, and now they have received it.

"Ice." One claps, celebrating.

"I hoped we'd see an iceberg." His friend cranes

his neck, although the dark night reveals nothing but water. "An iceberg with a polar bear."

Behind them, Colonel Gracie is lost in deep conversation with one of his friends.

"Colonel!" Edward calls to him. If anyone has the latest information, it will be Gracie.

We cut through the throng toward him, but then Edward draws up short, and I do too the next second, both of us noticing the same thing, both of us looking at our feet.

"The ship's list has grown rather steep while we were warming our hands." I am the one to say it.

Metal grinds above our heads and cuts off Edward's response. We look up, but we cannot see the A Deck from where we are standing.

"What is it?" The only explanation I can think of is unimaginable. "They are not preparing the lifeboats, are they?"

"Only one way to know."

Abandoning our quest to reach the Colonel who has walked farther away from us in the meantime, we return to the stairs.

We climb back to the Boat Deck, where a few more curious passengers roam the night now. On the port side, a group of burly crewmen are uncovering a boat. I can see Captain Smith on the Bridge, behind the glass.

"Should we talk to the captain?"

"Leave him to his work." Edward looks lost, looking from boat to boat as if counting them.

One of the quartermasters hurries by. "You'd better fetch your life vests." Then he is gone.

Edward tugs at my elbow. "The man is right. Come, my dear Helen."

On our way back down, we meet a dozen first-class passengers on their way up. Some are people we saw below minutes ago, but in the short time that passed, they all have miraculously procured life preservers.

An older man escorting his sleepy and protesting wife looks at us and pats the middle of his chest. "Captain's orders."

We push past them and go all the way to the B Deck, where Edward has his cabin, number fifty-eight. He gives me his own life vest, then steps across the hallway to a cabin with its door wide open.

The occupants have already fled. He grabs a life vest left behind on the small rug of the entry and drags the life preserver over his head.

"Do you suppose we might end up in the water?" The prospect is unimaginable.

"Let us hope not, but we must obey the captain."

While I fumble with the straps, he snatches up the rug and wraps it around my shoulders. "For added protection from the cold."

How long does he think we'll be forced to spend out of doors?

I have no chance to ask. Metal screeches above, then more screeching from farther away, then farther away yet. All the lifeboats that have been still swung out are being brought in and readied for boarding.

We rush back up to the Boat Deck, to the port side, where several boats are now uncovered and level with the deck.

Next to the boat closest to the Bridge, Captain Smith is talking to a dozen officers.

"Are they leaving the ship?" I grab Edward's arm. "Are they leaving us?"

"They are taking their orders."

There are crew members all over the deck. Shortly, however, most of them are sent below.

"First-class passengers only." The captain waves people forward, his every movement determined. "Ladies first." Then he returns to the Bridge, leaving the boats to the officers.

"A precaution only," a husband tells his wife behind us. "Merely out of an abundance of caution, my dear."

Yet I wonder.

The crew members the captain ordered below pass by us without meeting our eyes. Every expression bleak. They have the look of men who think we *are* sinking, and they have just been told to walk away from the lifeboats. Every mouth is grim.

"Gentlemen, please assist the women and children into the boats," one of the quartermasters orders, and when one man swings his own leg over, the quartermaster holds him off. "No men allowed."

The women, who until now thought the proceedings a drill, are silenced by disbelief. Then, as they step up one by one, the sudden prospect of having to climb in and dangle over the side, the long drop to that cold water, the idea of being separated from husbands and sons proves too much. A cry of protest goes up.

I spot René Harris pleading with one of the officers. "My arm is broken. I must have my husband with me. You must understand."

"No men allowed, madam."

An older lady tries next, holding a young man of twenty by the elbow. "Please, I must have my son."

"Women and children first." The officer is adamant.

The son hugs his mother. "As soon as they fix the problem, they shall bring you back up, Mother. We will not be long separated."

I do not know why I start counting the people as they go over the side, perhaps to soothe the building panic in my stomach. *One, two, three…* Twenty-seven women are lowered in that first boat that leaves the Boat Deck on the port side, lifeboat eight. The group includes my friend Emma Eliza Bucknell. When I catch her eye, I give her an encouraging wave and a smile.

They barely disappear from sight when a cry rings out. "A ship!"

An excited buzz spreads on deck, then a hushed silence. We are all praying. Within minutes, a loud boom rends the night like cannon fire, and the sky lights up above us. The captain must have ordered flares launched.

"There are multiple ships nearby," a passing

steward tells us. "The radio operator is sending out calls nonstop."

"We are saved," several ladies cry out. "We are saved, thank God." More than one pair of eyes around us mist over with tears from relief, mine included.

"Cease putting people in boats," a gentleman shouts above the noise. "When the rescue ships save us, they shall set up a bridge of planks, and we will all simply walk over. It shall be easier and safer."

The quartermaster ignores him. "Women and children in the boats. Captain's orders."

The scent of perfume, brandy, and cigars hangs in the air as people move around us. Husbands cajole their scared wives, and grown children their parents. Then, strands of music float through the night, and I search for the source, but cannot see the musicians beyond the crowd.

"Our circumstances cannot be that serious if the band is playing," I tell Edward. "Perhaps I should stay onboard."

"You must go." He pushes me toward lifeboat six, which Second Officer Charles Lightoller is in charge of filling.

"Lookout Fleet and Quartermaster Hitchins," Lightoller addresses the fresh-faced young man and the more grizzled seaman who flank him, "hop in. You will man the oars." He looks around, as if for another seaman, but there are none near, so then he holds out his hand toward the nearest women. "All right, ladies, it is time."

"Must we?"

"But a rescue ship is coming."

"I need my husband. I am feeling unwell."

"I cannot possibly," says another. "I am lightheaded."

"I also feel faint."

"Go." Edward pushes me forward.

I step up, pressing my hand against the flutters in my chest. My fingers rest on the bump of my mother's cameo, which I wore to dinner last night and forgot to unclip from my dress. It is a miniature portrait of her, with her name, *Mary Churchill Hungerford*, engraved on the back. I dig under my coat and unclasp it now, and while I am at it, I also tug my little silver flask from my coat pocket.

I thrust my treasures into Edward's hands. "I would not wish for these to fall into the water as I climb over the railing. We shall see each other soon. Hold on to these for me, would you, dearest Edward?"

I am determined to be brave, yet at the last moment, I hesitate. The thirty-foot lifeboat seems a fickle vessel in comparison to our giant of a ship. It sways too high, too precariously above the water. The men shall be safer on the ship than the ladies lowered in the night, then dragged back. The closer I stand, the more I agree with the gentleman who protested earlier. Rescue is on its way. They will reach us long before the *Titanic* can sink. *If* it can sink.

After all, how many times have we all heard her declared unsinkable?

One of the women in front of me climbs over the side, then jumps into the boat, screaming as she leaps. Then she rights herself, flashes back a half-embarrassed, half-reassuring smile, and she sits.

The next lady, an older woman, steps away, vehemently shaking her head. "I cannot."

All right. "I shall go next."

Edward and I exchange a brief embrace, cumbersome with the life jackets. I console myself with the thought that we shall be soon reunited.

"Stay safe," we tell each other at the same time.

Then he says, "The rescue ship is near."

I must turn my back on Edward to jump, and I do so with difficulty, but I manage in the end. The water is a dark abyss below, the surface of the ocean a terrifying distance away. *The open mouth of death.*

Oh, do not be maudlin, I scold myself. Yet I stand there, suddenly paralyzed, while the shrieks and arguments and fighting behind me fade away. All I can hear is the waves crushing against the side of the ship. They sound hungry, impatient to swallow us all. I cannot stop shivering.

"Jump!" Edward calls behind me. "We will be back together before you know it."

He is right.

Do not look down. I must not hold up the line. I push away, cursing my blasted corset, which limits crucial free movement. *Must women be forever hobbled?* "Oh!"

As I land, my foot wedges between the oars

stowed next to the gunwale, and when I fall down onto the bottom, my ankle snaps.

The pain is instant.

No, no, no.

"Hold on." Hands reach for me and assist me to an empty space on the bench. "Here. Are you hurt?"

"I have broken my ankle." The pain is too breathtaking for the injury to be anything less.

Of all the times for such a thing to happen.

I grit my teeth and tuck my feet under me, for the next woman is about to land.

"Unhand me at once, you brutes!" So much does she protest that she is tossed over into the boat by force in the end.

"Margaret." I reach for Mrs. Brown as she brushes off her coat with indignation at being manhandled. "It's Helen."

"I was trying to help up there. I could have helped some of those scared ladies if I weren't so rudely removed." She shoots a matronly glare upward, but the men who tossed her over are gone from the railing.

Room is made for her on a bench, and she peers at me in the dim light of the lanterns. "Are you unwell?"

"My ankle…" I attempt to roll it to assess the damage. The ensuing sharp pain makes me see stars. "Definitely fractured."

"Can you elevate your foot?" Margaret suggests.

"We have no room."

She concedes with a nod, at the same time as

Second Officer Charles Lightoller shouts above. "Away!"

We hold on to the bench as best as we can while the crew lowers our boat hand over hand. The lifeboat swings precariously.

Lord help us.

Margaret calls up, "We have only two seamen."

"I can help them, Captain," a man on deck volunteers. "I am a yachtsman."

"You may go if you are seaman enough to slide down the rope." Lightoller gives his conditional approval.

A gentleman swings out onto one of the ropes. Then something falls, a small thing, and hits the water below.

"My wallet!" he shouts as he slides down and hits the bottom hard, the last passenger in our boat.

I am glad I left my valuables with Edward.

"Thank you, Major Peuchen." Margaret Brown appears to know him. "I am glad you could join us. We can certainly use your help."

Our lifeboat touches down with a crash that rattles my bones and sends sharp pain through my ankle. Salt water sprays some of the passengers, but I remain dry, a small mercy. I peer up in the hope of catching a glimpse of Edward, but all I see are shadowy shapes by the railing, the night too dark.

The ship, our majestic *Titanic*… I can scarcely believe my eyes. "Is that the third deck the waves are lapping?"

Oh, God help us, it is… The *Titanic is* most definitely sinking. And I am not the only one to notice.

"She has sunk forty feet already," the major observes. "Where is that darned rescue ship?"

We can no longer see it. Is it possible that, frightened by the ice, they are sailing away?

A couple of the women break down crying, then more and more, as we begin to understand that we might have left the men behind to their death.

Edward. No! Oh, dearest Edward.

Anxiety lodges in my chest like a sharp shard of ice, and it cuts me with every ragged breath.

Among the twenty-four of us in the boat, there are only three men. Among the women, other than Margaret, I recognize Mrs. Rothschild and a few others. Most of us are from first class, save one woman who, based on her uniform, must be from the restaurant staff.

People introduce themselves, but I forget half the names almost immediately. The shock of our situation and the pain in my ankle distract me from everything else.

"Pull away! Go, go, go!" Lightoller shouts from above. "Pull away, but keep the boats together as much as you can."

His order stirs our men to movement. Major Peuchen grabs an oar, Lookout Fleet another, while quartermaster Robert Hichens handles the tiller in the back.

Peuchen calls back to the quartermaster, "Leave the steering to a woman and help us row, Hichens."

"I am in command," the quartermaster shouts back over our heads, huddled down as we are against the cold. "You are here to row in silence."

The two glare at each other. Our ship is sinking before our eyes, and the men who should be saving us are fighting each other instead of working together.

Heaven help us; they are no better than children. I am in too much pain to care whom I offend. "This is hardly the time to bicker, gentlemen!"

"Why did he send me away?" The woman beside me, in nothing but a silk kimono and a life vest, cries out for her husband. She grabs my hand and grips it until my bones protest. Desperation spills from her eyes and streaks down her cheeks. "William will find me, won't he?"

Other ladies begin calling out. "George?" "Wilson?" "Henry?"

"Edward!" I cannot resist either. I shout toward the next lowered boat, hoping to catch sight of him. "Edward Kent!"

He may yet make it down, assigned to a boat to assist the women, similarly to Major Peuchen.

Our acquaintance has been too brief. I pray that fate grants us the chance to know one another better.

"The boats are not filled." Margaret voices the thought I had earlier. "They are in such a hurry, they are lowering boats half empty."

I notice another thing. The vast majority of people in the boats are from first class. The Boat Deck can only be accessed from the A Deck, which is inaccessible to second- and third-class passengers. What will happen to them? I suddenly remember the Viking woman with her children in steerage.

"The boats are not filled!" I shout back toward the ship in vain. The men in charge are too far and too high up to hear me.

Major Peuchen and Lookout Fleet row us away from the *Titanic* with excruciating slowness. Two men are plainly not enough at the oars, but it shall be all right. We do not have to go far, just far enough to make room for the rest of the boats to be safely launched.

They hit the water, one after the other, a few nearly tipping out their precious cargo. I scan each one for Edward, but I cannot see well enough. Then the last one is on the ropes, sliding toward the water, and I catch the moment when the people on the ship realize it is the *last boat*.

The level of noise rises, but over the melee, I hear a sharp clap.

Margaret cranes her neck. "Was that a gunshot?"

A dark head appears at a porthole and draws our attention. A man wiggles through, then lunges for the lifeboat descending past him. Behind him follows another fellow.

They both succeed and claim two of the empty seats. They are saved.

Hold on, dearest Edward, hold on, hold on, I repeat silently, as fervently as a prayer, willing the *Titanic* to stay atop the waves, while I search the horizon for the rescue ship, which I spot once again. For some reason, the vessel is no nearer than when it was first spotted.

"What are they waiting for?" The major is as exasperated as I am.

Some of the people in the boat gasp, and I turn back to the *Titanic* in time to see another row of lights disappear under the waves. Deck by deck, the dark and hungry ocean is swallowing the portholes. The sight is too shocking to be comprehended.

Improbably, music floats over the water still. The notes fall like an offering cast upon the waves. The orchestra plays *Nearer, My God, to Thee*.

The hymn rips a sob from my heart that cracks open as I watch men jump into the icy waters. *Edward!* I cannot find him in the dark, but there are definitely men in the water, grabbing on to anything that floats, deck chairs for the most part. Those who can swim for the nearest boats.

Yes! "We must save them!"

Except, the people in the boats fight off the swimmers. "Away! Away! You will turn us over."

"Let them in!" I shout as I spot a head bob toward us. *Oh.* "It's the little gymnast!" The boy from the exercise room is still wearing his white flannel, which makes him more readily visible than the others who'd fallen in without a life vest. I hold my hand out, even though he is some thirty yards away. "Here!"

He struggles.

Margaret grabs an unused oar. "We must go back for him."

"We are coming." I grab another. "Hold on!"

The two of us row toward him, but Hichens orders Fleet and Peuchen to row away. The men are stronger, and unlike us, they know what they are doing.

"We will capsize, damn you. Halt at once!" Hichens shouts at us, his face puffed up. "Have sense. There will be a whirlpool when the *Titanic* sinks. She will drag us down with her. We must move away. We do not have a moment to spare. Do you women want to live?"

I row all the harder, my eyes on the struggling boy.

Margaret is not giving up either. She huffs and puffs with the effort.

"Where is your decency?" she shouts at Hichens.

"Quiet, you damnable woman." Then Hichens calls to the little gymnast. "We cannot take you on."

The boy stops but a dozen feet from us. He paddles the water, his lips dark. For an eternal moment, he watches us. "All right." His voice breaks. "God keep you all."

And then he stops fighting, and he is swallowed by the ocean.

"No!" I swirl back to fight Hichens, but at that moment, the *Titanic*'s stern lifts into the air. Then, incredibly, with a loud crack, the ship breaks apart between the second and third chimneys. And we all watch, frozen, as both halves slide into the ocean, the twisted stern after the bow.

None of us can draw a breath until all of her is

gone, then the women break down in great, heaving sobs.

The people in the water start calling out again. "Help!"

"My husband could be out there." Mrs. Lucien Smith, if I remember her name right, begs the quartermaster, "Please, sir. Have mercy. I see no whirlpool."

"They will rush us and swamp the boat. If we want to survive, we must think of ourselves."

"We are twenty-four here." I cannot move past the waste of it, the insanity of it all. "Sixty-five could fit in the boat." I remember Edward telling me that. "We have room."

"No."

"Row, if you want to save your men," Margaret orders the women as she begins handing out oars.

Those who can, row; some are beyond anything but sobbing, having collapsed.

We struggle, but progress little. We lack the skill, and so the boat moves in a slow, useless circle. Over the next hour, as we keep arguing with the men, the surface of the water falls silent. One by one, the swimmers slip away into the icy embrace of death.

"There. Done." Hichens throws up his hands. "Now will you be sensible and let us row to the rescue ship, where we should have been heading all along? Just the men. Ladies, restrain yourselves from interfering, if you would."

He considers us capable of little.

I refuse to relinquish my oar. "The more arms, the faster we shall reach our deliverance."

We do our best, but no matter how hard we work, how eagerly we row and row with bloody palms, we do not reach any closer to the light on the horizon. After a futile, soul-crushing hour, Hitchens lets go of the tiller.

"Stop. All is lost." He rubs his hand over his face. He seems to have aged a decade since our boat was lowered, his face haggard, his shoulders slumped. For several seconds, he stares forward in silence. Then he shifts his gaze over us. "We will never reach that ship. They must not have seen us. They must be sailing away. We are in the middle of the North Atlantic. We have no drinkable water, no food, no charts, no compass. We must accept our fate."

We are all in shock, freezing. I am in too much pain to think. My ankle throbs, jostled with every move I make. We float, bereft of hope, shivering.

I feel claustrophobic. I do not know how that is possible on the open sea. It is not the lack of space that boxes me in, but our circumstances. I am in a nightmare I cannot escape. I feel trapped, as if I am already sealed in my coffin.

"I saw it," Lookout Fleet mumbles, then he mumbles again, "I saw it first."

"Saw what?" Margaret asks.

"The iceberg. I was on duty. I reported it at once." He begs us to believe him. "I reported it."

Silence covers us, all of us probably thinking the same thing. *Why wasn't anything done at once?* No one is left alive to tell us. Captain Smith would have gone down with the ship, as is the duty of the captain.

The murderous cold steals under my clothes, under my skin, freezing the very heart of me. Right now, the frigid temperature is our worst enemy. Didn't someone say that there was more than one ship nearby? We must stay alive until we can be found. I rub my gloved hands together for heat, then I reach for my oar again. "Could we not keep rowing, if only to stay warm?"

Margaret joins me. "An excellent idea."

A few other women soon follow our example.

"We must do something. We cannot give up." I ignore the roaring pain in my ankle, which I must use to brace myself, and give the oar everything I have. "Row! Move!"

Hichens ignores us, but Major Peuchen shouts at me. "Why, you damnable woman? You don't even know which way we are heading."

I look up. "There." I grimly point at the sky. *Thank you, Edward.* "That is the North Star."

"And how would a woman know?" The great yachtsman scoffs without looking.

"Do consider staying quiet, Major," Margaret snaps at him, "if you have nothing useful to say."

We women row. The major seethes with fury. Hichens is lost to defeat, and Lookout Fleet will not do anything without an order from the quartermaster. We are in a pitiful state.

"Over there." I point to where a number of lifeboats bob on the water. "They are pairing up.

Should we search out a partner for mutual aid?" I ask Margaret.

"By all means. If the sea grows rougher, two boats lashed together will be more stable."

We row closer and then pull up to lifeboat sixteen. In the middle sits a man in white pajamas, looking like a snowman. Then again, we are all wearing white, more or less—our lifejackets. We look like brides on their way to meet their groom, who is death.

"Bailey, master-at-arms," the large man commanding the other boat introduces himself.

Lifeboat sixteen is more filled than ours, but none of the fifty or so fortunate is Edward. Many of them are crew and second- and third-class passengers. I recognize one of the stewards, Violet Jessup. She is a small woman, half frozen, yet holding a child she has saved somehow. She has the kind of capable hands that have cared for thousands of passengers on a hundred ships and now protect the babe with an unconscious competence. I admire her resilience.

The castaways in lifeboat sixteen are also mostly women. Some of the few men are wet. They must have been pulled from the water. Their teeth chatter as they shiver.

We have little conversation. We do not have the strength left. After an hour of floating together, the teeth chattering becomes unbearable, like skeleton bones rattling in a boneyard. I keep my head down and try to think of anything else. Then, one by one, the small moans and pitiful murmurs of the soaked and shivering men quiet, as they succumb to hypothermia and die in the arms of strangers.

Mothers still call for their children now and then, in both boats, desperately scanning the waves, but they receive no response. No voices have risen from the water in a while now. The people floating out there are all dead.

"Listen up." Quartermaster Hichens seizes control again. The crew members in the other boat look to him for direction. Major Peuchen might be a military man, but to the crew, he's just a passenger. "We could use another man over here. In case a storm rises and the boats are separated."

"I'll come." A stoker, black from coal dust, rises, then steps onto his bench and climbs over to us with care.

He is assigned an oar, but we are not ordered to row. Hitchens orders us to drift.

One woman will not cease calling for her child.

"Do quiet down, Madame de Villiers, for heaven's sake," someone reprimands her. "Your son wasn't even on the ship."

Her brain is addled from shock. She falls silent, but I am not certain it is an improvement. The silence brings us no comfort. Terror blankets us like ice on a pond, growing, spreading over the surface until no breathing hole remains.

"Once the fire was put out," the stoker's eyes are glassed over as he speaks, "I thought we were safe, I did."

"What fire?" I ask him, while Hichens clicks his tongue, annoyed at the both of us.

"The fire in one of the coal bunkers." The man responds without looking at me. "Coal caught on fire weeks before she sailed. We finally put it out on Saturday. We all thought we were that much safer. Didn't expect to sink on Sunday."

Hichens's arm comes up, as if he would hit the man if he could reach him. "Quiet."

The rest of us stare at the stoker in silence. There had been a fire on the ship the whole journey, and nobody thought to inform the passengers. I do not ask the quartermaster why, because if the response is *So the ladies wouldn't panic*, I might throw my oar at him.

We float in a dark nothingness under a moonless sky. Our unsinkable *Titanic* is gone, nothing left of the great ship but the flotsam. A deck chair drifts past us, a makeshift raft, with a babe placed carefully in the middle. Her pinched little face is white with frost. She has frozen to death.

As far as we can see in the dark, we see nothing but ice and our floating, silent dead.

CHAPTER 19

Madison
    November 9, 2024 (Saturday)

After I read Helen's notes about the *Titanic*'s sinking, my mind decides it doesn't need sleep. Or rather, that it needs something else more urgently, something only brushes and paint can give.

Flashes of a vision come to me. I paint what I can, then every few seconds, I lift the brush from the canvas, close my eyes, and wait for more.

The sky is dark. I am in the water, submerged in waves that can swallow me or carry me to shore. At first, I am scared, then I am not, because I realize I'm not in the middle of an emergency. This is life, at any given point, always.

People look for shortcuts, the secret to flying, but flying is for angels. Human life is bobbing on a rough sea. I must learn how to swim.

. . .

"I popped into your studio earlier," Oliver tells me in the break room over his tea and toast. "How long did you stay up last night?"

For the moment, it's just the two of us.

"I went to bed a few hours ago." Around five. "It's as if a gate has opened. I can paint in a way that I couldn't paint before. It's wild."

"You gave yourself permission."

"You might be right. Of course, part of me is still saying, *Now what?* I keep regressing and convincing myself that becoming an artist is impractical. It's the least practical occupation in the world. Creative occupations offer no predictability, no stability, no safety."

"Science is where it's at?" He humors me.

"That's the credo I was raised with. Science is measurable. Results of scientific experiments can be reliably duplicated. Art is unreliable. In art, anything can happen."

"How is that not good news?"

"I am scared of trusting my life to art?"

"If you're not scared, you're not living."

"My father always says only science is solid ground." Art is floating in the middle of the ocean on a scraggly raft. "Science is exact. When you find the cure for cancer, it's a provable fact: the cancer cells die, the patient recovers."

"Are you telling me you're unsure whether you've created something there?"

"I know I've created something, but…" Art depends on the validation of others. Your success is out of your hands, a frustrating aspect. "You can think you're the greatest artist in the world, and it means nothing if the world disagrees. Vincent van Gogh sold only a single painting before he died. People thought he was crazy."

"If you could choose between being a scientist who stays in the lab all her life and makes a great discovery and wins a bag of prizes, or you could be Vincent, with all the suffering he went through and all that he created, what would you choose?"

"Vincent." I wipe my eyes with the back of my wrist. "Why am I crying?"

"It's a relief when one speaks the truth out loud." He comes for me and draws me into his arms. His eyes are smiling. "The answer might be bewildering, but you have an answer. That is something."

He's as solid as if his sculptor cousin had carved him from stone, but warm and comforting instead of cold and rigid.

"I sense something else there." He watches me. "More than the impracticality of being an artist holds you back. What is it?"

His question is a bucket, bringing up my unexamined beliefs from the bottom of a deep well.

"My mother wanted to be an artist."

"Ah. She died before she could have made it?"

"Yes."

"She died of cancer. Why would you feel guilt over her death?"

355

How does he know I do? But, of course, he does. He knows because he's Oliver. "Some women get breast cancer because of the high hormones that are present in the body during pregnancy. PABO. Pregnancy-associated breast cancer."

"You believe it's unfair to your mother that you can be an artist when she never had the chance."

Because of me.

"But not because of you." Now he's a mind reader.

I don't want to talk about this. I wish I could take the whole conversation back.

"You have ghosts," he says. "Everybody has ghosts. Here's the rule. We don't serve the ghosts."

"What do we do with them?"

"We let them go."

"Just like that?"

"Ghosts don't mix well with the living. We each belong to our own realms."

"We let the ghosts go."

"With gratitude, if we can."

"And then?"

"You don't let anything hold you back. You let yourself loose on the world."

I picture what that might look like, a life without any tethers. That kind of freedom feels unreachable.

We have to stop talking like this, with all defenses down, no niceties, no guard rails. I inch back. My soul hurts when it's this bare. "Have you finished Helen's notes?"

"Not yet." Oliver accepts that I've gone as far as I'm willing to go for now.

"I read about the ship sinking last night. I keep going around in my head, from character to character. The guilt the captain and the ship's designer must have felt. The panic of the crew who knew they weren't going to make it onto the boats because there wasn't enough room. The second- and third-class passengers. The men who chose to stay behind to make space for the women. And even the people who made it into the lifeboats, what that night must have been on the water. The tragedy of it all is too enormous to comprehend."

"You have a good start."

For a moment, I'm confused, then I understand. My two paintings. To the casual observer, they'd look abstract, but of course, Oliver guessed what they're about. He saw what I saw in the dark swirls and waves.

"Are you finished?" he asks.

"Not yet."

That weekend, I paint canvas number three.

More infinity blue and heartbreak purple, all funeral-veil dark. Here and there, a mist of white floats distantly, softly under water. No stars. The stars are too far, out of reach now. The darker tones on the bottom of the canvas await, the kind and accepting grave of the deep.

I don't have official titles for the paintings, but

unofficially, I think of the one with the stars as *Hope*. The next one, eye level with the water, is *Acceptance*. And the third one, under the water, is *Peace*.

The three works look alike enough to be sisters, but they're not the same. Each has its own mood. I wanted to evoke feelings, to paint concepts instead of subjects, and I might just have succeeded.

I should be content. I should be empty. But the more I look at those three paintings, the more I realize that the *Titanic* isn't done with me yet. I'm not finished.

This time, the prospect of more empty canvases doesn't make me feel scared and overwhelmed. I feel excited.

CHAPTER 20

Helen
April 15, 1912 (Monday)

Dark waves lap the side of our boat, tasting us as they plan out how to best swallow us.

"What time is it?" Margaret Brown mutters.

All our lips are frozen stiff.

None of us can comprehend how it can still be dark. We have been floating in the freezing cold waters for an eternity. My slight queasiness the first day onboard the *Titanic* had quickly passed, but in a much smaller vessel that responds to every small wave, it returns with a vengeance.

Maybe we have died.

Maybe this is hell.

Major Peuchen checks his pocket watch at length. I suspect he has trouble telling the time with his brain frozen.

"Three thirty," he pronounces at last.

We groan at the thought that we still have hours left until daybreak. Then, as a light flashes on the southeast horizon, followed by a boom, we gasp as one.

"Did you see that?"

"Did you hear?"

Every back snaps straight, and every neck cranes.

"What is it?"

"A flash of lightning." A woman shudders. *Mrs. Norton?* "God save us from a storm."

The stoker who's come over from lifeboat sixteen and has been lying in the bottom of our boat, frozen insensible for some time now, bolts upright and shouts, "Cannon fire!"

Hichens kicks at him. "A shooting star, you idiot."

We all look into the distance, too scared to blink for fear of missing anything.

Dear God, please let it be a rescue ship.

There is a light there, there definitely is, and it is too early for the sun. Then the light grows, and it separates into orderly horizontal rows.

"Portholes!"

"It's a ship! A ship!"

More booms rent the silence of the night; more flashes light up the sky, clearly identifiable this time. *Rockets.*

The stoker presses his large, trembling hand against his heart. "They are signaling us. We are saved."

"Too far away," Hichens shrugs, unable to rouse

himself to hope. He has already told us that all was lost, and he appears reluctant to be proven wrong.

The major, too, slumps back into his seat. "She cannot reach us through the field of ice. She'll sink, same as the *Titanic*. And if she doesn't, she would still require the better part of a day to make this much headway." He nudges the woman slumped against him, half dead or entirely so. "We haven't that much time."

We are surrounded by death.

In the Guthrie flood, I saw maybe two dozen victims out of the hundred, and it overwhelmed me completely. Now I am surrounded by what must be a thousand dead men and women. The magnitude of the tragedy is incomprehensible.

And our lives, the people in the boat, are by no means guaranteed. We are hanging on by a thread. We barely survived the night so far. Hypothermia has us clutched firmly in its icy fist. We are all numb and stiff, on the edge of succumbing. Even the excitement of sighting the ship does not last past a few minutes. Soon people go back to staring in front of themselves at nothing.

Hichens, who at first fought to be in charge of the boat, could rouse us if he could be bothered to step up to actual leadership. The crew looks to him, and the passengers look to the crew. When on water, they are the professionals trained for such emergencies. But Hichens is withdrawn, muttering to himself, no longer looking at us. He acts as if we do not even exist.

Their dread conquers me. The cold whispers in my ear: *curl up, fall asleep.* Then a fainter voice, an ancestral voice, from a time long past, my great-great-great grandfather, Thomas Rogers, who crossed this same unmerciful ocean on the *Mayflower*: *Do not give up.* I shake off the heaviness, the darkness. I think of my children. I do not care what anyone else does, I am going home to my Edith and my Harry.

I tug the rug Edward wrapped around me tighter over my shoulders. If I could warm up one more degree, I might be able to think more clearly. I press my lips together to push blood into them. I need my lips to work to be able to speak.

"We shall row to the rescue ship." My voice is too weak. I call up what strength I have left and pour it all into my next words. "Let us meet our rescuers halfway. Rowing will warm us up, as it has before. I refuse to die within sight of help. Let us find our courage."

A few women stir. They blink at me as if waking from a dream.

Yes. Move. Think. Come out of the grave.

Once again, Margaret is first to reach for an oar. "Mrs. Candee is right. If we work together, we can save ourselves. Where is your spirit?"

Our first attempts do nothing but knock the two boats together.

"Hold." The stoker unties the boats. Half frozen, he moves stiffly.

"Here you go now." Margaret draws her sable stole from her own shoulders and wraps it around his legs. "Good man." She looks over the rest of us, her eyes settling on me as I struggle. "Two women to an oar." She nods resolutely, as if approving of her own idea. "One to steady it and one to push. That ought to do it."

Hichens moves, and I think he might help us yet, but no, he swipes at her. "Stop your foolishness, you insufferable witch."

I gasp at his ungentlemanly conduct, but Margaret is not cowed the least. She turns her whole body toward him while gripping her oar. "Put a hand on me, and I will pitch you overboard. I swear it."

"Accept your damned fate with dignity." The quartermaster's pride will not let him back down. "I will not die scrambling about the water like a coward."

"Then rest." Fury gives me the strength to counter. "Sleep while we ladies row you to safety." If not for the fear that my toes might freeze off, I would throw my boot at him. "As you are unwilling to help us, have the decency not to hinder us, at least."

"Stop your rambling, you shrew." His voice is as venomous as his gaze.

Even the stoker takes exception. "Sir. You are talking to ladies."

Either because Hichens is too cold or because he doesn't want to lose the support of his crew, he falls silent and leaves us to it.

"The worst is behind us." I raise my voice as I lean into the oar. "We did not go down with the

Titanic. We have survived the night. All we have to do now is reach our rescuers."

"She is unreachable!" Hichens shouts again.

"I do not care!" I shout right back at him. "I would rather die trying than simper in defeat. Have you not a shred of courage?"

We row. Our boat makes progress. We are not as fast as we would like, but with each stroke, we do take a bite out of the distance.

We are about a third of the way there when the wind rips into my hat. All night, the water has been flat, as if the ocean regretted its ghastly attack and was trying to convince us that the sinking of our ship has been but momentary madness. *My deepest apologies, messieurs and mesdames.*

Now the contrite lull is over, and waves rush across the surface, growing taller with each gust. My shoulders burn from effort, and so does my back. I shove the pain into the same compartment where I keep the pain of my ankle. *Better hurting than dead.*

Other boats row toward the rescue ship, some passing us, God keep them. I am glad for their passengers. There were times, in the still of the night, when I feared nobody but the people around me was left alive on the water.

"We might feel as if we are moving interminably slowly, but we are covering more distance than the ship," Margaret encourages. "Our smaller vessel can more easily maneuver between icebergs. You are making a great difference."

We row, huffing and grunting in the most unlady-like manner, and we none of us care.

"The *Carpathia*," Lookout Fleet calls out so suddenly, he even startles himself.

I believe him, although my eyes cannot yet read the name painted on the hull. "God bless the *Carpathia*."

We put that much more effort into our labors. Even Hitchens rouses himself.

We are on our last breath, our strength utterly spent, by the time we reach the rescue ship. Other lifeboats already bob empty by her side, their people safely discharged. Rope ladders hang from the opened gangway doors.

"We are saved. We are saved. We are saved." An older woman in the stern cannot stop muttering as she rocks in her seat. "We are saved."

Hichens navigates us to the ship's side, where we catch the ropes dropped for us. *We are saved.*

The major, too, comes alive. "Men, hold the boat fast for the ladies. Ladies, you must climb the rope ladder."

The bosun's chair is in use farther down the ship, in the aft.

A brave soul, a young woman in the bow, is first, with trembling arms and legs.

"I am not sure if I can manage," I whisper to Margaret. "I cannot put weight on my foot."

"We shall not leave you behind, my dear, so try as hard as you can." Her gaze bores into mine, as if she is pouring her own strength into me. "You can and will climb that darned ladder, Helen."

So I climb with a broken ankle. What other choice do I have? And I cry from the pain. Every step feels as if it might be my last before I lose purchase and I plummet.

An eternity passes as I dangle on the side of the ship in the wind. I can scarcely imagine how poor René Harris might manage this gauntlet with her broken arm. I hope she is already safe in a cabin above. I hope that by some miracle, she has been reunited with her Henry. And, oh, if they have Edward with them…

I grit my teeth and do not allow myself to quit. When I finally scramble to safety, pulled inside, I drop to my knees, gasping for air, eyes fixed on the worn boards under me.

"Are you all right?"

"Are you able to rise, madam?"

For several moments, I say nothing. I have nothing left to give.

"Welcome aboard the *Carpathia*." A man hauls me up without ceremony. "I am Purser Brown. You are in safe hands, ma'am."

"I am alive."

"Yes, you are, ma'am. You have survived."

"May I beg for a moment?" I lean against the wall when a crew member would escort me farther inside.

I look behind me. The vast ocean is dotted with ice and boats, both white, making the ones in the distance difficult to tell apart. The survivors of the

Titanic are spread out over what must be several miles. Debris floats on the water everywhere: furniture, empty food crates, luggage. Mixed in with the flotsam is the dead, the ones for whom the *Carpathia* arrived too late.

"Ma'am."

I hobble out of the way. Others are coming up behind me.

"You are injured." The crewman offers up his arm. "Let us find the doctor."

He carries half my weight as we stumble forward, then up a set of stairs to the C Deck, where he tells me where the sick bay and the doctor are located.

"René!" The sight of my friend outside the sickbay draws tears to my eyes. "Thank God."

Her own eyes are red wounds in her face. She must have wept through the night. "Helen."

I cannot bear to ask about her husband, and René cannot bear to speak about him. Tears roll down her face as she shakes her head.

We embrace.

"I am so sorry." I truly am. The cries of men begging for help in the water while those of us in the boats sat there still echo in my head. I do not know if I can ever, *ever*, forgive myself.

We cling to each other, reliving the terror, wishing desperately that we could wake up from the shared nightmare.

"Mrs. Candee! Mrs. Harris!" Mauritz Steffansson rushes toward me, the Southampton businessman, one of our coterie.

"Thank God." We all embrace, propriety be damned. Inside my heart, hope raises its stubborn, stubborn head. "The others?"

"Hugh Woolner made it. He was with me in lifeboat D. And I just saw Colonel Gracie. He is looking for you. He was not certain whether you left the *Titanic*." A pause. "He says he saw James Clinch drown."

James Clinch, who boarded with me in Cherbourg, one of Mrs. Astor's famous four hundred, the cream of New York Society. "I am so sorry. And Edward?" The news I most want to hear. "Mr. Kent?"

"I have not seen either of the Edwards, neither Kent nor Colley." The shadow on Mauritz's face grows darker. "I am coming from the deck. They have just rescued the last boat. Number twelve. She saved sixty. The last survivors. There will be no others."

"My Henry?" René begs, stricken.

"I am sorry."

"Did you look closely?" I grip his sleeve and demand. *The last boat.* "Did you look at each man?"

"I swear to you, I have."

"I shall search the *Carpathia*." I struggle to my feet, but immediately collapse.

"Mrs. Candee, you are hurt." Mauritz drops to one knee next to me. "What happened?"

"A stupid accident."

"What can I do to help?"

"Look for Henry and Edward. Look for all our friends."

I release Mauritz's hand and watch him go, until he disappears from sight. Then I turn back to René, who has collapsed.

"We shall not relinquish hope." I embrace her. "We must not. We must believe in miracles."

She nods and offers a vain smile. "Yes. Of course, dearest Helen. Yes."

We might, on our own, be able to admit that all hope is gone, but we are being brave for each other.

Both René and I are seen by the doctor, then settled into an empty cabin by the time Mauritz finds us again. This time, he brings Colonel Gracie along, and the London investor, Hugh Woolner. They look like a triumvirate of ghosts, all glad to be alive, but also deeply embarrassed to be so, with so many others gone.

We rejoice in their safety, but both René and I watch the door long after it closes, after the truth becomes clear that they found neither Edward nor Henry. And if they are not on the ship, then they were not saved.

René yields to grief at last. She covers her face as she sobs. My own heart breaks, and breaks, and breaks.

"Captain Roston has given up the search," Colonel Gracie shares in a low tone. "There can be no survivors left. The captain of the *Carpathia* is organizing a service for the dead. Would you ladies allow us to assist you up on the top deck?"

Too soon, too soon for a funeral. We are still struggling with acceptance; we are still fighting to break the surface of the nightmare. "Thank you, Colonel. I should like to attend."

When the time comes, they have to carry me on a chair. I have truly used up all my strength at last.

As the RMS *Carpathia* floats over the grave of the *Titanic*, Reverend Anderson, an Episcopalian, lifts up the living in thanksgiving and prays for the souls lost, assigning them to God's great mercy and care.

I find Edward Kent three days later, in New York, on the list of bodies recovered by the *MacKay-Bennett*.

#258 – MALE

Clothing: Grey coat, dress suit pants.

Effects: Silver flask; two gold signet rings; gold watch, gold eyeglasses, gold frame miniature of Mary Churchill Hungerford.

Love is savage and tender, and a rose, and a knife. Love is hopeless, and the only hope we have.

CHAPTER 21

Madison

December 13, 2024 (Friday)

Love is savage and tender, and a rose, and a knife. Love is hopeless, and the only hope we have.

The words Helen scribbled on the margin of her notes for her autobiography echo in my head as I sit through our morning meeting. I wish I could reach back through the years and hug her. I cried more over Edward Kent last night than I've ever cried over the loss of any boyfriend in the past.

After a quick update from Ramsey—where we only half pay attention, too excited about our upcoming Christmas break—Julia is off to finalize her reports on all the graves, while Eleanor and Oliver head to their labs. Ramsey waves at the documentary crew to follow them, but he holds me back.

"I stopped by your studio yesterday to see your

portraits. You've been working on a few other pieces."

"Oliver gifted me three canvases. He has an artist cousin who is up to his eyeballs in art supplies."

"You have talent beyond forensic art."

"Thank you?"

"The paintings have a certain ambiance, a bitter-sweet, nostalgic mood that fits TTP's brand."

I didn't paint the pieces for him, so I'm not sure I care, but still… "Positive feedback is always nice to hear."

"I'd like to remind you of the contract you signed. All the work you produce during the project at this facility is the property of TTP."

"My forensic portraits."

"All your work. Check your contract."

"The large paintings have nothing to do with TTP."

"They were inspired by what you have learned about the *Titanic* here."

Did Oliver tell him that? I'm not sure Ramsey is capable of that kind of insight. My paintings are abstract.

"I want them displayed at the reinterment cere-mony," he tells me with the confidence of a man who always gets what he wants, "and to feature them in our documentary. I want you to reenact parts of the painting process for the cameras. After the reinter-ment, the art can be part of our planned fifty-city traveling exhibit."

"What traveling exhibit?" How many ways are

they planning on milking this project? Stupid question. They'll make money on it for as long and in as many ways as they possibly can. "No."

The paintings are the beginning of something new for me. They're part of what I am becoming.

"I'm afraid this is nonnegotiable, Madison." Ramsey walks past me to the door. "Set up a convenient time with Maya for filming."

"What did you tell Ramsey about my paintings?"

"Nothing." Oliver puts down the osteometric board, types the measurements into his laptop, then gives me his undivided attention, unruffled and welcoming, as if I didn't just burst into his lab without knocking.

"He wants them. What the hell? And I have to give them to him. It's in my contract."

"He can't confiscate your art."

"I don't have money for lawyers." Normally, I appreciate his chill persona, but right now, I want Oliver to be outraged on my behalf.

"Fight him anyway."

"How?"

"For starters, you could remove the paintings from the building. Possession is two-thirds of the law, even in Canada."

"Sure. I'll drag three gargantuan canvases onto the plane and sneak them home for Christmas break. Have you been on a flight lately? If you can fit both butt cheeks into your seat, you're lucky."

"I'll keep them over at my place."

"I don't want to involve you in this. Anyway, if I take the paintings, Ramsey will probably sue me. That's why he keeps Chad Altman on retainer." I keep forgetting about Chad. We haven't seen the lawyer since September.

"The art is yours."

"Oh, I'm not giving up. I'm going to pull a Helen Candee. That woman didn't know the word *quit*."

"Where are you in her story?"

"They've been rescued from the lifeboats. If that were me, I would have stayed home for the rest of my life."

"Safety is overrated. The overvaluation of safety is the death of courage. Just think. What if the whole world is our heritage? Wouldn't it be a shame if we were too timid to claim it?"

"I don't know if I can process multiple life-altering questions on a single cup of coffee."

He nods. He doesn't push, and with a last look, I leave him.

In my studio, computer printouts of forty-four passengers look at me from the wall where I taped them, rough computer work, but they're here all the same, resurrected. The acrylic portraits I have so far are a lot more worked out, lined up on the shelves.

My three large paintings rest side by side against the wall opposite.

What am I to do with them?

I sit on the floor, in the middle, legs crisscross applesauce like a kindergartner's. The pose doesn't help me find any answers, but I do notice something from this new vantage point. A piece of paper is hiding under one of the shelves.

I fish it out. It's a page from Helen Candee's notes. I must have dropped it earlier.

Edward is buried in Forest Lawn Cemetery in Buffalo, New York. Thanks to my silver flask and my mother's miniature, he is not with the unclaimed dead in Halifax. It is the only satisfaction I have.

An investigation was opened into the wreck in New York the day after our arrival. I was not called to give an account of the night. None of the surviving female passengers were. On account of our sex, we were not allowed to testify.

I wrote my own account, published in Collier's Weekly *on the fourth of May.*

After lengthy hearings, the bulk of the blame was put on the British Board of Trade for insufficiently inspecting the ship. The captain and crew of the Californian *were condemned for watching our distress rockets and not coming to our aid. They sat but ten nautical miles from us while we were sinking, according to the papers.*

I spent the next few months at home in Washington. My ankle healed, but all through that summer, fall, and winter, I walked with a cane, limping.

Why me?
Why was I saved?

. . .

"Are you all right?" Ramsey is at my door. "I'm sorry about earlier." He's on the verge of being apologetic, closer to subdued than I've ever seen him. It's almost scary. "I want this project to succeed more than I've ever wanted anything. If sacrificing one of my kidneys made a difference, I'd do it."

I believe him.

"It's the *Titanic*." He spreads his arms wide, then drops them. "But, yes. I know. I got carried away."

"It's the *Titanic*. I get it."

"The biggest project I've ever been a part of." His eyes spark like a little boy's.

This is who Eleanor sees when she looks at him.

I push to my feet and lay the piece of paper on the table next to my paint brushes. "It's the grandest thing any of us will ever do."

"Right?" He brightens. "When are you flying out for our Christmas break?

"Tomorrow morning."

"I'd like to take you out for dinner tonight."

I don't want to talk about my paintings again. I don't want to have another argument. I stay silent.

An awkward laugh escapes him. "We've been working together all this time, but we haven't really gotten to know each other."

Wait.

What?

He means a date?

I recognize the look in his eyes. It's a little too intent for a business dinner.

Knock me over with a curling stick.

My brain stutters.

In what universe?

"We're having a going-away party for Julia. Since her job is finished, she won't be coming back," I say inanely, knowing Ramsey knows that. The graves have been processed. The bones are secured.

Julia has done what she could at the cemetery. Javier already delivered the wine for her goodbye party, and Oliver ordered a cake from his favorite bakery.

"When you return from break, then." Ramsey offers an easy alternative, then waits for my response, as if he hadn't just dropped a bomb on me.

CHAPTER 22

Helen
    Washington, DC
    February, 1913

"I fought hard against the despair and the cold to row that boat back from the mouth of death. I fought hard to climb the rope ladder with a fractured ankle, buffeted by the arctic wind. And after that, far fewer problems scared me than before. I was aware of injustice before, but not half as much as when I saw the bodies of those third-class passengers floating frozen in the water, never having been given a chance."

My visitors, Alice Paul and Lucy Burns, listen in my parlor in Washington, DC.

"I learned this much," I tell them, seated on my velvet sofa. "We women who rowed those boats that night were the equal of any man." I cannot believe nearly a year has passed since then. "Human fortitude is not distributed along the lines of sex. And neither is courage, nor intelligence."

"That is exactly what we need to make people understand." Lucy Burns is lit with passion from within. "We must show everyone that women are no longer willing to remain second-class."

"We must make a statement big enough that we cannot be ignored." Alice Paul leans in. "How about a march?"

The two young, impeccably dressed and groomed women are the newly appointed chairs of the National Woman Suffrage Association's Congressional Committee.

Our goal is to have the 1878 Susan B. Anthony Amendment finally passed, after thirty-five years.

The right of citizens of the United States to vote shall not be denied or abridged by the United States or by any State on account of sex.

"All right, Dr. Paul." I nod, warming to her idea. "A march it is, but when?"

Alice is twenty-eight years old and a recipient of a PhD. I call her Dr. Paul at every chance. I could not be prouder of her if she were my daughter. It fills my heart with joy to watch this next generation of women who know their worth refuse to take no for an answer.

Her posture changes; she grows an inch taller. She appreciates respect, especially from a woman who is her elder.

"I shall help in any way I am able." I am past

fifty-four. I want to spend the rest of my life serving in whatever capacity I can. I want my life to matter.

"How about the third of March?" Alice suggests.

I don't know. "The day before Woodrow Wilson's inauguration? Too many other events are happening already. Might be bad timing?"

"Imagine how many journalists will already be in Washington."

"Ah, you are a strategist." She will make the perfect leader.

"The newsmen might refuse to cover us, regardless," Lucy notes.

Alice is unconcerned. "They will not be able to resist thousands of women marching up Pennsylvania Avenue to the Capitol." Her eyes glint. "We could wear all red, to stand out even more."

"Let us not give our enemies an easy target. Red is not a color for respectable ladies. They would call us names." I do not have to say it; she knows what I mean. *Whores*. "How about white? The color of purity, since our cause *is* pure. White will show up sharp against a dark background in the papers."

Lucy hops to the edge of her seat, brimming with energy. "A pure white would work the best for the black-and-white photographs. It would be perfect, Mrs. Candee."

Alice agrees, then adds, "We shall create a true spectacle, but it is not enough for them to see us. They must hear us too. No more soft-spoken requests. Our voices must carry when we make our demands."

Lucy rises to a new level of excitement. Her shoes tap on the carpet. "What if we rode on horseback?"

Alice throws a veto. "A few thousand horses might be too difficult to control."

I agree. "We must also think of practical matters, such as the refuse we would leave behind. We *will* be criticized for everything."

"How about if only the leaders ride?" Lucy is not ready to give up on the wondrous image painted in her mind. "A dozen women?"

"The papers will criticize us for lack of decorum." I am the oldest in the room. I must be the voice of reason. Or must I? "Then again… Do men worry about decorum? No. When men want something, they go to war. They do not beg. They take what they feel is theirs. It is about time that we take what we want for our sex."

Lucy sighs. "We will all end up tossed in jail, won't we?"

She deserves the truth. "It is most possible. We must wear sturdy clothes and our most comfortable corsets. It will not be easy, but we will march anyway." I stand and raise my cup of tea in a toast to my coconspirators. "Ladies, sound the bugles!"

Alice and Lucy stand to toast with me. The winter sun, streaming through the window, paints us golden, and for a moment, we are Valkyries, warrior women.

March 3, 1913

. . .

"The horses mustn't rear up." I hold the reins tightly in my right hand. The early-March day in Washington DC, is bracing, though not freezing. "They cannot stumble. None of us must fall off. We must not give the men a reason to further ridicule us."

With my left hand, I adjust my skirt. "We cannot have an inch of stocking revealed above the boot."

That too is important. Not only must we fight, but we must wear long dresses and multiple petticoats and remain ladylike even in war.

I saw a union protest once. To say the men were disheveled would be an understatement. They came straight from the mines, covered in coal dust. Some of them must have paused for a pint on the way, because they were drunk. But men are weighed by a different measure. We women must be perfect to be heard—if we are heard at all. We must meet higher standards.

Seven of us sit atop our horses, all of us dressed in white, as are most of the women behind us. *Ten thousand* suffragettes march in three columns on Pennsylvania Avenue, each divided into various groups. Business Women, Pioneers, Teachers, Librarians, Lawyers, uphoald their banners, in addition to state delegations. White women, black women, and immigrants from every country, we march to the music of multiple bands.

Police line the street, which reassures us somewhat. We believe they are here to protect us.

"Can you imagine the press if one of us slipped off her horse?" Inez Milholland rides in front, on her white stallion, Gray Dawn. She is a Vassar graduate, a lawyer with a law degree from New York University, a symbol of what our sex could accomplish if only society would step out of our way.

"Women who cannot even manage to stay in their saddles," Jane Walker Burleson, an artist and a teacher, imitates the tone of an old man, "have no place leading anything, nor voting. The weaker sex best return to the kitchen."

I smile at her imitation, heartened by the crowd. "There might not be a woman left in her kitchen in all of Washington today."

We have twenty floats and innumerable signs and banners. We are, indeed, a great parade. We *could* be an army. We are not coming begging with hat in hand. We are issuing The Great Demand. What we want is right there on our first billboard on the first float.

We demand an amendment to the Constitution of the United States, enfranchising the women of this country.

"A quarter of a million people showed up to watch us march." I incline my head in appreciation. "Well done, Dr. Paul."

The thrill of a new day fills the air, a new chapter in history. We are breathing in hope and possibility. Nobody but nobody can deny that we can accomplish great deeds, that we can organize ourselves, that we have strength, and that we have solidarity.

Pride buoys me, nearly lifts me out of my saddle.

I am so light that I feel I could fly in the sky like an airship.

In an instant, however, everything changes.

Jeers rise above the joyful sounds of our parade.

Of course, not every spectator has come to support us. Some have come to ensure that we fail. A few have been cleverly lined up along the parade route all along, at even intervals, and now push among us from the side streets. This was organized.

What began as a celebration acquires a darker, uglier tone in a blink.

"Go home!" A burly, red-faced man in worn work clothes pushes his way toward me, veins bulging at his temples. He is as outraged as if I stole his dinner.

Another one, a few feet over, curls his palms against his mouth to yell louder. "Boo! Boo!"

"Unwomanly!" A banker in a bowler hat elbows his way forward.

"Ungodly!" This from a woman in all black. Her pinched face holds open hatred.

How do I tell her that we are doing this for her and her daughters? I can't. She is too busy throwing rocks at us to listen.

One rock narrowly misses me, brushing my horse's ear. He dances sideways. "Hoo." I hold on to him tightly.

"No need for all this circus." A bald, mean-eyed man in a baker's apron grabs my reins with one hand and his crotch with the other. "I've got what'll make you happy, honey." And then he grabs my knee, his hand as big as a bread shovel.

I raise my riding crop, but before I can bring it down, he yanks it from me. A minute ago, my worst fear was that my horse could stumble. Now I might yet be pulled from my saddle and raped in the street. "Get away!"

He swears at me, threatening violence.

"Why?" I demand, my words lost in the melee. I raise my voice to shout at him. "We are not here to take away anything from you. We merely wish to be acknowledged as equal human beings."

His fingers dig painfully into my thigh as he leers and laughs. "I'll give you what you need."

"Get away!" I kick at him, my boot connecting with his chest. Then I kick at him again until he stumbles back.

Behind me, our whole parade is in disarray and shambles. Everywhere, women are being grabbed and beaten.

I look for the policemen, but they are still standing on the sidelines and move not a finger. They watch with satisfaction as we flail. Some of them outright laugh.

"Help us!" I call to the nearest one, a hefty, dark-haired Italian.

He shrugs at me with contempt. "Wouldn't be in this pickle if you stayed home, would you, ma'am? A lesson to be learned."

Lucy Burns pulls her horse next to mine, fighting the swirling crowd. "Should we disperse, before someone is hurt?"

"Too late."

The fighting has spread the length of the street, men grabbing women, who are using flagpoles and banners to beat them back.

"Back off!" Lucy yells at a redheaded, hairy-armed drunk when she's attacked.

This time, I am ready. In a second, I have my hatpin in hand. I lean over and stab her attacker in the shoulder until he yowls and lets us be. Nobody will help us. We must fight our own battle. Since I have the high ground, I have an advantage. I help as many suffragettes who are on foot as I possibly can.

The brawl goes on for an hour before army troops arrive and drive off our cowardly attackers. The blessed soldiers clear the avenue, and we can continue on at last, ruffled, disheveled, but neither intimidated nor broken.

I ride ahead, glancing back now and then to make sure nobody falls away discouraged. I heard the crowd was judged to be five thousand women, but I think it's closer to ten, marching resolutely behind us. Their white dresses remind me of the ice on that fateful night a year ago on the Atlantic, but I do not shiver. *Watch out for us. We are not harmless. We might sink you yet.*

Lucy catches up to me and adjusts her bedraggled dress. She shakes her head at my appearance. I have not fared much better. "To think we spent so much time deciding what would look best in the papers." She laughs, and I laugh with her, because if we weren't laughing, we might be weeping.

"All right." I sit as straight and composed in my

saddle as if we were at the theatre. "So we have been attacked. The most important thing is, we are still here."

We pass by the White House, with its pristine white columns and the American flag whipping in the wind on top, a flag that represents and protects some of us more than others.

Yet I love that flag. "Do you think we shall ever have a female president?"

"Without a doubt, and very soon. As soon as we win the right to vote. Why should any of us cast a ballot to keep men ruling over us? The next president, after Wilson, will be a woman. This is 1913, not the Middle Ages."

We march all the way to Capitol Hill. At the bottom of the steps, Inez turns Gray Dawn around, and our eyes meet. We planned on stopping here. She has a speech prepared.

We find that we are not ready to stop, however. Not the seven of us, and not the other women. Not when we have come this far.

"To the top!" a strong voice calls out from the crowd.

"To the top!"

We nudge our steeds forward and climb the steps of the Capitol on horseback.

Is it so wild to ask that the greatest country in the world should be fair to all its citizens, regardless of sex?

We reach the top, but we do not jump out of the

saddle. We are not supplicants, but generals. We are not here to beg. We are here to conquer.

"Do you think you will have your own statue someday, on top of the steps, commemorating yesterday's achievement?" the reporter, a young man, asks me the day after our march, having come around to my house for an interview. "Is that the goal?" He does not know quite what to make of me. "To march into history?"

He is earnest and respectful, with a jaunty mustache that reminds me of Edward Kent.

I nearly burst out laughing at his question. How young he is, how naïve. "We are women," I beg him to understand. "Nobody will remember our names. History tends to only remember the men."

"There were plenty of women—"

"Name five."

"Cleopatra, the Amazons…"

"Nonfictional."

"Cleopatra… Surely, history won't forget Queen Victoria… Jean d'Arc!"

"Who else? In five thousand years of recorded history? Off the top of your head."

He racks his brain for another, grows embarrassed for a moment, then recovers. "You are fifty-four years old, and a grandmother. Will you now withdraw to focus on your family?"

"I am not retiring." I want not only to see the

world, but to change the world, in any small way I can, in what time I have left.

"Does the fierce opposition not scare you, Mrs. Candee?"

"Why should it? I promise you, I shall survive people's disapproval. I survived the sinking of the *Titanic*."

He nods at this. He has already asked several questions about the great ship and the disaster. "What will you do next?"

"Everything. I shall not leave life's cup half full, nor a quarter, young man. I am going to drink it to the last sip. I shall fight for justice."

CHAPTER 23

Madison

January 10, 2025

"Lunch?" Ramsey ambushes me in my studio, the first day we're back from Christmas break. He's gotten a haircut. He must have another taping coming up.

I'm in a good mood, refreshed. I managed to spend half a day with my grandmother and two whole hours with my father, counting the car ride to and from the grocery store. Other than that, I used most of my time to paint, and it was the strangest thing. As I moved the brush across the canvas, images appeared, as if they were pouring out of me, as if I was giving the canvas things hidden deep inside. But when I was done, I didn't feel empty. Just the opposite. Something traveled back on my arm, filling me with a quiet joy and contentment. As I built up the images, the act of painting built me. I have received more than I have given.

"I know a brewery not too far that has great microbrew and burgers," Ramsey says.

"We'd better not." I lower my camera. I've been taking photos of the finished paintings of the *Titanic*'s victims for TTP's website. "This project is going to unfold in the public eye. We wouldn't want any questions about what was and wasn't appropriate."

He blinks. "Right." To his credit, he doesn't push, but he does step farther inside. "You're talented." He examines my work. "You were the right choice." He looks around. "Where are the three big ones?"

He doesn't know about the other two, the ones I painted over the break, the ones that fill my heart, the ones where I might have actually accomplished something. "Drying. They need a few months before I can put on the final varnish layer for protection."

"Are these varnished?" He examines my small portraits.

"These are acrylic. Varnish protects paintings, but yellows with time, then you have to remove it as part of restoring the piece. Except, the solvent that removes the varnish also dissolves the acrylic paint under it. Oils are better at handling that process. I usually leave my acrylics as they are."

"There's a lot to this, huh?" He sounds surprised.

"I think there's more to every job than what meets the eye. Knowing that *more* separates the amateurs from the professionals."

When Ramsey is gone, the door closed behind

him, I return my attention to the people in my portraits. History calls them victims, but they were heroes, adventurers. Most were third-class passengers. These men and women fought for a better future for themselves and their families. They were people who dared.

"I *am* an artist," I tell them, and myself.

Feelings aren't a matter of decision. I can decide not to feel scared of spiders, but I will still scream if one drops into my lap. I can't necessarily decide to believe that I'm a good artist. I can, however, decide to act a certain way. My feelings might not be within my control, but my actions are. I can decide to *act* as if I believed in myself. And then, maybe, the feeling will come later.

I pick up my phone and dial.

Gail Winston, the PR director at Cyntinra, picks up. "Dr. McClain. I was about to call you. I received the photos you sent me before Christmas. How wonderful that our TTP project inspired you. We very much appreciate your participation, by the way."

"Please call me Madison. I'm grateful I can be a part of this project. I can honestly say that with every passing week, it means more and more to me." But that's not why I'm calling. "Did you have a chance to consider my suggestion?"

"We did."

The *we* sounds ominous. I picture a team meeting with a Ramsey-esque slideshow, with my paintings projected onto a screen, people stunned at my temerity, criticizing my composition and brushwork. *Who does she think she is?*

"We would love to offer you a per diem fee," Gail says, "in exchange for your five large paintings, to be displayed at the reinterment ceremony, and then at our *Titanic: The People* traveling exhibit."

The dollar figure she names renders me speechless. Their payment is a year's worth of income, but it's so much more than money. Somebody is willing to pay for images that were born in my head that I then translated to canvas. This is not copying and fleshing out computer sketches. This is all mine, from beginning to end. I *am* an artist. And for the first time ever, my art will be seen.

Johanna Bonger, Vincent van Gogh's sister-in-law, gave me the idea to contact TTP. After Vincent's death, instead of selling his art, Johanna exhibited the works in museums and galleries around the world. That way, she could share his vision without losing the pieces. She was brilliant, in so many ways.

"I'll have Chad Altman draw up a contract," Gail tells me. "Look it over and let me know what you think."

"Thank you. I will."

We talk for five more minutes, but I'm so numb with surprise over her offer that by the time we hang up, I can't remember what else we said. I'm going to need chocolate-covered marshmallows to process this. Break room vending machine it is.

Oliver catches me sailing past his door and joins me. "Where are we going?"

I tell him.

"The call of sugar is difficult to resist." He's filled with understanding. "Chocolate, specifically, has the ability to sing through time and space."

"I need to gather myself." I sound like a frazzled Victorian lady. I stop. We're outside the break room. "I painted a couple more pieces over the break." I recap my conversation with Gail for him. "I'm worried that I misunderstood something. I'm glad she'll send everything in email."

"Congratulations." Oliver picks me up and swings me around.

He's a gardener. He has the arms of a man who regularly digs deep holes and lifts large, dirt-filled pots. Three hoorays for landscape enthusiasts.

When he sets me down, we grin at each other. Joy throws sparks inside me like fireflies coming to life at dusk. I want…

I catch myself and step away. I don't want to start liking his arms around me too much. We only have eight weeks left on the job, then the reinterment ceremony in mid-March. After that, off we go. The TV series launches on April 14th, but we won't be gathered back together for that. By that point, our work will be long finished.

It'd be pointless to start anything with him. Nothing can come of our relationship. We don't even live in the same country.

"Anyway." I step into the break room. "I'm just here for celebratory chocolate."

"Let me get that." He pulls a fiver from his pocket. "My treat. Which one?"

I point.

He works the vending machine, waits through its rattling until the prize is dropped at last, then hands me the chocolate-covered marshmallows.

"Thank you." I share them with him.

"Are we holding our parties here now?" Eleanor peeks in from the hallway, looks from Oliver to me, and flashes me a knowing look. *Aha!*

It's not like that, I telegraph.

I know what I know, she telegraphs back as she walks in.

"Have you finished reading Helen's notes?" I ask her to knock her off track. "I read to the end over Christmas. I hope we don't have to hand the printout back. I want to save it to read her story again later."

"What did you think of her?"

"She didn't have an easy life, but she had a full life. She fought for what she believed in."

Eleanor smiles. "She sure did. You know, she lived to ninety. That looks good."

I'd offer her a marshmallow, but I'm chewing on the last one.

Oliver pops more money into the vending machine and pushes the button.

"Thank you, Oliver." Eleanor accepts his thoughtful offering. "Helen saw history happening. She was right in the middle of it all, and I don't think it was a coincidence for the most part. She *wanted* to be there. You know, she inspired me to live life to the fullest. She got me traveling."

We only just received her notes a few months ago and haven't gone anywhere since. "What do you mean?"

"Oh." She clicks her tongue. "I hate secrets. I don't have the memory to keep them. I remember everything I've learned in my career and things that happened twenty years ago, but I'll decide something one day and forget it the next. The truth is, I first read Helen's notes as a teenager. She's a distant relative. My mother ended up with her writings after her death."

Wow. "Does Ramsey know?"

"It's how he got hired onto the project. He pitched Helen's life story to a couple of studios as a movie. They turned him down. So did Cyntinra, but they had a *Titanic* project in development already, a new series. When he told them about Helen's papers and the family link, they offered him a job with TTP. His personal connection to the *Titanic* will be a surprise reveal at the end of the documentary. He didn't want me to tell you ahead of time. He wants your reactions to be authentic."

I really like Eleanor, but her son… I'm tired of the setups and the secrets.

I hope he won't stop by my studio again today, because I might throw some brushes at him.

. . .

"Today is the day," Ramsey tells us at our meeting the following morning. "TrinovarDNA is uploading the *Titanic* victims' records into their online database. They have a press release announced for eleven a.m."

"Are they going to notify the relatives or wait until people discover the records on their own?" I ask, instead of bringing up his family's connection to Helen. The cameras are rolling. If he wants the news to be a kind of gotcha moment at the end, I'm going to let him have that.

"Emails are being sent as we speak to every TrinovarDNA client who is a match to any of the victims. They'll also receive an invitation to the reinterment ceremony."

"And if they want the remains in a family plot somewhere?" Oliver brings up a good point.

"They'll have two months to protest the current plans," says Ramsey.

March 15, 2025

March sneaks up on us like a shark on mackerel. One second, we're barely back from Christmas break, the next, the interment ceremony is upon us. To say that the cemetery is mobbed is an understatement. Thankfully, we have police assistance for the event. The weather is perfect.

Ramsey claims the podium first. The representatives from Cyntinra and TrinovarDNA wait their turns in the wings. Two hundred relatives of the victims are in attendance, some still in disbelief, bewildered at their sudden connection to one of history's greatest tragedies. During the project, I didn't have a lot of time to think about the scope of what we were doing, but in hindsight, I'm in awe of all we have achieved.

Julia, Eleanor, Oliver, and I stand in the front, to the side. None of us were asked to speak. The two local archaeologists, Lily Mei Chen and Zuri Williams, stand with us. I wish I could have gotten to know them better, but they worked in the cemetery, so I rarely saw them. The only person who connected with them is Julia.

The media are in a feeding frenzy, elbowing each other out of the way. Our own camera crew, given preferential position inside the cordoned-off area, is filming everything for the documentary.

"And so, it is the greatest honor of my life to have been involved in this project, in the raising of the *Titanic*." Ramsey ends his speech, then invites the mayor to the podium.

"Halifax has always thought of the *Titanic* victims as our own dead," the man begins, somber in a black coat, with honest emotion in his voice. "We have always cared for the graves as if they were the graves of family."

Some of the relatives in attendance nod in appreciation; others look straight ahead, shell-shocked; a few have tears rolling down their faces.

"This was the right thing to do," the mayor tells

them. "Those nameless headstones needed names. The descendants deserved answers."

I lean toward Julia. "I know that for Cyntinra and TrinovarDNA, this is purely a PR opportunity. I didn't expect to be touched, but I am."

She nods. "The past is important, and so are our links to it. Lessons need to be passed on."

"I'm glad I didn't swipe that first email from TTP straight to spam." I'm glad I took a chance. "Want to know the truth? I took this project on to find myself."

Oliver smiles.

The question *What?* is on the tip of my tongue, but then I understand. A perfect version of me isn't wandering somewhere out there, waiting to be found. I'm not lost. I'm here.

The good news is the same as the bad news.

Helen's unfinished autobiography has it right. You don't *find* yourself. You *build* yourself. You must create the person you want to be.

People don't have some perfect template they were born with that they later forget. Even if you were happy at eight, you can't go back to eight years old and resurrect the people who made you happy then. You have to create your best thirty-year-old self with what materials you currently have, looking to the future, not the past. And it's the same when you're fifty or seventy.

From the grave site, we all go over to the expanded *Titanic* exhibit at the Maritime Museum of the

Atlantic, loaded onto buses. My paintings are directly across from the entrance, on the back wall in the first room, the first thing people see when they walk in.

Next to them is Helen Candee's original, unfinished autobiography, in a glass case. It's open to where the lifeboats are being lowered.

I want to touch the yellowed page, but I can't. "I wish she finished her story, all the way to the end. I would love to read what happened after she rode up the steps of the Capitol on horseback."

"She went and volunteered as a nurse with the Red Cross in Italy during World War I," Eleanor says. "She nursed the young Ernest Hemingway in Milan."

"No way."

Julia dips her chin, as if looking over imaginary glasses. "For real?"

"True story. I swear." Eleanor does a hand to heart. "Then she lived through World War II too. It's difficult to comprehend how much she must have seen. And she stayed true to her values and principles all the way."

"She survived the sinking of the *Titanic*, and it's the least interesting thing about her." My admiration for the woman cannot be overstated. "That's the kind of life I want to live."

"Step one," Oliver advises, "let go of everything that holds you back. Step two, let yourself loose on the world."

"You make it sound easy."

"Forward movement is as easy or difficult as you make it. The time is never right or optimal for anything. *Perfect* doesn't exist. You take the step because you decide to take it."

"Somewhere, a Zen monastery is missing its monk."

He laughs, interrupted by an "Excuse me," from one of the reporters attending the event. "Mind if I ask a couple of questions about the forensic science part of the project?"

As they step aside, Julia goes off in search of coffee, claiming the coffee on the plane was colored water. And then it's just Eleanor and me.

"How are you? For real?"

"More difficult to kill than the doctors anticipated."

"Have you told him yet?"

"I will. Soon." Her smile is serene, where I would be screaming against life's unfairness. "I want him to enjoy *this*"—she circles her head to indicate the scene around us—"to the fullest." She takes one of the visitors' chairs. "Let me sit a minute. You go and check out the exhibit."

"Are you sure?"

She is.

Curiosity draws me to a group of women who are looking at my paintings. I stop behind them, far enough so I don't necessarily look like I'm listening.

"You can tell the artist was feeling deeply," one of them says, a petite fifty-something. "It's like she tapped into what the passengers felt, and she was able to pass it on."

"I like *Hope*." Her friend leans forward. "The

starry sky. I can picture the passengers up on deck at night, looking up, on their way to the New World with so much hope in their hearts. My great-grandparents came over like that. They risked their lives on the journey so I could have it better. I don't think that generation ever got enough credit."

"The middle one is disturbing," the third woman puts in. "I can't look at it for long. All the emotion that emanates from the canvas sends chills up my spine. No people, just waves and ice, everything sharp and choppy. I can feel the danger and the chaos of the night."

"Then the peace," the petite fifty-something says of the last panel of my triptych. "The night was over. Every struggle has a finish. No matter what, peace waits for all of us at the end. I find that thought comforting."

Her friends hug her wordlessly, one after the other, and I wonder what fight she's fighting in her own life. I silently wish her strength for her battle.

Arm in arm, the women move on, and another group replaces them.

Oliver reappears at my elbow with his cousin, the sculptor, Javier Moreno. "Look who I found."

"What do you think about all this?" Javier, tall, with the build of a man who pounds stone all day, asks.

I met him once when he delivered wine to our accommodations at the office park, but we never really had a chance to chat. "I'm happy. My paintings are exhibited."

"That's the thing, isn't it?" His smile is warm and supportive. He wears charisma like a cape, making it impossible not to smile back as we walk toward the Hall of Portraits, the next room where the forty-four recently identified victims wait to introduce themselves.

I slow as I take them all in, the lost passengers and the people who came to meet them. A small crowd is admiring what I created. I want to pinch myself, but I don't dare, in case I wake up.

"If this is a dream, let me keep sleeping," I whisper.

"Do you think he was scared?" A little boy of maybe six looks spellbound, possibly at his great-great-grandfather. "What if penguins saved him, and he went to live with them?"

His mother hesitates whether to tell him that penguins live at the South Pole. In the end, she ruffles his hair. "Anything is possible."

We push through the crowd of descendants into the next room, which displays artifacts, including J.H.'s three silver coins and ring. Her name was Jane Holmes. She was on her way from Cornwall to New York to join her immigrant siblings.

We pass by the original menu for the last dinner on ship, then a violin, shoes, luggage.

"There were no suitcases in the lifeboats," Oliver says. "This one must have floated."

"The items are from various private collections around the world, on loan to TTP," I tell his cousin.

In the last room, flanking the exit that leads to the

gift shop, the final two of my large paintings are exhibited.

On the left side, forty-four people stand on deck in the aft of the ship as it pulls out of the harbor, waving to their loved ones. They are faceless, unidentified. We only see them from the back.

On the right side, they're shown from the opposite direction, looking right at the viewer, their faces as I have reconstructed them. They are mothers and fathers, sisters and brothers, old and young, alive once again.

An extended family is parked in front of the paintings, partially blocking the exit: the parents, three adult children with their own kids, and an old woman in a wheelchair. Silent tears roll down the thin skin of her cheeks that's like fine heirloom silk, softly wrinkled. She hugs her great-grandchildren to her, the youngest one climbing onto her lap.

Oliver catches me watching her. "What is it?"

"She makes me think of my own grandmother. This is what I've always wanted: a loving, genteel old lady. What I got was a grandmother who is a tank in attack mode. I used to be so desperate for affection…" I shrug off the memories. I'm fine now. I'm an adult.

"You wanted her to be your mother."

Yes. "I wanted a loving mother, and all I got was a grandmother on the bottle," I say in a low tone, more to myself than to him.

His eyes are sympathetic. "People can't give what they don't have."

The words make me want to cry, and I don't even know whether for myself or for my grandmother. In any case, I'm too old to cry in public like a kid whose lollipop was snatched.

"Mr. Moreno." A woman walks over to ask for Javier's autograph, cheezing at him as if she'd love a lot more than that. While they chat, Oliver nudges me.

"Hey. You did this." He gestures at the room at large. "The rest of us, our bit will be a footnote to the *Titanic*'s history. But you returned these people to their relatives. You made families whole. That's what you did."

His words fall softly on my heart. I'm not emotionally equipped for someone like him.

"You've given a gift to these families," he says. "That's as close to a miracle as any of us will ever experience."

The aurora borealis spreads through my chest, a mysterious, magical light that fills me up from the inside. I want to tell him that I'll miss him, but I stay silent. What would be the point? I'd like to make things easier for both of us rather than more difficult. "Thank you."

"When is your flight?"

"At six. I'm going to the airport straight from here." With a quick detour to pick up my suitcase at the hotel where we were given lodgings this time.

"May I drive you to the airport?"

A bespectacled gentleman interrupts with "Dr. McClain? I was hoping to talk to you when you have a minute. Dr. Robert Flynn, from Toronto University."

Oliver steps back. "Go ahead. I'll catch you later."

Javier is still in the clutches of his ardent fan—and not looking unhappy—so Oliver walks away, maybe to look for Julia and Helen. Or Jennifer, who is also here somewhere.

"We would like you to join the greatest project of your life." Dr. Flynn doesn't beat around the bush.

"That's what the last guy said."

Dr. Flynn laughs. "What would you think about Nun cho ga? Full funding. A tech billionaire wants to bring mammoths back. We're planning on recovering enough DNA to alter an African elephant embryo, then implant it back into the mother. Full reconstruction via forensic anthropology, full DNA sequencing. Reality TV series of the whole project. I'm told you know the drill. The funder wants original art of every step of the process, including giant scenes from the Pleistocene for the tourist center he's planning."

At least it's not Jurassic. A resurrected baby mammoth can't eat me, can she?

The project of my dreams. A few months ago, I wanted nothing more, wanted it with all my heart, and would have done anything to claw my way onto a Nun cho ga team.

Now…

"I'm sorry. I can't."

"But it's the greatest project of your life," he repeats.

"Thank you, but I'm going to try something

different next." I don't want to be part of a project that will bring back a mammoth just so the majestic animal could be a bored billionaire's latest plaything. If I ever walk into history, I want it to be through something else. I want to paint my own visions and ideas, even if I'll never be a true master. I want to cover blank canvases with life, create something from nothing. I want to make people feel awe. I want to make them think about the splendor of the universe, and that they're part of that splendor. I want them not to be scared of infinity but to forge ahead bravely.

I might fail.

In fact, failure is more likely than success.

"This is not an opportunity to miss," he reproaches.

"It's part of the human condition to have impossible dreams. What's the definition of courage if it's not to reach for the impossible instead of settling for something safe? I live in a country and at a time where I am free to choose the direction of my life. I shall choose to be brave."

He looks at me with confusion. "Are you sure?"

"I am. You won't have trouble filling the positions. People will beg to be on your team."

"Is there anything I can say to change your mind?"

"No. I'm sorry."

I walk out of the building without saying goodbye to anybody. I'll catch up with everyone on the phone later. I can't accept Oliver's offer of a ride. I don't want to cry at the airport. I don't want to drag out our parting. If I don't leave now, if he asks me to stay, I might. But I don't want to do that. I want to build the version of me that I can see in my head.

I walk to the sidewalk, then raise my hand for a cab without looking back.

Six months later
Rome, Italy

"The shadow must always be the darkest color on the painting, Signorina." Professoressa Bianchi tut-tuts at my canvas.

My teacher is the epitome of an Italian grandmother. She's also a great artist, with hundreds of works, many of them hanging in museums of contemporary art around the world.

"Better." She moves to the corner, where she's working on a small masterpiece while keeping an eye on us. "You all stay after class, yes?"

A dozen of us are scattered at various easels in her studio, all from different countries.

"Si, Professoressa," we respond as one.

"I am making saltimbocca alla romana. Veal wrapped in prosciutto crudo and sage." She kisses her fingertips. "And I have more of that wine you all liked the other night." She winks.

If ever I've met one of Bacchus's secret great-great-granddaughters, la professoressa is it. She does everything with unmeasured warmth, unbridled joy, and a sprinkle of mischief.

I thought TTP would be the adventure of my life, but this studio on the third floor of a seventeenth-century Roman villa might surpass even that project. I'm not sure anything will ever top this.

The fee TTP paid me for my work and is now paying for the continued use of my paintings is enough for the sabbatical of my dreams, a year split between Italy and France. I rented out my Boston house to a docent.

People who look for excuses find excuses. People who look for solutions find solutions.

"See how much better the contrast works?" Professoressa Bianchi circles back for another look. "The pomegranate jumps off the linen cloth. Now it's alive." We're painting a still life, with a tablecloth handwoven by her grandmother and pomegranates from her boyfriend's garden. "*Molto bene.*"

Her praise about levitates me off the floor. I am a different Madison in Rome from the Madison in Boston. I am an artist here. I came to make art. I was greeted as an artist in the very first class. It's easy to be an artist in Rome. Nobody here knows me as anything else.

She moves on, and I touch up where the light hits the tablecloth. The attic studio is hot, even with the windows open. They don't believe in air-conditioning here. I don't care. The view more than makes up for a few drops of sweat.

Terracotta tile covers the centuries-old buildings

around us, some with yellow stucco, some with amber, some with paprika, no two houses—or palaces—alike. Green ribbons of trees thread through the streets, and in the background, the famous dome of Saint Peter's Basilica stands outlined against the brilliant cerulean sky.

My insecurities melt away. I belong here now. All this beauty is mine.

Once the class is over, I'll record a quick update for my YouTube channel. My followers doubled in the past six months. They're enjoying this new phase of my life. They tell me they're inspired.

I like the idea of passing on inspiration. I received mine from Helen, who wasn't afraid of a damn thing as far as I can tell. After nursing Hemingway back to health during World War I in Milan, once the war ended, she traveled to Cambodia, China, Indonesia, and Japan. All that, a hundred years ago, when travel carried infinitely more risk than today, especially for women.

She rode through the jungles of Southeast Asia on an elephant called Effie. She wrote two acclaimed books about her adventures and received awards from the French government and the King of Cambodia. King George V and Queen Mary requested a private reading from her at Buckingham Palace.

Someone needs to write a book about that woman.

A text pings onto my phone from Oliver.

Progress today?

I send him a photo of my canvas.

I am so proud of you, he texts back.

In Paris, the work flows better, the translation of ideas onto canvas becomes easier. The second step is always less difficult than the first.

I miss Rome and Professoressa Bianchi, but in Paris, I have Jean-Philippe.

"Looser," he tells me in his raspy, movie-idol voice. I saw Michelangelo's David in Florence. It's not nothing, but… Sculptors around the world would cry tears of gratitude if my Parisian art teacher agreed to model for them. "You must hold the brush with the gentleness of a lover."

I flex and relax my fingers and let the paint glide across the canvas. Montmartre watches me from the open window, guiding my efforts from outside. The birds on the rooftops follow my daily progress. I imagine this is how long-ago pigeons watched Van Gogh, Valadon, and Renoir.

I'm painting in the city of the greatest of the great. I create during the day, go out for dancing and wine with some of the other students in the evening, and read half the night. I received a stack of books from la professoressa as a goodbye gift, stories about women artists who painted in Paris in the time of the Impressionists. I've finished the one about Suzanne Valadon and visited her studio too. Next are Mary Cassatt, Marie Bracquemond, Eva Gonzalès, and Berthe Morisot.

"See?" Jean-Phillipe's smile could melt the polar

ice cap. "Your colors are more clear, your lines more intentional, your composition more compelling. Super."

Last week, painting out on the street *en plein air*, I received an offer. A complete stranger looked at my art and judged me to be an artist. My painting is, right now, on its way to Finland with that tourist.

I am in love with Paris. I miss it already, and I haven't even left yet. Montmartre is exactly what I need, and so is Jean-Phillippe. It is my easy resistance to his charms that makes me realize at last that I am in love with Oliver. I think of him a hundred times a day, and collect stories to tell him when I see him next.

I don't call, though. I want to see his face when we talk. I want to be able to read his eyes. I paint, and for now, I just hold the promise of him in my heart.

My year in Europe is a time for me to find a way forward, but I do keep in regular touch with Dad. And one evening, after a particularly productive day, abuzz with endorphins and goodwill, I call my grandmother.

"When are you coming back?"

"Three more months." I mute the TV in the background. I've already seen the movie, *Sunflowers*, in English. I don't have to hear it in French again to know what's going on. "Thank you for sending me that photo of you and Grandpa." I'm practicing portraits and wanted old family photos to paint as a meditation on ancestors. I find lines in the faces of my family that are also my lines, and I think about their lives. I am the latest link in a long line of survivors who did the best they could. "I forgot how handsome he was."

"The devil in disguise."

"I'm sorry." And I am, because this is something I never had to experience. Dad might be neglectful, but he's never been abusive, either physically or verbally. A peaceful, safe home is all I have ever known, even if I did grow up without a mother.

"He drank and cursed and was none too pleasant to be around. Nothing but put-downs and criticism."

Pot, meet kettle.

"I know what you're thinking," my grandmother says, then pauses. When she speaks again, her tone is subdued. "I used to be different."

"I'm sure."

"Here's the thing. I had to match him or be chewed up and spit out. If he cursed me, I had to curse him back. If he smacked me, I had to smack him harder so he'd stop. We could be a wild beast and his victim, or two wild beasts that fought to a draw. And by the time he died, it was too late for me to go back." I can almost see her resigned shrug as she exhales a small cloud of cigarette smoke. "It's who I am."

I've never thought about it like that. A fissure opens in my chest, and it swallows all judgment. Sympathy wells up next. What a terrible way to live a life. "I'm sorry."

"The first time somebody raises a hand at you, you walk away."

"I know." It's not the first time she's given me this advice. It used to annoy me. Like, does she think I'm stupid? What kind of people does she think I hang out with? But now I understand.

She's giving me the advice she wishes she'd received herself, back when there'd still been time to save herself.

"What would you like from Paris?"

"*Hmpf.* Bring me a real French baguette."

"All right. Although it might be stale by the time I see you. You know what? I'll go to some lessons here, and when I get home, I'll bake you one fresh, hot out of the oven."

The following week, I join a baking class on top of my painting class. And then I go and learn about wine, to round out my French experience.

I only have a week left in Europe when Oliver's email pings onto my phone, a group mail, Julia and Eleanor also included.

Since we couldn't all meet for the premier, I'd love to invite you all again. How do you feel about watching the season finale together, at my place, in Halifax? Anyone up for a long weekend?

My response is brief: one word, three letters. *Yes.*

I'm the first one to arrive at Oliver's house. On either side of his front door, his pots of geraniums have greatly proliferated. His cottage looks like it's wearing red velvet. The seagulls above are the first ones to welcome me back. I close my eyes and inhale the salty scent of the bay for a moment.

"You're here." He stands in the opening doorway. His eyes are welcoming, clear, the color of the water behind me. His hair is a little longer, but not unkempt.

I'm vibrating with nerves.

He's as chill as ever.

Maybe he doesn't like me at all.

"Brought any artwork to show?" he asks as he ushers me into the foyer where the green continues.

"They're not here yet. I'm shipping them." In two steps, we're in the living room and I put down my bag under a potted palm. "I feel like I'm in Costa Rica."

"Are you finished with your travels?"

"Definitely not. Did you know that Helen Candee was still traveling at eighty and writing for National Geographic magazine? She was a founding member of the Society of Woman Geographers." *Awkward.* I move in for a friendly hug.

"Didn't know, doesn't surprise me." He lingers. "So, listen, I want to ask you something—"

A rap on the door startles us apart.

"Hello? Anybody home?"

Oliver lets in the new visitor.

Julia steps inside, visibly, obviously pregnant, her sporty body all motherly curves. She grins at me. "You're already here."

"You're glowing." I hurry over to embrace her. "Oh, wow."

She laughs. "Right?" Then to Oliver, "Didn't know you lived in a jungle. Nice."

Eleanor is right behind her. "We came together. Julia gave me a ride."

"You look great." I hug her even tighter. Her gray hair now has a lock of pink on each side to frame her face. "You look hip." We've kept in touch. I've held my breath as she survived three months past the doctor's predictions, then six, then nine. "How are you?"

Her smile is strong with courage. "The day is late, but there's still some sunshine left. This one," she nods toward Julia, her eyes sparkling with mischief, "gave me a reason to hang on. I'm determined to live to see my first grandchild."

"Ramsey is the father?" I don't mean to blurt the question as my eyes cut to Julia, but out it comes. Eleanor must be joking, obviously. They're going to laugh at me for even asking.

Julia's smile is straight from the Mona Lisa. "He's not a bad guy once you get talking away from work. He took me to dinner after the reinterment. One thing led to another. When the baby comes," she rests a hand on her belly, "we might move in together."

If anyone can keep Ramsey in line, it's Julia, so there is that. "Wow." I hug her again. "And I mean it as a good wow."

"Congratulations." Oliver finally gets in his own hugs. "How about we settle in? Let's get you off your feet."

We nest in his living room, chattering like a

troupe of spider monkeys in the treetops. I don't know what it is about his house, but I'm enveloped in instant peace. I feel surrounded by family.

He clicks on the TV. The title flashes onto the screen. *The Greatest Ship that Ever Sailed*. The season finale was just uploaded today.

We have all been watching the episodes on our own and discussing them online. TTP did well with the story. The show is a large-cast drama, with multiple story arcs and romances. It's nuanced and well acted.

"Drinks?" Oliver brings a tray from the kitchen. "The choices are wine and water."

Two minutes later, he returns with snacks.

Eleanor snuggles into the recliner, Julia on one end of the couch, while I sit in the middle. That leaves the spot on my other side for Oliver.

Like a teenager at the movies on her first date, my body buzzes with awareness, especially when his hand brushes against mine.

I miss half the episode. I'm going to have to rewatch later. My head is too full of other things: all I have learned, where I want to go next, Oliver.

Once it's over, we chat. We catch up. We celebrate each other. We promise to plan regular future get-togethers.

Dusk is falling outside by the time Julia and Eleanor rise to leave. We get in enough hugs to last us a few months. Oliver asks me to stay.

As the sky keeps darkening, a luminescent green

light begins to spread across the heavens. "Look!" I'm glued to the window. "It's magic."

He wraps his arms around me from behind and rests his chin on my shoulder. "It's the solar wind, carrying energetic charged particles from a solar flare or coronal mass ejection."

I'm not listening. I sink into his warmth. Tomorrow, I'll believe in science again. Right now, I just want to enjoy the magic of this night. I watch and I watch, until I am filled with wonder. And then my gaze falls on the clay pot with a small tree in front of me. "Why are you growing a pine tree on your windowsill?"

"*Pinopsia Wollemia*. Wollemi pine. Also known as the dinosaur tree, because they lived two hundred million years ago, in the time of the dinosaurs. I asked permission to plant it in the cemetery, in memory of the *Titanic* victims who were buried at sea and never made it back. I want their memory to be as enduring as the Wollemia."

Well, of course, I love him. "Earlier, before Julia and Eleanor got here. What were you going to ask me?"

"Boston University offered me a job, teaching forensics. Your old job. When you declined, they were only able to find a temporary fill-in." He steps back and gives me room to turn around in his arms. "Should I accept it? I could rent a room from you. What's so funny?"

Oh, fate does have a sense of humor. "I just sold my house."

"Of course you did."

"Why would you even consider a move?" He has a life here, a home, his garden, a thriving freelance business.

"I want to be where you are."

"How can everything be so simple for you? Why don't you tie yourself into a pretzel over every decision like normal people?"

"You can tie me into a pretzel if you want to." His tone turns suggestive.

Heaven help me. The look in his eyes. All right, so Oliver is definitely *not* a monk.

"What are you going to do next?" he asks.

"I'm going to let myself loose on the world," I say before I can decide it's incredibly arrogant or cringe sappy. "Why don't you come with me?"

His smile is brighter than the aurora borealis.

THE END

--If you enjoyed RAISING THE TITANIC, don't forget to check out GIRL BRAIDING HER HAIR, and THE SECRET LIFE OF SUNFLOWERS, next!

AUTHOR'S NOTE

The *Titanic*'s total capacity was 3,320 people. The ship carried twenty lifeboats with a capacity to hold 1,178 passengers. In the end, those boats saved 705 people. The deck was sufficient to hold enough lifeboats for every person onboard, but the decision was made to have only twenty so the space wouldn't look cluttered.

How much of the story is true? As with my previous books, most of the historical chapters are based on research. What facts I could find, I included. In some places, I had to fill in the gaps.

For example, I'm not sure about Helen's siblings. One source mentioned that she was the second oldest of five. Another said she was second of four. But her father's obituary says that he left behind two children, Helen and her brother. For the purposes of the book, I gave her two sisters and wrote what I thought might have happened. At the time, without penicillin and modern medical care, many young people were lost to various illnesses.

Some things I left out. One of the sources said Helen stood in the prow of the *Titanic* with Edward one evening, very much like the scene in the movie we've all seen. I didn't include that in my novel because I didn't want readers to think I was copying the movie.

The story of Dr. Ignaz Semmelweis, who identified that childbed fever was caused by bacteria transmitted by doctors, is all true. He was ridiculed and committed to an insane asylum. When he kept asserting his beliefs, the guards beat him, injuring his hand. He died two weeks later from gangrene. He was one of the best medical minds of his time, murdered because he was smarter than his contemporaries. He was vindicated years later when people finally accepted that he was right. Mothers stopped dying from childbed fever. The generations that followed called Semmelweis "the savior of mothers," until he was forgotten again.

The *Titanic* graves do exist, nameless to this day, in Halifax, Nova Scotia.

Helen Churchill Candee is buried in York Village, Maine.

Words cannot express how much I appreciate that you gave this book a chance and picked it up or downloaded it. THANK YOU!!! Without your support, I couldn't be writing anything. If you're on Facebook, please stop by and say hi. If you'd like to know when my next novel comes out, please sign up for my newsletter on my website. I promise not to overwhelm you with email. I think the last time I sent anything was six months ago. I'll only email you if another book is imminent.

And if you have a minute, please leave an online review. Reviews make a HUGE difference for authors.

THANK YOU!!!

Marta

P.S.:

If you'd like to read more about Helen Candee Churchill, I recommend her biography by Randy Bryan Bigham, available online.

If you'd like to find out more about the *Titanic*'s history and passengers, the Encyclopedia Titanica is a wonderful way to get lost in the past.

BOOK CLUB DISCUSSION QUESTIONS

Raising the Titanic – Book Club Discussion Questions

1.Identity and Legacy:

The project at the heart of the novel aims to restore names to the unnamed Titanic victims. How does the theme of reclaiming identity echo through both Madison's and Helen's storylines?

2.Science vs. Sensationalism:
The book juxtaposes rigorous forensic work with the demands of a documentary series. How do you feel about the ethical lines between honoring the dead and creating entertainment? Do you watch any 'real crime' shows that are doing something similar?

3.Madison's Transformation:
Madison begins the story lost—personally and

professionally. In what ways does the Titanic project give her purpose again? What are the key turning points in her personal arc?

4. Helen's Fight for Independence:

Helen challenges her era's expectations of women by seeking education and self-determination. How did her struggle resonate with you?

5. Truth Beneath the Surface:

Both the literal and metaphorical unearthing of long-buried stories plays a major role. What truths—personal, historical, or emotional—are revealed through the course of the book?

6. Connection Across Time:

The novel alternates between past and present. How did the dual timelines enrich the narrative? Did you find one storyline more emotionally compelling?

7. Team Dynamics:

The diverse team brought together for the exhumation and identification project comes from different disciplines and backgrounds. Who was your favorite supporting character, and why?

8. Madison's Humor & Voice:

Madison uses sarcasm and humor to cope with uncertainty. How did her inner voice affect your connection to her? Did it make her more relatable?

9.Ancestry and Belonging:

The project's goal is to connect the past with the present through DNA and genealogy. What does the novel suggest about our need to know where we come from? How does that shape who we are? Have you ever researched your own links to the past? Why?/Why not?

10.The Role of Women in History:

Helen is inspired by real historical figures like Clara Barton and Maria Mitchell. How does the book challenge the way women's roles have been written—or erased—from history? What are your favorite books/movies that feature strong female characters from the past?

Made in the USA
Middletown, DE
07 July 2025

10220007R00241